To Susan
With love
Jacqueline

when the **crow** sings

· A NOVEL ·

Jacqueline Wales

PANTULAN PRESS
NEW YORK, NY

Published by:
Pantulan Press
90 Pinehurst Avenue, #6D, New York, NY 10033 USA

ISBN-13: 978-0-9798598-0-9
ISBN-10: 0-9798598-0-8

Printed in Canada

Library of Congress Cataloging-in-Publication Data
is available from the publisher.

Library of Congress Control Number: 2007934974

This is a work of fiction. All of the characters, names, incidents,
organizations, and dialogue in this novel are either the products
of the author's imagination or are used fictitiously.

To
My mother GRACE

Your courage became mine

a few words of thanks

ANY CREATIVE ACT comes with great effort even if we call it pleasure. I worked on this book for twelve years nursing it through various stages of growth and destruction until I was satisfied with it. We are never totally satisfied, but I know one thing for sure, I gave it my best shot. This was not an easy book to write because so much of my history is tied up in it. But I did it. I'm proud of myself for completing it, and take comfort in the fact that my family will be the inheritors of the first piece of this Wales family history to make it into print.

There are many people who helped me on this journey—teachers, friends and family. My teachers were Deena Metzger, a kind, wise lady who challenged her students to find the heart of the story, to follow your own wisdom and never settle for less than the real thing. Patrick Horton, who believes that the magic of story is in the 'what about that matters' and who taught me to question every scene I created for authenticity. They both gave me the strength to continue with the work even when it seemed I was pulling the cart uphill myself.

I am blessed with great friends all over the world who cheered me on at all stages. In Los Angeles: Cathy Kaye, Carol Kleinman, Alice March, Shuli Wities, Lyn Avins, Didi Carr Reubin, Rabbi Steven Carr Reubin, Bert Kleinman, Tony Gwilliam, Marita Vincent and Laurel Quinn. In London: Della Hirsch, Dan Hirsch and Kay Woods. In Bali: Karen Waddell, Meghan Poppenheim, Anneke van Waesberghe, Lyn Schwaiko and Zoli Perry. In Amsterdam: Jetty van Gelder, Andy Miser, Peter March, Maia and Jenn Hahn. In Paris: Sally Katz, Jennifer Beder, Deborah Lillian, Nancy Heikin and Deborah Gallin. In Berlin: Renate Estiot. To all of you, you are the heart and soul of why I do what I do.

As for my family, they say the family you make is the one that really matters the most. It does to me. I have been blessed with five children in my life. My first daughter Laura was given up for adoption and it is that story that prompted me to write this book. My son Robert was born and raised in England by his father but who came back to his mother after a difficult separation. My California daughters Serena and Samara taught me how to be a mother and my step-daughter Virginia survived the trauma of moving from Bangkok to Los Angeles and my erratic step-parenting. To all of them, I am deeply grateful for the opportunity to learn what being a mother is all about. Last, but certainly not least, my husband Martin Rubin has watched me blossom and grow, has fought me and challenged me every step of the way and I definitely could not have done it without him. He has been my toughest critic and my greatest love of twenty-seven years and counting.

To all of you, thank you for being my family.

ADVICE ON LANGUAGE

When The Crow Sings is set in Scotland and much of the dialogue in this book is written in Scottish dialect. As a culture, we are all conditioned by how we speak to each other and I felt it was important that the characters speak to each other in a natural voice. The Scottish accent is very sing-song in its tone, and once you get the rhythm it will come naturally to your inner ear. As a musician, I always hear the music in people's language and that is part of the charm. Our language is part of who we are. We may change it to suit the culture in which we are living, but give a hefty shove to a person from another part of the country and the roots will shine through. Enjoy the song of Scotland. It has a lovely lilt. You will find a glossary of words at the end of the book.

This alone is what I wish for you: knowledge.
To understand each desire has an edge,
to know we are responsible for the lives
we change. No faith comes without cost,
no one believes without dying.
Now for the first time
I see clearly the trail you planted,
what ground opened to waste,
though you dreamed a wealth
Of flowers

        There are no curses—only mirrors
held up to the souls of god and mortals.
And so I give up this fate, too.
Believe in yourself,
go ahead—see where it gets you.

"Demeter's Prayer to Hades"
from *Mother Love* by Rita Dove

Edinburgh, January 7, 2000

Dear Lauren:

I've been struggling with the ways in which to tell you the story of how you came to be, and couldn't find a short story that would fit. The family history is too complicated. I decided in the end that you had to know the entire history to make any sense of it. It hasn't been easy but it's been worth the years it took me to put this down on paper.

Don't be too hard on Agnes when she delivers it. She was my reluctant messenger. I'm afraid I put her through the hoops on this one, but I didn't know any other way to make sure you got it. I would have come myself, but my health has not been so good, and I'm afraid I'm not doing well. I was diagnosed last year with breast cancer and it seems to be getting the better of me. I would have loved to have seen you. It's hard to believe you are twenty-four now. The years have gone away so fast. I was twenty when I had you, a silly wee lassie, as my auntie Agnes would have said. I didn't know what I was doing but I did know one thing. I wanted you to have the best chance in the world. I was working part-time jobs and living in bed-sitters. Not a good start for you or for me. I wanted to do the right thing. I hope you've had a good life. Your Mum and Dad have given you as much as they can, and I think it's a lot. They told Agnes you'd turned into a lovely young lady.

I'm sorry for all the trouble I caused them earlier in your life. I was definitely daft in the head. I missed you and I longed to be part of your life even if I couldn't be. I know it doesn't make any difference now, but I wanted you to know that. This book is my way of trying to make it up to you. We all need to know where we come from. It's the only way we have of knowing who we are. I can't tell you about your father because I didn't really know him. He was good looking and he had a sense of humor. I hope you've inherited that much. Judging from what I've heard, you've got brains too. I'm not sure who you got that from. Maybe it was me!

Some day you'll have babies of your own. I hope you have them under the right circumstances and give them all the chances in the world. Keep this book as a souvenir of your Scottish mother. It's got the wisdom of generations contained within it. I'm only sorry we have to find out at the end of our days.

For what it's worth this is our family story. It was a little more complicated than most. Don't let it frighten you. This has been a family of strong women. You are one of them. It was not an easy story to write but I hope I have done it justice. Much of what you will read is my interpretation of the events. Agnes told me many of the stories but she didn't live through all of them. She is a good soul. Be gentle with her and with yourself. It is the greatest gift we can give ourselves.

There is not much more I can say except to let you know that I love you and you are loved in so many ways.

Be well, my daughter. Live your life to the fullest. We only have one life to live.

With all my heart and love
Alison Napier
Your Mother

It is not unusual for strong winds to blow gales towards the ravaged east coast of Scotland, and fishermen know only too well that nature will have its own way. Too many wrecks lie beneath the surface and history repeats itself. Even in summer, the North Sea is unforgiving.

Scotland
1914

AS HUNGRY SEAGULLS wheel and dive over torn nets abandoned, fishing boats, buoyant with the weight of emptiness, clank and clatter against the harbor wall. Scattered among broken creel baskets, a gray spackled fish lies splayed, soft eye sockets blank, gazing at a red brick factory stuck between two dowager granite buildings.

Inside the factory, acrid stickiness mauls the nose, and voices yell above the din of grinding machines spitting out thick cords of black, tarred rope. A woman, stooped and gray beyond the tell of her age, pulls hand over hand, coiling the rope in a mounting pile at her feet. Ignoring the fine hemp pricks from the loose weave, which leave her hands chapped red and bleeding, and the charred smell of cooling tar on her palms, she throttles a sob, thinking of her daughter "cast out with the whores of Babylon," and continues to pull the rope roughly through her tortured hands.

On the open window frame, a seagull views her suspiciously, blinking its black ringed eye twice as if thinking of entering the pavilion. Screeching at the factory in protest at the noise, the seagull flaps its wings and lifts its plump body off the windowsill towards the sea.

When the bell rings to end her shift for the day, my great-grandmother gives one more pull on the rope and moans to herself, "How could I have sent her away?"

one

Lizzie grimaced as the silken gray hair ran across the raw cracked palms of her hands. Almost in tears, she called out, "C'mere, gie me a help wi' this. It's no go'in right this morning."

Her daughter, Effie, who was at that moment pulling her own hair into a tight bun, made a huffing sound and slouched toward her mother. The willful streak of teenage insult grated on Lizzie's nerves.

"Get a bloody move on, will you. You havenae got aw' morning. You'll be late for work and if you lose that job, I dinnae ken what's gonnie come o' you. I work myself raw trying to keep bread on the table and a roof ow'er oor heeds. Can you no have some sense, girl? It'll be you and the rope factory if you're no bloody lucky. C'mon, Effie, be quick aboot it. My hands are sare trying to get this up."

Effie took the pins from her mother's hands and noted that even in the dim light of the gas lamp her mother's hands were practically useless. She had no idea how she continued to work this way.

"Look at you—you're no even dressed yet. It's half past four and you've got half an oor to get there on time. You're gonnie be late. What was aw' that racket last night? You were tossing aboot something fierce. I couldnae sleep well because o' it. Are you feelin' aw' right?"

Effie finished her hair and moved away. "I'm aw' right. I winnie be long. It's always sae damn cauld in her," she said.

"Dinnae start complaining, lass. You keep moving—that'll keep you warm. C'mon now, say your prayers before you go. It's forgiveness we're aw' lookin' for, but I dinnae ken how much will be comin' your way wi' aw' that nonsense that runs roond your heed."

Effie always wondered how her mother knew about the stuff that ran round her head. She never understood all this business of sins and forgiveness, because, in her mind, she never had the time to commit any sins, and as for forgiveness, there was none coming her way anytime soon. With her father dead, her brother dead, and a mother who made sure every conceivable sin and then some was accounted for, she knew she was doomed to a life in hell.

Each morning, she had to kneel in front of the Virgin Mary and say a prayer for the departed.

Each morning, her mother reminded her that she was a sinner and the only way she could find redemption was in the arms of Jesus and his blessed mother, the Virgin Mary.

Each morning, she prayed for an end to her mother's complaints and hoped Jesus would forgive her for thinking such things.

Each morning, she prayed that someone would come along and fall in love with her so she could leave all this behind.

Yesterday, she thought her prayers had been answered. Someone had asked her for a walk.

With a "Hail Mary, full of grace, the Lord is with thee, blessed art thou amongst women, and blessed is the fruit of thy womb," Effie rose from the cold floor and put her coat on.

"Why does he want to see me?" she wondered, sneaking a glimpse in the mirror above the fireplace. In the dim glow of the gas lamp, the chicken pox scars on her face appeared as dull craters on the moon's surface. The clock on the sideboard chimed quarter to five as she headed toward the front door. Suddenly remembering the gaslight, she stepped back into the front room and turned the tap off. I better get out of here, she thought. She'll be down in a second to see what I'm doing if she doesn't hear the door close. She gazed at herself in the mirror one more time then pulled her headscarf closer to her forehead. "It'll have to do," she murmured.

Outside, a light breeze blew across the Forth estuary, pushing the slate gray clouds overhead toward a threat of rain in the dimness of the late summer morning light. She hoped it wouldn't rain today. She wanted a perfect summer day with lots of sunshine until midnight, and a full moon to finish it off. If she was going to walk, she wanted to be surrounded by birds and flowers and a fresh breeze that took all the stale fish smells out to sea. She had read somewhere that Scotland was green all year round and thought, "How stupid, wi' aw' that rain, how could it be anything else?"

She lived on the outskirts of Fisherrow, a small fishing village attached to the bigger town of Musselburgh, near the city of Edinburgh. Men married their boats during the summer months, hauling in fresh catches of herring, haddock, and cod. In their absence, the women mended nets, cleaned out their creels, and waited for the catch to come home. Loaded up with the herrings, haddock, and oysters, their baskets weighed eighty pounds or more and were hung from their foreheads by broad leather straps that made their neck muscles bulge under the weight. Their day ended at five o'clock, when they collected the fish and scrubbed out the creel, readying it for the next day. Wearing floral blouses, heavy navy skirts, and striped kirtles, heavy overskirts tied at the waist, under dark flannel capes dripping with salt water and fish blood, they were easy to spot. Their street cry of "Caller 'ou-ooh'" brought housewives to their doors in all kinds of weather to buy fresh caught oysters.

The children of Fisherrow dressed in heavy woolen sweaters with unwashed faces, were distinguished only by the number of times they missed school because they were needed at home to help with the nets. The smell of brine and decaying fish clung to their hair, their clothes, and the air they breathed. Effie's mother, Lizzie, had married a man who worked in the wire mills, and her grandmother, who still carried the creel at the age of fifty-two, never forgave her for breaking out of the family tradition, warning that it would only bring misfortune. Lizzie felt the only misfortune was being dragged into that life but held onto the fishing connection by going to work at Sinclair's Net Factory, where she was responsible for finishing the nets as they came off the machines. A destroyer of hands, the tarred black netting was coarse and made them bleed when the line ran through too quickly. Sometimes the nets were big enough to cover five football fields and took hours to check, but there was no point in complaining—there was always someone else waiting for your job. Lizzie was determined to give her daughter Effie the best chance possible, and put her into the bakery. She thought it would keep Effie clean and allow her to meet a better class of people.

As Effie hurried down Bridge Street toward the old bridge she saw two old fishermen with deep, craggy faces worn down by the cold and wind coming toward her. They touched their caps lightly as they went by. Effie knew better than to say something. All fishermen believed the fish would take flight and their boats would come home empty if a good morning was said. One word in the wrong direction, and everyone expected the worst. Priests, rats, salmon, and rabbits were all unmentionable, although it was unclear whether the priests or the rats were the worst.

Passing the newsagent's, a vibrant red poster with a man blowing fire out of his mouth for Cooke's Circus hung in the window. Effie remembered her dad, who had passed away five years earlier, taking her and her younger brother Duncan to the circus. She could still hear the hurdy-gurdy man and smell the wet piss sawdust that coated her shoes. The star attraction was a motorcar that fell thirty feet into a barrel of water while the heroine wrestled with a villain inside, trying to save her reputation. When the car hit the water, it splashed all over the theater, soaking the people dressed in their Sunday best in the front row. But it was "Mahatma, Mistress of Modern Miracles in the Most Mysterious and Bewildering Performance Ever Witnessed," that had Effie hooked. It was billed as "Anything You Want to Know. Ask Mahatma, Whose Marvelously Correct Replies Have Astounded the Whole Scientific World." Effie wanted to know if she would meet somebody handsome and get married. If she knew that she could prove her mother wrong. There was somebody was waiting for her after all. But when Mahatma pulled the first questioning person onstage, Effie decided she didn't need the rest of the world knowing how daft she was, so she kept still.

Her mother had said they were blasphemous for going to a circus on a Sunday before Christmas. They should have been in church praying and thanking Mary for her precious son and all the blessings he brought. It was a sin against all mothers in her book. Effie's dad had said, "There's nothin' wrong wi' a whistling Sunday from time to time. It gives the bairns a break." In his mind that was the blessing and she was a fool to believe any differently.

His interest in the Virgin Mary extended to the Admiral's Arms, where a small statue of her stood next to the bottle of Rose's Lime Juice. He told Effie's mother that he was going out to the Isle of May for some fishing, but Effie knew the nearest he got to catching anything was at the pub as he talked anybody he could into buying him a drink. He spent his days at the grind of Burton's Wire Mills, deafened by the sound of machinery, slowly polluted by the chemicals that coated the wire. Then his cough started. It came on slowly—an early harvest cherry-stained dribble—but it was not long before his handkerchiefs stiffened with abattoir red clots. They took him away on a gurney to the Free Hospital, saying he would be back as soon as his cough got better.

An old cabinet-type photograph sat on the sideboard that showed her mother and father on the day they were married. He stood behind the chair, with neatly combed hair and his cap in hand. She sat with her hands on her lap, holding her rosary. Neither one could raise a smile in the close confines of the photographer's studio on Princes Street in Edinburgh. Effie wasn't sure if their dour look was the cost of the photograph or the fact that both had resigned themselves to an unhappy life from the first day. She couldn't remember a time when she had seen them laugh together.

The sun spread its finger rays of pink dawn across the town in a delightful promise of rain. Red sky at night, shepherd's delight. Red sky in the morning, shepherd's warning, Effie hummed. A bird sang poignantly from the treetop above her head. Effie hurried her steps, glancing up the street leading to Our Lady of Loretto Church. Her mother was there regular as clockwork every night at five-thirty. The town was full of churches, but they were mostly Protestant in various guises. You had the Presbyterians, the Reformed, the Church of Scotland, the Free Church, and the Baptists. She hoped no one would ever ask her the difference because she didn't know. It seemed to her that Protestants had their politics and the Catholics had God.

Up ahead, the lights of the bakery cast a glow out onto the early morning pavement. The newsagent headlines screamed, "WAR IMMINENT!" Many of the young boys had started signing up for the grand adventure. Mr. Jenkins, the baker, had allowed his son to join the Territorials. He hoped the war wouldn't last—that Danny would be home in no time.

The clock above the town hall said seven o'clock, which was of no help because it always said seven o'clock. Effie started to run, knowing she was well and truly late now. After a year at the bakery, it would be her first time. Mr. Jenkins would know for sure something was wrong with her today.

The sound of the shop's bell was deafening at this hour. She looked hurriedly at the Hovis clock on the wall and saw it was five past five. As Effie came in the door, at the same time taking her coat off, Mr. Jenkins held out a cup of tea and a roll with butter, which he always prepared for her in the morning.

"You're a wee bit late this morning, Effie. Are you feeling aw' right?

"I'm awfy sorry I'm late, Mr. Jenkins," she said hurriedly, putting on her apron. "I didnae sleep sae well last night."

"I hope you're no comin' doon wi' anything, lass. I need your help in the shop."

"Oh, no, Mr. Jenkins. I'm fine. I havenae had a day sick in years."

"Aw' right then. Drink this quick and get on wi' the bread. Try to keep your heed straight the day. It wisnae aw' there yesterday."

"I'll be fine, Mr. Jenkins. Dinnae worry." She moved toward the big mixing bowl to mix the dough. "Have you heard fae Danny?"

"No, no yet. We hope he's aw' right. He's over in Tranent on some training scheme. He's accepted the king's shilling now, so there's no turning back. Mrs. Jenkins disnae feel sae good. They say the war'll be startin' anytime now. Can you imagine that? I dinnae ken if that Balfour doon there in England kens what's he day'in. Danny's got aw' kind o' notions aboot bein' a soldier—been daft aboot it since he was a bairn. I suppose we'll ken eventually." He piled up the wood in the fire and stood rubbing his lower back.

Effie took flour from a large cotton sack that lay against the brick wall and poured it into the bowl with a chipped china jug, scraping off the top of the flour with a large flat knife. "Aye, I imagine it must be hard no knowing what's gonnie happen."

Mr. Jenkins shook his head and turned toward the inside of the shop. "I'm goin' up the stairs to check on Maggie. You ken what to do."

Effie set about baking the rolls, buns, and bread for the day, arranging the shelves so that they looked neat and tempting. By six-thirty she would have at least three dozen rolls and a dozen loaves of bread ready to sell. Cakes came later in the morning when the rush was over.

The oven had been lit since three that morning, when Mr. Jenkins started work and it was warm in the back room. Effie took off her cardigan and rolled her shirt sleeves up before shaping the dough into rolls. The smell of yeast and baking bread was comforting. Taking care to form just the right amount of dough for each roll, she was unaware of the back door opening. She felt the cold draft on her neck and wondered if the old duster cat from next door had sneaked in to lick the milk from the jug again. She turned around, ready to chase it away, and jumped back in shock as the stranger with the dark piercing eyes and the thick shock of curly hair stuck his head around the door.

Effie grasped her rolling pin and backed up towards the oven. "What do you want?" she yelled hoarsely, looking to the curtain that led to the shop. Her mouth had gone as dry as a sailor's biscuit. "You cannie come in here. Mr. Jenkins winnie like it. You must leave," she whispered in panic.

He smiled coyly and put two fingers to his lips. "Sssh. Please see me tonight," he whispered.

"I can't. I'll get in trouble if I do that," she pleaded.

"Si te plait?" he said, putting both his hands together in a prayer motion. She hesitated, unsure what he was saying. Her eyes kept shifting from the curtain to the door. "If Mr. Jenkins sees you here, he's no gonnie like it," she whispered, lowering the rolling pin. Mr. Jenkins had already sent him away yesterday. She couldn't imagine what he was doing back again, and especially at this time of the day. He smiled at her again. "It must mean something," she thought.

Watching her hesitation, he jumped in. "Good, aux quai, the harbor at seven o'clock," he said, smiling under his wide mustache.

"I see you there." He closed the door, taking the smell of almond and vanilla with him.

The fire from the oven now felt like an inferno. The gluey dough had mixed with the sweat on her palms, and she had to rinse it off before she could go back to work. On automatic pilot, she set the rolls on their trays before placing them in the oven, and then stood staring at the wall. A thunderous clamoring started in her head, drowning out all other sounds.

"He wants to see me? Why does he want to see me? What will my Ma say? How could I be goin' oot wi' him? He's a tinker. Mr. Jenkins will go off his heed if he finds oot. He likes me. He's awfy handsome. Whae am I kiddin'?" She patted more rolls into shape and placed them on the tray. "Ma goes to church at five-thirty, but she's hame again by seven. If I'm no there, she'll go daft. What am I dayin even thinkin' aboot it? The neighbors will be talkin' for months. I dinnae ken whae he is. But he came back. That must mean something." She leaned toward the mirror above the bread shelves and saw her hair tied up in a scarf and her pink face shining back at her. "What can he be lookin' at?" she wondered.

Suddenly, she smelled the strong odor of burning bread, and rushed to the oven to take out the rolls, which had turned the color of rusty pipes. She tossed them off the tray and cursed herself for not paying attention. "Why would he be interested in taking me out?" she wondered aloud, looking behind her in case Mr. Jenkins was standing watching her.

His name was Loic Le Guellec, a farm worker from Brittany in France. The locals knew him as Onion Johnny, an itinerant onion seller who strolled the countryside with his bicycle heavily laden with tresses of onions. Throughout the length of Britain you could hear onion sellers call, "Des onions doux. Des onions frais. Venez acheter vos onions!" In their striped shirts, colorful scarves, and black berets, they brightened up the drab causeways of Scotland, sleeping wherever a dry spot could be found. They were considered lower than the gypsies whose campfires they regularly sat at, but they brought delicious onions and a willing smile that made them a charming part of the landscape as long as they minded their own business.

Loic smiled a lot to cover up the fact that his English was still poor after six years of roaming the Scottish countryside. His own language of Brittany was difficult for outsiders but the Scots spoke with a sing-song accent and shortened many of their words into unrecognizable patterns making it impossible for him to learn. It was doubtful he would ever speak English well. Asked why he came so far to sell onions, which they could buy for next to nothing at home, he always had the same response. "Nos onions sont doux," he would reply, "Our onions are sweeter," then shrug his thin shoulders and smile. He ploughed his wares in all weather and when asked why he needed to come so far from home, he would say because my father did it before me, or there is no work in France. Never did he say because he liked the life.

Yesterday, Effie had been in the front of the shop while Mr. Jenkins made cakes in the back. She saw him coming in the door and thought he was a tinker who probably didn't have any money. Taking off his beret as he approached the counter, Loic swept his thick black hair back from a young face that said he had seen too many miles and not enough beds to sleep in. He waited patiently until the last customer had left the shop before stepping forward. "I take a leetle bread today. Peut etre celui la?" he said, pointing at the shelf.

Effie looked confused for a moment. She turned to look at the bread then looked back at him with her mouth open to ask again what he wanted.

"You have des beaux yeux bleu," he said, smiling and pointing to his eyes. She blushed and looked down at the counter before turning her back to him, straightening her apron, then took a plain loaf from the shelf.

While she wrapped it in a square of brown paper, he leaned slightly forward holding his gaze on her face as she handed him the bread. "J'adore very much ton bread." Very slowly he passed her the money, brushing the palm of her hand with his fingers as he placed the coins in it. Effie felt a surge of electricity pass through her arm and recoiled quickly. He smiled again, held up the loaf, tipped his beret, and said, "Merci beaucoup," before turning and opening the shop door. Settling himself in front of the window, he took some sausage and onions from the bag on his bike, peeling them with great strokes of his knife and placing them between two hunks of bread.

Effie stood rooted to the spot, watching his back as he ate. "How can he eat raw onions?" she thought. "I'd have indigestion for a week." Loic turned around and gave a wave with his sandwich, munching and making nodding gestures with his head to tell her it was good. She flushed and looked intently at the yellow cakes on the front of the counter. "What's he playing at?" she wondered. She looked in the mirror that adverstised Hovis bread and pushed her headscarf back from her face. All her life people had told her she had very blue eyes, but nobody had told her they were "bose you" before.

"Are you all right, Effie?"

Startled, Effie snapped to attention. "Aye, it's aw' right. I was just lookin' to see if we needed anymare paper." She placed the brown sheets of paper into neat squares, and watched out of the corner of her eye as Loic finished his sandwich and stood up. Mr. Jenkins was leaning over the counter, reading a newspaper spread across the counter, when the bell above the door gave a little tinkle.

"Have you got something you need to be doing in the back, Effie?"

Effie looked up and then looked away as Loic came through the door. "Aye, Mr. Jenkins," she said, slowly, before going behind the yellow flowered curtain that separated the bakery from the shop.

Stepping forward reluctantly now that he was in the shop and Effie had been sent away, Loic approached Mr. Jenkins, who had stood up tall.

"What can I do for you, son?"

Loic took his beret off at once. "Please, I would like to see the young lady?"

"Effie's a bit busy right now. Is there something I can get for you?"

Loic smiled awkwardly. "Non, non, merci. Merci beaucoup. I would like her to walk with me," he stuttered.

"Oh, she's no available for walking. She's got her work. She's only a lassie, ye ken?" He brushed down the front of his apron with wide, flat hands. "I don't think you want to be doin' that."

Loic shifted his focus to the curtain and waited a moment. His smile vanished. "All right. Next time. Merci." He placed his beret on his head as he looked once more at the curtain before turning away.

Effie was practically breathing the curtain, standing with her arms folded across her ample breasts, listening to the exchange only a few feet from where she stood. She was almost in tears when she heard Mr. Jenkins send him away. Outside, Loic pointed his bicycle toward Edinburgh without looking back.

When she stepped into the shop, Mr. Jenkins said, "Well, fancy that. You need to be careful, Effie. These foreigners are always very friendly, but they're no like you and me. They're still strangers, no matter how friendly they seem to be."

Effie wasn't listening. Her mind floated on a sea of possibilities. He wanted to walk with her. He liked her. She glanced in the mirror again to see if she could see what he was looking at. The same moon-cratered face stared back at her with blue eyes sparkling behind a watery veil. This had to be an answer to her prayer.

The doorbell rang in the shop.

"Effie, are you listening? C'mon now, dinnae be daydreamin'. There's a customer in the shop. Would you serve her please?"

Effie slapped the flour off her hands and tried to concentrate on the woman. She had a sour mouth on her as she ordered a plain loaf. "Just make sure it disnae have too much burned bits on it. I dinnae like the heel too crisp." Effie selected the palest one on the shelf, one with hardly any crust, and twisted it tightly in the paper without saying anything. After the woman left, Effie went back to kneading the dough—and her thoughts.

Last night her mother had caught her reading the beauty tips in a woman's magazine. She had snatched it away, telling her there was no point in thinking about that nonsense. "You make do wi' what God has gi'en you," she said. "you winnie catch a man wi' your looks." Then her mother tore the magazine in two and tossed it into the fire. "That's aw' it's good fur," she yelled. When Effie started to cry, her mother told her to stop her sniveling. "It's only fish and chip dreams. It makes good wrapping paper. There's nae money in this hoose for aw' that nonsense."

"Well, she was wrong. He liked my eyes," Effie muttered.

Effie knew there were so many promises in that paper. A little color to lift up your dead hair. A little blackener to make your eyes sparkle. Some red to invite kisses on your lips. A corset to make your weight disappear. Everybody deserves love in the world, she thought. The books she read, the films she saw, all were about love conquering the tragedies in life. Someone out there would love her. Why not this handsome young man from France?

When Loic showed up at the bakery the following morning, Effie knew for sure it was a sign that he cared. Why would he come back again if he didn't? But her mind was spinning. Her mother would give her hell if she walked with him. Everybody would talk about her for months afterward. She'd be ruining her chances of meeting anybody in the town if she went with him. But she wanted to go so badly. It was only for a walk, she reasoned. There was no sin in that.

As the morning progressed her baking did not have the right touch. All the cakes were flatter than normal. The custard was too runny. The rolls were too crisp. Her arms lacked strength and could not beat for long periods. She was out of breath and tired. She gave out the wrong change three times until Mr. Jenkins took her aside and asked if there was anything wrong. Wistfully, she said that she was fine, but he wasn't satisfied. He kept pressing her for an answer. She began to cry and was about to send her home when Mrs. Jenkins came down the stairs. Putting her arms around Effie's shoulders, she led her upstairs.

The Jenkins's flat above the shop was as far from Effie's home as could be possible within a mile distance. The windows were hung with fine lace curtains that spread the sunshine in decorative curlicues across the heavy mahogany table polished to a high gloss in the middle of the room. Effie straightened out her skirt and apron and checked to see if her hands were clean.

"Sit yourself down, hen. I'll go make some tea," Mrs. Jenkins said.

Effie noticed an embroidered pillow that said, God Bless This House and sat down to the far side so as not to disturb the lay of the cushion. The grandfather clock clicked and clattered noisily in the silence of the room. Two china woolly dogs sat facing each other on the mantelpiece, each with a look of perpetual surprise on its face. In the corner was a large gramophone with a record on it. She'd never been in a house with music in the living room, but she dared not move to find out what the music was. On the sideboard was a picture of the Jenkins family on a picnic. They looked happy. Not for the first time did Effie feel ashamed of where she lived. The narrow windows of her house overlooking the street were lined with grease paper to keep people from looking in, but also served to stretch their nights and days into one continuous yearning for light.

Mrs. Jenkins returned with a tray holding two cups and saucers and a plate of biscuits that Effie had made that morning. She placed it on the small table in front of the couch and sat down, tossing the God Bless This House pillow aside.

She handed Effie tea and an Askit powder. "Here, take this—it'll make your headache feel better."

Effie didn't know how she knew about her headache, but thought maybe it was because all women have headaches when they've received an invitation to go out walking with a stranger. "I'll be aw' right, Mrs. Jenkins. I'm just feeling a wee bit under the weather."

"Aye, I know what you mean, hen. It's been hard wi' my Danny be'in' away." Effie nodded, pouring the Askit powder onto the tip of her tongue. The bitter taste almost made her sick, but she controlled the urge to choke and swallowed gulping down the hot tea.

"How is your mother these days? I haven't seen much of her."

"Oh, she's fine, Mrs. Jenkins. She's working."

"Aye, well, tell her to come in and visit us sometimes. You've been such a help to us during these last few months. I don't know how we could do without you now."

"That's awfy nice of you, Mrs. Jenkins. I'm just trying to do my job. It's no much."

"Well, it's no often we get someone to help us who can bake as well as you can, Effie. So, what's got into you today? Gordon says you don't seem to be your auld self at all. Are we workin' you too hard?" She patted Effie's hand and then held it.

Effie put her cup down on the tray and pulled her hand away. "It's nothing. I think I'm just a wee bit tired," she said.

"What's this I heard about one of these Ingin Johnnies coming into the shop yesterday? He asked to see you. Were you there when he came in?"

Effie nodded. "I was in the back."

"Fancy that, eh? I've never heard of that before. Usually they just bring around the onions and they don't say very much. It's one thing to be buying from them, and another to be go'in out with them. You have to be careful, you know. It's easy for young lassies to be confused. I don't know what the world is coming to."

Effie stood up and straightened her apron. "I'm sorry, I've got to go. Thanks for the tea and powder, Mrs. Jenkins. Mr. Jenkins will need me to help clean up the shop."

"Anytime, dear. If there is anything I can do for you, just ask. You're a pleasure to have around."

Effie went back downstairs to the shop, cleaned the shelves, scrubbed down the breadboards, and swept up the crumbs and flour that had spilled during the day. The last few customers came in for their evening bread, and she placed the unsold fruitcakes in the big tin storage bins in the back, before throwing the crumbs outside for the seagulls, who fought like scavengers for the scraps. When everything was looking neat, she put some more wood in the fire and put her coat on. It was only four o'clock, but she had to go home and cook dinner for her mother so she could get to church on time. In her more mean-spirited times, Effie wondered why she didn't get a job cleaning floors. She could be on her knees all day long with that.

She stopped at the greengrocer and bought potatoes, then bought some herrings from the old fishwife who sat on the corner with her basket. She would toss the herrings in flour and fry them, serving them with boiled potatoes and buttered bread. It was pretty much the same thing every night, only the fish varied. Some nights it was cod or sardines, but mostly it was herrings. She hated them but they were cheap.

Her mother always fretted about how much things cost and complained whenever Effie bought magazines instead of saving her money for when she got married. Since Effie had no idea when that would be, if it would be, she saw no reason to deny herself this simple pleasure. To her mother, the only book that was not a sin to read was the Bible, which she read every night before going to sleep. The library was Effie's sanctuary because she could read whatever she wanted.

For the next hour, the tug of war between going and not going to see Loic at the harbor drove her to distraction. She burned the potatoes, didn't cook the herrings all the way through, and spilled the cooking water on the floor. Lizzie yelled at her for being slovenly, careless, and useless. No one would want to marry a girl who couldn't cook. The house was a mess and the sheets weren't dry because she hadn't laid them out flat yesterday. If she would learn to do the washing better, then maybe she wouldn't look so bad in church. On and on she ranted, until Effie stopped listening and ate her dinner in silence. When they were finished, she yanked the plates off the table and put them in the sink but did not start to wash them immediately as she would normally have done. Instead, she put on her coat and tied a scarf around her neck.

"Where are you go'in at this time of night?" demanded Lizzie. "These dishes are no done yet. You never go oot at night. Where are you go'in, Effie?" she yelled as the front door slammed shut.

Effie launched herself across the street and broke into a run, almost singing with disbelief that she had just run out on her mother, feeling her rebellion thundering down the empty streets and across the windowpanes of fluttering curtains. Hitching up her skirt, she ran toward the Tolbooth and made no attempt to button her coat. There would be hell to pay later, but for now, she didn't care.

two

AT THE TOLBOOTH Tower, the clock hung like a summons at seven o'clock. As Effie passed the Free Church, the congregants were just going in for their meeting. All the shops in the High Street were closed and most people were having their tea. Approaching the bridge, a flock of seagulls wheeled and screeched above her head before flying out to the sea. Stepping onto the towpath, she walked slowly down the river, allowing the sunshine to warm her face. A pea green rowboat lay upside down with one oar next to it. She sat down on top of it and wondered what it would be like to just sail away on the Forth on a fine summer night like tonight and float away like the Owl and the Pussycat. On the steps opposite, young boys were skipping stones across the water, competing with each other to see who had the furthest reach and the biggest ripples.

"I'm off ma bloody heed," she muttered. "I cannie go see him. He's a tinker wi' nae hame and nae money." She pulled her skirt down over her legs and pulled her knees up towards her chest. She thought about the advertisement she had seen in the Musselburgh News the other week for immigration to Canada. It promised free land in Alberta or Saskatchewan for hardworking people. There was a great demand for labor all along the Canadian Pacific Railway. Maybe I can just run away wi' him there, she mused.

"Shite," she said aloud. "I cannie be sitting here thinking this. I better go hame. I'll have to say I'm sorry." She stood up and smoothed down her dress. "There's gonnie be hell to pay."

She walked back up to the bridge again, searching the windows of the houses for signs of fluttering curtains. Young lassies out walking by themselves at the quiet hour were always looked on with suspicion.

They were usually up to no good and the morning would bring the clatter of gossip at the doorways. The heels of her boots clacked on the pavement, and she had an urge to run on tiptoe. Her mouth was dry, and she wiped the sweat of her palms on her coat. When she got to the end of the bridge, she hesitated. If she went straight ahead, she'd be home in no time. She could get the dishes done and the place all tidied up and have a cup of tea ready for her mother when she came back from church. She looked down the street of narrow houses. If she went down Eskside, she could disappear into Fisherrow, and nobody would pay any attention to her, just a wee lassie on her way home from work.

"What am I gonnie dae?" she moaned.

Behind her she heard a bicycle bell and she jumped back. "Get off the road," yelled an old man carrying a ladder on the side of his bicycle. Quickly, she flew down Eskside towards the harbor wall gulping air as she ran.

❧❦❧

He was sitting with his legs crossed on a pile of drift netting, his bike parked alongside. The clink and clank of the fishing boats moored nearby swayed like music. She hesitated slightly, pulled her coat tighter around her, told herself this was all nonsense, and was about to turn back when she heard, "Bon soir, cherie," float across the broad expanse of the Links.

Loic stood up, smiled broadly, and moved towards her. "You come," he said excitedly.

Effie blushed and had an overwhelming urge to rush away, tear herself from the seduction of his voice. Loic was grinning. "Come, sit with me."

Flustered and embarrassed she said "I'm sorry, I cannie. My mother disnae ken I'm here. It was very nice o' you to invite me. I have to go now."

"Cherie, you come here. We have a nice seat. See?" He pointed towards the drift netting.

"No, no here. I think we have to walk," said Effie, shocked at her change of heart. She started walking fast, away from the bicycle and the netting. Summer fishing took most of the men into deeper waters, north of Musselburgh, which meant the town was quieter than normal. Only the clank of ropes and metal hooks singing in chorus from the remaining boats and the lighthouse sweeping over the dark sea showed signs of life.

Loic stopped and made a gesture for her to sit on a capstan next to him. Effie frowned and rushed on until she reached some steps leading down to another part of the harbor. "Why you go fast?" he asked, losing his smile.

Breathlessly, Effie answered, "I cannie be seen walkin' oot wi' you. I'll be the talk o' the toon the morn."

He stopped. "You no want walk with me?" he said, suddenly the injured party. "Why you come?"

Effie didn't really know why she had come when it came down to it. Her best response would have been that she was flattered he had asked.

"No, it's no that," she said defensively. "I cannie be seen oot wi' a stranger."

"But I no a stranger. I see you each time I come here," he said, puzzled.

"Aye, that's true, but it's no as if you come fae here. You ken what I mean?"

Loic missed the last part and was confused. "I see you the first time. I like you. You pretty. Pourquoi tu est pas content?"

The last part was completely lost on Effie. She sucked in her breath and her belly and said, "Och, you probably say that to aw' the girls you meet," and gave a short laugh.

"Non. We stop now," he said defiantly, taking off his jacket and placing it on the stone steps. "Assis-toi!" he commanded.

Effie was out of breath and stood looking at his jacket until he waved her to sit down. Carefully, she placed herself on the mossy steps a little distance away from him. She watched the waves scudding across the top of the water, before breaking at the bottom of the steps.

Loic pulled a bottle of red wine from his pocket and uncorked it before handing it to Effie. "Some wine, it is good for you," he said, smiling once more.

Effie shook her head. Her mother forbade any alcohol in the house because too many had destroyed themselves with the stuff. Her grandfather had killed himself falling off a boat because of it. The ironic thing was, he had been in the harbor when it happened.

"You taste—it's good," he urged.

Effie took the bottle and sniffed. It smelled musty. "Drink! It is good wine from my country."

She took a swig and screwed up her face. Her mouth puckered with the taste of vinegar.

"Plus. It is better. Good."

She took another swig and found he was right. It did get better. She took a great gulp and handed back the bottle.

"How many years you have?"

"Have I what?"

"You know, years?"

"Oh, that. I'll be fifteen in a couple of months," she giggled. "How old are you?"

"Tres âgé?" he said, gulping down some wine, a few drops of which dribbled on his unshaven chin.

"Is that auld?" Effie asked.

"Twenty," replied Loic, wiping himself with the scarf he wore around his neck.

Effie thought he was at least ten years older than her, but that must have been because of the beard. It made his face seem more aged. His deep-set eyes had a sad quality to them, but the skin around them looked young. He was tanned from being out in the sun all the time, like the fishermen, and he had a line where his scarf ended and his shirt began.

Taking a few onion threads from his pocket, he began to skillfully weave a braided necklace with long, elegant fingers. Effie watched with fascination until he was finished. He kneeled behind her to put it around her neck, and she squirmed under his touch, giggling. Reaching up to touch it, she noticed how remarkably smooth it felt. "Who would have thought that from an onion string," she crooned.

Letting his hand rest on her neck, he untied the scarf around her neck and pulled it slowly from her. "This is pretty. Many colors. Where you buy this?"

Effie bent down as if she were tying her bootlaces. "I made it," she said shyly.

"No!" he gasped. "C'est pas possible!"

"Aye, I did," she said more bravely, looking up at him. "I collect wee bits and put them together. It keeps me busy."

"Me, to keep this?" he asked, running the soft fabrics through his fingers.

"Och, what dae you want wi' an auld rag like that?"

"No, it is beautiful. Like you. It is for me of you." He slipped it around his neck, looking foolish in her rag cloth.

"What you do when you no work?"

"What do you do?" she countered.

"Sleep!"

"That's what ah dae," she said with a short, shrill laugh. She leaned back with her hands outstretched on the slippery moss behind her, feeling the effect of the wine relaxing her body.

He sidled closer to her and touched the edge of her coat. "You have brothers?" he asked.

"No, all gone," she sang lightly.

"You no have any men to fight the war for you?"

"No. None," said Effie smiling.

He slid in even closer but she didn't move, even when he touched her hand. She held her breath because she didn't know what else to do. All the women in her books knew exactly what to do, but Effie felt encased in stone. She had not been touched with affection since her father, who always gave her a good night pat and a kiss before she went to bed. Please, God, tell me what to do, she thought.

"You fae France?" she asked in a blurt of air.

"Oui. Je suis Français," he murmured sweetly and caressed her hand.

"Oh, aye," she responded, feeling every muscle in her body tightening up as she spoke. There it was again. The same surge she had felt in the bakery, like an electric shock. She pulled her hand back sharply.

"I dinnae ken what you think, but I'm no that kind o' lassie." She clasped her hands together but didn't attempt to stand up.

"Please, je suis desole. Sorry, sorry. No problem." He looked embarrassed and suddenly very young, and she took pity on him.

"It's aw' right, honest. I'm no sorry I came. I've been havin' a good time. It's just that . . ." She looked around the harbor and then down at the sea moving up the stairs. "What's it like in France?"

Loic took a swig from the bottle and then offered it to her again, but she refused. In broken English and French he told her of his brothers, who worked the farm; his sisters, who lived and worked in the big châteaux; and his mother, who had died the year before. Effie nodded when it seemed appropriate, but wasn't really catching much of the story.

He held out the bottle, which had only a little left in the bottom. "Perhaps you will be my French girl if you like wine. You would like to come and see my home? We have sands and sea too. This place is like my home," he said.

Effie took one more swig and handed the bottle back. He placed it on the ground and moved in closer to her once more, touching her hair. "Why you hide this every day?"

"It's fur ma work," she said, reaching up to pat it.

He slid out the comb that was holding the back of her hair in place, and her hair fell down towards her shoulders. She remembered a book where the heroine had long blonde hair that reached down to her knees and how everyone who saw it fell in love with her. She smiled at the thought as he stroked her hair lightly with his hand. With the other hand, he reached over to touch her breast.

Effie sat still, unable to move. She noticed a warm sensation, but she felt like an observer. Her hair was being pulled and stroked and her nipples were rising as he ran his fingertips over them, and she wanted to lie back and let him do what he wanted, let him kiss her and tell her how much he loved her.

And out of this whirr of desire, she heard the sins of the flesh sermon given by Father Fitzpatrick last weekend and knew she was doomed forever.

She pulled back slightly from his hand, but the wine confused the motion and she was moving towards him. He leaned in closer and she could smell the wine and onions on his breath. It smelled of exotic dishes from a faraway place she would never visit.

Suddenly, out of the reverie, her mother's voice scolded, "Whae would want a girl like you?" and she was sure that someone did. He was here right now, and it didn't matter how many sins were being committed—she would prove her mother wrong. Someone did want her and she wanted him, right now. Right here on this wet stone stair.

Her legs quivered and her hands were cold. She had an urge to stand up, to step out of the spell that bound her to this place, but instead she marveled at his ability to find his way in and out of the crevices and creases of her body that she never knew existed until now. Nothing in her romance novels had prepared her for this moment. The admonitions from the priest, from her mother, from their way of life sat on her like gravestones. She knew the sins of the flesh were evil and it was not pleasure she was feeling, but sins. Even so, she couldn't help it, she wanted to continue to feel his love. She did not want to wait for her rewards in heaven. She wanted them now.

When Loic raised her skirt and underskirt, she was beyond hope of stopping him. She wanted it more than she had ever wanted anything in her life, and neither the Virgin Mary, or her mother would stop her.

His callused fingers stroked their way in between her stockings and her knickers. He wanted her. She could feel the pulse on his fingertips. Sensations spread in bursts of rainbow colors between her thighs until, like a symphony, the pulse of it was running up and through her arms, her breasts, and her hair, and she was helpless to do anything about this passion she had read about in all the books of romance. A passion that promised to drown her. If this was falling in love, then she would do it. She would allow him to give what little pleasure she could find in life. She wanted with all her heart to be loved like this, night after night. All the stories she had read were true. Love was a blessing, a physical act next to God, and she would willingly give up her soul to surrender to the man who had inspired such intensity of feelings. With tenderness, he provoked every impulse she had ever had to be cherished.

And then with sudden horror, she realized that her stockings had holes in them and he would see them if he pulled her skirt up all the way. As her skirt rose higher and he began unbuttoning his trousers, all her sins came crashing down. "No, you can't! I can't! Please stop! I'm no go'in wi' you. It's no right."

"Sssh, cherie! Sssshh! I make you happy. Je t'aime. Je t'aime."

Blind from the tears that were spreading from ear to ear, she felt the first thrust and knew that God had come to punish her. The cold granite steps dug into her back as he thrust repeatedly into the tight virginal space. The colors of her rainbow changed to searing black streaks that she wanted to stop.

In a feeble voice, she cried, "Please, no. I cannie dae this. You have to stop," and tried pushing his weight off her. But even with her stout arms, she could not find the strength to throw off this lightweight man. Loic thrust a few more times before he groaned and convulsed on top of her. Believing he was dying, she scrambled from underneath him, pushing him back before rolling away. Surprised, he sat back on his heels, leaving his wilting penis dangling on the outside of his trousers. Placing it inside, he smiled at her. "Tout est bien, cherie," he said casually, holding the wine bottle out to her.

Effie struggled to sit up and pulled her knickers back into place, feeling the sticky wetness between her legs. It was like she was having her menses, and she wondered at the timing. She searched in her coat pocket for the grimy handkerchief she had forgotten to wash last week, ashamed that that was all she had.

"Cherie, I make you cry," said Loic, putting the bottle down.

Effie wiped her nose and sniffed, rolling onto her knees to stand up. "It's aw' ma fault. I'm sorry. It's aw' right. I shouldnae have been here." She stood up and clutched her coat around her, feeling the slow dribble of semen catch the top of her stockings and slither between her leg and the thick, coarse dark wool.

Suddenly, out across the water, the sounds of bells rang throughout the town and a small voice drifted across the harbor wall, yelling, "It's here. We're at war!"

Agnes couldn't believe she was on a plane to Los Angeles and desperately wanted to slam the manuscript down on the small table in front of her. "What a lot of shite," she muttered. "This is no my history." How could she. How could she write this? This is no right. I didnae tell her any o' this and she's made up aw' this. I telt her I didnae ken whae ma faither was, it was some Frenchman Ingin Johnny, but I never telt her this. My Ma would never have allowed anybody to dae that to her. What was she thinkin' putting aw' that doon? She smacked her lips together feeling an unbidden need to cry. She would not give in to it. This was just another sloppy story.

She adjusted herself in the tight constraints of the airplane seat, her ample body squeezed between the two armrests, and looked at the girl asleep two seats over. Her pregnant belly swelled in the cramped space pushing her naval upwards like a little hat through the thin cotton t-shirt she wore. That lassie should be at home, she thought. We're aw' stuffed in this wee space and I can hardly breathe.

Her niece Alison, had a good imagination all right, and she'd have something to say to her when she got back. Agnes had told her she wasn't interested in going on this journey; had refused to take the manuscript, but Alison had played the old guilt card and she had reluctantly accepted. It was hard to say no. The woman was dying in the hospital of cancer. Agnes told her, "You cannie be serious! I've never been further west than Blackpool. I'm seventy-six years auld. What about my blood pressure? What would I be doing going to California? I'm no sure I can even spell it. I've seen it on the telly and it looks hot and full of lassies with nae clothes on and police runnin' aroond wi' guns. I don't think I'd like it there. Besides, I dinnae like airplanes. It's no right to be gawn up in the air. I've never been on one and I dinnae want tae start now."

But Alison, in her usual way, managed to convince Agnes that she was the only one who could deliver the family story to the daughter she had given up for adoption. "She needs to know," said Alison.

"Why?" asked Agnes.

"Because we all need to know where we come from so we can know who we are," she said, pushing the manuscript across the bed towards Agnes.

three

FOR ALMOST SIX weeks Effie had done everything her mother asked her to do without objecting. She massaged her mother's hands each night with a special lanolin cream she had bought for herself, tolerated every complaint and every insult, and did not deviate in any way to and from work. With every stroke of her mother's dry, cracked sandpaper skin, Effie winced inwardly. This is my penance, she thought. She would not wander away again.

The image of Loic grunting on top of her, the searing pain of entry, and the cold, damp steps that cut her back like a knife ran in her head like a silent film without music in an endless loop. Each night was a whirligig of images and smells she wanted to forget. She would never touch red wine again as long as she lived.

She awoke with a terrible need to vomit but couldn't make it down the stairs before she threw up. Her nightgown was splattered with the undigested remains of last night's fish; her nose and mouth filled with the acid wash of barreled brine. She collapsed on the floor and began to cry.

Her mother Lizzie, ran down the stairs behind her. "Good God, Effie. What's the matter? Are you aw' right? For God's sake, would you look at the mess here. It stinks to high hell. It'll take days to get this smell out o' here."

Effie, shivering yet feeling overheated, stood up and began to take off her nightgown.

Lizzie grabbed a gray, slimy cloth from the kitchen sink and threw it at her. "Och, come up the stairs, will ye. Get something clean to put on yourself."

Naked, Effie walked up the stairs, clutching the stinking cloth to her breasts. She had not felt this sick in years, not since she had dysentery when she was eight years old. She had been feeling queasy for days now, and she wasn't sleeping well. Maybe she should go and see the doctor, but that cost too much.

"Here, cover yourself up, lass," said Lizzie gruffly, tossing her a clean nightgown. "You'll get your death o' cauld like that. Go doon and clean up that mess. I cannie put ma hands in it. You'll have to dae it yourself. Are you gonnie be able to go to your work?"

Effie nodded and went downstairs. She would go to her work, but soon Mr. Jenkins was going to have a word with her. She had not been her usual self, as he would have called it. She was tired all the time, she hated the vanilla smell of the cakes, and she didn't have much to say anymore. He kept asking if everything was all right, and she always said she was fine, but he didn't believe it.

Loic had vanished from the area after their walk, and she doubted he would ever come back. Now that France and Britain were at war, every able-bodied man was expected to sign up. What an idiot she was to think he would be her lover, her savior. Her mother was right. It was a fool's game. But every time the shop bell rang, she looked up expectantly. Mr. Jenkins saw the anxiety in her, read the nervousness in her body, and gently took her aside one day.

"He's no coming back, hen," he said quietly. Effie looked down at her shoes and nodded her head. "Would you like a wee cup of tea? I could use one myself."

She sat down by the bread bins and took her scarf from her head to wipe her eyes. "I'm just a wee bit tired, Mr. Jenkins," she said mournfully, "that's aw'. I'll be fine soon."

"I know, hen. That's aw' right. You just take your time there for a minute. I'll be all right by myself. The whole world is upside doon right now. My Maggie's beside herself as well, worried about oor Danny. I expect we'll aw' get through this, one way or the other."

The next morning, Effie awoke again with the sick feeling in her stomach, and also a fever. "I cannie stay in my bed, Ma. I'll no have a job to go back to the morrow if I stay away." She ran her hands over her tumid breasts and thought if she had the flu, she was going to die. She felt so tired, she couldn't think of anything else.

"You'll just have to deal with that one when you come to it," said Lizzie. "I'll go in there myself and tell him. He'll gie you a few days. You havenae had a day sick in aw' the time you've been wi' him. He'll be aw' right."

Effie launched herself from the bed towards the washing bowl that stood on the dresser and barely made it.

"Och, I've never seen anyone wi' the flu whae spews as much as you do. Can it be something else you've got?"

Effie shook her head and went back to bed. "I just feel like I'm slung ow'er a hard sea," she groaned.

Lizzie shook her head and took the bowl downstairs to the outside toilet. She had prayed fervently each morning that her lassie would be all right, had asked Mary to watch over her and not let anything happen to her. But the question that kept nagging at the back of her mind wouldn't let go, and she trembled at the thought of asking.

"Where did you go the night you ran oot the hoose, Effie?"

Effie lay facing the statue of the Virgin Mary and knew there were not enough Hail Marys for this one. Finally, there were sins to confess, but she couldn't do it in front of her mother. She couldn't do it in front of the priest. She had made a mistake she was sorry for. But it was her secret now. There was no forgiveness for lies.

"Nae whair," she said as innocently as she could. "I was just oot fur a walk. I needed some fresh air."

"You're lying to me, Effie. You came back in a right state that night. I saw it. You went to see somebody that night, didn't you?"

"I'm no lying, Ma. I didnae go anywhere that night."

"Dae you think I'm daft? I dinnae notice anything around here? I'm no the only one. Mrs. Jenkins said you had an Ingin Johnny come and see you. I saw her the day when I went to tell them you werenae well. She said she's been worried aboot you for weeks now. Dinnae lie to me, Effie. I cannie stand havin' people talkin' like that. There's something go'in on, I ken it."

She dragged Effie out of the bed and onto the floor in front of the statue of the Virgin Mary. The candles that stood on either side were cold. Effie's knees felt bruised as she stumbled to the floor.

"Tell me on the tears of Our Lady that there is nothing to ken," pleaded Lizzie. "Tell me on the blood of our Lord you havenae been keepin' something fae me. Tell me in the name of all that's holy, Effie. Tell me the truth. Did you go and do something daft wi' somebody? Did you gie yourself to somebody? You've got to tell me, Effie. Is that why you've no been well aw' these weeks? Is that it, Effie? Please, God, dinnae let it be," she beseeched, beginning to cry. "All ma life I've tried to be a good woman, Lord. All my life I've done my best. You took my man and my bairn, so dinnae take this one as well. She's all I've got. Dinnae take her as well." She was clutching at Effie, rocking back and forth on her heels, sobbing against her daughter's shoulder as Effie sat immutable on her knees. Lizzie pulled her face around to look at her. "Tell me you didnae dae it!" she screamed.

Agnes stared at the binder. "I dinnae ken where I am."

The pregnant girl leaned towards her. "You need to pull your table down. They're serving dinner now."

Agnes had turned a very bright shade of red and was sweating profusely.

The girl leaned across the spare seat and looked at the manuscript in Agnes's hands. "Are you all right?"

She gave a nod of her head.

"What are you reading?"

"A lot of shite!" said Agnes, feeling embarrassed at her outburst. "I'm sorry, I'm just a wee bit upset. Ma niece has written stuff aboot ma mother that I didnae ken. I dinnae ken what she was thinking, putting this stuff doon like this."

The girl nodded. "It must be painful."

"That's no even half of it, hen."

"Is it true?"

"No any truth I ken," said Agnes. "She just made it up."

"Sometimes the best stories are the ones we make up."

"Aye, and sometimes they're nothing but lies."

four

EFFIE RUBBED HER munitions uniform over the tin washboard letting the slick black, oily water flow into the sink. She would rather have been up to her elbows in flour, but these days were long gone. Factory work paid better and besides, there was a war on. Continuing to scrub the collar over the washboard, she scraped her knuckles against the corrugated edges and cursed quietly under her breath.

"I heard that," said Agnes. "That's a bad word."

Effie smiled. Her daughter was too smart sometimes. She was looking at a magazine and stopped at a picture of a young soldier coming home to a welcoming wife and children by the front door. "Why don't I have a daddy?" asked Agnes.

"I've told you before. He was away in the war." She pushed the rough cotton jacket harder up and down, trying to rub out every bit of grease and shell fillings. The kettle started boiling, spitting hot water. Effie rushed to take it from the black cast-iron hob over the fire.

"But is he comin' back?" she persisted.

Effie released the dirty water in the sink and poured in the hot water. Tossing the uniform into the enamel basin, she dried her hands on her apron and sat down, taking Agnes on her lap. "I think it's time you and I had a wee talk." She pulled her in closer. "Your daddy and . . ." She took a deep breath before taking the plunge. "He was sent away a long time ago, and he's never gonnie come back. I cannie explain it to you, but you have to understand that there's a lot of Daddies gone over there, and there's lots of wee girls who'll never get to see them again."

"Does that mean he's dead?"

Effie hugged her closer to her chest. "I dinnae ken what to dae wi' you," she laughed. "Aye," she said with a sigh. "He's deed." She shuddered as she said it, finally saying what she had been thinking for the last three and a half years. He died the moment he disappeared and left her.

Agnes sat quietly looking at the picture spread out on the floor in front of them. "Are we gonnie get another daddy one day?"

Effie gave a short laugh. "Aye, I'll get ye one for Christmas. Do you have any particular kind in mind?"

Climbing down from her knee, Agnes picked up the magazine with the smiling father, bag on his back, hugging his children as his wife watched with a beatific smile on her face. "Aye, one of these."

Effie roared with laughter. "I'll see what I can dae. Maybe you should go oot and pick one for me."

Agnes clutched her mother's waist and gave her a hug before flipping through the pictures again. "But what if I dinnae like him?"

"Dinnae you worry. I'll make sure he's a good one. He'll be just for you."

Effie finished rinsing her uniform and hung it up to dry. Each day was getting harder to continue alone. Agnes needed a father and Effie needed someone to help her out. She made enough to pay the rent and put food on the table, but there was nothing left. Lots of women were struggling with their men dead or missing, so she knew she wasn't alone, but it wasn't fair to Agnes to stay that way. What kind of life could she offer her by bringing her up herself? She was tired of always being alone. All her life she had been alone, and she longed for some company, but not with the idiots who frequented the pubs. She owed it to Agnes to make her life better, just as her mother had done by putting her into the bakery. Fat lot of good that did, she thought, looking at the drying uniform. I have to find a better way.

At the library Effie buried herself a little more deeply into the chair behind the stack of books that obscured the view of the men standing by the newspapers filling in time before the pub opened. She was engrossed in *Great Expectations* and had just come to the part where Pip discovers he has a benefactor who is willing to raise him with great expectations when, without warning, the books on the edge of the table tumbled to the floor. She jumped up and began to reach down for them at the same time as a young man with a thick mane of orange flaming hair apologized, struggling to bend down. "I'm sorry," he kept saying. "I didnae mean to disturb you." His face was contorted as he tried to get down on one knee. As Agnes raised her head to see who it was, they banged heads and the books dropped to the floor again. She saw him struggling to bend and took his arm. "It's aw' right, honest. I'll manage. You just get yourself up. I'll do it." She smiled at him shyly, noticing how the ginger hair and a red scarf around his neck created a halo of light around his worried face. He looked away, embarrassed, and lifted four books to place them securely on the table.

"I saw you the other day," he said shyly. "You come here a lot, don't you?"

"Aye, I come here once a week, usually." She pushed all the books further onto the table and sat down again. He stood awkwardly by the side of the table, looking at her.

Effie looked up at him and smiled uncomfortably. "You come here a lot too?"

"No much else I can do at this point," he said, shrugging a glance in the direction of his leg. "Got this at Ypres. Nasty place."

Effie stared into deep, dark pools of liquid, set like a blind person. "It must have been hard," she said, looking away.

"Aye, well. It's just one of these things," he said, brushing it aside.

She nodded and stacked the books again in neat piles.

"Aw' right then," he said, taking a tartan cap from his pocket.

Effie glanced at the clock on the wall and saw it was almost closing time at the library. She had to be getting back. Dottie Strachan, her neighbor, would be starting to wonder where she was, and Agnes would be getting tired.

He started to leave, and then hesitated. "Would you like a wee cup of tea? There's a café doon the road."

Effie looked at the clock again and picked up *Great Expectations*.

32

"I've got to get this checked oot," she said nervously. "My wee yin'll be waiting for me."

He looked disappointed. "Oh! Oh! You've got a man away? It's aw' right. I didnae mean to be a bother." He nodded and gave a small smile. "I'll be away then." He turned towards the library door. In the curve of his back and his broad shoulders, Effie saw there had once been a strong man.

"Wait!" she cried, "I've got fifteen minutes. I don't live so far away. It's no bother."

⟨⟩

Douglas Sharp had come back from the war in Europe as one of the walking wounded. He had been in the suicide ditches at Ypres when the yellow cloud floating over the mud-thick fields transfixed the embattled soldiers by its ethereal beauty. When the men around him began falling down, choking and coughing, their throats on fire and their bellies splitting wide with each breath, the deadly force of the mustard gas beauty came home to haunt him. Douglas had the sense to grab his coat and hold it to his face while the men around him died with the contents of their bellies fertilizing the mud that sucked them into oblivion.

When it was over, he was one of the lucky ones. Douglas lay temporarily blinded for three days under a mass of rotting bodies before anyone noticed him. His hip bone was shattered and the Army sent him home with a piece of shrapnel as a souvenir. His hip bone held in place by a metal pin, caused him to swing his leg a little too wide when he walked. He was the object of pity and amusement and any chance he might have felt for romantic attachment was lost in the shame of his physical state.

As Effie warmed to him and joined him each week for tea at the cafe, his courage returned and he asked her if she would be interested in staying with him. "It's not that I've got a lot to offer," he said humbly, "but I promise I can take care of you."

"You want me to marry you?" she said, surprised at the sudden offer.

"Aye, well, I probably wasn't thinking too well." He pushed the cup around the saucer, pulling the handle round and round, afraid to look up.

Effie sat up straight and put her hands on her lap, looking directly at Douglas. He looked as if he were reading the tea leaves in his cup. She leaned forward slightly. "But I haven't known you for a long time. I mean, it's a wee bit sudden, if you know what I mean."

He looked up and then looked down at the cup again as if expecting an answer to his conundrum any minute. "Aye, I know that," he muttered, "but I thought . . ." His voice trailed away and they both sat silent.

At the age of nineteen years going on thirty, Effie weighed fourteen stone and wore glasses, had a child who was smarter than she was, and couldn't remember the last time someone had asked her for anything except work. In the books she read, the films she saw, and the romances she heard about in the factory that made the girls cry, she knew that her heart had never been lost to anyone except Agnes. She had pined for Loic briefly, believing that perhaps he would return and rescue her from her fate. But soon after moving into Mrs. Bellingham's Home for Girls with Distressed Circumstances, she dismissed that fantasy forever. Too many girls were waiting to be rescued, and she didn't stand a chance. She was an ample girl grown into an ample woman. No longer were there spots on her face, but her chicken pox scars were still there, and although she had cut her hair to ear length, she was not handsome like many of the other girls, and her eyesight had failed shortly after the birth, requiring her to wear round, Bakelite glasses that slid down her nose at every opportunity.

He wasn't much of a talker, he didn't drink and he didn't smoke, and he wasn't betting on the horses. That was a good start. He had never forced himself upon her in any way. Granted, he had not spent any time with Agnes, but Effie thought she could do worse. Maybe Agnes would like him once she got to know him. But it bothered her that this was not the love she had always planned for herself.

"I dinnae ken, Douglas. I don't have much experience with this. I've been doing aw' right with just me and Agnes. It's a big responsibility for you. It can be hard when you've got a lot of mouths to feed. How are you gonnie manage it?"

"I think I've got it all figured oot," he began. "I'm gonnie get a job down at the gasworks. They're lookin' for someone to douse the coke. It's no a hard job, and I think I can dae it. It's a fair bit o' walkin', but the doctor said it was good for ma hip. I should be able to make a go o' it."

"How much money do they make a week?"

"Och, Effie. You dinnae have to worry aboot that. It'll be enough."

"Aye, well. I winnie gie up ma job sae fast."

"They're cutting back jobs, ye ken? This war's gonnie be finished soon."

"I'll just have to get another job," said Effie. "I've never been without a job. Something'll come up. But what aboot Agnes? Are you tellin' me you're aw' right wi' another man's bairn?"

"The wee yin needs a faither. You've said so yourself. I ken I'm no very good wi' bairns, but it disnae mean I cannie take care of them. I'm sure it will work out better as we go along."

Effie considered her options. In her neighborhood, men created children as casually as they had toast for their breakfasts, and discarded them just as easily as the crusts. Men were generally more interested in the three Bs than the three Rs. Betting, booze, and bed. Since Douglas preferred reading to boozing, maybe it would work out fine.

"So what do you think?" he asked expectantly. "Can we make a go of it?"

Effie put her hat on her head and pushed the pin into the back of it. "We'll see. I've got to be away to my work."

On Easter Sunday, Effie and Agnes took a basket of colored hard-boiled eggs, carefully rationed for weeks, and spent the morning chasing after them in Starbank Park. Pink, blue, and black eggs bounced and crashed down the green slope of the hill. Effie sat on the grass and watched Agnes fall on her knees as she ran after the eggs.

"You mind that dress, Agnes. I'm no gonnie be spending oors takin' oot the grass stains."

"Aye, Ma, I'll be careful," she yelled, running up the hill again, checking as she ran to see if there were any grass stains.

Agnes shouted "Look, Ma! Catch it, Ma!" as the eggs rolled down the hill, but Effie was looking the other way. Following her gaze down the path, Agnes saw a man who looked like he was trying to climb stairs because his left leg lifted awkwardly as he walked, his body rocking from side to side. Under his tartan tammy, his ginger hair exploded in all directions, and the ends of his red scarf bounced with his walk. He had his hands firmly stuck in his coat pockets as if they were supporting him. Agnes thought he looked like one of the clowns she had seen at the circus.

Effie waved and smiled at him, then picked at the blades of grass when he stopped next to her. Agnes called from the hill, "Here, Ma, catch the next one. The blue one. It's comin' doon the hill. Catch it!" But Effie ignored her, laughing and talking to the man with the ginger hair. The egg rolled to a stop beside her but she didn't pick it up. Agnes slowly descended the hill to stand next to her mother and picked up the egg to put back in the basket, the shell a crazy pattern of cracks in the pale blue skin. "You didn't catch the egg," she said.

"And whae do we have here?" asked the man, leaning his face down towards her.

Effie pulled Agnes in closer to her side. Agnes stepped behind her mother's skirt. She didn't like the man's eyes. They were too dark.

"Agnes, this is Douglas Sharp. Say hello."

"Och, you're no shy, are you?" offered Douglas. "Come on, come and say hello. I won't eat you, I promise." Reaching around Effie to chuck Agnes under the chin, she pulled away in horror at the man's familiarity.

"C'mon now, this is no like you. She's usually got more to say," said Effie apologetically, taking his extended hand to stand up. "Agnes, put all the eggs in the basket, we'll have them for our tea this afternoon."

Agnes picked up the remaining black and pink eggs and put them in the basket which her mother handed to her before taking the arm of the stranger. Pulling on her mother's arm to get her to lean down she said, "There's an awfy smell around here," she said quietly, looking at Douglas.

"Shush, Agnes. It's the gasworks. There's always a stink from them," said Effie casually.

"You didnae think it was me, did you? Away wi' you!" shouted Douglas. "Away wi' you." He scampered towards her and Agnes shrieked, running in front of them. Effie and Douglas both laughed as she ran in terror of this limping, blinded giant, hoping desperately her mother was not planning on making him the new daddy she was looking for.

❧❧

Two months later, Effie dressed Agnes for her wedding in a yellow and white floral dress that her employer had given her. True to her word, Effie had found a job as a maid as soon as the factory closed and refused to accept handouts except for this one occasion. Agnes hated the dress, and fussed over the ribbons on the sleeves, which were too tight. She was beginning to look a lot like her mother, except for the amber eyes of her father and dark raven hair that fell into voluptuous curls around her shoulders. "I hate this dress," she told Effie.

"Just today, Agnes, dinnae be difficult."

"A dinnae like it!" said Agnes stubbornly. "It itches and it's tight. Can't I wear something else."

"No, you can't. We're bloody lucky to have this much. You have to wear it today."

"I don't like it," screamed Agnes, "and I don't like him."

"Just wear the damn thing and let's get go'in," yelled Effie. "I've had enough o' your complaining, lass."

As Agnes began to cry, Effie also began to sob, putting her hands to her face, smearing her newly applied lipstick on the palms of her hands. "I'm sorry," she said mournfully. "It's no right, I ken." Reaching over, Agnes put her arms around her mother. "It's aw' right, Ma. I'll wear the dress, dinnae worry."

Effie wondered why this was not the happiest day of her life. Didn't all the books tell her that she should be wearing a white dress with lace and ribbons? Her husband would be handsome and she would be taken care of for the rest of her life? She had asked for a special day off work and was told she couldn't be spared for more than an afternoon, so she wore the navy blue cotton dress with the white Peter Pan collar that was her new uniform. All that was missing was the white apron. Douglas was right. The war was over, there were no jobs and the woman's place was back in the kitchen again. Effie's new job took her two hours away from home to the posh end of town. Because she spent ten hours a day washing dishes and polishing brass, her hands, previously thick with dirt under her nails, were now chapped and raw. She thought about the nights spent massaging her mother's hands; now even a little cold cream was unaffordable. Pulling on her white gloves, she smoothed down Agnes's hair.

"It'll be aw' right, hen, you'll see."

Douglas radiated cleanliness with a freshly shaved face and sheen of paraffin oil to control his thick red hair. He looked lost in the brown suit his father had left him when he died. The jacket was too big at the shoulders, and the pants were about three inches too long, causing his shoes to disappear under the broad sweep of the hem. He wore a white shirt vaguely fitting around the collar where his Adam's apple bounced when he swallowed. It was the first time Effie had seen him dressed up.

He stood awkwardly to the side as she approached him, and smiled uncomfortably at his mother before giving Effie a kiss on the cheek. His mother wore a tight black coat, which folded the flesh around her waist, and had a tight mouth to match. In all the times Effie had seen her, Douglas's mother had only smiled once, and that was on their first meeting and it was more a baring of teeth than an actual heart-felt smile. His sister, Meg, in a simple skirt and jacket made from turquoise blue cotton, stepped towards Effie and gave her hand a squeeze. "Are you all right, hen?" she asked consolingly. Effie gave a slight nervous smile and nodded, almost in tears.

"You'll be fine. Don't you worry. He's a good man."

Next to her stood Douglas's friend, Willie. Effie wondered which rag shop he had stopped at. He stood in yesterday's shave, wearing a navy striped suit shiny with age and grease and a shirt that had taken flight at the sight of water. His shoes were half-laced because the laces weren't long enough to cover all the lace holes, and a grimy handkerchief hung ludicrously out of the breast pocket.

She clutched her handbag to her belly and tried to smile, but it was kind of locked up in her jaw. Meg surprised her with a red carnation, as well as one for her brother. "There, that'll make it seem more real," Meg said, pushing it through her coat button. Effie gave her a small kiss and Meg squeezed her hand. "You'll be all right," she said softly.

Mounting the stairs to the registry office Agnes clutched her mother's hand trailing behind Douglas, who walked carefully lifting his specially made platform shoe, bringing both legs level with each other so that his movements were less jerky than before. Feeling the pull on the back of her coat, Effie turned and looked at Bertha, who gave a shake of her head in the direction of the registrar's office. "I'll take her," said Bertha. "Just for a wee while," said Effie softly to Agnes. "I'll be back in a minute."

Agnes began to cry, and Bertha told her not to be such a baby. Effie looked back briefly as Douglas opened the door to the office. He was followed by Willie, and Meg. Bertha sat outside with Agnes squeezed beside her, sobbing quietly.

Effie exchanged her vows with Douglas and took the simple gold band he placed on her finger. He kissed her politely on each cheek in a flourish of excitement, and she reciprocated before Meg came forth and kissed them both. Willie at least had the sense to stand back and do nothing.

When they emerged into the hallway, Agnes rushed towards her mother and smothered her face in her skirt. Bertha looked on disapprovingly. "You go and sit wi' your nannie," Effie said, pointing at Bertha. "I've still got to sign the book." Agnes stood resolutely beside her mother until she was allowed to go with her. There was no way she was going back to that old woman with the severe face and the cold mouth. This was not her nannie. She didn't have one.

Agnes awoke suddenly. "I cannie breathe." Anxiously, she clawed at the neck of her raincoat, which she had neglected to take off. "I've got to get off this plane." She struggled with the seat belt, which was pinching her belly, and looked down at the leftover food on the tray table, feeling sick to her stomach. Her palms were sweating as she took small gasps of breath, trying to get herself under control. "It's awfy hot in here," she said to no one in particular, fanning herself with her hands and wiping her top lip. I have to get some air or I'm go'in to pass oot.

The girl in the next seat had fallen asleep and lay with her head resting on her chest like a doll.

Craning her neck, Agnes looked over the top of the seats in front of her to see if she could see someone, anyone, who could help her out of her seat. She felt like a little girl trapped inside a room where the lock is broken, hammering away at it to get someone to let her out.

Seeing a flight attendant a few seats away, she started to wave. "Yoo hoo," she called several times. People turned around in their seats, then the girl awoke and asked what the matter was.

"You've got to let me oot, hen," said Agnes, trying to put the food tray on the spare seat. "I have to stand up now."

The girl quickly undid her seat belt and stood up out of the way, but Agnes was still blocked by the food on the tray. Just then the flight attendant arrived.

"Is there anything I can do for you?"

"Aye, hen, get me oot o' here. I dinnae like this flying business."

"It's all right," she soothed. "Come, we'll take you out of that seat." She lifted the trays from both the girl and Agnes, then handed them to another attendant nearby. The girl stood up and helped Agnes struggle out of the confines of the seat, and as she stood nature released the bubbles of stress that had built up over several hours, lingering unpleasantly in the air for several seconds.

"Oh, my God. I'm sorry. I dinnae ken where a am wi' aw' this. I'm really sorry." Agnes was almost in tears.

The flight attendant supported her arms as she stepped out into the aisle. *Passengers stared as she was led towards the front of the plane. An insistent lament kept repeating in her head: Just get me oot o' here, just let me go hame.* "*I dinnae want to go to California,*" *she whined like a child.*

After getting Agnes situated in a quiet section of first class, the attendant sat beside her and held her hand. "*I'll get someone to bring you a drink,*" *she said.* "*You'll be all right.*" *She signaled her colleague to bring some water.* "*Are you going to see somebody in your family?*" *She held Agnes's gaze in her eyes.*

"*I suppose so,*" *said Agnes, distracted by the size of the chair and all the buttons on it.* "*I dinnae ken how you dae it. Whae would take a job flying back and for'ard spending aw' their time in the sky? I like to ken where ma feet are planted.*"

"*You get used to it,*" *said the attendant.* "*It's not so bad. I get to see all kinds of countries and things I wouldn't see otherwise.*"

"*I can watch the telly if I want to see something different,*" *said Agnes.*

"*So what do you like to watch?*" *She had folded her hands in front of her as if in prayer.*

"*Och, it's aw' rubbish, isn't it?*" *said Agnes, beginning to breathe better. The flight attendant handed her a glass of water, which she accepted gratefully. Looking around her, Agnes took in the scale of her surroundings.* "*They seats are awfy big here. I suppose you pay a lot o' money to sit in these.*"

The attendant laughed. "*Yes, you do. Would you like to sit here for a while?*"

"*Oh no, hen, I cannie sit here. This is no for the likes o' me. I need to go back to ma cubbyhole.*"

"*I've never heard it called that before,*" *she laughed.* "*It will give you a breather for a little while.*"

"*No thanks, hen. I'll be aw' right now. I'm sorry I was a bother.*"

"*You're not a bother. Sometimes it's hard doing different things.*"

"*Aye, that's true, but well, what are you gonnie dae? You just get on wi' it, don't you?*" *She stood up and walked slowly back to the economy cabin.*

five

DOUGLAS FLINCHED AS a fire engine passed by outside, and drew his knees up to his chest into fetal position, waiting for the explosion of howitzers. Effie stirred in her sleep, worn out from the work of the day.

Getting out of bed, he sat by the open window dressed only in his vest and underpants, breathing in the cold night air. It was always the same nightmare. Davie Balfour saying he was off to see his wife before his head exploded. A wave of nausea forced his stomach muscles to contract, and he held back the urge to vomit by swallowing hard and forcing himself to concentrate on the street below. Cats meowed and howled in tin can fights, rattling the silence of the night; the man next door lay snoring loudly through the paper-thin walls. Mice played catch me if you can across the linoleum floor of the kitchen. He wished he smoked so he could do something with his hands, but he had never liked the taste of it. Waiting until his body registered frozen, he returned to bed, careful not to touch Effie for the first few minutes, delighting in the heat from her ample body.

After a while, he felt himself stir and touched the soft roll of her thigh. He continued touching her thigh, gently rubbing his hand over the dimples and grooves of her skin, until she surfaced from her heavy sleep and turned on her back. When she was asleep was the best way to get her to respond. She didn't have time for excuses then. He kissed her gently on the cheek and then rolled on top of her. Within five minutes, he had taken his pleasure and she had woken enough to kiss him and then roll back onto her side.

Although he had wanted her to stay home, she would not listen. She insisted that the only way to keep the rent paid and food on the table was if she worked. His wages were not enough to take care of them and his mother. He couldn't argue. His job was one of the lowest paid at the gasworks. When Effie complained about the lack of money, he told her he had to take care of his mother, otherwise she'd be living on the Parish. For all the good this marriage was doing her, Effie thought he should go live with his mother again. She worked from eight in the morning until six at night as a maid, but it took her two hours to get there each day and two hours back. When she came home she cooked the meal, read to Agnes, and spent the rest of the night doing washing or sewing. There wasn't much left over.

Douglas would have been hard pressed to say what he felt for Effie. Respect mingled with tenderness, but it did not run to the word love, because he wasn't sure he understood what that meant until the day she announced she was pregnant.

"Are you sure?" he said. He wanted to dance, to jump, but the shoe kept his leg weighed to the ground as he longed to set himself free from gravity. He couldn't get enough spring into his step, so he settled for swaying from side to side, taking Effie by the elbows and pulling her along. "You're no kiddin' me, are you? Oh, Effie, you cannie believe what this means to me. Aw these nights . . ." He lowered his voice and stopped dancing. "I never thought I'd get a chance to see a bairn o' mine. You are a bloody saint." He pulled her closer and gave her a wet kiss on the cheek.

Effie laughed and pulled away. "I dinnae ken aboot the saint stuff. There's too many saints in this world if you ask me. Would you stand still—you're making me dizzy!"

He was suddenly anxious. "Oh, do you want to sit doon? Can I get you something? Oh, Effie, what am I gonnie dae wi' a bairn?"

"You've already got one," she said, pulling Agnes towards her, "in case you havenae noticed."

Agnes giggled and held her mother's hand as Douglas pulled her round.

"Oh, Effie. You've made me the happiest man that ever walked the earth." He turned her around once more and then hugged her, causing her to let Agnes go.

"Aye, well, you'll get over it," said Effie, smiling from ear to ear and hugging him back.

"Do you hear that, wee yin?" he called over his shoulder. "your ma's gonnie have a wee brother for you."

"I dinnae ken if it's a laddie," said Effie.

Agnes had been watching the two of them jigging round the living room, giggling like children at a party. Effie held out her hands and pulled her from the chair and started dancing with her while singing "Mary Laurie," a party favorite. Agnes jumped up and down until the neighbor below started banging with the broom on her ceiling. The room grew quiet except for Effie, who was breathing hard.

Agnes watched her mother for signs of her belly getting bigger like she had seen other women who were having babies. "Are you going to have it tomorrow?" she asked.

"Dinnae be daft lassie," said Douglas. "We've aw' got to bide oor time. It'll be here soon enough."

⬥

It was almost nine o'clock, and Effie was still not home. Douglas paced the floor and kept looking out the window to see if she was coming. Maybe the bus had broken down, he thought. Maybe she's just been kept late. She was seven months pregnant and he'd told her she was getting too big to be going to work. "I'm still walking," she said.

He heard hammering on the door and a voice yelling, "Mr. Sharp, Mr. Sharp, you've got to come quick." A scruffy boy stood panting at the door. "Your wife has collapsed at the bus stop and she's in the infirmary."

"Jesus Christ, what's happened?"

"I dinnae ken, mister. I was just telt to go and get you. You've to come quick." He stood waiting expectantly with his cap in hand, but Douglas ignored him.

Grabbing Agnes from her bed, he wrapped her coat around her and ran across the street to Dottie Strachan's. "The wee laddie didnae say what was the matter. Keep an eye on her until I get back." Agnes watched him go, afraid for her mother.

"Is she coming back, Dottie?" she asked.

"Aye, hen, dinnae you worry. Your ma's made o' strong stuff. She'll be back."

When he entered the hospital ward, a nurse led him quietly to her bedside, screened off behind white curtains. Her dark hair on the white pillows looked like a stain on the sterile landscape. "She's resting now. We've given her a small sedative. She seems exhausted. The swelling in her ankles has gone halfway up her legs, which might have contributed to her collapse. She needs to get off her feet more."

Douglas nodded in agreement but said nothing. He had been telling her that for months, but she wasn't listening. She was determined she would stay busy until the end. Under the sheets, like a huge dome, her pregnant belly rose in great gasps as she slept. "Is the bairn going to be all right?"

"Yes, everything will be fine. The doctor will talk to you when he gets here on his rounds."

Effie's mouth was slightly open, making sissing sounds as she breathed out. There was a small cubby next to the bed, which had her coat sticking out of the bottom. He bent down to fold it and push it into the cupboard. It was difficult to make it fit, so he gave up and let it hang there, looking untidy amid the tightly bound blankets of the bed. He sat in the chair next to her bed for four hours, dozing off and on; the ward was awash in low lights and the sounds of coughing and moaning. As the curtains clinked open, Douglas struggled out of his sleepy state. Hastily, he rose from the chair and tried to straighten out his coat. Signaling him to sit down, the doctor went over to Effie and took her pulse. The nurse presented her chart and he studied it carefully before motioning Douglas to step outside.

"Is she going to be all right, doctor?"

"We want to make sure that she and the baby are doing well. We think she's about thirty-six weeks pregnant, would that be right?"

"I dinnae ken. I mean, we think she's about seven and a half months gone.

"Your wife is suffering from excessive edema, Mr. Sharp. It's a common complaint in pregnant women, but in some cases it can have dangerous effects on the health of the mother and the baby. Your wife is a little overweight, and we think that might be contributing to the problem. We think it would be better if we kept her here for observation and bed rest."

Douglas thanked the doctor and went back to pick up his cap from the top of the cubby. With all the daily ravages of her job erased from her face, she looked peaceful. Suddenly, he had an urge to throw himself on his knees by the side of the bed, to plead with her to be all right, that he would do everything he could for her if only she would be all right. The bairn would be all right. Instead, he patted her hand before picking up his cap and turned around. Effie mumbled something as the curtain closed behind him, but he didn't hear. "I'm aw' right, Douglas."

⸙

Agnes heard Douglas say "complications" and knew it was a big word that meant serious things, but her attention was on the movement of his hand rubbing hers very hard between his while he talked with his sister. She fidgeted, pulling away, but he held on tight.

Meg was biting the inside of her lip in a nervous way. "Is the bairn gonnie be aw' right?"

"They said she'd be aw' right, but I'm no sae sure. Effie disnae look great. You never can tell wi' they doctors. They only tell you what you want to hear most of the time."

Agnes pulled her hand away and moved closer to Meg, who leaned into her ear and whispered, "It's gonnie be all right. your no to worry aboot her. She just needs a wee rest."

⸙

Two days later, Effie's placenta ruptured and they pulled the baby out with forceps, ignoring the fact that there was a river of blood running off the table onto the floor. As her blood pressure fell, she passed out, so was unable to hear the yelling of her baby daughter, exhibiting a fine set of lungs.

When Douglas brought her home three weeks later, Effie had lost twenty pounds and the baby had gained two. The climb upstairs to their third-floor flat took ten minutes to complete because she kept stopping to catch her breath.

Agnes sat on the edge of the bed, listening intently for the turn of the key in the lock. Meg was in the kitchen making tea. When Agnes heard their voices, she flew towards the door. Douglas opened it first and came in carrying the baby, swaddled in the fine woolen blanket his mother had spent weeks making. Effie, leaning heavily on his arm, was thrown off balance when Agnes latched onto her legs and would not let go. Effie patted her head and pulled away from her, taking off her coat and scarf. Meg had taken the baby from Douglas and was making cooing noises at it. Agnes waited until her mother had sat down. "C'mere, hen," Effie said holding out her arms, "come and see your Ma."

Rushing headlong into her mother's breasts, Agnes sobbed "Dinnae go away again, Ma. Dinnae leave me here. Dinnae die, Ma."

"There, there, pet. What's got into you? I'm hame. I'm no go'in anywhere." She stroked her hair and took her handkerchief out of her sleeve and gave it to Agnes. She motioned for Meg to give her the baby and lifted Agnes away from her slightly to make room. Opening Agnes's arms, Effie placed the sleeping child there. "She's awfy wee, so be careful wi' her." Agnes held her cautiously and eyed her suspiciously.

"Is she gonnie stay?"

Meg started laughing. "Aye, of course she is, ye silly bugger."

Douglas came in with a cup of tea for everyone. "You need to gie your ma a break, wee yin. She's tired."

Agnes looked at her mother, who nodded. "Just sit over there wi' Grace. You'll be aw' right." Agnes sat with the small bundle wrapped tightly inside the blanket, with only her face showing, and thought she looked like a little doll. "Gracie," she whispered, leaning down to smell her face.

CRXP

While Effie was treading water in postpartum depression, Douglas swam in pride of ownership. He had a daughter, and he would love and cherish her more than anything he had ever cherished before. Agnes became the little mother to the crying child who demanded attention all day long. And while Effie withered away and tried to ignore the complaints of her child, Douglas was happiest when Grace was asleep in his arms and he could read a book.

It had been six weeks since Effie's return from the hospital, but her strength had not returned with her. Every chore was an effort of will, every attempt to move became a burden. The doctor said she should take some stout at night, but they couldn't afford it and she hated the taste of it anyway. Douglas encouraged her to go out and take some fresh air, but she only opened the window and stared out, ignoring the dishes, the dust, and the pail heavy with unwashed nappies that saturated the air with the heavy smell of urine.

Douglas came home from work and found Effie staring helplessly at Agnes, who was trying to give Grace a bottle, which she kept spitting out, flailing her tiny arms and legs bawling at the top of her lungs.

Dropping his lunchbox on the floor he yelled "That's it!" and dragged Effie up by the arm, forcing her into her coat. "You're gawn oot." Effie's protests were weak as a kitten meow as he dragged her down the stairs and led her into the street.

"I'm tired, Douglas. Dinnae make me dae this," The cold air blew her coat away from her and she pulled it back towards her. "Let me be."

"It's enough!" he shouted, aware of the stares of people passing by. "You cannie keep livin' your life like this." At the end of the block, Effie stood still, breathing hard and pulled her arm away from him. Her sallow face was spider-webbed red with cold as she beat him across the back. "I'm no gawn anywhere," she said defiantly. "It's freezin' oot here."

"That's mare like it," he said, before turning back to the house.

When they returned, Agnes was struggling to push a nappy

through the hand wringer and Grace was screaming. Douglas ran to pick her up. "What are you day'in?" he yelled. "Why didn't you pick her up?"

"I was just trying to make the nappies clean," Agnes cried, holding up the bucket with the nappies in it. "She disnae have any mare nappies. Her bum is aw' red and sare."

Effie took off her coat and hat, and then rolled up her sleeves. "Gie me the nappies," she said in a tired voice, taking the bucket from Agnes's hand. "Go get some cream for her bum."

When she was gone, Effie cried for ten minutes and then responded as if obsessed. Within days, the house was spotless, the washing was done, and the nappy rash began to disappear.

Agnes knew that the birth of Grace was hard on her mother, but it had never struck her that taking care of a baby could be difficult. It was always a natural thing to her. But somehow this was different and Agnes had known it from the beginning. Grace belonged to Douglas in a way she never would. She was his to dote over, and it was clear that Agnes could never belong to him.

From the moment Douglas knew he was expecting a child, he ignored Agnes all together. He didn't have to pretend anymore that he was her father. What she had always understood was now very clear. Her mother's depression had made her afraid she would never return to being the loving mother of the past. She was lonely and jealous as she watched Douglas with his new child. Her dream had been for a Daddy who made her feel special, but that never happened. She didn't realize until then that she had busied herself the same way her mother had busied herself. It made Agnes feel better to know she was making herself useful. How much of a habit that had become.

six

THE YELLOW INCANDESCENT light from the streetlamp made the top of the wardrobe glow. Douglas lay on his back, watching it flicker and change as the curtain blew with the breeze. He heard Grace sniff and make meowing sounds. He hoped she wasn't about to start. It had only been two hours since the last feeding, and it had been a long day at the gasworks. He rolled onto his side and put his arm around Effie's middle. She stirred as Grace's cries grew louder. Effie pulled away from him, but he held her back. "Let her greet for a while. She'll be aw' right for a few minutes. Just stay here."

"C'mon, Douglas. I've got to go." She pulled away and he felt his grip slip away.

"C'mon, Effie. Just a wee cuddle. It's cauld oot there."

"Dinnae be daft. She's probably hungry again. I've got to go to her." She pulled the blankets back, releasing the warm air. "I'll be back in a wee while. You keep it warm for me." She pulled her heavy body towards the edge of the bed.

"Why won't you be wi' me anymore?" he pleaded.

She turned around, surprised at the pain in his voice. "Och, you're being daft. I'm no go'in anywhere. I'll be back in a minute. Go to sleep." She patted his hand, which had reached across the bed, and stepped down onto the cold linoleum floor to take Grace from her cradle.

After a few minutes of feeding, Grace fell asleep again, and Effie, shivering, crawled back beneath the blankets and pulled herself towards Douglas, seeking heat. She put her arms around him, shivering a few minutes more, until slowly, Douglas began stroking her arms before rolling over towards her. Effie breathed a sigh and felt

51

him stiffen next to her. Her impulse was to pull over to the side of the bed, but thought it was all a matter of resignation really. If she let him have his way now and again, it would keep him happy. So she turned onto her back and allowed him to enter her. In a matter of minutes, it was over, and without passion she kissed him goodnight before turning over again, resisting the urge to go clean herself in the kitchen because it was too cold.

He touched her shoulder and said, "Thank you."

❧

When Effie became pregnant again, she was neither happy nor disappointed. This time there was no dance around the living room. Grace was only six months old. Effie worried what this would do to her physically and what it would do for them financially. However, an uneventful pregnancy gave her hope that somehow things would be fine.

A son, John, was born, but he lacked the robust spirit of his sister Grace. John was plagued with constant ear infections, colds, and bronchitis that eventually erupted into asthma, which was difficult to treat. Effie's attention turned to his care, and Douglas turned to Grace for affection. She was his princess; his beautiful child with glowing copper hair and brown eyes that sparkled when she was excited. Douglas liked to think her beauty derived from his side of the family. "Some people actually said I was handsome before the war," he said sheepishly.

"Och, away wi' ye," said Effie. "you're off your bloody heed. Do you think I married Douglas Fairbanks?"

"Well, you're no exactly Mary Pickford!"

"Tosh," said Effie.

Agnes also adored Grace. She was a real live doll to play with and each day she rushed home from school to be with her, took great delight in carrying her at every opportunity, and attended to her every voracious need. "You've made a rod for your back, ye ken that," said Effie watching her change Grace's nappy.

"She hasnae done anything o' the sort. She's a good little mother that yin," said Douglas, looking up from his book.

"Are you trying to tell me something, Douglas Sharp?"

"No, I wis just saying what a grand job she's do'in. I ken how hard it is for you wi' the wee yin."

"That wee yin needs a doctor again. I dinnae ken how we're gonnie keep payin' oot for this. I've got to find a job if we're gonnie make it. So dinnae go tellin' me that I'm no do'in my job."

"I was just saying, that's aw'."

"Aye well, then, just say it to somebody else. I'm day'in the best I can."

"We all are, Effie. It's no easy for any of us, right now. Half the bloody men on the street are oot of work. Do you no think I'm worried about it? The unemployment queue is half a mile long, all looking for anything they can get. I'm bloody lucky to have a job. Do you know what I do doon there all day? I'm shoveling coal into furnaces that would fry a man in ten seconds. Men are standin' around on street corners, smokin' rolled cigarettes made from the leftovers of the last ones. The Commies and the Irish are invading the docks, the railways, and the mines—everybody's going on strike. We fought for this country and died for this country, and got nothing back for our troubles. They tell us it will all change, but it won't be anytime soon. My job has a hundred men waiting for a chance at it. I don't want to be next."

"Just dinnae gie them an excuse," retorted Effie. "You've missed days lately and it's no good."

"Och, dinnae start, Effie."

What Douglas did not tell her was that he had already been fired three days before because he had not been able to keep up with his quota. When he confessed to her a week later, Effie took the news with typical resignation. She went looking for work and found it at Salveson's in the docks, cleaning their offices. Douglas had only one comment. "Whae's gonnie take care o' these bairns when you're oot working?"

Effie didn't miss a beat. "You are! I start at six and go until ten."

"I dinnae ken how to dae aw' that stuff. C'mon now, Effie, you cannie be serious."

"Get used to it! God knows how we're gonnie pay the rent. You're gonnie have to do the Means Test. We've got to dae something."

"Och, no that, Effie! I'll get next to nothing."

"It's either that or starve. You choose!"

Effie went to work and Douglas resigned himself to sitting at home taking care of the children. But it was Agnes who took up the mothering. It was a natural progression for her, given that she had been taking care of Grace since birth. She fed them, changed them, made sure there was nothing in the way that would choke them, burn them, or cut them, and gave them a bath in the kitchen sink without dropping them. She played shops with Grace, gave John his medicine, and picked them up as soon as they cried. She seemed happy to be busy, but at night she would sometimes cry because she missed her mother.

As the number of the strikes and discontent grew throughout the country, Douglas retreated into his books. He made enough for the rent from the Parish, but that was all. Effie kept the bread on the table, but not much else. His mother complained that she missed his wee contribution, and was tired of burning something that resembled coal, but was mostly dross, hardly throwing out any heat at all. Things would have been better if Douglas had been able to take over his father's coal business after he died, she said, but took no notice of the miners' strikes that had been crippling the country.

Eight years after the end of the Great War, the promise of a better future looked grimmer than ever.

Douglas complained bitterly to Effie that all the sacrifices had been a waste of lives. There was no future he could see that would make it worthwhile. He said strikes were a waste of time. Nothing changed much afterwards and anyone who had the "sousy-heed" to believe otherwise would be sadly disillusioned. Effie had to agree; everyone was borrowing just to keep the children from starving. An air of general resignation set in. Effie was grateful she still had a job to go to.

With no work Douglas spent more time at the library during the day, and at night he and Agnes took care of Grace and John. He brought children's books home and encouraged Agnes to read to Grace at night. After years of ignoring her, they were now in partnership. Agnes liked being "the little mother," as Douglas had taken to calling her. Grace called her "Nessie" after she discovered the story of the Loch Ness Monster. Douglas said, "Just like the Loch, she's long and deep." Agnes had no idea what he meant by that.

Effie, preoccupied with running the household and making ends meet was less interested in conversation. She spoke in brief memorandums: Would you? Could you? Did you? It was a marriage of convenience, but there was nothing convenient about his unemployment or his constant state of pain. Effie told him to see the doctor, but he said it made no difference. He needed more than painkillers.

To Douglas, his failure as a providing husband was held up to him every day as Effie left for work and he faced another day with nothing to do but make the tea for the children and clean their faces before they went to bed. His nightmares had subsided, but once in a while he would be hurled across a muddy field amid bullets and mud. At these times, he awoke heavy with sweat, breathing hard, sometimes yelling, and would disturb John, who slept at the bottom of the bed. Then he would be up for the rest of the night because he couldn't settle down again.

He lived for Grace, whose name he had chosen, and who he regularly thought of as his "saving grace." She was the only one worth living for, the only one who really loved him. The way he held her on his knees, stroking her back, playing finger games, stealing her nose, singing little songs in his gravelly off-key voice—all gave him such delight. Grace responded with songs for him, prancing in front of him as if she were a ballet dancer, hiding his glasses and his books, tying his shoelaces together, and doing all manner of other mischievous things to get his attention. She was the light to which all the moths gathered to meet their fate. Agnes loved her sister but saw how she had everyone wrapped round her little finger. Whatever Grace wanted, Douglas would do his best to give it to her. His dark eyes cast shadows over everything except Grace. It was magical to watch the transformation that brought fire and light to his face. She was his "wee doll" and Agnes was "the wee ma." Agnes loved the attention but hated the distinction."

Effie joined in with, "You've spoiled her. She thinks we're aw' gonnie dance aroond her.

"Naebody's dancing in this hoose except her," retorted Douglas. The truth was Grace learned at an early age that her mother was only available for practical matters—for feeding, for bathing, for dressing—and wasted no time on cuddles and kisses, which she craved. Agnes played games with her, but Agnes was busy taking care of John most of the time because of his breathing problems. She called him the "wheezy yin" and took great delight in mimicking his struggle to get breath into his lungs, which made John angry and even wheezier.

As they grew older, the goading became a sport that both participated in, to their ruin. She blamed him for everything she did wrong, and he took to throwing cutlery at her when there was nobody looking. Fist fights broke out occasionally, ending with a red cheek or a bruise on the arm that was quickly covered up with a lie that he had bumped into something when he blamed Grace. Douglas always believed her.

"You always take her side," he whined.

"Och, you're a laddie. You can stand up fur yourself," Douglas scolded.

"She gets off wi' it aw' the time."

"You're just jealous," called out Grace

John wasn't the only one that Grace had begun to annoy. Agnes resented the tricks Grace played, including stealing Agnes's gloves, lipsticks, hair combs. When Agnes found them at the bottom of the drawer under Grace's clothes, Douglas chose to take sides with Grace, saying she must have put them there accidentally. There was nothing Grace could do wrong in his eyes. It was always a mistake or a misunderstanding.

It had not yet turned five-thirty in the morning, but Effie was already shuffling around the scullery, putting clothes into the big basin, first searching through the pockets for handkerchiefs and marbles that had been forgotten. The kettle was boiling on the back of the cast-iron range, sending a plume of steam up the chimney. "Agnes, make sure that Grace has her schoolbooks before she leaves. She's aye forgettin' them. Gie her a piece and sugar as well. She needs to eat something, otherwise she's aw' ower the place."

Agnes had just stumbled into the warm kitchen, sleepy eyed from having been up with John most of the night. He had been having trouble breathing again and was propped up in front of the open window to help him. She had lain next to him most of the night to keep him warm, but had remained half-frozen nonetheless. "Aye, Ma, but I cannie make her, ye ken that."

"Just see what you can dae before you go to your work. I'm away to the steamie wi' the washin'. I dinnae ken what time I'll be finished. Make sure John's got his medicine fur his breathin'. That's another day he's gonnie miss the school. Ask Douglas to help him wi' his sums. I'll be back at my usual time."

"Aye, Ma."

Effie lifted the heavy aluminum basin loaded up with clothes and bed linen into the pram frame that Douglas had fashioned out of old wheels and a metal bar. Pushing it out the front door, she yelled back loud enough for the neighbors to hear, "You'd think somebody wid clean that toilet oot here now and again. It's stinkin'." Pushing the pram to the edge of the stairs, she called to Agnes, "Here, gie me a hand wi' this doon the stairs. I'll be glad when we get oot of this bloody tenement and into a proper hoose. It's aboot bloody time the council gave us something."

Douglas arrived to help but she brushed him aside then started to bump it down the stairs when Agnes ran to the front of it and lifted.

"It's heavy, Ma!"

"C'mon, let's get it doon the stairs. I've no got aw' morning."

Agnes backed down the stairs one at a time. "It's freezin' this morning."

"Put a coat on next time."

"But you've only got a thin coat on. Where's your big one?"

"It's nae matter. I'll get warmed up soon enough at the steamie."

"But where's your coat, Ma?"

"I lent it to somebody."

"You didnae pawn it, did you?"

"Dinnae be daft—whae would want it?" She could not tell Agnes that she had done just that, for a mere sixpence.

They huffed and humped the pram downstairs, and when Agnes set it down, she stopped a moment before letting Effie past.

"Ma, I was wondering."

"What, Agnes? C'mon, it's cauld doon here."

"Can I go to the music hall wi' the lassies fae work? There's a wee man wae sings aw' these Harry Lauder songs. I just thought . . ."

"This is the second time you've been oot this week. You better no be gettin' up to any nonsense. Whae's gonnie take care of the bairns the night?"

"Douglas is at hame. He can dae it? There's no much to dae."

Effie started to push the pram towards the front step. "Aw' right. Just dinnae go gettin' hame late. You're only fifteen."

Agnes started running up the stairs. "Ta, Ma. You're great!"

"Hmmph," snarled Effie as she pulled up the collar of her coat and began pushing the basin up the road, feeling the aching in her feet with each step.

Agnes remembered the rattling wheels of the pram along the dark streets in the early hours of the morning, the milkman shoving his barrow with morning cold frosted glass bottles in metal crates clanking over uneven cobblestones, the yellow light of the trams shining through the fog and the welcome rush of hot steam that enveloped you when you reached the wash house, affectionately called 'The Steamie' by the women who toiled over the mangles and the boiling vats of soap and water, spicing up the day with gossip. There's a good reason they call these television programs 'soap operas' she thought. Thank God these days were over.

The music halls were all the rage. For tuppence you could sit in the Gods, way up in the highest balcony, and see all the favorite music hall stars of the day. It was simple fun. The actors made fun of themselves, made fun of the audience, and everyone felt they were part of the act. Agnes remembered how much she used to enjoy these nights out. Life was simple then.

seven

DOUGLAS FINISHED DOING homework with John. Grace had claimed she had none. "It's no due until next week," she lied.

"Aw' right. It had better be," he said before telling John it was bedtime. "It's hers as well," he whined.

"Aye, A ken that, but it's you I'm tellin' to get intae bed. She's gawn in a minute. C'mere, Gracie, while I take care o' these knuckles. I've telt you before aboot fighting. I hope the other yin has worse than this." He took hold of her hand and stroked the back of it tenderly.

"When can I get intae ma ain room? It's no fair. She gets aw' the good bits."

"Do you see a room go'in' spare here? Just go to sleep, will ye. I'm no here to be arguing wi' a nine-year-auld."

Grace giggled and then winced as he stroked her knuckles individually with Vaseline. "There, that should do you. Dinnae be fighting anymare, Grace. It's no worth it."

John was watching from the bed. "What if I cannie sleep?"

"Just go to sleep. Your mother'll be hame soon."

Grace slid from the chair and stood awkwardly holding her back. "I didnae start it, Dad."

"I ken that, hen, you just have to be careful."

Shona Cogan, the school bully, had given Grace the nudge at school. The nudge was a heavy elbow to the side or back, depending on which angle one was standing at. It meant "get lost" and most girls responded by leaving. Grace was standing with her back to Shona and almost fell over with the impact. She swung around and punched her on the shoulder as Shona grabbed her hair. "Are they the ribbons your daddy bought you?" she sang. "Daddy's lassie disnae want anybody touching them." She pulled the ribbon bow and pulled some hair with it. Grace let out a yell and swung her fist at Shona's head, but missed. Grabbing her, Shona pushed her down to the ground, causing her to graze her knuckles as she landed. With a roar, Grace bounced to her feet and kicked Shona in the shins. When she bent over in reaction, Grace slapped her face. She was about to move in again when the crowd opened up to let Toothless Tooley, the science teacher, step into the circle. "What kind of behavior is this for young ladies?" he lisped, red faced and bloated. Snatching them by the collar, he pushed them in front of him towards his classroom.

They stood to attention, eyeing each other with silent curses, as he went to his desk drawer. Well known for his sadism, Toothless Tooley pulled out a twin-tongued leather belt that he had decorated with eyes on each fork of the belt; it was one of his greatest pleasures. Shona threw Grace a look that said she would have to be up first, but Tooley stood in front of Shona. "Hold out your hands," he commanded. After the third lashing, Shona had tears in her eyes. By the fourth one, the tears were falling down her face. Her hands and her wrists had red welts from the weight of it.

Grace prepared herself for the slaughter. After the third lashing, she bit her tongue, but she refused to let Shona see her cry. When Tooley noticed only a grimace at the fourth lashing, he gave her an extra one, "For good luck," he said. "Now, I want you to write out five hundred times, 'I will not fight in the playground again.'" Grace thought he was lacking in imagination if that was all he could come up with for them to write about.

Grace kissed her father goodnight and stuck her tongue out at John, who was watching from his bed in the living room. He turned over and she closed the bedroom door.

Douglas went into the scullery to pour a cup of tea. Agnes had washed the dishes but had not dried them, so he put them away in the cupboard before taking the teapot from the back of the stove. The tea was bitter because it had been stewing for a few hours, so he tossed it down the sink, regretting the waste of tea. The plate of stewed meat and potatoes that Agnes had left for Effie lay congealed on the plate. He picked up a sock that had fallen to the floor and put it back in the pile of newly washed clothes. She'll be up till midnight ironing, he thought. I wish she would learn to leave it until the morning.

Making a fresh pot, he took it into the living room where John lay asleep, twisted into his blanket, holding it to his face as he always did when asleep. He stirred the coals in the fireplace and then groaned as he sat down. The pain in his hip was getting worse, but he had long ago given up complaining because nobody listened. Effie was impatient with him and gave him no room to seek solace. "When are you gonnie get a job?" she asked today. For the thousandth time, he told her he was looking and he was not alone. "I'm no caring aboot them oot there," she said dismissively. "I just want to see to ma own."

He had been out of work for three years with only a few odd jobs here and there. Despair hugged him in a caul that seemed unbreakable. Depressed would have been the diagnosis if anyone had thought it was a problem.

He looked at the bedroom door and saw a small light coming from under it. She's awake still, he thought, picking up his book. His hip ground savagely in its socket as he turned in the chair, and he stood up again. There was no peace from the discomfort; the best he could do was to walk it off if his hip got to be too uncomfortable. He stared at the door again. He wished Grace wouldn't fight so much. She was always getting into some kind of trouble, usually because she had too big a mouth on her. He walked around the small living room, straightening out the dishes on the table, picking up John's jumper that lay on the seat and folding it neatly for the morning. Effie liked her house tidy and he did his best to keep it that way, but it wasn't easy. The bairns were always leaving their stuff lying around.

He looked at the clock, which showed just past nine. Effie was due to arrive home in an hour or so. He'd been trying for a long time to get her to change her job. Now that the bairns were older, she didn't need to work nights—she could find a day job. But she refused. She liked the company and she liked the job. There was no discussion.

"How did I end up like this?" he said to himself angrily. He was going to take over his dad's coal business when he came back from the war. There was good money in that if you had the right customers, and his dad had always done well. Everybody always needed coal. Well, I lost that opportunity, he thought bitterly, staring out the window at his own reflection. What's happening to me? I look like an old man! Effie never really looked at him anymore when they talked. On those rare occasions when they did talk, it was always about what they didn't have, or what he should be doing. She just didn't seem to understand that he was doing the best he could. He didn't know how to do it any differently. He walked the floor twice then hesitated by the bedroom door. Maybe I'll just give her a wee cuddle, he thought.

She was dozing with the light on when the bedroom door opened and thought it was Agnes, hoping she wasn't coming to bed. She liked it when she could have it to herself. She didn't get the sweaty smell of her or the wide hips bumping up against her. Agnes snored at night, sometimes so bad that Grace kicked her all night long to get her to shut up. She prayed it wasn't Douglas.

The light from the living room brightened the bedroom, then quickly extinguished as Douglas closed the door behind him. She heard a scraping and the drag of his leg across the floor and held her breath light so he would think she was asleep.

"Gracie, you sleeping, hen?" he murmured. "Gracie?" He leaned over to touch her hair. "Sweet dreams, ma beauty." Stroking her hair, his callused hands caught on it and pulled a few strands.

Grace winced as a current of fear ran through her body, curling her up inside and out, ending in fists held tightly by her sides. Just lie still, she thought calmly. He'll think you're asleep and go away. But another part of her was stammering, No! No! Go away. No again! Dinnae move, just dinnae move and he'll go away. Her curled fists stretched out the grazed flesh of her knuckles and she let the pain of them keep her connected.

Douglas sat down on the edge of the bed and as he did, the loose springs of the metal base creaked under his weight. He leaned in towards her, kissing her head, lingering on the smell of her hair, touching the fine strands of copper curls laid out on the pillow like a wreath of autumn leaves.

His heavy breathing followed his hand down to her shoulders and under the blanket pulled up to her chin. She curled deeper inside herself, knowing what was coming next; it was always the same. He was only coming for a goodnight kiss, she told herself, but it was always something more. Pulling the blanket down from her face, he stroked the front of her pajama jacket and then undid the button. Grace was still curled up but he pulled her gently backwards. She kept her eyes closed, refusing to look at him as he did this. Exposing her bare chest, he rubbed his forefinger over her nipple in circles, and then held himself as if he wanted to go to the toilet.

Straining to control every breath, she was caught in the cross fire of something she desperately wanted to escape from and yet was inextricably drawn to; the pleasure in her body. She felt as if she were exploding and determined to shut it all out, to turn away, to pretend that it wasn't happening, he wasn't there.

She had an intense desire to squirm and she wanted to thrust upwards, but instead, she lay perfectly still, as if she were dead.

If she complained, her Ma would have said she was a big girl now, but she didn't want to be a big girl. She was a little girl, her daddy's little girl. He said so when he rubbed her back. She was special to him, his favorite. Agnes and John didn't get presents or sweeties from him. She was the one he bought ribbons for. She was his little girl. Ma said she was spoiled, but Ma was never home.

He was pulling her hand out from under the covers. "Just a wee bit, hen," he murmured. Taking her curled fist, he pulled out her fingers one by one. "This little piggy went to market," he intoned in their favorite game. Moaning softly, he rubbed his leg with his left hand and made jerking movements with her extended hand inside his trousers, lying so close to her that she could feel his breath on her breast. Her hand ached from the pushing and the skin was on fire where he rubbed against the grazed knuckles

No, Daddy! she screamed in her mind. Don't do this.

She knew this was wrong. This was not a cuddle anymore. This was something else. This touch was thick and soft at the same time, and he was pushing her so hard where Toothless Tooley had belted her, it was hurting all over again. A weak murmur rose from her mouth, excited him more as he rubbed more vigorously.

"Oh, hen, you're ma wee yin. My bonnie lassie," he said breathing hard. "You love your daddy, don't you? Oh, hen, you love meeee," he said urgently, rubbing frantically on her hand sheathed over the thick, pulsing part that pissed in the sink in the middle of the night. His breath was so hot on her hair, and she finally could stand it no longer. She pulled her arm back, leaving him gasping and moaning.

Suddenly, a shaft of light spread across the bed as the room door opened. Douglas withdrew his hand instantly and pushed the covers over Grace, clumsily pushing himself off the edge of the bed, causing it to creak fiercely. Grace trembled under the bed covers.

"Oh! Oh! Agnes," he grunted. "I was just saying goodnight to oor Grace." He moved towards the door, which was being blocked by Agnes. "You're back early, aren't you?" He was red faced and sweaty, with tufts of red hair sticking out in different directions from the bald spot at the top of his head.

"What's go'in on here?" Agnes stood defiantly in the doorway blocking his way.

"I was just saying good night to ma bairn," he said weakly, reaching to his pants to make sure the buttons were done up. "Go to sleep, Grace," he said as he pushed past Agnes.

Grace curled up into a ball clutching her pajama jacket to her, stroking her injured hand gently, and began to cry silently.

The man singing the Harry Lauder songs was funny and entertaining, but Agnes thought he couldn't sing if his life depended on it. Her friends wanted her to stay out later, but there was nothing to do.

Agnes had never been one to stand on street corners chatting about nothing in particular, so she went home.

John was asleep in the corner, twisted in the blanket, so she adjusted it and turned him over. She wondered where Douglas was and thought he was probably in the toilet outside. The fire was getting low, so she put a couple of lumps on top. It wasn't like Douglas to let the fire get so low. She was going to the kitchen and was passing the bedroom door when she heard a moan. Thinking Grace was having some trouble, she opened the door.

Douglas often went to say good night to Grace and sometimes sat down to read to her, but he didn't usually lie on the bed beside her. Something about this wasn't right. Agnes wondered if someone had crept into the house from outside, and then heard the moaning sound again, and in the dim light she saw Grace on her back with Douglas pushing himself towards her. When he got off the bed, she noticed his trousers were unbuttoned. She was surprised at first, then realizing what she was looking at, the disgust rose like bile in her throat.

⚜

Filling the kettle with water, she was letting it run over the top when she heard him behind her.

"Aye, hen," he said quickly. "You're back early. The picture wisnae very good?" He checked his trousers and pulled down his sweater. "Making a cup of tea? I could use one myself. Your mother also. She'll be hame soon."

Agnes reeled around to face him, holding the black enamel kettle in her hand as if ready to swing. "What was go'in on in there?"

"Och, dinnae get aw' worked up. She couldnae get to sleep. I wis gi'en her a wee back rub. You ken how she likes that."

"You're no right, ye ken that. I dinnae understand you. She's eleven years auld."

"Aye, well, you're no the first one," he said.

"I dinnae ken what you were do'in, but if my Ma gets wind o' this . . ."

He grabbed her by the arm and held it tight. "You mind your ane bloody business, you hear me. Dinnae you go poking your nose where it's no wanted. You didnae see anything, so get it oot o' your mind. You didnae see nothing, you hear me. Nothing!"

Agnes pulled away then slammed the kettle down on the stove top, causing the water to sizzle on the griddle. As they stood facing each other across the kitchen, it was almost possible to touch the silence.

The click in the front door announced Effie's return. Douglas picked up the cups from the cupboard and Agnes stood still watching him.

"You didnae see anything," he hissed.

"You bastard," she said through gritted teeth.

⁊⁊

Seeing Agnes first, Effie said, "You're hame early? It wisnae any good?"

Agnes said nothing.

"What's gawn on here?" she asked, shedding her coat. "Are you two havin' one o' your sessions?"

"Ask him!" said Agnes.

"What is it?" asked Effie, puzzled and a little concerned.

"Nothing," he said, taking the tea caddy down from the shelf. "Just get your coat off and sit doon."

Effie looked from one to the other and then sighed. "I havenae got the strength for this," she said sorrowfully. "I'm fair wheekit. Just gie me ma dinner. I've got the ironing to dae before I go to ma bed."

Agnes took the plate of food in her hand and had every urge in the world to throw it at him, but bent down to put it in the oven.

Effie took off her headscarf and ran her fingers through her hair. "Dinnae bother heatin' it, hen. It'll be fine as it is."

Agnes put her mother's dinner down in front of her and as she did, Effie gave a huge yawn and closed her eyes. "Make me a cup o' tea, Douglas," she murmured. "Make yourself useful."

Douglas made no attempt to do anything. He was staring at Agnes.

67

"I'll get it, Ma," said Agnes bitterly. "He's too busy gawkin' at nothing."

He had never been physically violent, but at that moment, he had a tremendous urge to smack Agnes across the face. For the first time since the war, he was afraid. One word from her to Effie, and his whole house of cards would tumble down. "You better get to your bed," he admonished as she came towards him to make tea.

Agnes narrowed her eyes and turned back towards Effie. "Ma . . . ," she hesitated. Douglas took a sharp intake of breath and waited. It felt like he was back in the trenches and they were waiting for an incoming to shatter their lives.

"I'll be up early the morn, so dinnae worry aboot the bairns. I'll get them ready for the school. You should get some sleep."

"Och, I'll be aw' right. Dinnae worry aboot me."

Agnes rubbed her mother's back. "But I do worry aboot you," she said, looking directly at Douglas. "You're no gettin' enough sleep. You'll be ill if you're no careful."

"Aye, and so will you," said Douglas, pouring boiling water into the pot.

"Since when did you take an interest in my life?" said Agnes.

"Och, dinnae get started again, you two. I'm too bloody tired."

"I'll talk to you the morn," said Agnes to no one in particular as she left the kitchen in a hurry to go to the toilet. Amid the smell of urine and cold stone, she vomited into the bowl. How could he, she wept. To his own daughter!

When Agnes returned to the bedroom, Grace was lying on her side with her back to the door, holding her hands together as if in a prayer sealed by searing heat. The bed sagged to one side as Agnes sat down, causing Grace to roll backwards slightly. Pulling Grace towards her, Agnes demanded, "What was he do'in to you?"

Grace turned a tearful face and said, "It wisnae ma fault. He said it was just a cuddle."

As Agnes took her hands, Grace winced, and Agnes noticed the grazed knuckles. "Did he dae this as well?" She stroked the palm of Grace's hand and bit down on her lower lip. "How come ye didnae tell me, Gracie? I had no idea," she said as gently as she could. "How long has it been?"

Grace pulled her hand back.

"Why didn't you tell me, Gracie?"

Grace stared at the ceiling. "It was only a cuddle," she intoned. "I didnae mean it."

Agnes sat quietly for a minute before saying, "What are we going to do about this? Did he—you know?"

Grace's sobs made her chest bounce like hiccups.

"He's a bastard, ye ken that?" She reached hesitantly towards Grace and lay down. "We better no let Ma ken aboot this. She'll go off her heed and she's got enough on her plate for now. I'm feard for her and you," she said quietly, then pulled Grace towards her body and said, "C'mon, hen. It'll be all right."

Grace turned to sit up. "Where were you, Agnes?"

"I'm no your ma, Gracie," said Agnes in a tired voice, putting herself into a spooning position close to Grace's body. "Let's go to sleep."

Over the next few weeks, Grace moved around the house like a wraith, saying nothing, pale and anxious most of the time. Even John's teasing did not get a reaction from her. She stayed out late in the street and when she came home it was to eat and then go to bed. Effie asked "Are you no feelin' well?" and Grace replied, "Leave me alane."

Agnes stood at the foot of the stairs watching the kids play 'stote the ba' up and down the street, the ball bouncing from one player to the next. Grace stood to the side watching them, sucking on the ends of her hair.

"You cannie keep acting this way, you ken that, don't you? Ma's worried sick aboot you. If you're no careful, she's gonnie get wind that something's up. You have to get over it, Gracie."

"What fur? He disnae even look at me anymare. It's no ma fault that this happened, but he disnae even want to talk to me."

Agnes looked around the street and leaned in closer to Grace in case somebody was coming down the stairs. "Well he shouldnae," she growled. "If I as much as see that slimy bastard come near you again, I dinnae ken what I'll be responsible fur. I telt him to mind himself. Do you realize what he did to you? He's your faither."

Grace looked down at the stone steps, studying the cracks that lay between each paving stone.

"Och, you're off your bloody heed if you think he's worth it. He's no well, I've always thought that, but this is wrong. Do you understand that?"

Grace pulled on her lower lip and twisted her hair around her fingers. "Aye," she said in a low voice, "but whae's gonnie gie me sweeties now?"

"If that's aw' you're worried aboot, I'll gie them to you. Just stay away fae him, Gracie. He's no to be trusted anymare."

Douglas was going over John's homework for the umpteenth time. "Och, how many times do you have to have it banged intae your heed, laddie. Nine times nine is no ninety-nine!" John bit the end of the pencil and studied the sheet of paper with his sums on it. "You're no go'in oot until you can show me you've got it."

Effie looked up from her knitting and stared over her glasses at Agnes, who was playing solitaire with a pack of cards. "Agnes, hen, would you go and make Douglas a cup of tea. His nerves seem to be gettin' a wee bit shattered over there."

Douglas looked at her before taking the sheet of sums from John. "He can get it himself."

Effie smiled. "I ken that, but you can get me one at the same time. You two seem to be gettin' on like a hoose on fire fur ages now. What's go'in on?"

"Nothing," said Agnes, concentrating on the cards.

Effie looked from one to the other and shook her head. "It disnae matter. I'm off to the Assembly Rooms shortly. They've got a women's special go'in on."

"What's a women's special?" asked Douglas.

"Nane o' your bloody business—that's what makes it special," said Agnes.

Effie laughed, then turned serious. "Would one o' you keep an eye on Gracie? She's gawn to her bed early again, which is no like her. I dinnae ken what's come ow'er her these last few weeks. I'm worried aboot her. She's awfy peeky."

"She'll be fine," said Douglas, turning his attention back to John. "Now you, let me see what you've done. Have you got the answer yet?"

Effie shook her head and got up to put her coat on.

"I think so," said John. "Can I go oot to play?" He slid the sheet of paper over towards his father, nervously biting the pencil, which was beginning to shred at the ends.

"You've got three more sums here that's no right. Do you think ye'll get through the school wi' work like this? I dinnae want you filing up at the Broo' lookin' for a job wi' nae qualifications. You'd better get yourself better applied to this work, lad, otherwise you're gonnie find yourself wi nothin'. You hear me?"

John nodded his head and waited a few more minutes. "But can I go oot for a wee while? It's still light ootside."

"Just you mind what I've been saying. It looks like you've got the answer on this one. I'll gie ye half an oor. Away ye go."

❧

Douglas was reading the Daily Mail when Agnes came back in from the kitchen with a cup of tea for herself and nothing for him. Setting it down by the side of the fire, she reached forward and yanked the newspaper from his hands.

"What're you do'in?" he yelled, gathering up the paper again.

Agnes yanked it down again. "You think you've got off wi' it, don't you?"

Douglas picked up the newspaper from the floor and folded it back into its original format. He refused to look her in the eyes.

"Dinnae get started!" he warned.

"It's you whae started this," she hissed, spit oozing from her lips

"You dinnae ken what you're talkin' aboot. You think you ken everything, don't you? Well, you don't. You're just a bairn."

"Aye, a bairn whae's developed eyes in the back o' her heed!" she spat. "You think I dinnae ken anything, but you're wrong. She telt me. I saw her after you'd finished wi' her. She's a bloody bairn. What where you thinkin'? I dinnae understand what you were after."

He stood up from his chair and tossed the newspaper he had been clutching into the fire. "You better mind your ane bloody business, lassie. If you were mine, I'd wallop you for that mouth." He bent over her and she lifted her fist ready to strike his face. He leered at her "Go on, do it. You can't, can you? You're your mother's wee lassie."

She swung her fist and it connected with his jaw, making a large cracking sound as it bounced off the edge. Her eyes were blazing. "I thank God I'm no your lassie."

He staggered back towards the chair again and collapsed into it, letting all the air out of his body, like a balloon deflating. "It wisnae like you thought," he said weakly.

The bedroom door opened and Grace stood in the doorway. Seeing Agnes bending over Douglas in his face, she rushed forward and pulled at the back of her jumper. Agnes was still ranting. "I'm no your daughter, so I dinnae matter to you. You've never cared much aboot me. I've watched you all these years. I've just been somebody you tolerated. But your ain daughter! Did you ever think aboot that? Are you no ashamed o' yourself?"

Grace pulled harder on the jumper until Agnes began to back away. Then Grace rushed forward to her father, tossing herself into his lap. "She disnae mean it, Daddy. Please, Daddy, tell her you didnae mean it?"

He pushed her to one side and stood up. Agnes backed up a few steps and let him pass. She was shaking from the violence in her. "Don't you touch my sister again," she hissed in a voice she did not recognize.

Agnes let out an explosive "ppppffff" as the plastic cup in her hand cracked under her tight grip. It was as if it were yesterday. She could not believe that she had actually punched him. All she remembered was her anger and how for the first time in her life, she knew what it was like to wish someone dead. She shivered at the memory and kept her eyes shut tight, replaying the scene in her mind. It was the scariest thing she had ever done, and she had worried that he would take his revenge on her, but he never did.

She had opened the box, now Agnes was being subjected to the awful truth of something she had long ago decided to forget. She should have minded her own business when Alison told her it was her responsibility to tell the truth about the history. She had been living with the secrets all her life and couldn't figure out why she had given them up now. *How can I know myself if I don't know where I come from,* begged Alison. But not like this.

Grace was just as much her child as Effie's. Agnes had protected her, nurtured her, but she had failed her. Agnes wanted to save her mother from heartache, remembering how empty she had been when she came home from the hospital after Grace was born—Agnes never wanted to see that look on her mother's face again. "I failed her," she murmured, shuddering and pulling her coat around her.

Family secrets. There was a reason no one spoke about them. The shame of it was just as fresh today as it was fifty years or more ago.

eight

THEY HAD WAITED seventeen years and could hardly believe their luck when the letter came. They were assigned a flat in Granton with four bedrooms and an indoor toilet with a bathtub. There would be no more smelly lavvy for Effie to clean again. Situated near the gasworks tower and the surrounding warehouses, the view from the living room window was worth every bit of industrial pollution. Across the water to the small dab of land they called Burntisland, the boats ploughed back and forth from Granton harbor. Effie thought they were moving to paradise.

Before the papers were signed, she began to pack up their meager household, embarrassed at the furniture that by now was distressed beyond repair. "We need a new couch," she told Douglas. "And a new dining room set. This one is so full of scars and cracks it won't stand to be moved." Douglas told her it was enough to get the moving van. They might be moving their stuff on the back of a hand cart if they were not careful. Grace complained that it was too far away from her friends. John complained that he didn't want to move to a new school. Effie didn't like the corporation nicotine yellow on the walls and had Douglas paint them all white before they moved in.

Once they were settled into the flat, Effie sat long hours at the window, staring at the view out onto the water. In all her years growing up in Musselburgh, she never had a view of the water and she enjoyed watching the boats. There was also a back green where she could hang out her washing and not worry about it flapping against the side of the building when the wind blew. The Edinburgh Corporation had planted trees to give a sense of park in the backyard. It would be a good place to sit in the summer time.

There was only one complaint. "It's bloody queer, I know," said Effie, "but there's no fighting in the stairs at night, nobody to trip over, fallen down drunk. It's awfy quiet around here."

"I'm sure it'll no last long," said Douglas. "All the riff-raff from Leith will be here in no time."

Grace and Agnes still shared a bed, but John finally had a room of his own. He set about putting up his collection of Players cigarette cards on the walls. He had built up a fine collection of kings and queens of England and a history of naval uniforms. He wanted to join the Navy when he grew up. Grace made fun of his collection and said he stood no chance of getting in the Navy because he couldn't swim. As for her, she carefully put up her favorite film star cards and film magazine cutouts of Lucille Ball, Bette Davis, Ronald Coleman and Clark Gable.

Agnes carefully arranged her small pots of African violets on the windowsill and told Grace she wanted their room tidy. No more mountains of clothes and dirty underwear on the floor and no more pieces of chewing gum on the bed. It was a desire that would find no satisfaction.

By age sixteen, Grace had worked at the Co-Op, the sweet shop, the dress shop, and the wool mill. She never settled down in any of them, and either left or was fired because of laziness, lateness, or stealing. Effie had enough. "When are you going to keep a job, Gracie? Fleming's is looking for people."

"I'm no gawn in there. You come oot wi' your hands and your skin aw blue fae the ink."

"You better get something. You cannie expect us to be keepin' you. No at your age," said Effie.

Douglas shook his head. "Dinnae be sae stupid, lass. If you cannie keep a job, how dae you expect to get anywhere?"

"I dinnae see you go'in anywhare! Where do you think I'm gawn? There's naewhare to go. It's aw' the bloody same. I just want to get oot o' this hoose."

"You watch your mouth, lass," barked Effie. "This hoose has kept a roof ow'er your heed, so dinnae get sae bloody gabby aboot what you think you're gonnie be day'in."

Grace huffed and hunched her shoulders before picking up her coat. "Whare do you think you're gawn?"

"Oot."

"Och, no again." She looked at Douglas to get a response, but his head was behind a newspaper.

John sat quietly reading in the corner and looked up when the door slammed. "She's gawn to the King's Heed. She's always in there wi' the fellies. I saw her the other night walkin' in there wi' them."

Douglas looked up sharply. "What are you sayin'?"

"Nothin'. I just ken I saw her the other night."

Effie stood in front of him with her hands firmly on her hips. "I'll never understand that lassie, ye ken. Why don't you get your fat arse doon there and see what she's day'in."

Douglas rustled his newspaper but stayed hidden behind it. "There's no much I can dae," he said softly. "You seem to have everything handled around here. She always does as she bloody well pleases anyway."

"And whae's fault is that? I hope you're no blamin' me. I'm no the one whae ignores everything that's go'in on."

John put down his book. "I'm away oot." He had heard this argument too many times and it bored him.

"You as well. Where are you gawn?"

"Ma pals are waiting fur me at the chippy. I'll no be long."

"You're aye hangin' aboot at that chippy. It's amazing ye dinnae turn intae one," grunted Douglas.

"Och, let him go," sighed Effie. "He's no the one whae's lookin' fur trouble."

Douglas folded his newspaper and stood up. "I've had enough o' sittin' here listening to this shite."

Effie blocked his way. "I used to think you were a help, but I dinnae understand you now. You've just gi'en up. How in the hell's name is she ever gonnie amount to much if we just sit here and let her get on wi' it? She cannie even keep a job for five minutes. What am I gonnie dae wi' her?"

"It disnae help when you tell her she's nae bloody good. She just might want to prove that to you."

"Dinnae go blamin' me," said Effie. "This is no ma fault. She's been runnin' wild since she was twelve years auld and you've done nothin' to stop it."

Douglas thrust the folded newspaper at her. "What was I supposed to dae—tie her up and keep her in? Dinnae be daft. I'm no the only one whae's at fault."

"Dinnae start that again. I've been oot keepin' these bairns in shoes when you couldnae, and I've kept food on this table when you couldnae. Dinnae start wi' me. I'm no the one whae's been oot o' work mare times than I've been in it. You're two of a kind."

⟪✦⟫

Agnes was in the kitchen listening to the broadcast of "The Coughing Horror" on the weekly Fu Manchu show. There was lots of hissing going on, so she leaned in closer to the small Bakelite box to better hear. As the voices started to rise in the next room, she turned up the volume, increasing the hissing, making the voices less audible. From the living room, she heard her mother yell, "Agnes!" She tried to ignore it, concentrating on the program. "Agnes!" It was louder and more insistent.

She sighed and turned the volume down before turning it off then walked into the living room. Effie and Douglas were glaring at each other. "Go intae Leith and see if you can find oor Grace. John says she's in that pub, the Kings Heed. If she is, I'll have her heed when she comes in. If she's no there, try the chippy."

"Aye, maybe she'll bring us aw' back fish suppers," quipped Douglas. Effie threw him a dirty look.

"Do you want me to come wi' you?" he asked.

Agnes shook her head. "What fur?"

⟪✦⟫

The pub was wall to wall with sweating, beer-saturated men, bleating on their barstools. On the other side of the thick wall was the snug bar, entered from the street and euphemistically called the "family

77

section," although no children were allowed. According to the die-hards, this was not a place for a man to sit down and share his drinking with a woman, unless he had no shame. No self-respecting man would be taking his wife into a pub. Agnes pushed her way through the crowd and amid the red velvet glow of bar stools and smoke, she saw Grace sitting in the corner with her friend Ellen. Both of them clearly underage, but no one seemed to care. Beside them sat a young man who had combed his hair to one side to obscure the fact that he was going bald. Agnes squeezed her solid mass through the crowd of bodies smelling of beer, sawdust, and toiled sweat and planted herself in front of the table with her hands firmly in her coat pockets. Grace was half-turned towards Ellen making a joke. Ellen looked up at Agnes and Grace turned her head. "Aw, Agnes. What are you do'in here? Did she send you? Can you no just let me be?"

Agnes held firm. "C'mon."

Grace started talking to Ellen again.

"I'm no movin' until you come, Gracie."

"Come and sit doon. Have a wee drink. It'll no kill you, ye ken."

Agnes dug her hands further into her coat pockets. "Let's go."

"Why don't you get a boyfriend, Agnes. Get yourself somebody to marry. You're gettin' auld." Grace waved her hand across the room and started to laugh. "There's dozens o' fellics oot there lookin' fur a wife. I bet you could find somebody whae'd want you." She shoved the boy with the balding head. "Here, Charlie! Want to get married to ma sister?"

Agnes flushed the same color as the red velvet of the chair. Charlie wiped his hand across his pieces of hair and smiled at her."

"C'mon. Let's go. I'm tired o' makin' up excuses for you. I'm missin' my wireless show because o' you."

"Just tell her you cannie find me."

"No. Not this time. Let's go, now." Agnes pulled her hands out of her pockets and reached across the table to grab Grace's arm.

"I'm comin'," she growled. "Let me go." She gave Ellen a look of extreme annoyance and raised her eyes upwards. "I'm sorry, I've got to go wi' ma sister," she said. Ellen moved out of her way as she stood up and moved towards the bar. She had seen it before when Grace started yelling. It was not pretty. Everyone in the bar started to get in on the fight until they were chucked out. This pub had been good for them up to now. "Dinnae start, Grace," she hissed.

Grace marched ahead of Agnes through the crowd. "Gawn hame early the night, Gracie," some wise guy shouted. "Nae time for a bit o' nooky before you go?" She gave him the two fingers up sign, enraged and ready to split someone in two. Agnes was right behind her. "Dinnae let your mother keep you hame for long, hen. We'll miss you."

Agnes elbowed someone who was standing grumbling about all these women whae should be better off at hame. "C'mon, I'm sick to death o' aw' this runnin' around after you. I dinnae ken why I have to get the job." The pub door swung open and the fresh night air washed away the clammy atmosphere.

Grace dragged her feet towards the tram stop. "I dinnae ken why you have to come oot. I'm no day'in anything."

Agnes pushed her forward. "Just get moving. I'm sick to death o' this, ye ken." She stopped at the tram stop and peered through the fine drizzle to see if the tram was coming. "You dinnae seem to understand what you do to yourself. You're asking for it, ye ken that? We're aw' worried sick aboot you, him included. If you're no careful, Gracie, you'll end up deed one day. Do you think we like runnin' around after you?"

"We aw' end up deed, Agnes. He's no worried aboot me. I dinnae see him comin' oot to find me."

"You ken bloody well he won't step foot in a bar. It's time you got a grip. Stop aw' this nonsense."

"Aye, well!" Grace muttered. "Here's the tram." She jumped on it before it had stopped completely and ran upstairs. Agnes sat downstairs. She had managed to get Grace out of the bar and on her way home—that was all that counted.

⁂

Grace began to vomit at four o'clock in the morning and was still vomiting at six. "It's the flu," she said to Agnes, in between trips to the toilet.

"It's no any flu I've seen," said Effie. "You better stay in your bed the day and see what happens."

"I've never felt sae ill in aw' ma life."

"Have you had your period?" asked Agnes when they were alone in the bedroom.

"What's that got to dae wi' it?"

"Dinnae be sae daft, Gracie."

"I'm just ill, that's aw'. Dinnae go makin' stuff up."

"I'm no the one whae's sick as a dug," said Agnes. She closed the bedroom door. "You're no, are you?" she asked.

"No what?"

"You ken what I'm askin'."

"Och, you're just as bad as she is. I'll be fine the morn."

❧

The following three days, Grace was sick every morning and nauseous most of the day, but by the fourth day she was feeling better and went out.

She was gone until the early hours of the morning and crept into the flat hoping they would all be asleep. Effie was waiting for her, dozing in the chair.

"Where have you been?"

"I didnae mean to be oot sae late," stammered Grace.

"Sae late. It's five-thirty in the morning, lass. Where have you been?"

Grace suddenly turned and ran to the bathroom. Effie was right behind her, watching as she vomited into the toilet bowl.

"You've gone and done it, haven't you? Were you that stupid, Gracie? Could you no ken that you'd get in trouble?" said Effie softly, taking her into the kitchen.

Grace sat at the kitchen table looking at her mother, who loomed over her. Nervously, Grace played with her fingers and then reached into her coat pocket to hold out some money. "Maybe that'll help," she said slowly, holding out three pounds.

"Where did you get that?" asked Effie nervously.

"Last night's wages."

"Where? You havenae had a job for weeks now. Where did ye get money fae?" A sick feeling rose in Effie. "Oh, no, Gracie. No that. How could you? I cannie believe you'd be sae stupid." She sat down heavily in the chair across from her.

Grace put the money down on the table. "That'll keep the roof ower ma heed," she said sarcastically.

Horrified, Effie said, "Fur God's sake, I never meant it like that, Gracie. No like that. I thought you were being stupid, but no that stupid. What were you thinkin'?"

Grace began to titter nervously.

"What's sae funny? said Effie. "Do you think this a laughing matter?"

Grace swallowed hard on the hysteria that was clambering furiously at the back of her head. Her body convulsed in gales of laughter stifled inside pursed lips. Then the tears began to flow. Effie watched in amazement, disgust, and fear for her daughter.

"Do you want me to leave?" she said.

Effie responded slowly in a small voice. "Where would you go? You cannie leave. We'll just have to do the best we can."

"But I dinnae want to be pregnant, Ma," she bubbled. "I dinnae want a bairn."

Effie stood and took the soiled dishcloth from the sink and swiped Grace's face with it. "You've got a lot o' growing up to be day'in."

༺❉༻

Grace sat in the pub nursing a gin and bitter lemon, smoking her fourth cigarette in a row, bouncing her leg up and down. Frances McIlveney, a scrawny, bird-beaked girl with bright red lipstick, was sitting next to her, sipping a shandy. "It's no gawn away, hen. There's nae point in sitting there worryin' yourself aboot it. You've done it, so you might as well get on wi' it, or ye can dae as I did and go see somebody."

Grace stopped her leg bouncing and ground the butt into the ashtray. "What do you mean?"

"You ken what I mean." She leaned in towards Grace, whispering, "There's help if you need it. I can gie you the address."

Grace pulled back from her bad breath. "Och, I cannie be day'in that. They stick aw' kinds of things up ye. Och, naw."

"Suit yourself, but you better get used to it. It's no gawn away."

"I wish I was deed," groaned Grace.

"Och, dinnae be daft. It's no the end o' the world."

"How would you ken?"

"It's just no, that's aw'."

Three days later, Grace ran into Frances on the Junction Road. "I need a favor."

⚬⚬⚬

Grace stepped into the dark alley thick with damp stone and hundred-year-old piss and pulled her coat collar closer to her neck. An old man, unshaved and wearing dirty overalls, sat on the steps at the entrance to the stairs smoking a cigarette. He nodded to her in a half-alert way as she stepped past him into the gloom of the stairwell. Like so many of the tenements there were no lights on, so she used the wall to guide her, feeling her way up the stairs one by one.

She stopped halfway and, as if on queue, a grizzled voice rose from the bottom. "She's on the third flair!"

Her feet wore lead boots sinking deeper with each step into the sand-filled cavern of her dry mouth. There was not enough saliva to swallow. Frances had said it wasn't very nice, but this was worse than anything she could have imagined. Something wet littered the stairs, sticking to her shoes, and the crumbling plaster walls were damp. Hanging over everything was a bitter, clinging smell like dead rats.

As she reached the landing, she almost fell when her foot came down too heavily expecting another step. She slowly groped her way to the outline of the first door feeling her hands scabby dirty from running along the wall. Frances had said, "Whatever you do, don't make a noise at that door. The auld man'll throw you doon the stairs." She tiptoed past it, breathing shallow in case he could hear her. At the next door, she stuck her hand out and grasped a cold brass doorknob. She jumped back and almost slipped on the wet floor. Frances had said she would know she was there. The doorknob was the sign.

She was feeling dizzy from holding her breath. "What if it disnae work? I'm so bloody stupid." She shivered and made a fist to knock, but held back. She was crying softly and wiped her nose with the back of her hand then slithered back against the wall into the darkest corner. She heard muffled voices on the other side of the door. As the door opened, she pressed herself into the wall, trying to disappear. In the glow of the door, a sallow-faced young woman came out leaning on a heavyset woman. "Let that be a lesson to you," she was saying to the young woman. "Just hope to Christ this is the end o' it." In the darkness of the landing, they looked like ghosts gliding past and gave her only a cursory glance.

Grace looked beyond the open door to the gaslit room. Who uses gaslight these days she wondered, taking a few steps forward. The smell from the house was a mixture of carbolic mixed with vomit. Grace managed to stifle an overwhelming surge of nausea.

"Is there anyone there?" a woman shouted cheerfully. "You might as well come in because it won't do you much good out there."

Grace hesitated. How bad can it be? she thought. It'll be ow'er in a minute and I'll get on wi' ma life.

Then the voice changed to something rough and unforgiving. "If you're comin' in, then do it. If your no, then close the bloody door and go away. Dinnae waste ma time."

Grace jumped back, grabbing hold of the banister then threw herself down the stairs two at a time, not caring if she missed any. She banged into the two women slowly making their way down the stairs. The older woman shouted, "Aye, run away, hen. Serves you bloody right."

The old man sucked on his cigarette and nodded at her as she flew past him. "Couldnae dae it?" he muttered to himself.

Agnes was surprised to find her mother sitting in the darkened kitchen holding a pudding bowl in her lap; her hands covered in flour and her face covered in tears which she wiped away when Agnes turned on the light. "What's the matter, Ma?" she said anxiously. "Are you no feelin' well? Do you want me to fetch the doctor?"

83

"Naw, I'll be aw' right. I'm just tired." She slapped her hands together to take the flour of them. "I've been watching the birds out the window," she said, reaching into her pinafore pocket for a handkerchief. She blew her nose then started to beat the cake mixture once more. "That lassie goes flyin' aboot wi' her coat wide open, her belly growing bigger every day, and she disnae look like she could gie a damn aboot anything. What do you think I've done wrong?"

Agnes got down on her knees in front of her mother. "Och, dinnae be stupid, Ma. She's got a mind o' her ane, and naebody can tell her different. It's no your fault. She's aye been that way."

"Maybe I could have been a wee bit stronger wi' her? No left you wi' it so much," she said.

"It's no anything I couldnae dae, Ma. You're no thinkin' right."

"Aye, I suppose, but I'm no sure it was a good idea, that's aw'. You're almost twenty-two and you're no even close to findin' anybody to marry. Maybe if I'd gi'en you a bit mare room."

"Och, dinnae be daft. I'm a big lassie and I can dae as I want. There's naebody oot there I'd want anyway. They're aw' daft in the heed wi' the fitba, the horses, or the drink. I dinnae need any o' that."

Effie sat silently for a few minutes and Agnes rose to get her a cup of tea. "Did you ever wonder why there was nae faither for you before Douglas?" she said.

Agnes poured the tea carefully, placing two spoons of sugar and milk into it. She did not turn around from the counter. "You said my faither was killed in the war."

"Aye, I did, but I didnae really mean it that way."

Agnes sat down opposite her mother at the small kitchen table, still holding the cups. "What did you mean?"

"Your faither was somebody I hardly knew."

"You dinnae have to dae this, Ma," she said.

"I ken, but aw' this business has me aw' stirred up. I was a stupid wee lassie as well, ye ken." Effie was staring at the bowl on her lap. "Probably no much better than oor Grace, that's what makes it sae hard. I didnae ken any better, but I never regretted it because o' you. I'm just sorry I've no gi'en you a lot o' time. Douglas hasnae been much o' a faither to you and I ken that."

Agnes wanted her mother to stop. "It's aw' right Ma. We've done aw' right, haven't we? It's no your fault."

"Sometimes I dinnae ken whaese fault it is. I'm just trying to keep it aw' the gether and there's no much thanks for it, but you've done for they bairns and now I look at them and nane o' them could gie a damn." She sniffed and wiped her eyes with her sleeve. "I dinnae ken what to dae aboot Gracie."

"She'll have to figure that one oot for herself, that's aw'. All you can do is keep an eye on her. I'm there to help if I can."

She patted Effie's arm and stood up. "What are we celebrating?" she asked, looking at the cake batter.

"You're awfy daft sometimes, ye ken that? It's your birthday the morn."

"Oh, that," said Agnes.

Effie looked out the kitchen window and saw the tree outside was thick with starlings deafening the evening air with their chorus. "I want to tell you about your father," she said.

As she began to tell the story of Loic, she struggled with the remembrance of what had passed between them and the regret of their encounter, but when she spoke of her mother her voice descended into sorrow. "She never let me leave the house except when I went to ma work or I was oot wi' her. I didnae have an easy time wi' your granny, that's why you never met her. I was sorry I lied to you when I said she was dead. She didnae want me hame wi' a bairn. I was only fifteen. I was really innocent in these days. I didnae ken that no havin' your period meant you were pregnant. She didnae want the neighbors talkin' aboot me and asked Father Fitzpatrick to find me a hame in Edinburgh. When you were born, I had no intention of gi'en you away. To her I was dead, so I thought she should be too. I was sorry I never saw my Ma again, but I've never been sorry I kept you. As for your faither, well, aw' the men went away to the war, so it widnae surprise me if he did die in it." She stared wistfully at the branches of the tree moving slightly in the breeze. "They birds make an awfy racket."

Agnes asked quietly, "Why did you marry Douglas?"

Effie leaned in slightly. "Do you remember you askin' me for a daddy?"

Agnes shook her head.

"Well, you did, and although I thought we were do'in all right, I knew I had to gie you somebody. Women are no supposed to live on their ane wi' bairns unless they're a widow. I was a young lassie. I had to tell so many lies aboot you and me. I didnae make a good choice, did I?"

Agnes sipped on her tea and said nothing.

"He's never been much o' a faither to you and I'm sorry for that. But I dinnae understand him and Gracie. He used to think the sun shone out of her bum, and now look at them. They hardly speak to each other. There's so much silence in this hoose, and I just cannie make sense o' it."

Agnes bit her lower lip. For one long expansive moment she was ready to tell all. But this confession was already too painful. She could see her mother struggling with the depth of her guilt and shame, burying herself in a place she could not come back from easily. Agnes struggled with the weight of her mother's shame. It was hers also and she didn't know how to deal with that.

She paused for a moment, and in the time that it took for her to continue, Agnes knocked over the cup with her elbow, spilling the tea. Rising hastily, she grabbed the dish towel from the back of the chair and began mopping it up.

"Look, there's nae point to this," Agnes said nervously, "you're makin' yourself daft for nothing. C'mon, drink your tea."

Effie stood, hesitatating before her. "I ken . . ." she said. Agnes held her breath. "I've no done everything I could do," she continued. "I hope you can understand that."

"It's aw' right, Ma," Agnes sighed. "I'm fine. I've always been able to fend fur myself."

"Just dinnae tell Grace or John anything. I dinnae want them to ken aboot this. This is between you and me. You're the only one I've got to answer to," she said urgently. "I havenae even told Douglas the whole story."

Agnes looked directly into her mother's eyes and said, "Dinnae worry. I'll no tell anybody."

Below, long white-capped waves broke the surface of the ocean. In the cabin of the airplane most of the passengers were asleep, and the only sound evident was that of the engines. Agnes closed her eyes for a minute to relieve the pressure that was building behind them. *I kept that secret,* she thought, *until now. Now everybody's going to know it.* She smacked her lips together and clenched her fist. An urge to strike out barreled through her body and she felt sick. *Now everyone knows. How am I going to tell ma bairns. What am I going to tell them?* In her need to protect, Agnes had lied to the one person she loved more than anyone else in the world, continuing to hold to that lie through all the years and the tragedies that followed.

Telling Alison that she did not know her father and the circumstances of her birth was never meant to be broadcast to the world. She wasn't even sure why she had told her, but like everything else in this book, Alison managed to capture the reality without having actually been there. How she did that, Agnes had no idea. But now that it was written down for everyone to see, she would have to tell her children about it.

Thinking back to that day of the confession, she felt sure that somehow her mother knew about Douglas and Grace. Maybe not in the details, but she knew something had gone on between them. Agnes would never know for sure because after that day there was never any mention.

All her life she had judged Grace's behavior when it was clear she was in no position to judge anyone. She had betrayed her mother; she had betrayed Grace by keeping the secret. Effie had been dead for thirty years, and she wished she could bring her back to tell her how sorry she was that she had not told her the truth. She should have let her mother deal with it herself.

How dare Alison assume this information was hers to do with as she pleased? Not this. This was nobody's business but her own.

nine

GRACE'S DAUGHTER RITA was born prematurely weighing less than four pounds. She was diagnosed with congenital heart disease, otherwise known as hole in the heart syndrome. Grace said she was the one with the hole in the heart. The color of the baby's skin was milky moonlight blue and the circles under her eyes would have looked natural on a raccoon. The doctors warned that any signs of respiratory distress should be attended to immediately. It was best to keep her quiet, not to excite her, and not to expose her to too much variation in the weather in case of colds.

Keeping her quiet was not a problem. She was a placid child who cried very little and slept for long periods. The weather was a different problem. Damp was a permanent state of being in Scotland because of rain that was spitting, drizzling, or pouring. She was kept indoors as much as possible and only taken out on dry days when she could be left lying in the direct sunlight "to put some color on her cheeks," said Effie. The child was like a magnet, inextricably drawing people towards her, attracted by the quiet pulse of her existence, until Effie told them to leave her alone. She would not have her breathed on by strangers.

Douglas devised a makeshift bed from the bottom of a chest of drawers, and then decided she needed a proper bed and went foraging for pieces of wood to make a cradle. He carved her initials on the end of the bed. A neat "RS" with small vines wrapped around them, each notch carved with the greatest effort to make it perfect for his angel grandchild.

Effie swaddled her in a blanket made of finely knit wool she had spent months knitting and put her on a strict feeding schedule every three hours, which everyone, including John, took turns regardless of what time of night it was. All the child had to do was whimper and there was someone picking her up, cuddling her and walking her.

All, except Grace. The screaming during the delivery was a nightmare she had woken from, and only the physical existence of the child was enough to prove that it was real. But it did not belong to her, and no amount of verbal abuse would make her change her mind.

For the first time in her life, she went eagerly to work every day as a bus conductress. She could pretend her life was normal; that there were no responsibilities beyond the present moment. In her neat uniform with the ticket machine strapped in front of her, she rang up tickets all day, made cute banter with the passengers and flattered the men who hung about on the platform below the stairs trying to catch a glimpse of her legs as she ran up and down. Many joked about a date with her, but she was savvy enough to know that one mention of a child and they would disappear in the dust from their shoes.

Agnes marveled at how Grace could sleep the sleep of the dead, ignoring Rita's cries at three a.m. as she struggled out of the bed to feed her. No matter how hard she nudged, Grace would resolutely pretend she was sleeping, clinging tenaciously to the side of the bed as Agnes nudged her with her backside to get out of bed and feed her daughter. Grace didn't see any reason to be getting out of bed at three if she was getting out of bed at five to get to the depot by five-thirty. "I'll take the nine o'clock the night," she agreed, but would usually miss it because she was out with her pals.

As usual, Effie would have the last word. "I'm no your servant, ye ken. If it wisnae fur the fact that that wee yin is so good, I dinnae ken what we'd dae. You're bloody useless. This is the third time this week you've no been here when you should be. When are you gonnie grow up? This bairn deserves better."

"I'll dae the nappies," she said cheerfully. "That's one less thing you have to do." She picked up the bucket and began rinsing them under the tap. "Jesus Christ, these things burn my eyes."

"Aye, a wee whiff o' what's good for you. When you get them rinsed, put them in the boiling pail and keep them there."

Grace lifted them into the boiling pot that covered the top of the stove, pushing them down with a large wooden stick, slurping the edges into the water causing it to spill over. "I've got a date the night," she announced, pushing the rising gray material downwards.

Effie was in the middle of chopping onions, tears streaming down her face. "You're no go'in anywhere the night," she sniffed.

Douglas looked up from the newspaper. "Di ye ken that Chamberlain is trying to keep Hitler fae startin' another war? If it's anything like the last one, it'll be the high jump for the likes o' us. That man's no well. He's walked intae Austria and Czechoslovakia and now he thinks he can take Poland. God help us all."

Effie sliced through the carrots. "Aye, I've been see'in it at the pictures. They say we're aw' gonnie be in it soon. I heard they're lookin' for women to sign up for the Women's Volunteer Service to gie a hand."

"Bloody shite. You'll sit around and gab while you knit socks and make cups of tea to gie oot."

"We aw' did oor stint in the first one, so I dinnae think it'll be different in this one. The only difference is, you winnie be gawn."

"Bloody right aboot that. They've taken ma pound of flesh." He absently rubbed his hip and shifted position in his chair.

"Do you really think they're gonnie go fur it?"

"Has to be, hasn't it? We've no been puttin' up aw' these blackout curtains for nothin'. I signed up for the ARP the day. I've got to go aroond and check if there's nae chinks in the windaes. If I find any, I've got to report it."

"You never telt me or talked to me aboot it!"

"Och, away wi' you, woman. I dinnae have to ask you for everything."

"When do you start?"

"I dinnae ken. I'm waitin' fur the letter."

"We got one the day. It says we've aw' got to go doon to the library and get oor gas masks. Have you seen them yet? Wee square boxes wi' a bit o' string. It says we're supposed to take them wherever we go or we get a fine. Next thing you know, they'll be charging us for breathing. They're even talking aboot evacuating bairns fae England."

"Dinnae you go thinkin' we're gonnie take bairns in here. We've got enough. As fur these gas masks, God help us. If they start that again, nane o' us'll be alive."

Grace was standing quietly poking the boiling nappies as they talked. "Do you think they'll let me join up?"

Douglas raised his head from the newspaper and stammered, "Join up what? Dinnae be daft! First of all, you're no auld enough, and secondly, you've got a bairn. Get that idea oot o' your heed."

"I'd rather be gawn there than sittin' in this hoose wi' you lot," she muttered.

"What was that?" frowned Effie. "Get that bairn's nappy changed. That's useful."

"I'm no stupid," said Grace picking up Rita and bouncing her into the air. The child began to hiccup with laughter.

"You mind that bairn. Dinnae go gettin' her aw' worked up. And if you're changin' her, dinnae leave her arse stickin' oot like you did the last time. There was shite everywhere."

Grace folded the nappy into two triangles and placed it between her legs. "She's got a red bum."

"Put cream on it! It's lying right there."

Grace saw the jar, took a thick dab of it on her fingers, screwing up her face at the feel of it in her nails, then gently rubbed it over the tender rash. "I was thinking."

"Wonders'll never cease," said Effie.

Grace ignored her. "I ken you said I was too young, but I bet you they'll take me when I'm eighteen. I think I've got to help dae ma duty for the country," she said patriotically.

Douglas looked up. "Since when did you get sae bloody eager to serve your country? You cannie even serve your ane bloody family. What kind of help do you think you'd be?"

Grace looked at Douglas and turned her mouth down. "It's better than sitting here aw' day, isn't it?" She stuck the safety pin into the nappy and caught the sharp end on her fingers as it came through the other side. "Fuck!" she shouted, making Rita jump.

"Mind that bairn and mind your mooth. It's amazing she disnae greet when you dae that to her."

Grace ignored her and started singing to Rita:

"Just a wee deoch and doris, just a wee drop that's aw'
Just a wee deoch and doris, afore ye gang awah'
There's a wee wifie waitin' in a wee but and ben
If you can say "it's a braw bricht moonlicht nicht,
Then your aw'richt, ye ken."

Shivering, Agnes felt immensely tired as she let herself drift with the hum of the airplane engines. It felt like a warm womb, everyone nestled into tight spaces, waiting for the moment of release.

Thinking about these days during the Great War, it was easy for people to believe that Effie had been widowed at a very early age, and she was content to leave it at that. Grace never thought to invent anything. At birth, her child belonged to the family, and the family had been more than willing to take it on. At seventeen, Grace was incapable of taking on the responsibilities of a child, let alone one with a disability. Agnes thought she was still a child herself—selfish and cavalier about everything.

A quiet life was all Agnes ever desired, and as she grew older it was what she got. She thought she was content. Now she wasn't so sure. It was almost as if she had read too far and couldn't turn back. She was sucked into the life of this thing, and the more it revealed about her family history, the more exposed she felt.

ten

THE SUMMER HAD been long and hot. Windows flung wide open invited the whole street to eavesdrop on the what, where, and how of each other's lives. Arguments, lovemaking, and what you were having for your tea were all public domain. Everyone sat either at the window, leaning on well-scrubbed windowsills, or on the stone stairs that led into the building. The back green became a place for sunbathing in between the gray sheets, stringy towels, and worn dungarees. Rita was laid out in the sun each day and was beginning to take on a more natural color. Although still frail, she had put on more weight and was moving around like a normal child, albeit closely guarded by Effie or Agnes. Grace worked hard on rapidly multiplying the number of freckles on her skin with a regular smearing of baby oil. The long mauve nights disturbed children accustomed to going to bed when it was dark. Murmured conversations about the possibility of war sat heavy on those who remembered the last one which had ended twenty-one years ago. Mothers were anxious for their sons and husbands, daughters were eager to discover new freedoms, and sons were full of bravado for the number of Nazis they would kill.

One Sunday morning, quiet with the sound of church bells in the distance, Agnes leaned out the window, cooling herself with a fan she had made out of cardboard. Effie was putting away the breakfast dishes, and John was trying not to cut his face shaving using the metal door of the bathroom cabinet as his mirror. Grace was singing to Rita. Douglas was fiddling with the radio dial when he yelled "Will ye aw' hud your wheesht!"

The Bakelite radio sizzled and crackled as he tuned in to the sound of Big Ben chiming eleven o'clock. The voice of Neville Chamberlain hissed and popped on the airwaves. "This morning, the British ambassador in Berlin handed the German government . . ."

Grace was bouncing Rita on her knee. "Pack up your troubles in your old kit bag and smile, smile, smile . . . ," she sang, drowning out the words on the radio.

" . . . withdraw their troops from Poland . . ."

"Shut up, Gracie, for Christ's sake. This is important." Agnes, sitting on the chair next to John, was leaning towards the radio. Grace fell silent but Rita was still humming.

"Sssshh!" said Effie.

" . . . no such undertaking has been received and that consequently this country is at war with Germany . . ."

There was a stunned silence in the room until Grace stood up and handed Rita to Agnes. "Well, I guess that's it then. I might as well see how I can be useful."

"Good God, what's gonnie become o' us now?" moaned Agnes, holding Rita so tight that she squirmed to get down.

Douglas turned the radio off, pushing his hands behind his suspender belt, his veins turning to ice water as he stood contemplating the street below. From outside, a voice yelled, "We're aw' fur the high jump now!" Sighing, Douglas felt the darkness sweep over him again.

"Och, it'll be over in nae time," said John. "We'll get these Jerries runnin'. I'm away to see if I can join up."

Douglas swung round and gripped him by the arm. "You're no gawn anywhere, you hear! Just dinnae get any big ideas. I dinnae want to hear you've gone anywhere. If it's anything like the last yin . . ." His voice trailed away and there was a moment of intense silence until a small voice sang "Pack up your troubles in your old kit bag" out of tune.

Rita was sitting on the floor, bouncing her doll on her knee as she sang. "Pack up your troubles in your old kit bag and smile, smile, smile."

Effie looked at Agnes and they both started laughing. "See what you've done?" said Agnes to Grace, who picked Rita up from the floor. "Maybe we should send you ow'er to Germany. You'll sort them oot, won't you?" Rita gurgled and hiccuped as Grace tickled her.

"You mind that bairn," cautioned Effie. "God help us aw'."

"She's do'in great, aren't you?" squealed Grace, struck by a sudden burst of euphoria. "We're off to war," she sang.

❧

Recruiting took place in every Labor Exchange, church hall, and local government office. Posters went up all over the place advertising what YOU could do for the war effort. Placards demanded that people pay attention to the three Rs: Run to cover, Remain under cover, then Relax and Recover. "Someone cannie count," John said. "There's four R's in that slogan. Nae mare reading, writing, and 'rithmetic fur me?"

"No you don't laddie," said Douglas. "You get hunkered doon wi' the schooling. I'll see to that." John shrugged his shoulders and buried himself deeper into his math homework. After years of feeling ignored, John basked in the attention of his father, but it did not escape him that Grace was no longer the center of attention and had not been for years. He did his best to please his father by bringing home good school results and was the first to stay on at school· beyond the general leaving certificate at age fourteen. Douglas always told him he would do better than anyone else in the family.

Even if John had not noticed his sister's flirtations and attention grabbing on the streets and in the bars, all his pals did. "Your sister's a cracker," said his friend Dan. John thumped him on the arm and shoved him to one side.

"Do you fancy her?" he asked angrily.

"Aye, right!" said Dan. "She's got a bairn and if I wisnae careful she'd gie me one too. No thanks."

Many of the boys told him how beautiful his sister was but he couldn't see it. She was all red hair and freckles and he hated to see how casual she was with herself on the street, teasing the boys, throwing herself around and daring them to come get her. Embarrassed and ashamed, she had all them all right where she wanted them. It was sickening, but he wished he could have had some of that carefree attitude. His life was too serious and he was too timid. Grace took the risks that turned heads and brightened the tongues of bored lives. John fell somewhere between duty and obligation, feeling confused and strangled by it.

Douglas was now out with the ARP every night. It was his job to make sure everyone had their blackout curtains on securely. With all the streetlights disconnected for the duration of the war, he trained his night vision to see into the dark stairwells and knock on doors to tell them their curtains were not fastened securely. The first warning was free. "This is the second time I've had to find my way up here," he said, whistling wheezily from the climb to the top of the tenement building. "You should know better. I'm supposed to fine you." The second warning was supposed to cost as much as five pounds, but he never had the heart. "I'll let you go this time, but don't make me climb these stairs again. It's killing me, let alone you."

The bombs might have been falling in London and destroying much of the city, but in Scotland, it was more likely to be an accident that killed or maimed you. Many people were run over by cars because the drivers couldn't see anyone on the dark roads, or they broke their ankles falling off the pavement because they couldn't see the edge. The City Corporation took up the issue and began painting white lines on the edges of the pavement and on the lampposts. Douglas found himself with a bucket of paint and a paintbrush as part of his duties.

Effie continued cleaning at night and took a job with the WVS during the day, knitting and making tea, just as Douglas had predicted. Children were evacuated from the south of England to Scotland, arriving by the hundreds at Waverley Station in Edinburgh, holding tight to the hands of a brother or sister, occasionally with a mother, clutching small suitcases, laundry bags, and sometimes plain brown paper packets tied up with string. They all carried gas masks in little brown boxes around their necks and wore tags labeled with their names and addresses. Most of the children looked dazed, and a few were openly sobbing. Effie saw a small girl about six years old standing in the middle of a melee on the platform, people busy moving around her, looking frightened and holding her brown paper parcel tight. "It's aw'right my darlin'" she said, taking her hand. "We'll find where you belong," and led her towards the meeting point at the front of the station where stray kids met with their unobservant chaperones. It broke her heart to see the little ones clinging to the skirts of the volunteers, crying for their mothers. More than once she was tempted to take one or two home.

While Effie was at Waverley Station worrying about the children, she missed all the action down by the water near Granton. At two-thirty in the afternoon, passengers on a train crossing the Firth of Forth Bridge leaned out of the windows to get a better view of Royal Air Force planes opening fire on each other, dropping bombs into the water. On shore, children stopped playing and people left their work to get a glimpse of the valiant RAF in action. John was looking at a Join the Navy poster in the newsagent's, dreaming about joining. He heard the clatter of guns across the water and as he turned to look, one of the planes went hurtling towards the water near the Isle of May and a parachute opened in the sky. It seemed like an awful waste of an aircraft, he thought, and he hoped the airman could swim. He thought it was a practice run.

The following day The Scotsman newspaper reported it was the first enemy action on the River Forth, an intercept of German planes returning from an attempt to bomb Rosyth Shipyards. Not one siren sounded during the fight.

"But you had to see it, Ma. It was something," said John. "There was aw' these Jerries and they wis flashing aw' their guns at each other, go'in back and for'art. It was great. When the Jerry plane went intae the water, it was aw' black and smoky. We didnae ken whether to cheer or no, so we didnae dae anything. It was queer."

"Aye, bloody queer," said Effie. "We could be deed in oor beds for aw' they care."

"Never mind, Ma. The whole war might go like that," piped up Grace.

"Nae bloody chance," said Douglas. "There's gonnie be a lot o' deed yins before this is aw' ower."

"Cheerful Charlie there," said Grace, playing with Rita's hair. "You ken Nellie?" she asked Effie.

Effie shook her head in the negative.

"Well, she's got herself joined up wi' the WAFs. Frances is gawn as well. I was wondering if it widnae be a good idea for me. I ken I've got a bairn, so dinnae throw that one at me. But they seem to think we're aw' needed now. I think you could manage."

"Oh, you do, do you? Dinnae get me started."

Grace continued twirling Rita's hair into little ringlets, which caused her to pull away. "Well, you see, it's like this. . . ."

"Och, dinnae tell me! Have you signed up? You've got to be jokin' me! What am I gonnie dae wi' you, Gracie? You think you can just do what you please." She threw down the clothes she was folding and went through to the bedroom.

Agnes was shaking her head at Grace. Douglas said, "Now see what you've done. Can you no leave things alane, Gracie? I dinnae understand you."

"There's nae surprise there," she said.

"It's no fair," whined John. "She's no supposed to be gawn anywhere. She's the one whae's got a bairn that we're aw' payin' fur."

"You shut up, eedjit," yelled Grace. "Naebody would have you because you're sae stupid. You widnae ken what to dae withoot your daddy."

He lunged at her and made to hit her. Grace backed away. "Go on then—you cannie, can you?" she taunted. "Aw' these books are making you soft in the heed."

"At least I dinnae have to work on the buses," he bellowed. "I at least finished at the school."

"Och, dinnae kid yourself," Grace snarled. "You widnae be anywhere if he hudnae made you."

"Well at least I'm no gawn oot on the streets like a whore."

Grace lunged for him and slapped him across the face. "That's the last time you'll call me that," she hissed.

"Aw' the laddies in the street think you're on the game," John yelled.

Douglas stepped between them. "Stop it, Gracie. You're no gawn anywhere, and neither are you," he said to John. "You need to get a better tongue in your mooth."

"We'll see whether I go or no," said Grace bitterly, putting on her coat to go out.

"Where are you going?" asked Agnes.

"Ma! She's gawn oot," yelled John.

"You've got such a big gob, ye ken that," Grace said, punching John as she walked past him.

"Where are you gawn?" shouted Effie.

"Away fae here."

❧

Dressed in a black checked coat, cinched tight at the waist, a brown felt hat with a feather sticking out the side, and peek-a-boo shoes that exposed her toes, Grace looked as if she had stepped out of a magazine. Inside her small brown leather suitcase was a change of underwear, a hairbrush and curlers, a tube of Revlon red lipstick that some sailor had given her, and her sign-up paper. She hoped there would be no need for a change of clothes since she hadn't brought any. She was promised real stockings with her new uniform; that was all she wanted. Thousands of men and women were gathered on the platforms saying good-bye to family and loved ones. The noise was deafening as trains chugged in and out, blowing steam and soot over everything.

She had said good-bye to Effie and Douglas at home. Effie had given her a quick peck and a hug. Douglas said, "You watch yourself," but made no attempt to touch her. Rita had learned the word sing but interpreted it as sig and was pulling on Grace's coat, smiling up at her. "Sig. Sig," she said.

"She wants you to sing," said Agnes.

"I can see that," Grace replied with tears in her eyes, patting Rita's head. "No now," she said quietly, then reached down to give her an almost empty lipstick case before kissing her on the lips, leaving a smudged heart-shape mark.

Standing on the station platform, Grace took Agnes's arm. "Do you think I'm do'in the right thing?"

"You're a bit late for that," she said. "You're do'in what you think is right. I cannie tell you if it is or no. You widnae listen so dinnae ask me now. I'm no your keeper. There's a war on. The rules are no the same. Just try to take care of yourself, that's aw'. We'll aw' be here when you get back." She awkwardly took Grace's hand and then impulsively reached forward to kiss her cheek. Grace was surprised and stepped back before reaching over to her, holding on tight. Just as quickly, she let go, waving her hand as she walked away.

"Cheerio! I'll be back in nae time," she said chirpily. She rushed off down the platform towards the waiting train and a sign that said "Women's Royal Air Force Scunthorpe."

❧

Six months later, Grace came home without any warning. She refused to discuss what had happened, but it seemed she was home for good, dishonorably discharged.

"What did you dae?" asked Agnes in the quiet time before going to sleep. "It must have been bad if they drummed you oot."

"It's no worth talking aboot," she said, turning over in the bed. "Now I've got your fat arse to lie up against."

"Och, you havenae changed, have you?"

But she had. Two months previous Grace had found herself in military terms 'being pregnant without permissions," which was subject to immediate dishonorable discharge. She had tried to cover it up because he was a colonel in the Special Services of the Air Force and the other girls told her not to tell because she wouldn't be believed. He'd call her a liar and she would get tossed out anyway. But morning sickness and fatigue made her condition impossible to hide. She was reported to the C.O. who told her it was unfortunate, but she had to go home. Grace anguished in the days following, knowing full well she could not return pregnant, so she did the one thing she said she would never do. She bled for two weeks while living in a dreary bed-sitter in Scunthorpe with only the clothes she had arrived in. On the train home, she vowed no one would ever get to know about it, not even Agnes. But lying here next to her, she yearned to hold onto her sister's broad expansive body, to tell her everything that had happened, to find something that would give her some comfort.

Agnes sat looking at the page in her hand remembering when Grace had told her the truth. It was on a visit to York, right after her hysterectomy when they were going over some old pictures.

There was one with Grace linking arms with a bunch of pals in their uniforms, caps askew, smiles on their faces, ready for the adventure. "They were the days," she said sadly.

"I dinnae ken what it is aboot me, but I'm glad they did this hysterectomy. Having bairns has been like a curse for me. I didnae even have to try. You see aw' these women whae desperately want bairns, and all I had to do was open my legs wide enough and there it was."

"What happened back then, Gracie?" Agnes urged.

"It was an awfy business," she said shuddering, and then began to weep. When she finished with the story, she smiled wanly before flipping through the pictures and pausing at one of Rita. "She was a bonnie bairn," she said.

"Aye," said Agnes. "We aw' loved her."

eleven

Effie wasted no time in telling Grace it was probably something she did. Confused and disappointed in her one more time, she made it clear that she was to return to work immediately. Grace went to work at the factory making uniforms for the Army. For once, she did not argue but instead obeyed all the rules. She showed up for work on time, came home when she was supposed to, and became the model mother. She made Rita's meals, played makeup and dress up, sang songs and read stories. By the time she was two years old, Rita could sing a dozen songs.

Grace learned all her favorite songs from the radio and the pictures. Her favorite movies were musicals and romance. Tyrone Power, Errol Flynn, Clark Gable, Ginger Rogers, and Fred Astaire were her favorites. When she was young, she had dreamed of becoming a star, singing and dancing her way around the world. Now she was singing in the pub on a Saturday night.

"You should sing at the picture hoose in between the shows," said Jeanie Ranson. "You'd be good."

"Och, away wi' you. Everybody else is singing. Just look around you."

"Naw, seriously. Let me hear you sing that one again. You know, "The Glory of Love." I love that song."

Grace put her head back and closed her eyes. Slowly and with a sultry voice, she began. "You've got to give a little, take a little, and let your poor heart break a little . . ."

As she sang, her voice soared, lost in the emotion, lost in the lyrics of the song, rising and falling in perfect pitch and mood. She paid no attention to what was happening around her until she stopped and realized that the whole pub had been listening to her sing. Suddenly, everybody burst into a cacophony of applause and whistles and yells, cutting through the thick smoke of cigarettes and the moldy smell of beer.

Jeanie had tears in her eyes. "My God, Grace. Where did you get that fae? That was incredible. Gie us another yin."

There were shouts for more, but Grace laughed nervously and said no, she needed a drink first. Immediately there was a round of drinks brought to the table, and a tall, blonde, square-jawed American, with a dimple in his chin like Kirk Douglas, approached. He held up his drink and saluted her. "May I sit down, Miss?"

"It's a free world," Grace giggled, spreading her hand across the seat next to her.

"Well, we're working on trying to keep it that way, at least," he joked as he sat down.

The Americans had been arriving at the docks in droves, with easy smiles and an armful of chewing gum and the biggest prize of all—nylons—which they gave away in return for favors. As part of the special operations forces they were not technically in the war, but were quietly lending a hand to the Allies. Grace had drunk with quite a few of them and enjoyed their friendly, easygoing temperaments, but was careful to keep them at arm's length when they got too friendly. The Scottish guys thought they had too much money and too much gab but were always eager to accept the free drinks they so generously supplied. Grace loved their accents, the clean uniforms, and their well-scrubbed faces. They admired her long curly auburn hair and long legs and told her she should be in Hollywood. Flattery usually went a long way with Grace, but she had learned to give nothing in return except amusement. Lingering at the back of her mind, she hoped one of them would fall in love with her and take her back to Philadelphia or Oklahoma or wherever it was they came from. Life in America, like in the movies, was glamorous, rich, and comfortable.

"That's one helluva voice you've got there, young lady. Where did you learn to sing like that?"

"Och, away wi' you, Yank! What are you after?"

"Now that's no way to treat a visitor to your country, is it? Didn't anybody tell you there's a war on? We're the friendly guys, remember?" He put his drink down and asked if Grace and Jeanie would like another one.

"Gin and tonic," they giggled.

"Which one is gin, and which one is tonic?" He surveyed them both with his head tilted to the side. "Hmmm. I think you're the gin," he said looking at Jeanie, "and I'd say . . ." He hesitated a moment, surveying Grace from head to toe. Touching her lightly on the knee, he said, "You're definitely the tonic!"

"I'd say you're already three sheets and the only tonic you're gonnie get is in your heed," said Grace. "However, darling, I'll be whatever you want me to be the night. Just gie me a drink and bring one fur ma pal here and she'll be happy."

He stood up and saluted once more and left for the bar. He came back with the gin and tonics and a friend. He introduced himself as Hank from Des Moines, and his friend as Brad from New York City. Lighting up cigarettes which they offered all round, they said, "All we want is another song."

"Aye, that's what they aw' say," said Jeanie.

Brad produced a pair of nylons, pulling them delicately one by one from his jacket pocket and swinging them in front of Grace's face. "Just one song," he asked.

Grace took the nylons carefully from his hands and put her hand inside the nylon to admire the golden color. "For you, dear, anything, as the song goes," she sang, then launched into "Darn That Dream" and "It's a Sin to Tell a Lie." Brad said she could sing at the new club Village Vanguard in New York City. She could give Billie Holiday a run for her money. All the best jazz singers performed there. By closing time at the pub, Grace had forgotten all about Leith and was well on her way to New York City. All things seemed possible in the glow of gin and tonic haze.

Grace was just getting out of bed when Agnes returned from her night shift smelling of grease and gunmetal. "I hope you left the bed warm," she joked.

"Aye, barely," Grace said yawning. "The wee yin wisnae sae good last night."

"I was just in the living room. She's as right as rain, playing. Ma didnae say anything."

"That's a surprise. I wisnae in the good books at one o'clock this morning."

"Aw, Gracie. You didnae go oot again did you? I thought you had stopped aw' that nonsense." Agnes took off her greasy overalls and shrugged her way into her nightgown.

"I didnae dae anything. I was just oot talkin' and singin'."

"Singin'!"

"Aye, I had a good wee singsong last night wi' some American fellies. They were aw' right. I didnae dae anything. I behaved myself." She twisted herself into the hard elastic corset. "I hate these things."

"Why do you wear them? Your no the one whae needs to be hudding anything in."

Grace grunted and swore, then relaxed into the shape of the thing. "I'm gonnie be late as usual," she said, "but see my new nylons." She held them up for Agnes to see.

"What did you have to do for them?"

"Sing. That's all. I've finished wi' aw' that nonsense."

"You're off your bloody heed," said Agnes.

Opening the living room door, Grace found Rita standing on a chair, looking in the mirror above the fireplace and putting on lipstick. In off moments, she was constantly astonished at how beautiful this child of hers had turned out to be. Her brown eyes had flecks of green in them, which Effie said was the mark of fairies. Rita put out her arms to be lifted down but Grace lifted her and put her face into Rita's neck holding her close, breathing in the slightly wet wooly smell of her. She had an urge to stand there all day like that, but Effie walked in and she put her down immediately.

"Aye, I see you're up. We havenae got much for breakfast the day. I've run oot o' almost everything and I'm no sure we've got enough coupons for what I need. See what you can scrounge up the day when you're oot. Thank God there's enough milk and orange juice for the bairn."

106

"It's aw' right. I'll get something doon at the work."

"You come right hame the night? I dinnae want a repeat o' last night."

"I wisnae up to anything last night, ye ken. I wis singing. My pals telt me there's a job at the picture hoose. I'm thinkin' o' gawn there."

"Never mind the singin'," said Effie dismissively. "Just make sure you're hame the night. I'm gawn doon the bingo wi' Agnes. She's got her day off." She bent down to wipe Rita's face. "Drop her off at the nursery. I've got to go help some bairns fae London. You should see the state o' some of them. We think we've no got much. It's a bloody shame."

Agnes came in dressed in nightgown and curlers. "Are we still gawn to the church bingo the night? I told Bessie I'd be gawn."

Just then Effie focused in on Rita. "Would you look at that red stain aroond her mooth! What kinda dye dae they put in these things?" She rubbed hard and Rita pulled away. "She'll have to dae, I suppose. Take her now, Gracie. You're gonnie be late."

"I'll see you the night," she called, as she bent down to pick up Rita and put her into the push chair to bump down the stairs.

"You watch that wee yin," Effie called out.

"Aye, Ma," said Grace, closing the front door.

Calls of "legs eleven" and "bees knees" during the game of bingo were not meant as flattering remarks. Agnes wasn't looking for a husband, but huddled over her board next to her friend Bessie, she wondered aloud if she would ever meet anyone she liked.

Bessie looked up from her numbers and said, "I've got just the laddie fur you, hen. He's ma cousin William fae York and he's comin' next weekend because he's on the trainin' up the North somewhere. You must have heard me mention him before. I think you'll like him."

Agnes shook her head. "I dinnae ken, Bessie. They're aw' galoots, the fellies I've met. I dinnae want to be set up wi' another yin."

"Och, he's no like that at aw'. He didnae leave school 'til he was sixteen! Imagine that. He's a teetotaler as well," she said proudly, "which is a pity because there's no much tea aroond right now. Just come ow'er. I winnie tell him your comin'."

"I'm no sure. I widnae ken what to say to him."

"Och, dinnae worry aboot that. He's no much o' a talker either. You'll probably hit it off aw' right. Just be yourself, if ye ken what I mean."

"All the sixes, sixty-six!"

"Bingo!" shouted Bessie, jumping up and down, pulling on Agnes's arm.

Effie worried that Agnes was becoming too much like her, frittering her time away watching over Rita, knitting cardigans and jumpers, and going out to the pictures or bingo when she had a wee bit extra, and urged her to go out more often. She was surprised when Agnes appeared in the living room dressed in a soft yellow print dress that she had bought at Goldberg's department store before the war.

"You look awfy braw the day," said Effie, admiring Agnes as she brushed her hair. "Is there a boyfriend you haven't told me aboot?"

"It's no anything special. I'm just gawn ow'er to Bessie's fur some tea."

"Are ye wearing that nice cardigan you knitted for yourself? You ken, the one wi' the yellow flowers on the front? It'll look nice wi' that dress you've got on."

"I think Gracie's gone off wi' it. I cannie find it anywhere."

Effie clucked her tongue against the roof of her mouth. "I thought I saw her go oot the other day in a yellow cardigan. She cannie leave anything alane, can she?"

Agnes shrugged and picked up the white one. "I suppose that'll have to do."

"You look lovely, hen. Whae is it?"

"Och, it's naebody. Bessie's got a cousin she wants me to see." She glanced one more time in the mirror and shrugged her shoulders. I suppose I'll do, she thought.

❧

For late September, the weather was extremely agreeable. The sun laid a high gloss on the burnished copper leaves of the trees, and flowers were still forcing themselves through the cracks in the pavements. Agnes stepped outside and lingered a few moments, letting the sun give her face a glow, before setting out for Bessie's house a few streets away. Some children played with chalk on the pavements, and it seemed like the heat threw a blanket on the day hushing all the normal sounds of a Sunday afternoon.

In Bessie's house the windows were open, curtains fluttering in the breeze, but it was not quiet. The living room looked like it was bursting apart. Bessie's cousin William, a tall, lean young man wearing Army khakis and thick, round glasses, sat nearest the window. He looked out of place amongst the brawny torsos of Bessie's brother Tam and his friend Stuart, home on leave from the Navy. The priest, Father Reid, had been invited over after mass for a cup of tea and Mrs. Green's famous rock cakes, made from flour, water, and a dab of jam. In his white collar and dark robes, he was flushed with the heat. Bessie's mother apologized for the lack of food in the house, and said she would love to have served sandwiches. The priest said they were all grateful for everything—it didn't matter what they had.

"You can get a pint easier than you can a cup of tea these days," said Tam, which made everyone laugh.

Agnes arrived as they were enjoying the joke, and felt as if she were intruding. "Come in, Agnes, dinnae be shy, now," said Mrs. Green. "you ken everybody, except William." She nodded towards William, who was puffing on his pipe. "Sit yourself down if you can find a chair." She pointed in William's direction, towards the empty chair. Agnes blushed and squeezed in next to Bessie.

"I like that dress you're wearing, hen. It suits you well."

"Och, Ma, leave her."

"I wis just sayin'," said Mrs. Green, a little hurt.

Agnes pulled her dress down over her knees and placed her hands on her lap.

William uncrossed his legs, stood up, and stuck his hand out towards her. Agnes looked up from her lap briefly, shook his hand, and looked down again.

"Aw right, William," said Tam. "It's only Agnes. you dinnae need to shake her hand. She's one o' the family, aren't ye, hen?"

William smiled shyly and let Agnes's hand drop.

"You always have the right thing to say, don't you, Tam?" cried Bessie.

"Aye, ye can always count on me, kiddo."

Father Reid smiled beatifically and asked Agnes why he didn't see her in church.

"Oh, we're no Catholic, father. My ma disnae believe in it," she blurted out, and immediately regretted it since Mrs. Green was a devout practicing Catholic.

The priest nodded his head. "It's never too late."

Mrs. Green came in from the kitchen carrying the tea and the rock cakes. Within minutes the cakes were all gone. Agnes nibbled delicately on hers, thinking how much better her mother's were. She glanced in William's direction to see if he was eating his, and found it untouched.

Tam and Stuart were discussing football and who was going to win the Cup this year. Would it be Hibs or Hearts? Stuart was a Hearts fan, but Tam thought the Glasgow team, Celtic, was actually the better team. Stuart couldn't agree. There was nobody better than Hearts. They asked William what he thought. He said it would be difficult to give an opinion because it could only be interpreted as an invitation to a wager as to who was best, and since he had no knowledge of either one, it would not be fair.

Tam raised his eyebrows. "Is that a fact?"

William sucked on his pipe, leisurely folding his arms and crossed his legs.

"So do you like football?" ventured Stuart.

"Mmmm. Tha's not bad when there's a final going on. It can get quite exciting."

"Quite exciting! You haven't lived yet, my boy. It's the best time in the world when your team is winning," said Tam. "You cannie imagine how it feels until you're there wi' the noise bouncing off the bridge of your nose when the fans go mad, the sheer joy when the final goal rushes home. Oh, it's sweet, it is. Do you ken what that means, William?"

"I think tha' I can see what you mean," he demurred.

Agnes drank her tea and watched, amused by William's accent and his ability to take the piss out of Tam.

Father Reid, who had been forgotten in the melee, supped his tea and remarked it was a shame these young ones weren't out enjoying the weather.

William stopped sucking and put the pipe down on the window-sill. "It is a lovely day outside," he announced. "Maybe we should go for a walk." He looked directly at Agnes, his eyes steady behind his wire-framed glasses. "Would thee and Bessie like to go walking?"

Agnes looked at Bessie, who shrugged her shoulders.

Tam took the lead also. "Och, we're away off now as well, Ma. I think we'll go doon the Atlas Hotel. Are you sure you widnae rather have a pint wi' us, William? They lassies are aw' daft in the heed."

"No, I'll leave you two to your pleasures," he said, reaching over to take his jacket from behind Agnes. His close presence made her shiver.

"Did you get that stripe on your jacket for good conduct?" asked Mrs. Green.

"No, Auntie Norma, I just knew how to peel the potatoes the right way," he joked.

"Och, away wi' ye."

Agnes was staring at William when Bessie gave her a push. "C'mon, the afternoon is no waiting for you, ye ken. Let's go oot while the sun still kens it's supposed to be oot. It's hot in here. They houses hold the heat like stone water bottles."

On the street, William placed himself on the outside nearest the road, and Bessie placed Agnes next to him, holding her arm as they walked.

"It's awfy quiet aroond here on a Sunday," said Agnes, looking for something to say. They continued past the butcher's shop and the bakery, both with empty windows. Mr. Price, the draper, had a sign up saying there were remnants of a blue and white checked cotton that looked like mattress ticking, available for coupons.

"A could make a nice dress out of that," said Agnes.

"Aye, only if you want to sleep in it," giggled Bessie.

Agnes nudged her friend with an elbow. "I could do an ice cream about now."

"Keep dreamin', hen. You're no gettin' one." She nudged her back towards William, forcing him to step out onto the road.

"Do you two always talk to each other like that?"

"Only when she's feelin' daft," replied Bessie.

"Shut up, you!" To cover up her embarrassment, Agnes asked him how long he would be in Edinburgh.

"Just for the weekend. I've got some training to do up North. Tha' don't tell us much, just where to report. I can't imagine I'll be doing much beyond the paperwork because of my eyesight. What are you doing? Are you in service?"

"We're Canaries," offered Bessie.

"Canaries?"

"Aye, we fill the shells wi' the TNT. It turns you yellow after a while. We'll look like we've been on holiday and got the sun."

"And when do you think you'll be coming back?" ventured Agnes.

"Hard to say, pet. I'll just have to see what happens."

Agnes blushed and wished she did not turn red every time a man spoke to her.

Bessie suddenly remembered that she had to do something at home. "I have to go back. You two go on without me. I'll catch up later," she said breezily, turning away before Agnes could register her distress that her friend was leaving her.

"We might as well walk," he said. "I'm in need of fresh air."

"Aye, me too," said Agnes slowly, looking down at the shoes she was wearing. She had decided on shoes with heels for the day and they were definitely not for walking in. By the time they stopped at a quiet field, they had walked halfway across Edinburgh and the blisters were making it hard on her heels. They talked about each other's family and she found out he only had his mother. She learned what he hoped to do after the war, and he had coaxed her into saying that what she wanted the most out of life was to get married and have children. She took her shoes off to feel the cool grass on her stockinged feet, and he laid his jacket down for her to sit on and placed himself close to her. "Tha's feet look sore," he said noticing the blisters that Agnes reached down to rub.

"It's all right," she said. "I've had worse." He touched her foot gently and she pulled it towards her. He looked apologetic.

"I'm not sure how long the war will be going on, but I would like it if tha' would write me a letter from time to time." He loosened his tie a little at the neck and wiped his forehead with his hankerchief. "Just from time to time. If you felt like it," he repeated.

"I'm no a great letter writer," she said, picking at imaginary lint on her dress. "Probably because I dinnae have anybody to write to."

He lifted her hand and kissed it. "Now you do."

She let her hand hang in his, but she was quivering and hoped he would not notice.

"I've had a good time today with thee."

Agnes smiled and leaned in a little more towards him, feeling giddy with the pleasure of his company. "I've enjoyed it also. Thanks very much."

He kissed her lightly on the lips causing her to sweat and tremble in the rush of confusion that swamped her senses, leaning a little more closely to his body, hungry for more.

It's awfy hot in here, thought Agnes, pulling on the neck of her jumper. If I didnae ken better, I'd say I was having the change o' life again.

The last part, about her and William, was a lovely piece of romance but she wasn't sure it was entirely that way, although she remembered clearly her awkwardness and his gentle approach. He was so handsome in those days and Alison was right—she had fallen in love with him almost immediately. Looking out the window, Agnes noticed that the ocean had disappeared and there was nothing but great gusts of white fluff punctuated with streaks of sunlight. When does it get dark? she wondered.

twelve

WITHIN TWO WEEKS after William's departure, letters began to arrive three or four times a week. He said he was in a beautiful place in Scotland, but he couldn't tell her where because it was a secret. All his letters were delivered with a London postmark. He said he missed her and would try to see her again as soon as possible. Each time a letter came, she opened it nervously, half-expecting him to tell her it was over, he had met someone else. But after two months of correspondence, he wrote to say he had a weekend pass and could she come to England to see him.

Agnes panicked. "How can I go to England? I've never been anywhere."

"Well, it's aboot time ye did," Bessie said, filing down the casings at work, trying not to breathe in too deeply because it stung her lungs. "I think he's serious, hen."

"But I cannie go to England—he'll have to come here. I'm no gettin' on a train. Anyway, I dinnae have the money fur aw' that. What if he thinks I dinnae want to see him? What'll I do?"

"He'll understand, and if he wants to see you, he'll figure it oot."

"My ma's gonnie go off her heed when I tell her. She thinks I'm an auld maid."

"She does not. She just thinks it's time you got yourself a bloody life."

"If he comes, it'll be the first time I've ever had a laddie at the hoose."

"So!"

William was sympathetic and agreed he would come to Scotland on the overnight train. He would stay with his aunt Norma and come for tea in the afternoon.

The household went crazy with cleaning and baking. Effie saved up her sugar and margarine rations so she could bake a cake for him, and fussed over the fact that she couldn't possibly get it light and fluffy with no butter and only dried eggs. Douglas shaved and put on a clean shirt and polished his shoes. Grace helped Agnes curl her hair the night before and gave her back the yellow cardigan she had "borrowed" a few months earlier. She wanted to lend her a dress, but Agnes was considerably bigger in the bust than Grace, so there wasn't much chance of her getting into it. Instead, she helped her choose a dress that was a little shorter in the length than she was used to. Agnes thought she was showing a bit too much, but Grace said she'd seen women at funerals in less than that. Rita was tired that day and was having a little trouble breathing, so they placed her on the couch. Effie told Grace and John they had to go out once they had met him. The house was too crowded with everyone in it anyway.

Agnes flew back and forth to the window for over an hour, check-ing in the mirror every time she passed it to make sure she looked all right. When she caught sight of his lanky figure sloping up the street, he was carrying flowers. She panicked again. Was there a jug big enough to put them in? She straightened out the tablecloth where a wrinkle had developed and moved the plates a few inches before declaring, "He's coming!" Everyone rose at once, and Grace ran to the window to get a look, with Effie straining behind her.

"Will you get away fae the windae. He'll see you," said Douglas. "The poor laddie'll feel like he's on the parade ground."

"No bad," declared Grace.

Agnes adjusted her dress downwards. "Do I look okay?" She was flushed in the face.

"Dinnae you worry. He's gettin' a good yin. You look great," said Grace.

Agnes met William at the front door, and he held out the bouquet of flowers to her, nervously adjusting his tie with his free hand. She took them with a small chuckle, and he gave her a little peck on the cheek. She flushed bright red and felt pools of sweat start spreading in her underarms. She wished she had some baby powder to put on. "You better come in," she said. "They're aw' itchin' to meet you."

As soon as he came in the door Effie stood up, closely followed by Douglas. She patted down her apron and said, "Pleased to meet you." Douglas stuck out his hand and lurched forward to meet him. "Good to have you here, son."

Grace sat on the couch beside Rita and said, "Hello," but stayed quiet.

William stepped forward to shake her hand, and then leaned over Rita, taking a small lollipop from his pocket. "How are you, young lady?" he asked, placing it in her hand.

John stepped forward and shook his hand also, then said he had to go out. "Gracie, you're comin' as well, aren't ye?"

Grace, who had been watching William's every move, was delighted to see Agnes behave like a schoolgirl, standing by the door looking like she was afraid to come into the room. Grace wanted to give her a drink to get her to relax, but since that was not an option, she stood up. "Save me a bit o' the cake," said Grace.

In a house of short people, William seemed to touch the ceiling. "Sit doon, laddie," said Effie. "We're no used to visitors, so you'll have to forgive the mess." She waved her hand around the meticulously clean living room. Everything sparkled, just the way she had seen it at the Jenkins house on that long-ago afternoon. She brought in the tea and the cake on a tray and set it down on the table, which was carefully covered in a lace runner.

Agnes sat close to Rita as she fed her a small piece of cake. There was an awkward silence as everyone waited to start the conversation. "So, you're here on leave, are you, son?" asked Effie.

William munched on the cake and nodded his head. "Tha's good cake," he mumbled with his mouth full. Gradually, the conversation picked up and soon Effie was getting all the news about his family and his job on the Signals Corps. He said he didn't imagine there would be much combat for him, but he was torn between wanting to fight and being glad he didn't have to.

"You're better off staying hame," said Douglas. "It's no something you want to go to if you dinnae have to. I ken, I wis there."

"Och, dinnae start that again, will you," warned Effie.

William and Agnes exchanged glances, both desperate to leave. Agnes broke the ice first. "I'm sorry, Ma. I think I'd like to go oot for a walk wi' William."

"Oh, I'm sorry, son. I've been rabbiting on here like an auld widow and no gi'en you much room to yourselves. Away ye go. We'll see you later."

They both bounded down the stairs, and at the bottom William grabbed hold of her and held her tight in a kiss. She thought she was going to faint when he let her go, but she pressed herself towards him again, inhaling the fragrance of his Old Spice aftershave, hungry for his love, seizing him in her arms, not wanting to let him go. Her desire was so overwhelming that Agnes stepped back out of breath, longing like she had never longed for anything before. "What are we going to do?" she asked.

"Marry me," he said, holding her in his gaze.

"Oh. William. Are you sure?"

"Never been more."

"Oh, aye," was all she could manage. "Oh, aye."

"As soon as I can get leave again. I'll ask permission. I'm sure they'll give it to me."

"Soon," she said dreamily.

When she returned that night, Grace was already in bed. Agnes threw off her clothes and left them hanging at the end of the bed on the railing.

"You must have had a good time," said Grace sleepily.

Agnes put on her nightgown and searched for her cold cream to put on her face. "He wants to mirry me," she said, unable to hide the excitement in her voice.

"Aye, I suppose he does," said Grace yawning, "but no the morn, so get intae bed. Did you see Ma? She's aw' excited. I think she's got you married already."

"I'm gonnie get married!"

118

"No now, Agnes. Go to sleep."

Agnes crawled into bed and lay in the dark, listening to Grace breathing. She thought about the long walk they had taken out to Corstorphine Hill on their first meeting. How her feet had hurt but she didn't notice all the miles. When he kissed her good-bye he promised he would write, but she didn't really expect him to. He had stroked her cheek and she had tasted tobacco when she kissed him. Now he was telling her he loved her. Nobody had ever told her that before. She didn't know what to say at first, but then realized she loved him too, and told him she would be a good wife to him. He said he had no doubt because he had seen the way she had taken care of Rita and how she was concerned about her mother. There was no doubt she would be an excellent mother as well. Feeling suddenly anxious and excited at the same time, Agnes threw off the covers.

"Och, for Christ's sake, Agnes, make up your mind," yelled Grace, pulling the covers back towards her.

Agnes' imagination was already in bed with William playing all the possibilities of what it would be like to be his wife. She had slept in this bed with Grace for as long as she could remember. They knew each other's bodies as if they were one. She would miss Grace with all her fussing, her aggravating, selfish ways, the mess in the bedroom, and the way she made everyone laugh when she sang. Agnes turned onto her side. Perhaps it was time for her to give up being the little mother around the house and experience a life of her own instead.

—⁂—

Agnes remembered her early days with William as a time of waiting and hoping. She wasn't like Grace, who seemed to have more boyfriends than spit on a griddle and toasted them just as quickly. If Agnes knew one thing, it was that love came with marriage and then children followed. It wasn't that she didn't have anyone ask her out—she'd tried a few boyfriends. It was just that she never found any of them particularly attractive. From what she could see, men only wanted to have a good time, and seeing what happened to Grace made her feel it was even more important that she wait for the right man to come along.

She missed William. He was a good husband and good father and for forty-two years he had stayed that way. It was strange to be reading about him like it was a romance novel. So much of their relationship was not about romance but was more practical, and here was Alison trying to make a silk purse out of a sow's ear, with it sounding so much better than it actually was.

thirteen

THE ALARM WENT off as usual at five a.m. Grace searched for the little hammer and slid it to the side, shutting off the ringing bell, and then rolled off the edge of the bed. Grabbing her clothes in the dark, she struck her toe on the bed leg and cursed. A sudden spill of tears left her bewildered and afraid. Agnes turned over and moaned in her sleep as Grace slid to the floor, wiping her eyes on the sheet. She had slept badly, contrary to her usual way of sleeping through everything, and had lain for hours staring into the pitch-blackness. With Douglas, the ARP monitor, there was not a chink of light coming through his windows.

She watched the rise and fall of the outline of Agnes under the covers. For as long as she could remember, they had shared a bed. It was warm in winter and overbearing during the summer. All night she had thought about getting the bed to herself if Agnes went off to get married, but now she wasn't sure if she wanted it. She wiped her face with the sheet, pushed her blouse into her pants, and yanked up the zip, pulling the belt extra tight around her waist. She was being bloody stupid, she thought, pulling the hairbrush through her tight curls before grabbing her shoes and leaving the room. The house was still quiet as she closed the outside door with a solitary click and cursed herself for being late again.

Tommy, the chargehand at the factory, had to tell her twice to pay attention to the seams of the jackets she was working on. Grace wanted to throw the damned jackets at him and deliberately stitched them twice on the same line. They won't be able to move in these, she thought. The noise of the sewing machines was giving her a headache. All day she was irritable and snappy with her responses, until Tommy asked if she was getting her period.

"Nane o' your bloody business," she replied.

"Nae need to be miserable, hen. Fancy a drink the night? That'll cheer you up."

"Get lost!"

"Aw, c'mon, it'll be good for you," he coaxed.

"I'm no in the mood," she said, but on the way home, she changed her mind.

When she entered the pub, she saw Andy Galbraith and Robb Johanssen throwing darts in the far corner. Her friends Lizzie Dalgliesh and Nora Thompson were sitting in their usual place, a small table on the side under the Guinness sign, and waved for her to come over, but she shook her head and said no, and went to stand at the bar. It was cold in the bar and at least half the chairs were empty, but that was not surprising since so many of the laddies had signed up and there wasn't much money around. At the end of the bar was a loud group of men in Army uniform. They waved at her as she stood waiting for her order to be taken by the barman, Guffie, so called because he took no guff from anyone in his bar. She ordered a half-pint of beer and took a seat on a bar stool. "Is there nae peace aroond here," complained an old man, moving down the bar. "Women in pubs should be barred."

"Auld men should keep their opinions to themselves!" muttered Grace. Then she saw Alex Glendon sliding down the bar towards her.

"All alone, Gracie?" he sneered.

She nodded and sipped her beer. Alex was a fat, beer-bellied man with a loud voice and a bad attitude, who fancied himself the ladies' man, but his clothes were frayed at the cuffs and his collarless shirt with buttons bulging made him look like he was tied up with string. Most women wouldn't give him the time of day. Most men thought he was an arrogant bastard who was always getting into fights. He edged closer to her and pulled a stool out to sit down. "This is no right, Gracie. I cannie have you standin' here like this. C'mere, have a wee yin wi' me."

"No thanks."

"Aw, c'mon, Grace, you cannie be withoot a man fur company. You can have a wee yin wi' me."

Grace moved her body to turn her back to him, crossing her legs on the stool. She was searching in her bag for cigarettes when he appeared by her side and offered her one of his. She accepted it and he lit it for her, giving a flourish with the match. His face was sweaty and his breath black with nicotine.

"It's a pity you women have taken to hiding your legs in these troosers. I've always thought you had nice legs, Gracie."

"Go away, Alex," she said wearily. "I'm no in the mood."

"Will you gie us a wee song? Just a wee yin for me, and for everybody else in here." He swept his hand around the room. "Do you want a wee song fae Gracie?" he said loudly.

The old man down the bar said, "You're drunk. Leave the lassie alane."

He ignored the man. "Och, it's no like you, hen. C'mon, just for auld Alex." He stood next to her and put his hand on her knee. She pulled it away. "Och, dinnae be like that. I just want to be nice. I know you really want to be ma lassie the night." He leaned in tighter as Grace leaned away to avoid his breath.

Just then the bar door swung open and John swaggered in, closely followed by his friends Eddie Sinclair and Bobby Merton hanging on the arm of the girl who worked at the chip shop. Bobby was laughing with the girl and Eddie was looking down the bar at Grace. "Your sister's here."

"I can see that," said John. "I'm gawn somewhere else."

"Dinnae be daft," jostled Eddie. "I want a pint." He waved to Guffie to come down the bar.

Alex leaned into Grace's face. "Just a wee song, Gracie, I'll no bother you again, I promise. I love the way you sing. I heard you the other night at the picture hoose. Naebody does it better, you ken that." He placed his hand on her shoulder and she shrugged, but he did not remove it. In a loud voice, he announced to the pub, "What dae you think? Should we have Gracie sing us a song?"

A few hearty voices shouted back, "Aye, c'mon hen, gie us a song."

Grace turned around and saw John at the far end of the bar staring at her. She lifted Alex's arm off her shoulder, but he plopped it back down again. She wondered how he managed to be this drunk at seven o'clock at night. The boys in uniform were all looking at Grace now and were cheering her on to sing. Andy and Rob stopped throwing darts and were watching her to see what she was going to do. "Leave her alane," yelled Nora. Grace was still staring at John. He had told her the other night that he was going to join the Air Force and she'd said, "Good riddance to bad rubbish. I hope your plane crashes."

Alex followed her gaze down the bar. "Is that no your brother standing there? C'mon, son, have a drink wi' us," he yelled, waving his free hand.

John stood hunched over the bar, sipping his beer. The chippy girl was laughing and pointing at Alex and Grace. "Your sister's at it again," she crowed, giving him a dig in the arm. John spun round on her and shoved her away. "Watch it," she said pushing him back. Slamming his glass down on the counter, he began to walk down the bar.

Eddie followed him and took his arm. "Aw' right, John, you werenae thinkin' o' taking a drink wi' your sister and that galoot, were you?"

"Shut your trap," he hissed.

Grace pushed Alex upright and away from her. He staggered back and almost fell over. "Och, I was just havin' a bit of fun," he whined.

John's face looked ready to explode. Grace saw he was about to get into deep trouble if he took on Alex Glendon and thought it was strange that John was stepping into a fight. She mouthed "no," and shook her head.

Alex followed her gaze. "Is that your wee brother," he slurred.

Eddie pulled on John's arm again. "You're no gonnie go in there. He'll have your heed. He's drunk. Let it be."

John shrugged him off and then stopped. Grace had turned away and begun to sing.

"Be sure it's true when you say 'I love you.' It's a sin to tell a lie." The rhapsody of her voice floated over the clinking glasses and loud bleating voices, causing them to descend into silence. "Millions of hearts have been broken, just because these words were spoken."

She closed her eyes and seemed to float on the bar stool. Everyone had their eyes on her, except John. He had turned towards the door. "What a waste," he said under his breath.

Lizzie was sobbing into her hankie. "She makes me greet every time she sings that." Nora gave her a dig and told her to get over herself.

Andy stood riveted by her performance. "God, can she sing," he muttered.

When the song was finished, Grace sat for a minute before opening her eyes. She looked like she'd drunk too much.

Suddenly, the pub broke into applause and the old man at the bar said, "No bad, hen, no bad." Alex took advantage of the moment and landed her a kiss on the mouth, which brought her back to center again. "Och, get away, will you," she snarled.

Shouts of "Gie us another one, Grace" were joined by "Aye, another yin," from the uniforms as they began stamping their feet until the whole bar seemed like it was rocking.

John grabbed hold of Eddie and left Bobby and his girlfriend locked in tongue exchanges. "C'mon. I telt you I didnae want to stop here. I'm away oot. It's too crowded for me."

Eddie's voice followed him. "Your sister's got a lot of different talents, you ken that."

John hurled himself through the swing door, banging into Nellie as she was coming in. "Oh, aye, John. Nae apologies needed," she yelled at his back.

Grace got down from her stool and began to leave. "You're no gawn hame already, are you?" asked Nellie. "I just got here."

"I've had enough. I've got to get hame," she muttered.

A note on the mantelpiece said: *Ma's sorting clothes up at the WVS office, Douglas is out looking for 'chinks' so make sure the curtains are closed right. I've gone to see Bessie with Rita. See you later. Agnes.*

Grace crumpled up the piece of paper and threw it on the fire, which was burning low. She stoked it and placed a few more briquettes on top then went to make herself some tea, measuring very carefully the half teaspoon of mostly tea dust into the pot. I'll be glad when this war's over, she thought. I could kill for a piece and jam right now.

Settling in front of the fire, she picked up the newspaper and read the headlines. The British Expeditionary Forces were making progress in France; a bomb had landed in the backyard of someone in Lancaster, but had not exploded; Chanel was producing exquisite wartime fashions despite the restrictions; and sugar was now rationed. She put the paper down and closed her eyes, listening to the ticking of the clock. She was dozing when she heard the key turn in the door and felt annoyed at the interruption. Keeping her eyes closed, she hoped they would be quiet and leave her alone although there was fat chance of that in this house, she thought.

John slammed the door and immediately Grace felt irritated. "Could you no be a bit quieter when you come in? I'm trying to sleep," she grumbled keeping her eyes shut.

"Well, sleep in your bed then. It's ma hoose as well," said John, shrugging himself out of his jacket and getting caught in the sleeve as he twisted it back and forth. "Shite, gie me a hand wi' this, will you."

Turning around to see what was going on, she saw him twisting himself violently out of his coat and throw it to the floor.

"You're drunk!"

"Fuck you, Gracie."

He staggered a few steps towards her. "That was quite a show the night. You must think you're Vera Lynn or something."

"Get lost, John. Learn how to manage your booze better." He stood next to her, swaying slightly, staring down at her.

"I can see why the fellies think you're a charmer. You wear aw' these jumpers dead tight and naebody needs an imagination. You think you're the Marlene Dietrich of Leith, don't you? The singing whore." He reached down and clutched at her breast. Grace leaped from the chair.

"What are you day'in?" she yelled, smacking his hand out of the way. "Leave me be."

He staggered back a few paces as she pulled away from him, and then came forward again, his face shiny with perspiration, his jaw slack. "You've always fancied yourself, haven't you? You think everybody's just gonnie let you get away wi' everything, don't you? Every laddie oot there kens your name. You're the talk o' the toon. Aw' up and doon Leith Walk, everybody kens whae Gracie Sharp is."

"You're drunk. Get away fae me." She punched him on the arm, causing him to stagger, but he smiled and stood his ground.

"That bairn disnae ken whae its mother is half the time. Do you ken whae's payin' these doctor's bills? We are! But you dinnae seem to care. No! Oor Grace gets to go oot and do it wi' whae ever she pleases. Don't you, Gracie?"

She hesitated then stepped back towards the window. "I dinnae want to talk to you."

"That's a laugh. We never talk. Don't you get that?" He was holding onto the mantelpiece, trying to keep himself upright. Grace watched him sway and was almost ready to push him into a seat.

"Why d'you dae it, Gracie?" His voice softened slightly to a whine. "Why're aw' these fellies always after you?" He staggered forward and put his hand on her shoulder.

Her natural instinct was to shove him away, but the sound in his voice was so hurt, he was like a little boy—she was unsure how to respond. Taking his hand away from her shoulder softly, she started to turn around. "You've got it all wrong," she said quietly.

"What is it then, Gracie?" he said, anger rising in his voice. "Is it aw' that feely stuff?" He grabbed her arm and twisted it up her back.

Surprised and shaken, she let out a yell and twisted herself towards him, breathing the smell of his sweat and the beer. She could see dribble running out of the side of his mouth as he pulled her towards him in a viselike grip. She punched him with her free hand and pushed him, but he grabbed hold of that one too. Suddenly, he was no longer staggering, but had all his strength contained in the grasp of her arms.

"Let me go, John." Her voice began to rise another octave in panic.

"You're drunk. Let me go." She tussled but his grip was too strong. It had been years since they were physically violent with one another. When he was younger, she took great delight in watching him squirm as she tossed kitchen knives in his direction, only just missing the target deliberately, but the intent was still the same. She tried pulling herself out of his range, but he was pushing her across the living room towards the open bedroom door.

"C'mon, John. Dinnae be daft. Let me go." She was almost in tears.

"I think you like this," he leered, then began to giggle. "Just like the fellies at the pub. They dinnae ken how to let go either, do they? I saw you with that stupid bastard Alex Glendon. They're aw' eedjits. Half-baked drunks. Do you like them like that, Gracie?"

She pulled and twisted her body, but it was beginning to hurt her shoulder even more. "Please, John. Dinnae be daft. They'll aw' be hame in a minute."

He continued pulling her towards the bedroom. "You want to ken something? Aw' they laddies oot there think I'm the eedjit because ma sister couldnae care less. You've got aw' they laddies dancin' aroond you. Makes you feel good, doesn't it?"

"Let me go."

"I'll let you go when I'm finished," he sneered, kicking open the bedroom door.

Grace wriggled in his arms, digging her heels into the wooden floor, but slid hopelessly along with him. "Let me go! Let me go! Where are taking me? You dinnae ken what your day'in." She wrestled one arm away from him and held onto the doorjamb now terrified of what was happening. He was still pulling her, and with a final wrench, they stumbled towards the bed.

"No!" she screamed, but he belted her around the mouth and she fell silent, stunned from the blow, onto her knees. He tumbled after her and knocked the crib that Rita slept in on one side. Grabbing her up again, he tried to get her to the bed. "Good God, John," she mumbled through her swelling lip, "dinnae dae this."

She fell once more onto the floor, her shoulder aching from the pressure of being held, and noticed his unzipped pants with his penis protruding out of it. "Aw no, John!" she moaned helplessly, the swell of her lip dulling the sounds from her mouth "You cannie."

He threw her flat on her back, and she heard a crack as the weight of him landed on top of her and she lost consciousness for a minute. In an instant he was digging his fingers into the side of her pants and jamming himself into her. She howled with the impact, but it only encouraged him.

"See this, Gracie. Feel this. It's how you like it, isn't it?" He groaned and thrust harder into her.

Grace felt as if she were floating above, listening to the sounds of an animal rutting in the mud, moving with each bang, bang, bang, but not entirely there. A pain shot through her shoulder and her mouth was dribbling, and somewhere she could hear moans. The moaning was like a song floating without a melody.

Suddenly, she landed back in her body, screaming and pushing with her hips for him to get off her.

"This is the only kind of fuckin' you understand, isn't it?" he snarled. "You're the cheap whore whae gets everybody to love you. Well, love this." He viciously grabbed her hair and slammed her head against the floor, gasped and groaning before collapsing on top of her, banging her forehead with his head.

She coughed and screamed at the same time, shoving him with all her might to roll out from underneath him. Her shoulder was burning, aching with pain, as she rolled into a ball on the floor and he stood up.

"That's us aw' settled now, Gracie."

She made a kicking motion on the floor as he stepped away. "You're no very good at fightin' back, are you? I guess that's why you get intae aw' that trouble." He laughed, buttoned up his trousers, and swept his hair back from his face, before staggering into the living room and grabbing his jacket. As the front door thudded shut, leaving only the sound of her soft weeping, Grace vowed she'd kill the bastard.

"Och, no!" gasped Agnes. "It's no right! How could she do this?" She stifled a sob and bit down on her trembling lip. This was too painful, too public. Agnes had told Alison it was rumored that Grace had been raped by her brother, she never said it had actually happened, and here Alison had written it as if it were gospel. In all her years, she had never read such muck as this. She had been so stupid to tell Alison any of it. What was she thinking? There was so much she wanted to pull back, to deny, but now she couldn't. She felt betrayed, but the betrayal was hers. She had betrayed Grace, and now the whole world was going to learn about it.

Alison had said it was everybody's business because they were all in the same family. Nobody could escape. It mattered because all the secrets and lies of others left gaps within each of us. Like ghosts, it haunted each generations ignorance repeating the same thing over and over again. Alison had said the truth would set us free as if the hippie axiom of full disclosure would make a damned difference. What kind of truth was this?

Agnes couldn't tell where the fiction began and where the truth ended. She was caught in a spider's web of hearsay masquerading as truth that was actually the truth as written down. She didn't know anymore what she had told Alison. She was confused and afraid. How could I have been so stupid not to see how this would turn out?

fourteen

SHE PUSHED HERSELF up onto her elbow and felt the pain rip through her shoulder. Moaning, she struggled to get off the floor and grabbed hold of the end of the bed with her good arm. "He's broken my arm," she sobbed, feeling the slow crawl of his semen dripping down the inside of her leg as she stood up. Listening for the sounds of anyone in the house, she limped to the kitchen and took the scrubbing brush that cleaned the floor from the bucket under the sink and a bottle of bleach and began brushing her legs. With each hard stroke she intoned, "It wisnae ma fault," scrubbing until the pain in her arm and the pain in her legs from the scrubbing were equal, until the skin had turned bright pink and she could no longer feel the thunderous ache in her body—praying the whole time that no one would come home and find her this way.

She put on Agnes' flannel nightgown, then moved slowly onto the bed and curled up into the fetal position with her hands clasped between her legs, rocking slightly to the rhythm of "I didn't dae anything" in her head.

When Agnes returned with Rita from her visit to Bessie's, she was surprised to see all the lights on, but nobody home. Placing the sleeping child on the couch, she went to make sure her bed was ready. Opening the bedroom door, she was shocked to see the upturned cot with all the bedding strewn across the floor, but even more surprised to see Grace curled up on the bed.

"What's been go'in' on here?" she demanded in a loud voice.

131

There was no response from Grace. She picked up the cot with some difficulty and put the bedding back into place. "You're drunk, aren't you?" she snorted.

In the quiet moment of waiting for a response, she heard a soft muttering from the bed that was different from Grace snoring. A fluttering of panic settled on her breast as she leaned over her and pulled on her shoulder, sighing, "When are you gonnie learn?" Picking up the distinct smell of bleach, she asked, "Have you been day'in a washing? Wonders'll never cease."

Grace mumbled something Agnes did not hear.

"What!" she said impatiently. "It better be good, Gracie. I'm tired."

"John!" Grace began weeping.

"What aboot him? Has something happened to him?"

Grace turned over with difficulty towards her. Tears streamed down her face as she said, "I didnae dae anything! I really didnae!"

"Dae what? What are you talkin' aboot?" She came closer towards the bed and gasped when she saw the swollen forehead and lips. "Good God! What happened?" Sitting down next to her sister, she reached over to touch her. Seeing Grace flinch, she removed her hand.

"It wisnae ma fault. I didnae ask fur it."

In frustration, Agnes rose from the bed. "I dinnae understand you. Did you get in a fight the night? You're in an awfy mess."

"He fucked me," she whimpered. "He fucked me, Agnes!"

"Whae did?"

"John!"

Agnes recoiled. "Have you been drinkin'?"

"I didnae dae anything. It wisnae ma fault."

Agnes stepped over to the door and looked back to see if anyone had come in or if Rita had awoken. "I dinnae ken what you're sayin'," she whispered. "Dinnae be tellin' me stuff like that, Gracie. I cannie be day'in wi' aw' that shite."

Grace was weeping now, struggling to sit up with one arm. "You dinnae have to believe me. I ken what happened."

"What happened? You're no telling me . . . ," began Agnes, then held back, afraid to put the rest of that thought in place.

Grace sat on the edge of the bed, holding her arm, rocking slightly.

"See this? My arm could be broken. He fuckin' raped me!" she spat. "Look at me, Agnes! I didnae dae this to myself." She held her wounded arm tight to her body.

"Sssshh!" said Agnes urgently, looking back towards Rita, who was snuggled up tight on the couch in her coat and hat, sucking her thumb. Grace's face was blotchy yellow deepening towards purple. All of her parts were disheveled like she had walked into a moving van. In the raw light of the overhead bulb, she could see the pink scratches on her legs that the brush had made.

"Turn the light off," Grace cried.

Agnes flicked the switch and went forward to touch her sister's hair. Grace winced. "Aw, Gracie, John couldnae have done this," she said softly. "No this."

She sat down softly beside her and held her hand.

"What are we gonnie dae?" wept Grace.

"We cannie talk aboot this, Gracie. You'll have to be strong."

"I'm gonnie kill him." She gripped the sheet between her fingers and felt the pain in her shoulder worsen.

"Dinnae be daft," said Agnes soothingly. "I'll find oot what this was aw' aboot." Grace moaned and Agnes held her hand for a few minutes before pushing her gently down onto the bed. "It'll be aw' right," she whispered.

Agnes waited up for Effie to give her the news.

"There's been a wee bit of bother the night."

"What kind o' bother?"

"Oor Gracie was belted by one o' these laddies fae the pub."

Effie rose from the chair in the direction of the bedroom. "It's aw' right, Ma. She's sleepin' now, so leave her be. I just wanted to tell you aboot it so you didnae get a fright the morn. She's gonnie look a right sight. It wisnae anybody she kens."

Effie sat down again slowly and sighed deeply. "I wish to God . . . she just cannie seem to keep herself clear o' trouble. Did she go to the polis?"

"Naw. He was gone before she could dae anything."

"Naebody stepped in to catch the bastard?"

"Naw. It was outside. I dinnae think anybody seen it."

"How could she be sae stupid?"

"It wisnae her fault, Ma."

Effie sighed and allowed a small tear to slip down the side of her face before brushing it aside. "I dinnae ken what to think anymare."

When Effie went to wake John for his work the following morning, the bed was empty. "If he's run off to join the Navy I'll kill him myself," she said. She went to wake Douglas. "You better go find him." He groaned "I've only been in my bed since three o'clock, will you leave me alane woman. He's a laddie, probably out wi' his mates."

Grace emerged from the bedroom around eight o'clock and said she would not be going to work that day. Effie nearly dropped to her knees when she saw her. "Och, Gracie," she wailed, almost crying. "Whae done this to you?" She rushed to the sink to get some icy cold water on a cloth and made a move to put it on her face. Grace waved her away.

"I'm fine."

"Have you looked at yourself? You look like you had a run in wi' a bus."

"The bus might have stopped if I had." She attempted a smile, but her lip hurt when stretched. Her arm and shoulder were feeling better this morning, although there was still a throbbing when she tried to raise it above her head.

"Do you no ken whae it wis?"

Grace looked away and in a low voice said, "No. If I meet him again though, I'll let him have it."

Rita stood frightened by Effie's side, holding tight to her skirt. "You're making the bairn feard wi' that face."

"I ken, Ma! C'mere, hen, it's aw' right."

Rita held on stubbornly for a few minutes, but when Grace was seated by the fire, she placed herself carefully by her side and reached her hand towards the swollen lip. "Ma's right," she said slowly, patting it gently.

Grace winced but said nothing, only took her hand down and held it for a moment before turning away, tears in her eyes.

"You should be gawn to the hospital wi' that mess. I'll walk you up there if you like."

"Nae hospital. you ken I hate these places. I'll be aw' right eventually."

"Suit yourself. I think you need some attention."

"Aye, later."

"Wait till your faither sees you. He's gonnie have a fit."

"Yeah, right. I'm gawn back to ma bed."

⁕

Douglas was polishing his boots for his shift that afternoon. It was essential the ARP wardens looked smart. They had to give a good impression of authority. Effie had told him what had happened to Grace and he thought he was prepared, but he couldn't help gasping when she entered the living room. "Jesus Christ. Whae did that to you?"

By now her face was a blotchy yellow-purple combination, her eyes small and swollen from crying, her freckles dull in comparison.

"Do you no ken whae he is? This is unbelievable. A lassie gets battered and naebody sees it. That disnae sound right to me. I'm gawn doon to the polis. This is no right."

"Dinnae bother, Dad. It's too late now."

"This is no right," he repeated.

⁕

When Agnes returned from the munitions factory around nine in the evening, John had still not returned and Effie was putting her coat on. "It's too much, you ken that. First oor Gracie last night, and now he's gawn somewhere."

Douglas tinkered with the radio, waiting for the news to start.

"I hope he hasnae been stupid and signed up. If he did I'll kill him before the Jerries do. He's no auld enough, and he kens that. I hope he's only wi' a pal somewhere." The radio crackled and the voice of Richard Dimbleby gave the latest report on the war in France. Douglas had his ear clapped to the side of the radio. Britain was making progress but there were no details of what that meant. It was a valiant struggle, which translated into thousands killed. Douglas shook his head. "Same old shite." He looked up to see Effie standing in the middle of the room with her coat on.

"Where are you gawn, woman? You've got nae idea where he could be."

"Somebody's got to ken."

"You're no gawn oot there," said Agnes. "I'll go. You ken aw' the roads in the dark now, Douglas. You can come wi' me."

"Aye, aw' right. I'll get ma coat, but I think we're gawn oot fur nothing. He'll be hame soon enough."

Effie sat down and picked up some socks for darning, worrying the needle through the hole. "Dinnae come hame withoot him. I winnie be able to sleep until I ken what's go'in on."

For two hours, Agnes and Douglas scoured the pubs and dance halls of Leith asking for John. All his friends shook their heads and said, "Naw, havenae seen him." Agnes had a headache from sniffing carbon steel all day and was tired of being pushed and nudged as they made their way through each crowd. She would happily have left John to rot, but her mother would have been beside herself with grief if she didn't know what had happened to him. Outside the Palace picture house they saw Bobby Merton with his girlfriend from the chip shop. "Aye, he was doon the road wi' us the day," he said merrily. "He signed up for the Air Force."

"The Air Force!" Douglas exploded. "Why the bloody Air Force?" He threw his cap down on the ground. "What did I tell him? What did I say? How could he be so bloody stupid? Where is he?"

Bobby walked away with his girlfriend hanging on his arm.

"Dinnae ken, Mr. Sharp, but you could try Eddie Sinclair's hoose on Lochend Road, next to St. Anthony's. Up the stairs, second floor. He might be there."

Agnes picked up his hat and gave it back to him. "Are you sure you want to do this?"

"My life is no worth livin' if I dinnae have something to go hame wi'. I'm gonnie kill the stupid bastard myself."

They walked in silence until they arrived next to St. Anthony's school. Agnes had never seen Douglas so mad. He had limped up the hill dragging his bad side, and when they stopped he stood with his hands on his knees, breathing hard. She thought he was going to have a heart attack. "I'll go. You wait here. If he's there, I'll bring him doon."

The staircase was poorly lit and when she arrived at the second floor, she peered through the dimness to find the brass plate with the name Sinclair on it.

She rang the doorbell twice before Eddie answered. "Where is he?" she demanded.

"Aye, nice to see you to, Agnes."

"Dinnae gie me that. Where is he?"

"I dinnae ken."

"I dinnae believe you," she said, pushing her way into the front hall.

Eddie's father came out from the living room holding a model train; his glasses perched on the end of his nose, he peered at Agnes. "What's go'in on?"

"I'm sorry to bother you, Mr. Sinclair, but I'm here fur ma brother. He's got to come hame."

Eddie stood behind her shaking his head at his father in a 'no' motion "He disnae want to. He's feard fae his faither."

"He'll be feard, aw' right," said Agnes fiercely. "But it'll no be his faither whae's the problem. Where is he?"

John came through the living room and stood meekly between Mr. Sinclair and Eddie. "Go home, Agnes. I'm no coming. I've signed up the day and there's nothing any of youse can dae aboot it."

Agnes snatched at his arm. "C'mere you!" She pulled him towards the front door as he looked expectantly at Mr. Sinclair and his son.

"You better do as she says, son," said Mr. Sinclair, taking his glasses off. "You cannie be joining up if your faither doesn't want it."

Taking his jacket from the coat hook, he stepped outside with Agnes and she shut the door behind him.

"How could you have been sae bloody stupid? What where you thinkin' aboot? I've got a good mind to hang you oot to dry, you ken that. I cannie believe what you've done."

"It was only signing up, Agnes. I'm only six months short, so what's the big deal?

"Are you kiddin' me? You better no be kiddin' me. You ken what I'm talking aboot. Signing up is the only way you can get oot o' this mess, isn't it? If she gets her hands on you, she'll kill you herself. How could you? I dinnae even want to talk to you, you're beyond words, you ken that?"

He hung his head but said nothing.

"I just cannie believe it. Your ane sister! Get doon they stairs now!"

"Is he there?"

"Aye, he's there aw'right. What where you thinking? You've broken their hearts, you ken that."

He looked up sharply. "Do they ken?"

"Naw. You're bloody lucky, they dinnae ken and that's the way it'll stay. I dinnae understand. How could you?" She started to turn away in disgust, then swung round and gripped him by the collar. "Get doon the stairs right now. He needs to see you so he can tell Ma you're aw' right. Get doon there right now and see him."

She pushed him towards the edge of the stair and he pulled back. "Let me go. I'm no gawn doon."

"You're gawn doon, aw' right. You're gonnie tell her you're sorry. Get doon these stairs." She was practically hauling him down. "You can show your bloody shame to your faither," she hissed.

Douglas stood in the cold street, huddled inside his coat, breathing out great puffs of cold air, trying to control the panic that constricted his breathing, ignoring the violations of the blackout laws as John stood holding the street door open with his foot, allowing a small sliver of light to escape through the crack.

"I'm off the morn," he said brazenly, sticking his chin out, "and I have to be there at six o'clock. There's nae mare to be said."

"What's got into you?" Douglas kept asking. "Why can you no come home? Why did you sign up when you knew I didn't want you to? I dinnae ken who this person standing in front of me is. I dinnae ken what I'm gonnie tell your mother."

"I'm sorry," said John, "but I cannie come hame. You have to understand that. Tell Ma I'm sorry."

Agnes stood watching John with one hand on the door and his face turned downwards looking at the pavement. Suddenly, Douglas pulled him from the door, grabbing him in a fierce bear hug. "I dinnae ken what it is your runnin' away fae, but I hope it isnae something you're gonnie regret fur the rest o' your life." He smacked him on the side of the head, and then turned his back, heading downhill towards Leith Academy. He had thought at one point that his son might get far enough ahead to go there, but there was not the slightest chance in hell now that anybody in his family would see the inside of that place.

As they walked through the dark streets, he realized he would have to lie to Effie, that only a half-truth would do. He told her John had already left. She cried for a week until she rationalized he was doing his duty.

Effie had just finished washing her hands and face in the bathroom when the door burst open and Grace launched herself towards the toilet bowl, making loud choking sounds.

"Och, no again! I cannie believe you!"

Grace hung over the toilet bowl while her mother watched, hands on her hips. "That's it! I'm finished wi' you, you ken that. You've done what you've bloody well liked aw' your bloody life, and see what happens. You throw yourself aroond and you leave other people to pick up the mess. Well, I'm no pickin' it up anymare, you hear?"

"It wisnae ma fault!"

"Whaese fault wis it then? Are you the Virgin Mary? Dinnae be sae bloody stupid, Gracie."

"It's no what you think," she wailed pathetically.

Agnes stood in the doorway and watched.

Effie stood with her arms folded across her chest, her eyes turning the color of steel. "You're on your own! That's it! There's a bairn oot there whae's always in the bloody hospital and I spend mare time running after her than I do anything else. I'll no let you dae it to me again." She brushed past Agnes leaving Grace with her head bent over the bowl muttering, "It wisnae ma fault."

Grace looked wretched sitting on the toilet seat, holding her belly, her hair hanging without a note of curl, her freckles blotted out by panic.

"She disnae understand yet," Agnes said apologetically, "but gie her time. I'll help you as best I can, but I'm no gonnie be here for much longer."

"My life is over," Grace droned.

"Dinnae be daft! There's a lot worse things happening oot there than what you've got."

"I cannie dae this again!"

"You can and you will!" said Agnes. "Now get up!"

Agnes found her mother standing at the sink, staring out the window. "You found out?"

Effie reeled around on her. "You kent and you said not a word!"

"Aye, I kent," she said apologetically. "She told me yesterday. It's no her fault, you ken?"

"She keeps sayin' that, but I cannie believe it. That lassie asks for everything she gets."

"No this time, she didnae. That night she got beaten up, the laddie forced her. She disnae have a choice in this one, Ma. She's gettin' the rough end o' the stick."

"How come you ken sae much aboot this?"

"Because she telt me, that's how. She was feard of tellin' you. She didnae want this, Ma."

Effie sat down heavily on the chair. "There's only so many times I can stand up and get on wi' it. I'm no lifting a finger this time. I'm sick and tired o' aw' this. She's gonnie have to learn herself what it is to take care o' a bairn."

Agnes smacked her lips together and bit back an intense desire to spill out the truth, save Grace from the harshness of wrong judgments—after all, she reasoned, John was gone and was not coming back anytime soon. But just as she had hesitated when Grace was molested by Douglas, she had hesitated again, and the moment was gone. She had already lied and there was no swallowing that one.

Agnes covered her face with her hands and began to tremble. She wanted desperately to be off this plane, to be out of this story. "I didnae ask to go into ma family history like this," she muttered into her hands.

The girl in the next seat rubbed her arm. "Are you all right? You should stop reading this. It's making you sick." She sat a few minutes gently stroking her until Agnes sat back with a huge sigh.

"It's . . . I dinnae ken where I am wi' this. That's been the problem wi' this aw' along. I'm reading it like I was reading a book, but it's got ma name in it, and the names o' aw' the people I grew up wi', and nane o' it was supposed to be seen like this."

The girl took the pages from her hand and placed them on the tray table. "Maybe you should take a nap. We'll be there soon. Only five more hours."

"God, I want to be home again," said Agnes.

fifteen

WILLIAM WROTE TO Agnes and said he was being shipped out in two weeks. He couldn't say where, but he knew it was somewhere warm because they had been issued with lightweight uniforms. If they were to get married, it would have to be now, and if she agreed, he had arranged special permission with his C.O. to have three days' leave. He wondered if she could come down to York for the ceremony.

Agnes broke out in hives thinking about leaving home. Effie told her she was making a big fuss about nothing and dabbed her skin with calamine lotion. "But I cannie leave you Ma. Whae's gonnie help pay for Rita? I cannie get married and no have you there."

Effie said it would be nice to be there but it wasn't important. Agnes would not hear of it. "I'm no gettin' married withoot you, and that's that."

She wrote to William and said it would have to be in Scotland, or they would have to wait. She couldn't do it without her mother being there.

When the telegram arrived Effie was relieved it was not about John. Agnes ran around the house waving the piece of paper in the air. It read: We'll do a registrar in Scotland stop we can do a proper wedding after this thing is all over stop expect me in ten days' times stop I love you stop.

"Ten days! How can I be ready for a wedding in ten days?"

"What is there to dae?" asked Effie. "You go doon to the registrar's office and put up the banns. Everybody day'in it because naebody's got any options these days. You'll be aw' right."

"But Ma, I've got nothin' to wear."

"We'll find you something nice, dinnae you worry."

143

꿈

For the next ten days, Agnes worried about her clothes, her hair, and the tea they would serve after the wedding. Bessie told Agnes her mother was so excited she was already planning on making cakes. Agnes told her to tell her mother to do something else. As for the clothes, Bessie would help. She was a dab hand with the needle, and she could fix almost anything, even if it was an old pair of curtains.

Effie, who was in charge of the clothes drive for the WVS, found a beautiful two-piece navy suit. Her supervisor told her not to mention it when she put it in her bag. The war was taking its toll on everyone's waistlines, so a few nips and tucks with the material was necessary to make it fit. Grace loaned her a beige blouse and a pair of stockings she had been hoarding, and Douglas polished her shoes until they looked like new.

"What am I gonnie dae wi' ma hair? It's aw' ower the place." She pulled on the wiry strands that stuck out in all directions.

"Dinnae you worry, hen. We'll gie you a Toni," said Bessie. "We'll have you gorgeous in nae time, won't we, Grace?"

"I'll even paint your toenails if you like," piped up Grace.

"Och, I hate perms and I cannie keep polish on ma fingers for mare than five minutes withoot smudging it."

"Well, we're no havin' you turnin' up fur this wedding looking like who-flung-dung," said Bessie.

Agnes, Grace, Rita, and Bessie were sitting on the bed painting their fingers and toes. Rita was moving around so much, they sent her to see Effie after they had painted her fingernails. Grace carefully applied each brushstroke with precision after filing her sister's nails to a smooth edge. "He'll wonder whaese claws he's got himself intae," she joked.

"Aye, watch oot, William. She's gonnie rake your back like a gairden," said Bessie, folding over with laughter.

"Och, shut up, the both o' you's."

"Oooh, I think she's nervous," giggled Bessie.

Grace leaned towards Agnes and said in a low voice, "I dinnae want you to get aw' upset here, but do you ken what you're in fur the morn's night? I mean, have you done it yet?"

Agnes punched Grace and then remembered her nails, "Och, look what you've made me dae now." She held up her middle finger and showed where it had been smudged.

"Nae bother—give it here. But seriously," she continued while wiping off the nail polish, "do you ken? You might be the first virgin bride in the hoose. Did you ever think aboot that?"

Agnes paused slightly, pulling her hand away. "What do you mean?"

"Keep still. I cannie dae this wi' you moving." Agnes waited to see what Grace would say next. "It's different for everybody, but what I'm sayin' is, dinnae expect too much. Sometimes they get too much beer in them and they have a few problems, if you ken what I mean." She and Bessie started giggling.

"He disnae drink!"

"Aye, but he might be nervous. It is your first time, isn't it?"

"What dae you take me fur? You ken the answer as well as I do," she said.

"Aye, I do," she sputtered, having a hard time controlling her laughter.

"You were just trying to get my goat, that's what."

"I think everybody's nerves are a wee bit tight right now," said Bessie. "We need a wee sherry or something."

"We dinnae have any sherry," Grace said, "but Ma keeps a wee bottle of whisky under the sink. She says it's for medicinal purposes when Rita gets a cauld, but I'm no so sure. I think she nips on it. I'll go get it."

"She'll chase you, you ken," shouted Agnes as Grace left the room.

Effie was bent over a bowl beating eggs, margarine, and sugar together, her forearm veins bulging with the effort of keeping up a decent speed. "Where did you get eggs?" asked Grace.

"You can get anything, if you ken the right people, or you can afford it," winked Effie.

"Oh, ho! Been loitering wi' the hoi polloi, have you?"

"Enough o' your cheek, lass. You lot sound like you're havin' a grand time in there."

"Me come," said Rita, putting her finger into the bowl for a lick and looking at Grace.

"No the now. We're busy." She was bending down to look under the sink.

"What are you lookin' fur? There's nothin' in there."

From the back of the shelf, Grace found a half-empty bottle of whisky. "Somebody's been nipping at this," she said, holding up the bottle.

"Where are you gawn wi' that? That's ma medicine fur the wee yin."

"Agnes needs medicine the night otherwise she's no gawnie sleep."

"Dinnae make her daft and dinnae drink it aw'. That's aw'—I'm no gonnie get anymare for a long time to come."

Grace pretended to swig the whole bottle back and brushed Rita's hair with the top of her hand as she walked past.

Agnes took a taste and felt as if her whole body had been set on fire. "Whae drinks this?" she gasped with an airy voice. "Nae wonder people go off their heeds wi' this stuff."

"Dinnae think aboot it," said Bessie, sniffing her glass before sipping it. "Wow!" she said with the same gasping sound.

Grace put her taste into a small thimble glass and shot it back. "I prefer gin myself, but I guess this'll have to do." There was no trace of discomfort in her voice.

After two small nips, Agnes was a new woman. "I wonder what he looks like wi' nae claes on," she joked.

"Skinny, wi' a long ding-dong," cracked Grace.

"You better make sure you ring the bell loud and long," screamed Bessie.

Agnes put her hands up to her face and roared with laughter until the tears started down her face. Then she started to cry for real and said she was sorry she was leaving the house and everybody.

Grace put her arms around Agnes, nestling her against her swollen belly, and reminded her she wasn't going anywhere yet. All that was changing was her name. "He's daft aboot you. Just think—you're gawnie be Mrs. William Rankin. You'll be A. Rankin, just like the fruit and vegetable store up the toon. You're a nice peach, aren't you?"

Agnes pulled away and gave Grace a poke in the belly. "You're the one whae's full o' fruit," she said, instantly regretting her choice of words.

"Aye, and it's gettin' riper by the minute," Grace responded softly, singing a few bars of "Strange Fruit" by Billie Holiday.

William looked handsome in his Army uniform, buttons gleaming and shoes polished, but his eyes looked a little glazed. Bessie's brother Tam had whisked him off to the pub for his stag night, although William had protested that he didn't drink. In Tam's opinion, it would be a shame if he never found out what he was missing on his last night of freedom. Tam had managed to give him a night he would remember, but one he would rather forget. He had no memory of coming home, only of sitting with a group of men who asked a girl to sit on his lap. He remembered she had bright coral lipstick and deep blue eye shadow with thick black lashes, but that was all. He awoke in the morning with an imprint of her lipstick on his forehead and a noise like a goods train rushing through his head.

Agnes had slept like a baby as Grace had predicted. She was a few minutes late after fussing with almost every aspect of herself for over an hour. Eventually, Grace and Effie told her she was brilliant, and they should go or he would think she wasn't coming. She had never looked so well dressed in her life in the navy blue suit, beige blouse, tan stockings, and black shoes, carrying a black bag. She wore a blue garter on her left thigh that Mrs. Green had saved for Bessie's wedding, but since Agnes was the first one to the post, she could use it. Clutching a small bouquet of African violets that Bessie had thrust into her hand, she was almost in tears as they approached the building.

The registrar's office was full of excited, weeping couples, taking oaths and signing the book before the rush to war. Agnes felt shy taking William's hand in front of her family. An old man who looked thoroughly bored with the proceedings told them to hurry along. When she said, "I do," William took her in his arms and kissed her in front of everyone. She didn't know where to look when he was finished, so she giggled and held his hand even tighter. Mrs. Green sniffed into her handkerchief and wished William's mother could have been there for this, but she hated traveling and wouldn't even get on a bus. Effie wiped her eyes, and Douglas put his arm around her and squeezed her tight. It was the first affectionate moment they had had in years where she did not withdraw.

The sign said "no confetti" but Grace paid no notice when she whispered to Rita to throw it at her auntie Agnes. She threw up her hands but couldn't get the confetti high enough to hit their heads, sending horseshoes and hearts cascading to the floor, to the annoyance of the registrar. Outside, Grace emptied the box on their heads. Confetti stuck to William's brilliantine hair like a multicolored hat. As was customary at weddings, he took a few pennies out of his pocket and threw them to the waiting children, who came every Saturday for the poor-oot of coins, scattering and shoving each other to see who could get the most. Agnes was almost skipping as they ran to catch the bus back home for tea.

That night, Agnes had her first taste of a hotel. It was shabby and the room was poorly lit, but she was thankful for that since she didn't want him to see her naked. She undressed in the dark —a habit that would continue for the rest of their married life. She would come to know every inch of his body by touch but would never know what it looked like without underwear. First night jitters quickly melted in their embrace and as they drifted off to sleep with their arms around each other, William promised he would do better after the war was over.

In the morning, Mr. and Mrs. William Rankin arrived at a photographer's studio on Princess Street, where they stood by a green leafy wall next to a short Ionic column and smiled for the camera. At Waverley Station, he promised he would be back as soon as possible. But in a time of promises, they were difficult to keep. It would be two years before he returned.

Watching the train slowly puff its way out of the station towards London, Agnes had never felt so lonely in her life.

The story of her wedding night was wonderful, but all Agnes could remember was how nervous she had been and how she had kept asking Grace if she was doing the right thing. It wasn't as if she had known him for long, at least not in person. She had been wise enough to know that letters can be deceiving, but there had been something special with William since the beginning. She felt as if they were made for each other. He was kind, generous, and always thoughtful. In all her married life, she never had any reason to complain. He had cared for his family as much as any man could.

Alison had said she hated her mother, mostly for all the things she didn't tell her. She also thought her mother didn't really care for her. All they ever did was fight. Agnes thought that was a bit unfair and tried to reassure her by saying all daughters feel that way about their mothers. When her daughter Shirley said she was going to London to become a model, Agnes had argued relentlessly that it was a mistake, but William insisted she find her own way. Shirley left hating her mother for what she said was her rigid ways. Six months later, she was back, saying it was not for her and she was sorry for everything she had said.

Now, Alison wanted to apologize to the daughter she had given up for adoption. To explain how things happen. She didn't want to be judged badly. "Like you're judging your mother," Agnes said. But this story was a love story. A daughter who longed to be loved and had found a way to love. Alison said she gave her away because she did not want her to be raised with lies, with secrets, and most especially with the anger at being trapped in circumstances she could not break free from. She wanted to make sure her daughter would understand that. She wanted to be forgiven for the choices she made. Agnes wondered if that was possible.

sixteen

THE BIRTHDAY PARTY had a cake, candles, and a couple of balloons that Agnes found as leftovers from a wedding at the Assembly Rooms. Effie found a doll among the Toys for Needy Children box. She always thought that was a ridiculous idea since everywhere she looked, children needed something. This doll had all its hair intact and eyes in their sockets, which was more than could be said for many of the broken-down kind that came their way. It was wearing a hand-sewn dress made from gingham and lace and hand-knitted bootees on its feet. It was in such good condition that it looked as if it had come straight from the toy shop.

Douglas had taken up carving and now filled his time whittling away at odd pieces of wood. He carved an intricate whistle with doves on each side and put Rita's initials on the bottom of it. Agnes gave up an entire month's sweet rations to buy her a box of candied cigarettes, and Grace produced a small green leather handbag with a broken zip and the remains of a red lipstick.

Rita gasped when she saw the doll, taking it gently from Effie's outstretched arms, cradling it and making shushing sounds to its make-believe cries. She clapped her hands with delight at the cigarettes and put them in her mouth, puffing extravagantly while trying to make smoke rings as she saw her mother do, then swung the green handbag over her shoulder before Grace pointed out the lipstick inside. Pulling a chair in front of the mirror above the fireplace, she leaned towards it, carefully applying the lipstick as she had seen her mother do thousands of times, smearing her top lip before sucking her top and bottom lips together, and placed a kiss on the mirror as she had once seen her mother do. Carefully putting the lipstick back into her handbag, she took Douglas's whistle and blew a short, sharp sound that made Grace hold her ears. Her newly applied lipstick left a ring of red around the mouthpiece. Taking the candied cigarette between her first two fingers of the right hand, she made a smoke ring with her mouth, blowing out the imaginary smoke before pulling her hand towards the ceiling. Everyone collapsed in gales of laughter as she mimicked her mother perfectly. "She's only missing the high heels," laughed Effie. Grace found a pair under the chair and Rita paraded through the living room, puffing on her cigarette, pushing streaks of red hair away from her face, scuffling along in her mother's high heels, enjoying every minute of making the family laugh. Grace didn't know whether to laugh or cry.

Grace put her feet up on the pouffe in front of the chair. Rita ran towards her and lost her balance in the heels, falling into Grace's enormously pregnant belly, "Easy, easy," she shouted, "that's it! Enough o' that!" Grace lifted the child and took the shoes off her, before setting her down on the floor. Rita looked confused and then hurt at the sudden sea change in her mother's attitude.

As the mood in the room collapsed, Effie said, "C'mere, hen, come to Nannie." Effie took the doll on her knee and put a newly knitted dress on it. "See what I've got for you."

Quickly, Rita clambered onto her grandmother's knee and gathered the doll to her chest. Effie told her she would knit a cardigan for the dolly.

❧

A few days later, Rita was coming home from the nursery in the late afternoon with Grace, who was anxious to get home because it looked like rain and she was tired from being on her feet all day. Rita tried to get out of the pram. "My bag," she said, over and over again, as Grace tried to hurry along the road.

"It's gawnie rain any minute. We've got to get hame."

"No, I want ma bag," she insisted.

"C'mon then, let's be quick aboot it." She pushed the pram back in the direction of the nursery, but before they reached the door, the gray skies blackened to night and it began to pour. With no raincoats and no umbrellas, they were both soaked through.

"My God, look at the state o' her," cried Effie when they arrived home. As she placed Rita in front of the fire to dry her, rubbing her hair with a towel, she asked, "Could you no have waited until it stopped?"

Grace shook off her coat and hung it over the top of the door. "She wanted her bag," she said sorrowfully. "I didnae mean fur us to get soaked."

"I hope she disnae catch her death o' cauld," said Effie, putting her into her pajamas. "Go fix her a toddy, just to be safe."

"We drank aw' the whisky at Agnes's wedding night," said Grace nervously.

"Aw, naw," sighed Effie.

Agnes heard the wheezing sound first and knew they were in for a difficult night. She gave Grace a dig in the back. "Grace, get up. She's wheezing."

"Mmmm," was her response. Agnes shoved her and got out of bed. "Whaaat!" came the sleepy reply.

"She's no well!"

"Neither am I," said Grace, feeling a kick from the child in her belly.

Effie made a poultice from mustard to send heat into Rita's chest and placed her high on the pillows, but the wheezing continued throughout the night. She pounded her back with quick, short thumping motions as she had seen the doctors do from time to time, but nothing moved. Her face developed the familiar blue color and her eyes had dark circles under them. After two days, she sent for the doctor.

Dr. Preston had been their family doctor for years, knew Rita's condition well, and would normally have suggested they wait a few days to see what happened. When he arrived, he offered to take Effie and Rita to the hospital in his car. Grace and Agnes were both at work.

In the waiting room, Effie alternated between the hard wooden chair rubbed to a shine from all the years of waiting, and the hallway, her slippers making shooshing sounds on the tile floor. When Douglas arrived, she told him, "They've no got much hope."

"Och, they've said that before and she's always come through."

"No this time. It's 'newmonie. They're just trying to keep her comfortable."

Douglas turned away and began studying the parrot pictures on the wall meant to brighten up the pallid green room they sat in. Swollen with anger about the unfairness of life, he turned to Effie and punched his fist into the palm of his hand. "Why? What did she ever dae wrong? What has she done to deserve this? All she ever brought us was goodness. She never did anybody any harm, did she?"

Effie, used to anger as a defense, said "My mother used to say it was all in the hands of God. Well, aw' I can say is, if this is God's way, then I dinnae think much aboot his choices."

Agnes came home from work and was told by the neighbor downstairs that Rita had been taken to the hospital. She left a note for Grace.

Sitting by the bedside, Agnes held Rita's hand, stroking the back of it, murmuring a quiet song, willing the child to breathe easy as her chest rose and fell in long washes of agonizing gusts. She had hardly eaten or slept during the last two days, while Grace had gone about her daily life as if everything was going to be all right. She was a fair weather mother, showing up for the parties, the good times, the easy times, but disappearing when it got difficult. She was mother in name only. In truth, Rita had several mothers, but right now the one who should be here was not. Agnes wiped away the tear that fell onto the sheet. She hadn't heard from William in over a month and despaired that something had happened to him. Her mind was a whirlwind of all the worst things that could have happened.

When Grace returned she read the note but was dead tired and her feet were killing her from serving tea all day in the canteen at the factory. I'll just sit a wee while, she thought. Lying on the pouffe was the green handbag. She picked it up before putting her feet on the cushion, and clasped it to her chest. "What was I thinkin' gi'en her that? If I hadnae gi'en her it, we wid have been hame before the rain got us," she moaned. After a few minutes, she closed her eyes and fell asleep, with the tightening of her unborn child's feet kicking her ribs.

She awoke with a jolt and without warning she knew she had to be at the hospital. Holding onto the green bag, she grabbed her coat off the hook, raced downstairs, and prayed a bus was coming. Stamping her feet at the bus stop, she was chilled to the bone by the cold wind blowing in off the water. She was shivering when the bus showed up ten minutes later. "You're late," she told the bus conductor.

"What's the hurry, Mrs.? Your bun aboot ready?" he said. Grace said nothing more, shuffling to the front to take a seat, wiping the window with her hand occasionally to clear away the condensation.

At the hospital, the receptionist thought Grace had come to deliver a baby and was set to put her into a wheelchair. It took her another five minutes to clear the confusion and find out where Rita was. Grace passed the waiting room where Effie and Douglas sat, heading straight for the ward, out of breath. Effie saw her and rushed to stop her. "You cannie go in there!" But Grace continued without heeding her.

A shadow fell across the bed and woke Agnes from her reverie.

"You can leave her now. I'll stay," Grace whispered.

Agnes stood up, shocked and surprised to see Grace standing beside her. She hesitated, "Are you sure?"

Grace gave a wan smile and leaned towards the bed as Agnes moved out of the way. Rita lay tucked into white sheets and blankets with her hands on top by her sides. Her chest rose and fell in tight gasps as little whistling noises escaped her soft lips. Her long black eyelashes fluttered occasionally, but her eyes never opened. On her cheeks were two red stains of color. She looked like the kind of doll that was treasured and handed down from generation to generation until it fell apart. The kind every little girl imagined she would want.

Grace touched the auburn hair so much like her own, then rearranged it to frame her daughter's pale face. Taking Rita's hands she placed them over the green handbag before leaning in to kiss her forehead.

Agnes stood behind, astonished at the sensitivity of her sister's affections. Quietly, she left the room and went back to the waiting room to sit with Effie and Douglas.

Sitting by the bedside, Grace pushed herself as close as her pregnant belly would allow and placed her hand on top of her daughter's. She sat that way for several minutes until Rita shuddered and the sensation reverberated down Grace's arm, culminating in a violent movement of the baby in her womb. Grace gasped, annoyed that the baby should intrude on such a moment, before realizing Rita's chest no longer moved up and down. Stillness had descended on her. For a moment, Grace sat silently watching the sleeping face of her child, then panicked. She picked up Rita's fingers and let them drop softly onto the handbag. Standing up and leaning over as far as she could to feel Rita's breath with her face she found none, and as she pulled back her knees began to soften and she sat down heavily. "Dinnae die on me," she pleaded, placing her hand on her mouth to feel the breath. Here was the truth of why she hated hospitals. People died in them, they were a place of loss, not of hope. She had always known this. Eventually, it always caught up with you. "You cannie be deed," she said and sat for a few minutes longer holding her hand, letting the tears fall and feeling the trembling of the child in her belly. Reaching into the green handbag she pulled out the red lipstick inside. Rolling up what remained of it she put some on her index finger and slowly applied it to Rita's lips with expert care. Then, replacing the lipstick inside the handbag, she leaned in once more to kiss her daughter, taking the imprint of the lipstick on her lips before stepping away.

Outside the window, Agnes, Effie, and Douglas watched. "What's she day'in?" asked Douglas.

"Sssshh," said Agnes.

Effie caught the sob in her throat, but could not stop the tears. God did have a sense of humor after all. As Grace stepped out of the room, Agnes took her mother's shoulder and led her into the room. Douglas, drained of all his will to walk, stood rooted to the spot. Grace stepped past them without saying a word.

Agnes had told Alison it was the most extraordinary thing she had ever seen anybody do—putting lipstick on a dead bairn. Her impulse to stop Grace was tempered by the understanding that this was the only true intimacy she had ever had with her child.

Grace had kept the handbag after Rita's death, putting it in her closet next to her underclothes. Agnes thought it had been lost for many years but it was found when Grace died. It still had the dried-up lipstick case inside it. Alison was about to throw it away when Agnes told her what it was. Agnes told her Grace kept the bag for sentimental reasons but Alison thought it was because it had belonged to the only child in her life that she had loved without consequence.

seventeen

EFFIE MADE ARRANGEMENTS for the funeral and waited for Grace to go into labor. It was as if there were some cosmic joke, a game of checkers where you just moved the pieces around the board until you took one. Gaining and losing. Agnes wasn't sure if her mother could stand the losing. Everyone tried to ignore what was uppermost on their minds. No one wanted another baby coming into the household. For a family that had never professed love, they had all been in love with this angel child.

Two days after the funeral, Grace was taking down the washing from the line in the back green. As she reached up to take out a peg from the sheet, a crescendo of pain mounted her abdomen and a puddle of water splattered her feet. "Ma!" she shouted weakly. All the windows were closed, so she slowly climbed the stairs to the second floor and collapsed onto her knees at the front door.

She could hear the sound of "COOOAL! COOOAL!" as the coalman did his rounds. She reached up to open the door and shouted, "MA!" Effie did not hear her, so she called again in a louder voice.

"Wha . . ." Effie's irritated voice turned to concern as she came into the hallway. "Oh, my God," she exclaimed as she rushed to pick Grace up. "The lassie's in labor! Douglas! Go get the doctor."

Effie lifted her with difficulty and ordered Douglas to get his coat on. "We better get her there as quick as possible," he said, then heard the sound of "COOOAL" coming from downstairs. "The coalman is outside—he'll take us."

As Grace gasped for breath in between contractions, she yelled, "I'm no gawn in a coal cart."

"You're gawn in a coal cart unless you want to gie this bairn oot

157

on the street," said Douglas, coming up behind them as they slowly descended the stairs.

The coalman was astounded at the three people scurrying towards him. One was obviously pregnant and very much in trouble, if he was not mistaken. He'd had five bairns of his own, so he could recognize the signs by now.

"You have to take us to the hospital," urged Effie.

He took off his blackened cap and scratched his head with blackened hands, surveying the situation. "I dinnae have to dae anything."

"For the love of God, she's almost there," begged Douglas.

He looked at Grace, who was now pink in the face and perspiring badly. "Aw right. In you get. I just hope she disnae gie oot up here."

Grace and Effie clambered onto the wooden seat next to the coalman and Douglas sat on the back of the cart on top of a pile of coal. "I hope I'm no gawnie have a blackie fur a bairn," Grace gasped, feeling the steady movement of the horse's gait moving forward.

The smell of coal dust and the sheen of the black pony took Douglas back to the days with his dad. He inhaled the familiar smell of coal and watched the driver's hands expertly handle the reins. They were thick, muscled hands pitted with black and gray, his nails outlined in black lines. The pores of his skin shone like creased black diamonds where his shirt ended and his neck began, and his hair was matted with coal dust, making it stick to his head where he carried the sacks up stairs. He urged the horse on faster, but the horse, not used to going beyond a trot, refused to pick up speed.

Douglas saw the horse was well groomed, just the way his dad would have kept it. The man would be out in the wee hours of the morning brushing him down, ready for the day, and at night, he would not go to bed until his horse had had his feed and a dust off. He felt like a small boy again as he clung to the side and listened to the click clack of the hooves on the cobbled stones.

Grace was moaning loudly as they reached the hospital, grabbing hold of Effie's sleeves to ease the pain. "I can feel it!" Her eyes rolled in her head, and she bit her lower lip.

"Just hold it a minute, hen, otherwise you'll get mare than a blackie fur a bairn," called the driver. "You'll get the whole world watching

158

you," he said, anxiously pulling the horse to a standstill.

They slid down off the seat and staggered into the reception area. "Quick," yelled Effie. "She says she can feel it."

Two hours later she was trying to push when the nurse saw the umbilical cord emerge from the cervix and knew they were in deep trouble. Grace had no memory of what came next and awoke in the recovery room with a tremendous pain in her belly. Her first thought was, Oh no! I've no had it yet. The nurse came into view and told her not to move. "You've been stitched up," she said gravely. "It'll be a while before you can get back to normal."

Grace rolled her head from side to side feeling like someone had packed it with cotton wool. "Is the bairn . . . ?" she slurred.

"Oh, aye. Right as rain. She's got a good set of lungs on her. You must be a singer to have one like that. You just rest. You'll need all your strength when the anesthesia wears off."

Grace slumped back into a never-never land of sliding images and ghostly voices telling her she was for the high jump now.

She was moved to the ward and was settled onto a hard plastic-sheeted mattress and laid out flat like a corpse. To the side of the bed lay an empty crib. She was dimly aware of chairs scraping across the polished floor and metal trays clanging before she opened her eyes to the blinding ceiling lights. Her head shuddered with a booming sound, so she closed her eyes again and drifted away once more.

When she awoke there was a baby crying next to her, and Effie was standing by, giving the crib a shake. Seeing Grace open her eyes, she greeted her with, "Aye, you're awake. You all right?" then added bitterly, "You've got yourself another lassie."

Grace lifted her head from the mattress and stretched her neck to have a look. She saw a flurry of red hair and gasped.

Effie caught the look and said quickly, "It's aw' right, she hasnae come back."

Grace relaxed back down again and felt the wide gash in her belly, which seemed to stretch into an ugly smile. "What happened?"

"The bairn widnae come oot, so they cut her oot o' you."

The child's cries did not diminish, but instead became quite lusty. "Could you pick her up?" she begged. "She's gi'en me a sare heed."

"Get used to it. There's a lot mare to come," said Effie impatiently, giving the crib a shake.

She was putting on her hat as Agnes arrived. "Is naebody picking that bairn up?" she asked.

Effie put on her coat. "She's just had a caesarean, Ma, so how can you expect her to lift the bairn out of the crib?" She looked at Grace, who had turned her face away from them both.

"Is she aw' right?" she asked Effie.

"Aye, she'll survive. I'm away. I've got to get the dinner on." She gave one more shake of the crib, before picking up her handbag. "This is your problem, no mine," she said to Grace. "You're gonnie have to learn how to deal wi' it."

Agnes gave Grace a look of pity, giving a light push to the crib. By now, the child was using its full lung power. All the women in the ward began to wonder when somebody would pick up the baby.

Effie shrugged. "I've got to go." As she turned to leave, she looked back and her lower lip began to tremble. She wanted with all her heart to pick the child up, but she couldn't give Grace the excuse to leave her with the burden one more time. She would not do it again.

Agnes stood silently watching her mother go, her shoulders slumped towards her chest, and knew the terrible toll this was taking. She didn't think it was fair of her to be so harsh on Grace, but there was no way for her to sympathize with circumstances she didn't understand. If she knew, perhaps she would feel differently. But then, perhaps she would never have believed the truth.

Grace lay with her eyebrows pinched into a fierce frown, her lips in a grimace. The wail of the child was like machine gun fire on her mind. "Make it go away," she pleaded.

"You have to take her," said Agnes pushing the crib.

"I cannie," said Grace weakly.

From across the ward, the sound of clicking heels with a mission strode towards them. "What's this?" demanded the nursing sister. "I won't have my patients disturbed because nobody will pick this child up." She reached into the crib and with expert ease wrapped the baby tighter into its swaddling blanket and placed it firmly in Grace's arms as if handing her a parcel from the butcher. "I know you've just had a caesarean, but that's no excuse not to hold your baby. All babies need to be held." She plumped the pillow behind her head and placed another one behind it, sitting Grace up a little.

Wincing with the painful movement on her abdomen, Grace looked at the squalling face of her child and made a motion with her arms up and down. The baby's cries began to diminish to a hiccup.

Agnes closed her eyes briefly and when she opened them again, Grace's face had relaxed as great globs of tears fell onto the blanket of the sleeping child.

"I ken it's hard for you, Grace," she whispered, "but I cannie dae it this time, neither can Ma. You'll have to learn. It's the only way. This bairn needs you."

Grace looked down at the infant and then back at Agnes before gazing at the harsh ceiling lights. "Where do I go from here? Ma chest is as hard as rocks, I'm sare aw' ow'er, and I'm scared," she said with a little girl voice.

"Aye, we aw' are, but we've just got to get on wi' it, hen."

"I hope he rots in hell," said Grace venomously. "I hope he never comes back."

At that moment, Agnes felt attached to a bat with a rubber string and she was the ball that was banging and pulling without end. Taking the baby from Grace's arms, she lingered with it for a moment before putting it back into the crib. "She looks like you. It's that red hair thing you've aw' got." She didn't want to say the baby looked liked John.

Grace shivered. "Just my bloody luck."

"All right, lass. I think you've lain in that bed long enough. You can get up to the toilet today." The nurse took hold of the corner of the sheet and blanket and yanked it back to expose Grace's white legs beneath the pink nightgown she was wearing. Easing her out of bed, the nurse held her elbow as she gingerly searched for the floor and her slippers. She groaned as the abdominal muscles cranked into action and her wound cracked open. "How old are you?"

Breathing deeply, Grace shuffled alongside the nurse. "Twenty-one," she gasped.

"Och, you're just a young thing. Have they given you the key to the door yet?" At age 21, the tradition of giving a young person the key to the door was a moot point in her life. "Don't worry," said the nurse, "we'll have you out of here in no time."

In the bathroom a deep porcelain bath was filled with water. Lifting Grace's nightgown over her head, the nurse placed her hand on her belly. "This will sting," she said, then whisked the sticky plaster off in one swipe. Grace meowed like a cat in protest. "It's coming along nicely," she said. "You'll soon be a new woman. You won't even notice it in a few months. Now let me help you get into the bath but don't sit down. It's not time yet." Grace wondered how she could even get her legs up to step into the bathtub but the nurse assured her it was easy. Once Grace was installed she bustled on briskly, squeezing a cloth with hot water and rubbing soap on it before washing Grace's back.

Grace looked down at the long vertical black gash in her belly, which looked like a mouth sewn up to keep it quiet. Running her hand softly over the wound, all the hurt of the last years spread in the yawn of the opening. She was losing her youth to children and had lost any opportunity for a life of her own. Nobody would want her with a scar down her belly and a daughter. Now more than ever, she was used goods, lying for the rest of her life every time someone asked her who the father was. If she had been free after Rita died, it could have changed things. She began to weep softly as the nurse ran the rough cloth over her body.

"There, there now. What's this?" said the nurse softly. "We can't have you getting all upset like this. I know this must hurt, but it'll get better, I promise you." She continued rubbing on Grace's chest and stomach, carefully avoiding the wound.

Not anytime soon, thought Grace.

Sitting under the big plaque celebrating the opening of the hospital in 1645, Grace stared at the queues of people waiting their turn for emergency treatment. She held the child tightly swaddled inside the blanket that had once swaddled Rita. It had been white and soft; now it was yellow and hard. The child's face was barely visible inside of it.

When Agnes arrived to take her home, Grace looked like someone had placed a sign around her neck saying "waiting for collection." Her hair was lank, her face pale, and she wore no lipstick, which surprised Agnes because Grace always took the time to put on her lipstick.

"Have you been waitin' a long time?"

Grace shrugged. "C'mon then, let's be gawn hame. It's cauld outside, so fasten up your coat." She held out her arms to take the baby, but Grace looked at her blankly. "Your coat, Grace," she urged again. As if coming out of a dream state, Grace handed her the baby, buttoned up her coat, and held out her arms again to take the baby back.

Agnes picked up the small suitcase containing her nightclothes and proceeded to push her way through the hospital doors.

When they arrived home, Effie was sitting by the fireside knitting socks for soldiers. Douglas was asleep but awoke when he heard them enter. Neither one of them rose from their chairs.

"Aye, aw' right?" said Effie by way of recognition. "I've made the bed up in there if you want to put her doon."

Grace put her down on the couch and took her coat off. Agnes placed the small suitcase in the bedroom and returned.

"Do you need to rest, Grace?"

Grace shook her head and unwarapped the baby from the shawl. Agnes stood watching for a moment. "What are you do'in?"

"She needs changed."

"But she's sleepin'," said Agnes, as if she needed to explain.

Grace continued unwrapping the child until the change of air disturbed her and she let out a cry.

The sudden noise of the child's cry seemed to rouse everyone into action. Douglas got up and went to the bathroom. Effie put down her knitting and went into the kitchen. Agnes sat alone in the living room with Grace and the now howling child, bare from the waist down.

"Do we have any nappies?" Grace asked innocently.

"Aye, I suppose we've got some left over fae the wee yin," said Agnes, going to the bedroom to look. "Did they no gie you some when you left the hospital?"

In a dull voice she said, "I'm no sure—maybe in the case."

Agnes brought the suitcase back into the living room and found inside a change of nappy, a small can of dried milk, a glass bottle, and a teat. "Looks like they sent you hame prepared. Better put that on her before she gets a cauld." She handed Grace the cloth nappy, which was almost as big as the baby, and watched as she deftly folded it into a square and without a word lifted both the baby's feet at once and stuck the nappy under her behind. Agnes watched her sister going through the motions, feeling a prickling sensation at the back of her eyes, blinking away the possibility of tears. Gulping back the emotion, she asked, "Does she have a name yet?"

"You choose."

"Dinnae be stupid," said Effie, who had just entered the conversation. "She's yours so you have to choose her name."

Grace shrugged her shoulders and looked across at the book lying on the table. Napoleon's Army by Harriet Townsend. "You can call her Harriet," she said, and finished pinning the nappy before pulling down the nightgown and pulling the drawstring at the bottom and swaddling her back into the blanket.

"Could you put the kettle on?" she asked Effie. "She'll need feeding."

"I've already done that," she replied curtly, and sat down with her knitting again. Grace placed the baby down on the couch again and picked up the can and the bottle. Agnes looked at her mother and said nothing. Douglas returned from the bathroom and stopped to look at the child before picking up his book from the table.

Agnes sat in silence watching the two of them keep their distance and wondered how they were going to survive in this atmosphere. Harriet was crying, so she picked her up and rocked her as she walked. Per wee thing, she thought. You dinnae stand a chance.

Douglas looked as if he were reading his book, but the cries of the baby felt like needles piercing his skin. At the hospital he had taken one look at her wisps of red hair, and knew he could not love her as he had loved Rita. He closed his eyes against the vision and wanted Rita back with every breath he took. This child could not be a substitute for her.

Douglas wanted to tell Grace to leave, to take the burden away from them. But for as much as they had suffered, he knew instinctively his daughter was suffering more. He could see the life had been knocked out of her, but he did not see how much he had contributed. He thought her life was wasted. She could have been somebody with that magnificent singing voice, but now there wasn't a chance in hell she was going to get anywhere. Not with another bairn on her hands.

Effie held the knitting needles tightly between her fingers, and the stitches were getting increasingly smaller and tighter as she knit. It was the exact opposite of everything she knew. Only by relaxing could you knit properly. It was tension that held the knitting together, but if the tension was too tight, then you couldn't get the needles through the stitches, which cut down on your speed. The members of the knitting circle said she was a maniac knitter, which was fine with her—it kept her hands busy but let her mind wander. Now she wanted her mind to be quiet. Never in her life had she been able to stand by and see someone struggle. Leaving Grace to fend for herself was an act of sheer will that was crippling her. She knew it was a cruel rejection, but they had invested too much last time and look what had happened. It was painful to think of letting another child take Rita's place, but if anything were to happen to this child or to Grace, she would be the first to show up. But not now. Now was too soon.

For the next six months, Grace fed the baby on time, washed the nappies, and learned how to knit. She repaired clothes that Effie brought home from the clothes drive and even managed to make soup for the family. The baby slept only two to three hours at a time and cried every day from five o'clock at night until eight. Grace took to it on automatic pilot, never daring to ask herself how she was feeling. She rested when the child rested, and otherwise buried herself in the minutiae of the day. In her mother's silence, she felt the resounding blame for Rita's death. It could have been any one of them, but it was her luck that day.

Only Agnes seemed to care. Agnes took turns when she could to feed Harriet, giving Grace a break to wash her hair or read a magazine. In the silences of the day, Grace felt as if her body was encased in concrete and her mind a basin filled with slops. She cared little for her appearance and rarely went out unless she had to. She sat by the window smoking cigarettes, ignoring the friendly waves from the neighbors as they walked by.

Douglas was tired of wandering the streets at night looking for blackout violations and found a job in the shipyards of Henry Robb as a fitter's mate building ships for the Navy. He was exhausted from little sleep and his hip ached most of the time, but like most men, he was doing his bit for the war effort and that was all that counted.

John wrote from France, "things are no very good, so I don't think I can be home soon." Douglas complained about the lack of letters and asked if there were no postboxes over there. When the baby was born, Agnes wrote to him 'it's a girl' and left it unsigned. Grace muttered under her breath, "He's no deed yet?" Effie fretted about whether he would make it back alive.

William wrote irregularly telling Agnes how much he missed her sweet face and how he thought about her every day and couldn't wait until he could come back home again. It was the one thing that made life bearable. The newspapers were full of the latest terrifying news of the bombardment of London, and she was glad to know he wasn't there, praying he wasn't somewhere worse. He sent a picture of himself in uniform and said he looked a little gawky. Agnes thought he looked handsome although a little thin. Something she would try to remedy in later years. He asked her to send another picture of herself because he had lost the one she had given him when his barrack was bombarded. She went straight to the photographers that weekend and sent it. Each night she kissed their wedding picture lightly and placed it next to her bed. Saying good night she trembled slightly at the thought of his imaginary touch.

Agnes pushed the food tray to one side. "They dinnae give you much to eat, do they," she said to the girl next to her.

"I eat it, but it's not very good," she said. "You look like you're reading a book. Did you write it?"

"Oh, no, hen. I couldn't write this. It takes more imagination than I've got, that's for sure. My niece is the writer. What an imagination that lassie has." Agnes laughed and said, "she makes up all these stories about our family. Some of them are real but the rest, I dinnae ken where she gets it from."

"A good imagination can get you in trouble," said the girl.

"Aye, and I'm going to have to talk with her when I see her." Staring out the window, she thought, *I didnae kiss his picture at all. I just used to look at it and wish he were with me. That's all I told her.* She smiled at the reminiscence then felt sad. John was a bastard but he was still her brother no matter what he did. His death from a heart attack at age fifty-six was a cruel blow to his young family, but Grace was pleased. She didn't deserve the punishment she got and that bairn of hers didn't deserve to be born. There were so many bairns who didn't ask to be born and too many mothers who should never have had them. It was Grace's bad luck that she got them in spades.

eighteen

Grace rarely picked up a book, so Effie was surprised when she began reading to Harriet at night, taking her through the pictures one by one and rarely complaining when she asked for the same book each night. Effie began to think there was hope for her daughter after all, but nobody, except Agnes, noticed that Grace was deep in.

Douglas had fallen in love with Harriet by the time she was crawling and fussing around his ankles. She was cute, and no matter how much he looked for someone else, there was no mistaking she had her mother's looks right down to each minute freckle across her cheeks and nose. If he looked very closely, he would have seen that she had his son's freckles also, but nobody was counting.

The latest movies from Hollywood blurred the edges of unhappiness and made Grace forget about where she was and how miserable life was. The picture house's nicotine-stained curtains and piss-soaked floor strewn with chewing gum, newspapers, cigarette butts, slippery condoms, and crackling buckie shells gave way to satin and chiffon swirls of gowns adorning the bodies of goddesses of the screen. It allowed Grace to project her dreams of a better life to the characters she adored. But before a film would even start, the organ player would rise creakily from the pit in front of the stage and the singer would fill the auditorium with valiant war songs. Next the Pathe cock would crow the news of casualties, battles, victories, and extermination of people in places most people could hardly pronounce. At last the trailers would blaze eye-catching headlines across the screen and taunt the viewer with the thrills of what was to come. Finally, after all the booing and hissing died down, the main event. It was then Grace could drift off into the make-believe worlds of heroes, heroines, and adventures. She was Mrs. Miniver bravely fighting the war on her own; she was Charlotte Vale in *Now, Voyager,* on board an ocean liner, trying to figure out what a rich woman should do with her life. When Bambi's mother was killed, she cried, knowing there was no justice. She sank herself into every film she saw and left believing that all things were possible in the pictures.

Nellie grabbed hold of her arm as they came out of the Palace. "Dinnae go hame. Let's have a wee drink."

Grace pulled away. "My ma'll have a fit."

"Since when did that stop you before?"

She hesitated for just a moment. "It's no the same anymare."

"Just a wee yin, Grace. It winnae kill you fur once."

"Aw' right, just a wee yin."

"That's the lassie I remember," said Nellie as they strode down the road arm in arm.

The bar was crowded with Saturday night special girls, all done up in their finest Pan-cake makeup stockings lined with eyebrow pencil marks to make it look like a seam. The men strutted like peacocks in grease, taking their chances among the Yanks crowding out the bar in their tan uniforms and loud voices.

Grace ordered a drink and was side-swiped by a sailor who lost his land legs in a collision with a beer glass. "Hiya, sweetheart!"

"Hi yourself," she said, doing her best to ignore him and poking Nellie in the ribs. They both giggled, took their drinks, and slid across the room to the furthest corner. There was a group of people singing "I Love a Lassie," clutching at each other as they swayed from side to side. Grace watched them and sipped her beer.

"Did you ken they're lookin' fur a singer at the Eldo on Saturday nights?" said Nellie.

"What are you tellin' me fur?"

"Well, I thought you could do it. Somebody mentioned your name the other day and said it was a waste that you didnae get oot and dae mare singing."

"Shite!"

"Naw! Seriously, why don't you gie it a go?"

A flicker of hesitation passed over Grace's face. Effie would never let her away with that. But maybe this was a chance she should take.

"I think Andy Galbraith has something to dae wi' it. That'd be great if you got it, Gracie. Hearing you sing, what a braw thing that would be."

"I've still got my ma to deal wi'."

"Och, I'll put a good word in fur you."

"You'll need more than a word wi' her. You'll have to swear your life away."

Effie was in the middle of putting a spoon of mince and tatties in her mouth and almost choked. "You're off your heed. A job singing! How dae you think you can dae that?"

"It's only Saturday night, Ma. They'll even pay me for it."

"Aye, well, it might keep you in cigarettes."

"It's no like I've got anything to do on Saturdays."

Effie spooned another mouthful of food. "What aboot the wee yin?"

"Aw, Ma! Dinnae be like that. It's only a Saturday night."

"Aye, Saturday night. That's the start. Pretty soon it'll be Monday, Tuesday, Wednesday as well. It's aw' it takes to get you intae trouble."

Effie lifted Harriet out of her high chair and put her down on the floor. She ran towards Douglas with a book in her hand. "Gaga, book!"

He reached down, put her on his knee, and opened the picture book. It was the same book every night but she never seemed to notice.

"Didn't you ever dream?" implored Grace.

For a moment, Effie glanced at Douglas immersed in the book with Harriet. "Aye, I did," she said weakly, scraping the last spoonful of mince off the plate. "It disnae matter what I say, you'll do what you want."

Grace jumped up and without hesitation kissed her mother on the cheek.

"Aw' right. Aw' right," said Effie, waving her away. "Just dinnae make me regret it."

"Thanks, Ma. I winnie let you doon."

Douglas continued reading to Harriet but raised his eyebrows in Effie's direction and shook his head from side to side.

༺✦༻

If Effie had known what the Eldorado dance hall was like, she would never have let Grace out. The girls sucked up the walls while the men crawled, shimmied, and groped their way among them. For Grace the biggest surprise was the band. They were all girls. She found it difficult to imagine they didn't have a singer among them, but Andy Galbraith had told her no one could put a candle to her in the voice department. He had insisted she take the job, but told her not to expect too much money. Grace would have done it for nothing.

For the first few sessions, Grace missed the beat starting the song, but the girls were forgiving and she was quick to catch up. When Grace got over her nervousness, her voice captured all the loneliness, heartache, and love of her audience and the musicians went along with her. Grace embraced the songs like a lover and charmed her way back into the lives of her family. Effie pretended to ignore her when she was practicing her songs, but she was listening with an aching heart. If she hadn't been sae stupid, she thought, she could have done something with her life.

Harriet began to sing along with her mother and soon she was dancing. Douglas watched them with delight. He had never imagined that joy could reinvent itself in the house after Rita's death, but watching this little Shirley Temple dance made him fall in love all over again. Agnes applauded Grace, danced with Harriet, and felt empty inside. She longed for William to come home.

༺✦༻

It had been two years since she had seen William, but he wrote every week and sent her a few shillings from his pay. For someone who was supposed to be stuck to a desk job because of his eyesight, she was surprised when he wrote to say he was going to Italy, but he could have a week's leave. Would she come down to York to meet his mother since she had been upset that William had married and she still hadn't met Agnes. He would send her the money for her fare.

"What'll I do?" she asked Grace.

"Do! What a stupid thing to ask. You'll go, that's what."

"But I've never been on a train before, and it's hard to get a ticket unless it's an emergency journey."

"It is an emergency. Your husband's been like a bloody ghost. Dinnae be daft. Get oot o' here. It's good for you."

Agnes wrote she'd come and hoped his mother would approve of her. William wrote back with a five pound note and said, "She'll love you, just like I do."

It took six hours to get to York and at each railway station, men and women in smart uniforms heavy with kit bags congregated on the platforms and stood in the aisles because all the carriages were full. Agnes had been lucky to get a seat at Waverley station because Grace shoved a man out of the way when he was about to sit down.

As she stepped off the train, William was pacing the platform and rushed to greet her. Breathlessly, he lifted her off the ground, smothering her with kisses, paying no attention to the people passing. They were not alone. Hundreds of couples were doing the same thing on almost every platform in every station. Passion and loneliness mixed with anxiety knocked down any restraints in society.

William's mother, Doris, was a small woman who was rarely seen without an apron because she seldom left the house, except to go shopping. She welcomed Agnes like a long lost daughter, wiping the tears from her eyes as she kissed her on the cheek, then made it clear her offer of help was not needed when it came time to make the tea. Agnes, unused to doing nothing, twiddled with the corner of her cardigan as she sat on the couch. William sat contentedly in the corner window sucking on his pipe, watching her every move. "Maybe we should go oot and leave your mother in peace," suggested Agnes.

"Tha's not a bad idea," he said with twinkling eyes, "but she'll not hear of it." Doris arrived with the tea and set it down in front of Agnes. "Does ta ivver wek up early an' can't get back ta sleep?" she said.

"Sorry?"

"I's hev a hard tawm sleepin'. Does ta sleep well?"

"Oh, aye. Like a bairn," said Agnes, cottoning on to the question. She had heard there was a strong accent in Edinburgh, but this was a foreign language.

"Ti war during thi time when the bombs flay," Doris said, pulling her pinny up to her face to wipe away the tears. "T'hard when my boy is gone."

Agnes pursed her lips and waited. She had no idea what Doris had just said. She looked to William for encouragement, but he just nodded his head and rose to go into the garden. Don't leave me now, she thought.

Doris poured the tea and continued on for about another ten minutes until Agnes could not stand it any longer.

"I'll go see what William is do'in," she said apologetically. "He might need some help."

William was pulling some weeds that were supposed to be vegetables in his mother's Victory Garden. "Did she tak t'ears off you?" he asked, laughing.

"Dinnae you start," said Agnes, looking back towards the house. "I couldnae understand what she was saying. I thought you were bad."

William sat back on his heels and roared with laughter. "C'mere," he said, holding out his dirty hands towards her. Even on his knees he could hug her waist easily. "you'll have t'get used t'it." He pulled her down and kissed her.

She pulled away, glancing back at the house. "Your mother'll see us."

"Aye, she will that, lass, but we're married, remember?"

Agnes blushed and looked towards the kitchen window. She could not see Doris behind the curtain, smiling.

In the two years since William had been home, there was much

173

fallen to neglect. He fixed the leaks in the Anderson shelter, now overgrown with grass, and packed the walls with cardboard to make it warmer. So far York had managed to escape the same kind of bombing he'd seen in London, but he knew it was only a matter of time before Hitler came at Britain in strength.

Basking in the pleasure of being together, they walked for hours along the River Ouse, As they stood in the nave of York Minster, where the floors had run red with the blood of royalty during the War of the Roses, Agnes gaped upwards, with chills running down her spine. Above and behind her, magnificent vaulted ceilings soared towards the heavens and windows shone like jewels in the light cast from the setting sun. Agnes had been raised to believe the church was all nonsense, but standing here in this, she wasn't so sure. She felt almost afraid and irrelevant and leaned towards William as he held tight to her arm. "Tis lovely, t'int it?" he said. Agnes nodded dumbly. "Come. You have to see this." He pulled her past the magnificent choir stall and the boarded-up windows where previously the famous Five Sisters stained glass had stood before the war. As he raised his face upwards, Agnes followed his gaze.

Above their heads, an umbrella-shaped roof shimmered in spokes of iridescent red, blue, and gold shining in tribute to glory. If she had never understood the word humble before, she knew what it was now. Never in her life had she been in a place with such beauty. In an instant she knew she wanted a church wedding. She wanted to wear a wedding dress and have the organ play and hold flowers in her hand and have a flower girl bearing the ring. She turned to William and held him fiercely. "You'll come back to me," she whispered urgently, on the verge of tears. "You come back and we'll get married proper. Dinnae you forget."

"Not a chance," he replied, hugging her tightly to his chest.

"She's such a bloody romantic," Agnes mumbled. *I telt her York Minster was one of the loveliest I had ever seen, but I didnae tell her it like this. This is like Brief Encounter when Trevor Howard meets Celia Johnson for the first time and takes that grit out of her eye. You just know there's going to be some passion involved. We weren't like that at all. She smiled remembering how it was. I was so young then. I really did think he was my knight at that moment. That lassie in Los Angeles is gonnie think this is aw' rubbish. I widnae be a bit surprised if she didn't believe a word of it. I'm no sure I do."*

nineteen

In May 1945 the war was over.

"He's comin' hame! I cannie believe it. We're gonnie be the gether again." Agnes shouted, frantically pacing the small living room, holding the letter in her hand. "What am I gonnie dae? He'll be here in three weeks. He tells me I have to be ready. What am I gonnie dae? He's got a job."

Effie raised herself slowly from the chair, tired from all the celebrations that had been going on for days in the street. "You need to calm doon. It's no for another three weeks."

Agnes folded the letter and put it in her pocket as she looked out the window. There was still some bunting tied to the lampposts and a couple of men staggered up the street, hanging on each other's shoulders, swaying from side to side. "I'm no sure I want to live in York," she said quietly.

Effie came behind her and placed her hands gently on her shoulders. "First of all, you have to go where he's go'in. He's your man. Secondly, if the man's got a job, then that's it. It's what he kens. His Ma is all alone doon there. She'll need him. I've got aw' these other buggers to bother wi'. You dinnae need to be here for me." She took Agnes's face in her hands and stared into her face. "You've been wantin' to go for a long time, hen. This is your chance."

Agnes pulled away from her mother's grip. "But I dinnae ken, Ma. It's a long way fae here. I widnae be able to come up very often."

"Well, I'll just have to come doon to you, won't I," said Effie. "It'll gie me a chance to get oot o' here."

Harriet came from the bedroom, rubbing her eyes. "What's Auntie Agnes shoutin' aboot?"

176

Agnes swept her in her arms. "My man's comin' hame," she laughed through tears. "He's comin' hame." Then she twirled Harriet until she was giggling and dizzy.

Effie caught hold of her as she staggered across the room. "I would like to hear fae that son o' mine," she said slowly. "Nae word fae him in months. I hope this disnae mean anything."

"I widnae worry aboot him. If there was anything, you'd be gettin' one o' these telegrams," said Agnes breathlessly.

A week later a letter postmarked Berlin arrived. John said he had signed up for special duties and would be there for a few more months. If everything went well, he could come home for a visit. He hoped everyone was in good health.

"But why Germany? It's an awfy place to be," said Effie.

"They have to be rebuilt as well, you ken," said Douglas. "It's a good thing he's no comin' hame. There's nae bloody work. Same old bloody story; you get oot there and gie your life and limb to these buggers, then they screw you when you come hame. All promises and nothin' but wind to show for it. It makes you sick."

The rule of last in, first out applied. When the need for ships was reduced, Douglas was one of the first to go. With nothing to fall back on and his hip in constant pain, depression returned and he buried himself in books once more. Not even Harriet could lift him out of his slump. For both him and Effie, the best years of their lives had passed by without them noticing they were supposed to be good. He hoped that Agnes's husband would take care of her properly. As for Grace, he wondered if she would ever leave their house. There had to be someone out there who would be willing to take her on with a child.

"Are you leaving the bed?" asked Grace.

"Dinnae be daft, Gracie," said Agnes, irritated.

"I was just wondering, that's aw'."

"Sometimes I wonder aboot you," said Agnes, taking her blouses from the chest of drawers and folding them neatly into piles. Grace sat on the bed watching her, smoking a cigarette.

"Sometimes I wonder about me," said Grace distantly.

"I'll be glad to get rid o' your nasty cigarette smell fae ma claes."

"Och, dinnae worry yourself. You forget your man smokes a pipe. Whae are you kiddin'?"

"That's different."

"Suit yourself," she said, stubbing the butt out in the ashtray by the bed.

Agnes stood in the hallway with her two suitcases. "Have you got everything?" asked Effie.

"It's no the end of the earth, you ken. You can come back anytime you want," said Grace. Effie picked up one of the cases and started towards the front door.

"Where you gawn, Auntie Agnes?" asked Harriet

"I'm gawn to my ain hoose, hen," said Agnes, gently caressing her hair.

She looked confused. "But you live here."

"You'll see her again," said Grace blinking back the tears.

Effie shouted "C'mon, let's go. That train's no gonnie wait for you."

Agnes held Grace's hand and said, "Dinnae let me doon," then bent down to kiss Harriet. "You take care of your mother," then turned to go, stifling the greatest urge she had ever had to stay home.

"Cheerio," shouted Harriet.

The lump in Agnes's throat reduced her reply to a whisper. "Cheerio."

At the station, Effie shoved a bag of sandwiches into her hand. "Dinnae you forget we're here," she admonished.

Agnes stood clutching the sandwich bag, afraid to step up onto the railway carriage. Douglas stood by Effie's side, then placed the suitcases on the train. "Away you go. It'll no wait for you."

Agnes nodded and then kissed her mother briefly on the cheek before climbing aboard. "You'll come soon?" she asked.

"I'll do my best," she answered, withdrawing to Douglas's side.

"You better get your seat," he said.

Most of the window shades were drawn and people were sleeping or watching the movie. Agnes felt hot in the raincoat she had not taken off since getting on the plane. She was also dying to go to the toilet so she excused herself, putting the manuscript on the empty seat that lay between her and the pregnant girl. As she walked down the aisle of the plane the cabin attendant who had taken care of her earlier was in the galley. "Would you like a cup of tea?" she asked.

"Oh aye, hen. I'd love one. Is this plane gonnie get there anytime soon? It's an awfy long way to go. If I had kent it was going to be this long, I dinnae think I would have come."

"Are you going on holiday?"

"No, really. I'm takin' a book to a wee lassie who disnae really want it."

"It's a long way to go to deliver a book. Couldn't you just send it?"

"I wish I could have, but it was my niece's idea. She's in the hospital and cannie come herself so she asked me. It's for her daughter."

"It must be pretty important."

"I suppose. You'll have to excuse me dear, but I've got to go to the toilet before I burst. Just leave my tea there and I'll get it in a minute."

twenty

GRACE LIFTED HER glass to her eye, giving a warped view of the man sitting at the table opposite. "He looks like Clark Gable."

"Naw! Errol Flynn."

"Clark Gable!"

"He could look like Tyrone Power for aw' you care."

Grace put the glass down on the table and adjusted her stockings before uncrossing her legs. Davie Wishart was watching her and smiled. "Aye, no bad, Gracie."

"Keep dreamin', you!"

"He's no interested in the likes o' you, said Nellie, "anyway, he's no much interested in anybody."

"How do you ken?"

"Because I've tried, that's how," said Nellie. "He's just no there. I was telt it was because of the war, but he looks aw' right to me. He's an awfy dancer, do you ken that?"

Sauntering to the other side of the room, Grace stood at the man's table and leaned in slightly. "Would you like to dance wi' me? Somebody telt me you werenae bad."

Kenny Napier looked up into the deep brown eyes of Grace Sharp and smirked. "They're telling you lies."

"Aw, Kenny. Watch oot. You're in trouble now," said his friend

"Shut up, you!" barked Grace. "You're just jealous 'cause it's no you I'm askin'."

"Whoa! Fighting words. You better watch it, Kenny. She's serious."

"Whae said I could dance?" he said, looking around him. The man made a pumping motion with his arms and hands.

"Well, are you or no?"

"A challenge, my lad. Are you gonnie take her up on it? If you are, button up tight."

Grace jutted her chin forward towards him. "Shut your gob, fatso."

"Ooh! The name's Mike, just in case you're interested."

Kenny stood up and took her arm, leading her towards the dance floor. "I'm only day'in this because you ken how to sing. I hope you can dance as well."

"If you follow the lighthouse, son, you're gonnie wreck the boat," said Mike making swirling gestures with his hips.

Holding the small of her back, Kenny took two paces, and without effort, she followed his lead and glided easily across the floor in a parallel flow of legs moving in unison, elegantly stepping backwards and forwards. Grace moved her whole body to embrace his and felt they could have waltzed, tangoed, and shimmied the whole night. Once the music ended, Grace was breathless and astounded when he dropped her hand and walked back to his table without turning around.

To hide her embarrassment, she went quickly to the bandstand and spoke to the bandleader. A few minutes later she had the whole dance floor moving like a field of seaweed in motion with the current as she crooned "You'll Never Know Just How Much I Love You." Kenny sipped his beer and watched her with no sign of emotion on his face until one of his friends nudged him and his beer spilled onto his trousers. "Aw, c'mon," he growled, searching for his handkerchief to wipe up the wet mess. "These are new troosers."

"Did you get them out of Burton's window?" said Mike

At the end of the night, Grace brushed past him on her way to the toilet. "Thanks for the dance the night. Maybe next time you can stay long enough for me to catch ma breath."

He gave a slight shake of his head. "Aye, maybe."

Grace smiled and pushed her hair back from her face before walking on. Behind her she could hear a roar of "Whooaaa!" from the boys sitting at the table. She wiggled in her high heels and stuck her middle finger up behind her back. Nellie told her not to get started again. She'd only get in trouble.

The following week, Grace came down from the stage and almost tripped over him. Taking a step backwards, she exclaimed, "Och, it's you. Still hanging oot wi' that galloot wi' the big mooth."

"Hmmm. Very funny." His face registered a slight smile and he walked away.

"Have you taken any mare dancin' lessons since last week?"

He hesitated and then turned around. "Why? You ready for another go?"

Grace put out her hands and they waltzed onto the floor. Just like the last time, their bodies followed every crease of syncopated movement across the floor, dedicating each step as if they had done it a thousand times. This time he didn't turn away when the music stopped. He held her close to him, catching the bristles of his cheek against the softness of her hair. Towards the end of the next dance, Grace felt him stiffen and then drop her hand. "Sorry. I've got to go. I'll see you."

At his table sat a small blonde with big breasts, wearing a face that looked as if it had just bitten into a sour apple. He sat down next to her and when she sat on his lap, he brushed her aside. She pointed in Grace's direction and she saw Kenny shrug. The girl was waving her hands about and he ignored her until she turned and walked away. Grace went back on stage and sang slow numbers until the bandleader told her to change the tempo.

It was three weeks before she saw him again alone in the pub. "What have I got to lose?" she told Nellie.

"Everything, if you're no careful," she counseled.

She took her shandy and left Nellie talking to some fellow who had been asking her out for weeks. Kenny wasn't paying any attention to anybody. He was smoking a cigarette in the palm of his hand, the way workers do when they don't want to get caught. He didn't look up when she approached.

"Hiya! Can I sit doon here?" she said cheerfully.

"Suit yourself."

"I havenae seen you at the Eldo lately," she said.

"No."

"Everything aw' right?" She sat down next to him and put her drink on his table.

"Aye," he offered, dragging on his cigarette.

"Sometimes I dinnae feel like gawn but I have to sing," she offered, as if the singing was a burden.

"Aye. You're no bad."

"Thanks. You're no a bad dancer either."

He shrugged. "It's no hard."

The conversation stumbled along for another fifteen minutes, interspersed with long periods of silence as he smoked his cigarettes and sipped his beer. Grace babbled on about work and the people she knew. She remarked on him being a sharp dresser and said he must have got it in the Army. He said, "Aye," and left it at that. He was well known in Leith for being the best-dressed man in town with empty pockets and an empty mind.

"Well, nice to see you," he said politely. "I've got to go hame."

"Aye!" said Grace standing up. "Me as well. My ma expects me to be hame." She cringed as she said it, cursing her useless attempt to charm him. He was already walking away from her as she staggered to catch up. That was a bloody washout wasn't it, you stupid bugger, she thought, walking out the door with him.

As soon as the door had swung shut, the gossip began. "Fancy that. Kenny Napier wi' Gracie. I hope he kens what he's day'in."

"Och, leave it alane. I hope she kens what she's gettin' intae," said Nellie.

Kenny knew she was following him and said nothing until he reached the corner before turning and saying, "Cheerio." Grace tried to look nonchalant and turned up Bernard Street in the opposite direction. She didn't know if it was his Eroll Flynn good looks or the fact that she had not been with anyone who mattered in years, but every part of her yearned to follow him. Pulling up her coat collar against the fog, she headed for the bus stop. I'll find a way, she thought. I'll get him to notice me.

Grace heard the voices before she opened the living room door. She wondered who it was since they rarely had visitors. Her steps froze when she saw John sitting in the chair next to the fire, with Harriet on his knee. Effie was ecstatic. "Look, Gracie! See whae's here. He's hame."

Creased and pressed, not a hair out of place, his face livid with a scar that sliced through a midden smirk. John was home. All the air left the room as she tried to control the burning desire to snatch Harriet away from him and run from the house.

"Hello, Grace," he said slowly, putting Harriet down on the floor. She was playing with a new wooden doll.

A small distant voice said, "Are you planning on stayin' long?"

"Staying long! He just got here," burst out Douglas. "Where have you been?"

"I wis just oot for a drink wi' ma pals."

"You havenae changed, have you?" said John.

Grace sat down opposite him on the couch next to her mother and pulled Harriet towards her, sitting her down on the couch close beside her. Bending the arms and legs of the doll at the joints, turning its head and bending the body at the waist, Harriet was trying to get it to dance. "See Ma! It's dancin'."

Grace patted her head and said, "Nice," but she wasn't really there.

"You wouldnae believe how much she's changed," said Effie proudly, looking at Grace. "She's got a job singing three nights a week and she's back on the buses."

Grace wasn't listening. "You'll break that if you're no careful," she yelled, snatching the doll from Harriet's hands. Effie took the doll and put it back together again properly.

"Will you make me some claes for it, Nannie?"

"Aye, we cannie have it naked, can we?"

Douglas leaned towards John. "How did it happen, son?" he said in a hushed voice.

"Och, dinnae start, Douglas. That's no something we want to be

184

hearing wi' the bairn here," said Effie, who did not want to know the story. He was home, he was alive, it was all that mattered.

John rubbed his face where a long livid scar ran down the left cheek. "It's a long story, Dad. I'll tell you later."

Douglas shook his head. "Aye, you're right. Maybe later."

Grace thought he'd gotten off lightly. The bayonet or whatever it was had been aimed too high.

"Do you have anymare like this, Uncle John?"

She cringed at her daughter's use of "Uncle John" and thought, You bastard. You're no hame five minutes and she's aw' over you.

"No, that's it, hen. Maybe the morn' I'll get you some sweeties."

"Yippee!" she exclaimed, laughing and clapping her hands.

"C'mon, it's time for your bed. Let's go." Grace jerked her across the room.

"No! I dinnae want to go. I'm no tired yet. I want to be wi' Uncle John."

"I'll read you a story," she said gruffly.

"You can leave the bairn, Gracie. I'll put her to her bed," said Effie.

"No, it's getting late and she needs to sleep. Say good night."

Harriet whined all the way to the bedroom until Grace pulled out her favorite book and began to read. Within minutes she was asleep, but her mother lay in bed weeping softly, praying he wouldn't stay too long.

❧

It was the prodigal son returned. Effie waited hand and foot and he could do no wrong. She washed and ironed for him, and fed him whatever was available with limited rations. She gave him money for cigarettes and drinks and told him there was no hurry to get a job. So he settled himself at home, taking it all without a single thank-you.

Douglas sat huddled with him at the table afraid to know the details but asking anyway what had happened to John's face. He was told it was a drunken brawl with a Sicilian over a girl. John was in the hospital for a month. There was also a six-month internment in a prisoner of war camp in Italy. He said he was glad to be alive, but he did not say he was glad to be home.

The tension hung like a steel curtain between Grace and John. They avoided contact as much as possible, brushing past each other in the hallway saying nothing, averting their eyes. Grace felt her skin crawl each time he was near, and stayed in her bedroom as much as possible when home or stayed out at the pub or Nellie's house. It drove her crazy when she heard him and Harriet laughing together and would interrupt their fun by dragging Harriet away. The anger between them sung like a live electrical wire, and nobody could figure out what was going on.

"What is it between you two?" asked Effie one day. "You never have a civil word to say to each other. I dinnae ken what's go'in on, but I sure as hell would like it to be done wi'."

Grace finished rolling a skein of wool. "It's your imagination," she said quickly.

"I dinnae think so," said Effie, who looked at John reading the newspaper. "Can you tell me what's gawn on," she exploded, hitting the newspaper.

"What! Dinnae look at me. It's no ma problem. It's hers." He lifted the newspaper higher so he could hide his reddening face. The last few weeks had been unbearable at home. Every time he came in, he wondered if she would be there. Each time she came near him, he caught the distinct smell of fear and loathing that reminded him of being in the prison camp. He didn't know how long he could take being in the same house as her.

"Where's ma daddy?"

Grace placed the cup down on the table and looked at her daughter, ignoring the stunned silence from the other members of the family. "He went away," she said simply.

"Where?"

"To the war," she said impatiently. "C'mere, let me brush your hair." She snatched a hairbrush from the top of the sideboard.

"Is he no comin' back?" she asked innocently.

"No," said Grace curtly.

"Well, then, Uncle John can be my daddy, can't you?" She bounced towards him. "Can't you, Uncle John?"

He smiled and held his arms out to her. Grace wanted to take the hairbrush and whip his face into a froth of scars. Gripping the handle tight, she fought to control the anger by grinding her teeth. A habit she would develop more with each passing year and that would lead to insufferable headaches.

He looked towards her briefly and then looked back at Harriet. "Naw, I dinnae think so. You've got your nannie and gaga here. That's aw' you need."

Harriet looked at Effie and then Douglas before coming back to John. "But everybody has to have a daddy, don't they?"

Grace leaped forward with the brush in hand and pulled Harriet towards her. "I told you to come and have your hair brushed," she said, proceeding to drag the brush from the front of the child's hair to the back without stopping for the knots. Harriet cried out in pain and begged her to stop.

John said pleadingly, "Easy, Grace."

Grace could not stop and continued brushing until the hair was done.

Effie said, "What's got into you?"

Grace thrust Harriet into her coat and announced they were going out.

"Where to at this time o' night?"

"Nellie's," she said, slamming the door behind her.

—⟋⟍—

I wisnae there for that, thought Agnes, Where did she find that oot? She cannie go aboot tellin' people this. I mean, a story's a story, but this is no real. She can't be serious. What am I going to tell that lassie in Los Angeles. Her mother's a liar. I don't think that will go down well. She placed her hands over her eyes and shut them tight. All my life I told nobody about this stuff and here it is for everybody to read about. I don't know how much more I can take of this.

twenty-one

THE LAST PLACE she expected to see Kenny Napier was on her bus at eight o'clock in the morning. He was dressed for work in dungarees, an oilskin jacket, and work boots. His hair was immaculately combed and greased and his mustache neatly trimmed. She saw him waiting at the bus stop as they approached and quickly looked in the window behind the driver to see if her hair was a mess, straightening her cap. She rang up a ticket before turning around just as he was sitting down. She feigned surprise. "What are you day'in here? Aren't you supposed to be at your work?"

"I didnae ken you worked on the buses," he said with an Errol Flynn smile. Then his face grew serious. "I'm off to the hospital. Ma sister's been taken wi' the pleurisy."

"I hope she's gawnie be aw' right."

"Hard to tell. I'll find oot mare the day."

"You havenae been dancin' for a while."

"Naw, there's no been much o' the doe, rae, me," he said, smiling.

The bus lurched to a stop and she stumbled slightly towards him before standing upright again. An old woman, bundled up in heavy wool scarves, was having trouble stepping up onto the platform so Grace pulled her onboard and got her seated. She held out the money in her hand to pay for the ticket but Grace had already turned away to speak to Kenny again. "You're supposed to be working here, no chattin' wi' your boyfriend," shouted the woman. Grace rang up the ticket and threw the pennies into her leather satchel.

"Everybody's got an opinion," she said, holding the pole that connected the seats, leaning in towards him. "It's hard when you've got somebody in the hospital. I dinnae like they places myself. I had a wee yin whae was always in and oot."

"Is she aw' right now?"

"Naw. She died a few years ago," she said, looking out the window

He shook his head slowly and followed her gaze out the window. "I've got to go," she said hurriedly. "There's the inspector." She ran upstairs to collect some money.

Kenny was waiting on the platform as she came down. "Would you like a drink the night doon the fit 'o' the Walk? I can meet you ootside Woolies."

"Aye," she said breathlessly. "I can meet you at seven."

He nodded and gave a wave as he jumped off before the bus had stopped completely.

Grace knew from the moment she met him that she loved him. She had fallen in love before but it usually involved some confusion between love and lust. This time there was no mistaking. There was something in his dark, brooding nature that compelled her into his arms, to glide across the dance floor like the proverbial two peas in a pod. When she was in his arms, nothing could break the intimacy that settled her hips against his stepping in time to the music, not admitting one misstep or crushed toe. He wore his good looks and dark temperament like a well worn mahogany table, keeping his secrets discreetly hidden. She was the Queen of Hearts, willing to break the hearts of others but holding hers tightly in her hand. He loved her flamboyant nature and the magnificent sweep of her Rita Hayworth red hair curled about her shoulders. She longed for him each day and thought only of how to make him marry her. He said he fancied her but couldn't afford her.

"She's got a bairn," said his sister Cathy.

"She has not. She said it was deed. You dinnae ken what you're talkin' aboot," Kenny said indignantly.

"She's got another yin. Ask her."

He hesitated a moment and in the space of time he took to answer, he could only think of one thing to say. "So! I'm no gonnie marry her. I'm just gawn oot wi' her."

"Aye, you'll see. That's what they aw' say."

"You're talkin' shite," he said, turning his back on her, but feeling unsettled at this piece of news. After his father died during the Great War, his mother had raised the family of four girls and a boy by taking in washing. After the last war, it had become his responsibility to keep food on the table. He wasn't taking anyone else's burden, least of all with a child. To be truthful, he really didn't care much for children. They were a nuisance factor he could do without. The Victorian axiom of being seen and not heard was fine with him. Having been raised with sisters who fought and complained most of the time, he was happiest left alone in the company of men. Women found him attractive and called him Clark Gable or Errol Flynn, but he was prone to moods and hid the fact that he was woefully ignorant of anything approaching interesting conversation by remaining silent, having learned at an early age that his opinions didn't matter very much. In a later time, he would have been diagnosed depressive, but in movie parlance, he was the strong, silent type. In contrast to Grace, he was water to her fire. No one in their right minds would have thought of putting them together.

"You cannie go oot the night, Gracie. You've been away oot far too much these days. You have to hunker doon and stay hame wi' the wee yin. I'm no watchin' her anymare. You started wi' three nights oot a week and now you've got it up to aboot five. It's no good enough."

"But Kenny wants to meet me the night."

"Whae's this Kenny laddie you seem sae daft aboot?"

"I've telt you. He lives on Bernard Street."

"A Leither? What does he dae?"

"He works in the docks."

"Och, no, Gracie. No a docker. They're mare oot o' work than in it."

"It's aw' right, Ma. We're no gettin' married."

"At your age, there's no much left."

Grace rubbed Harriet's hair roughly with the towel, feeling irritated at the reminder that she wasn't getting any younger. "C'mon, Ma, just this once. I'll get her ready for her bed."

"You must be daft aboot this laddie if your wantin' to spend aw' your time wi' him. Why does he no come here to see you?"

"Aye, he will, but . . ."

"But what?"

"It's just that I havenae asked him, that's aw'."

"It's no like you to be gawn oot wi' anybody for long."

"He might no want to come."

"Well, if he disnae, he's no very serious, is he?"

"Aw' right, Ma. I get the message."

Grace struggled with what to tell him about Harriet. She never brought her up in conversation and if she invited him home, he would probably run away. "Maybe I can tell him it's my sister," she told Nellie.

"You're oot o' your mind, you ken that? He'll see through you in ten seconds flat and then you'll be in it because you lied to him. Do you no think he kens aboot it aw'ready. I mean, it's no exactly a well-kept secret, is it? Just tell him, Gracie, and see what happens. You might be surprised. I think he's daft aboot you."

"Do you think so? Whae wid tell him?"

"Aw, c'mon now, Gracie. You're being a bit stupid, aren't you. She's five years auld and you've been seen at the shops wi' her a lot of times. Everybody kens he's gawn oot wi' you. Somebody must have telt him by now."

"But I've been really good wi' him, Nellie. I havenae done anything wi' him and I havenae let him. I want to mirry him. I dinnae want to ruin ma chances."

"Well, what can I tell you, hen. Look at me. Seven months pregnant and a man I cannie stand. Just dinnae start the lying. You'll no get him day'in that."

❧

"It's my ma, you ken. She wants to meet you. I telt her it wisnae anything serious, but she said aw' the same, she'd like it if you came for a cup o' tea. She's no one for anything stronger, I'm afraid. But if you dinnae want to come, that's aw' right. I mean, naebody's saying you have to come if you dinnae want to."

"I cannie figure you oot. On the one hand, you're invitin' me, and on the other, you're no. Is there something here you're no tellin' me?"

"No, naw, it's nothing really. It's just that, well, I dinnae ken how to tell you, but I've got a wee ssss . . . well, it's just that, there's something I havenae told you yet," she sped up the last part as if her constipation had just improved.

"I ken," he said.

"Ken what?" she asked stupidly.

"I ken you've got a bairn. I've kent it all along."

"How come you never telt me?" she said indignantly.

"How come I didnae tell you?" he intoned. "That's no my job. That's yours."

"I wis gettin' to it," she said innocently. "I just didnae want to rush things."

"We've been gawn oot fur six months, Gracie. It's no rushin' things."

"Whae telt you?"

"My sister Cathy saw you wi' the bairn, but she wisnae the only one. Everybody kens, Gracie."

Grace opened and closed her mouth a few times like a fish. "There's nae bloody secrets in this toon. Everybody kens what's gawn oan. Your life is a bloody open book." She stamped down the street and then returned to stare into his face. "So where does that leave us now? Is that it, are we finished? Are you gawnie be runnin' doon the street now? If you are, you might get gawn now. Get on wi' it." She was clenching her fists and stamping around not looking at him. He stood casually against the wall of the fishmongers watching her.

"When you've finished," he said slowly. "I didnae say I wis gawn anywhere yet, and when I do, it'll be because I want to, no because

193

you telt me. I've kent aboot your bairn for months now, but I was waitin' for you to tell me. We're no serious, are we? Dinnae tell me you're gettin' serious. We're just havin' a bit o' fun, aren't we? Nothing's changed, has it?"

"Nothing's changed," she said petulantly. "I dinnae understand you. How could you no have telt me you kent?"

"Me! Tell you! I think you've got to be kiddin'."

Grace walked around in circles then strode back towards him.

"You're always so fucking secretive Kenny. You never talk aboot anything. So is this it? Are we finished?" she demanded.

He smoked his cigarette and slowly said, "When would you like me to come?"

She rushed towards him, causing him to stagger under her weight, kissing him deeply until he was wrapped in her embrace and forgot what it was they were talking about. He began kneading her arse and she moaned and thrust towards him. In the darkness of the cold, damp stone building, a fever that had been held in check for months erupted. She wanted him to love her, to be with her, to inhabit every part of her body, to be hers, and she wanted him now because tomorrow he might decide to leave. With her stroking him like a musician playing an instrument, singing softly into his ears, he was reminded of the stories they told at sea of the mermaids who claimed the lives of sailors. He was back on the dance floor melting rhythmically with each step, wanting with every part of his body to be inside of her. With the sweet smell of Evening in Paris in her hair and hands that easily found his aching, yearning muscles straining with desire, this fiery redhead was threatening to ruin his life with lust. "Wait a minute, Gracie. C'mon now." He pulled back and held her arms but she wasn't going to stop. She didn't care, there was only this moment, and she was going to take it, to take the risk and dissolve herself into him. "You cannie," she said breathlessly. "Come to me," she pleaded. Kenny heard all the alarm bells ringing, but his yearning knew no reason as he raised her dress lifting her onto him with strong arms used to hauling sacks of grain and cement, believing for that moment that this was all he had ever wanted in life.

Agnes had to get out of this straightjacket they called a seat. Her whole body felt as if it were being melded into the narrow chair she was in, and her feet felt too big for her shoes. "I've got to get up for a while," she said apologetically.

The girl slid herself out to the aisle. The man in front had reclined his seat to its maximum, and it was hard to stand up. Agnes tried to squeeze out but couldn't so she leaned over. "I'm sorry," she began. The sleeping head in front jerked up and glared at her. "I cannie get oot," she said.

He grunted and then pulled his seat up as she grabbed the back of it to support herself. He glared again and said, "Do you mind?"

"There's no much I can dae, son," she said without apology.

Once out in the aisle, the circulation in her legs returned, giving her pins and needles down her feet. She heaved a big sigh and looked at the girl who was making a face at the back of the man's head. Agnes pursed her lips and nodded her head before walking to the back of the plane. She squeezed through a group of people to the toilet and then locked herself into the tiny box. I look terrible, she thought, unusually critical of her appearance. She washed her hands twice just to make sure they were clean and then splashed some water on her face. She sniffed the hand lotion and blew her nose before patting her hair into place. "I have to get off this plane," she murmured.

twenty-two

DOUGLAS HAD DEVELOPED a talent for carving wood animals out of scrap wood he found down at the docks. He had quite a collection of dogs and cats, and he was now learning how to do horses by studying books on anatomy. The small tools in his thick hands looked like miniatures, but he found elegance in turning the wood and peace of mind unlike anything he had ever done before. It didn't seem to matter that he was out of work again. It gave him time to expand his knowledge. The afternoon of Kenny's arrival, he had just finished a Noah's Ark boat and was working on making a giraffe.

Harriet was on the floor marching the cats and dogs up and down the ramp when Kenny came in dressed to perfection in a suit and tie. Effie glanced at Douglas, who was sitting in his collarless shirt with suspenders draped around his waist. Effie had on her apron and brown rabbit slippers with the fluffy bobble on top. Grace had dressed in a brown suit cut tight across the bust and narrow in the hips that she had borrowed from someone at work who was now too fat for it.

Effie had the impression that everyone, except Kenny, was underdressed and they were furious with Grace for not telling her he was coming.

"Say hello, Harriet," said Grace, standing on the other side of the room next to Kenny.

"Hello! Whae are you?"

Kenny bent down to look carefully at the figures on the boat. "I'm Kenny. Nice cats and dogs." He straightened up and shook hands with Douglas, who continued his whittling, and Effie, who was self-consciously taking off her apron and fluffing up her hair. Grace coughed to shake up the atmosphere and offered a cup of tea. Kenny accepted and then looked around for somewhere to sit, opting for the couch next to Harriet.

Douglas, still whittling, asked, "Do you ken much aboot wood-work, son?"

"No, no much."

"Helps the mind."

Kenny clasped his hands together and leaned forward, picking up a dog to get a closer look.

"Gracie tells me you're in the docks?" said Effie, sitting down across from him. "Have you got much work these days?"

"It's aw' right, up and doon, but you get used to it." He ran his finger down the crease in his pants and found an imaginary piece of fluff to wipe off.

"Do you make any money doon there?" asked Douglas, flicking bits of wood shavings onto the newspaper that lay at his feet.

"It depends," said Kenny, looking around to see if Grace was coming back from the kitchen. Harriet played happily next to his feet, ignoring everyone.

"It's hard, I ken. I've been trying for months to find something and I havenae found anything yet. I've got a bum hip which bothers me a lot of the time."

"Och, dinnae start on that," grumbled Effie.

"What? I'm no day'in anything," he said. "Did you dae any fight-ing, son?"

"Aye, some."

"I got this in the first one." He banged his fist against his hip. "That was an awfy war."

Kenny nodded and said nothing, praying Grace would come back with the tea and let him out of there.

Effie stood up and went towards the kitchen. "Dinnae let him go oan aboot the war, son. He's like a broken bloody record."

"I am no," Douglas argued.

Grace was putting the teacups on the tray to carry through to the living room. "Why didn't you tell us he was coming?" hissed Effie in a low voice.

"I didnae ken for sure," said Grace, pouring water into the teapot.

"Fine mess we're in," said Effie, making sandwiches from potted meat.

"It never bothered you before," said Grace, picking up the tray.

Kenny studied the dog and found the details of the face exquisite. The puppy eyes were doleful as if waiting for an instruction.

Effie returned carrying the sandwiches. "Grace tells me you live in Bernard Street. That must make it easy to get to your work on time."

"Aye, missus, it does, but I dinnae like gettin' oot o' bed too early." He smiled at her.

"You should laugh mare often son, it gies you a good face. Did anybody ever tell you? You look like Errol Flynn?"

He laughed and shook his head. "Naw, Clark Gable."

He bent down towards Harriet. "How old are you?"

"Five and half, going on forty," said Effie.

"I'm no five and half—I'm gonnie be six. How auld are you?" said Harriet indignantly.

"Just like her mother," said Douglas. "She's got an answer for everything."

Kenny wrinkled his forehead and rubbed his carefully shaven cheek. "My Ma says I'm twenty-five but I'm really go'in on ten. Does that make me auld?"

"Oh, aye," Harriet responded. "You're aulder than God. That's what I hear my nana sayin' all the time."

Effie blushed and stirred milk into her tea. Grace offered him a potted meat sandwich and a cup of tea with sugar in it, which he drank and ate in silence. When he was done, Grace stood up and said they had to go.

"But he just got here," said Effie.

"Aye, well, there's a picture we want to see. I'll no be late." With her eyes she urged him to stand up. He straightened out his pant legs as he stood up and leaned forward to shake Effie's hand with a thick, firm grasp—it made Effie just a little uncomfortable.

Douglas put the wood down on the paper and stood up to shake his hand. "Awfy nice to meet you. She disnae usually let us meet her fellies. We hope you can come ow'er again."

Effie looked at him and wondered who her husband had suddenly turned into. "Awfy nice to meet you." He never asked anybody to come back.

"Oor Grace is a handfae, but I'm sure you can manage," he said jokingly.

"Daaad!"

"Can I come?" said Harriet.

"No, you're stayin' here wi' Nana and Gaga. I'll see you later," said Grace a little too quick.

"C'mere, hen. I'll make you another giraffe like the last yin," said Douglas.

Grace cinched up her coat and put on her hat with the feather sticking out the side and then pushed Kenny towards the door. "We'll see you."

Effie watched from the window as Grace, holding Kenny's arm, swayed from side to side in her high-heeled shoes. They made a handsome couple; she hoped he would be good to her.

❧

They went to see *Duel in the Sun,* and while Jennifer Jones was struggling with Gregory Peck, Grace was trying to figure out how she was going to get Kenny to marry her. She was now twenty-seven, well on her way to spinsterhood and her affection for him bordered on obsession as he filled up each moment of her waking life and her dreams. A year older than her, Kenny was not in a hurry to get married. He said he liked his single life because there was nobody to bother him except his family. "Anyway," he told her, "I have to wait until I can afford a wife."

She held his hand throughout the picture, rubbing his hard knuckles trying to soften them up. She thought he had done well with the bairn, had showed an interest, but it was hard to tell what way he would go. She continued rubbing his hand until he pulled it away with a tug and lit a cigarette. He ignored the sigh in the dark that came from Grace. No, he wasn't going to be around anytime soon for marriage, she thought. He's not as daft about me as I am about him.

After the film he said he would walk her home. Grace knew that a walk home with Kenny was more like a jog because he walked so fast, so she deliberately put her weight on his arm to slow him down.

"I've got something to tell you," she said breathlessly. Kenny continued walking. "You have to slow doon, Kenny. I'm oot o' breath."

He stopped completely. "If it's aboot your bairn, I dinnae want to discuss it."

"I wis . . . I mean, I wis . . ."

"C'mon, Grace, you've been up to something aw' night. What's go'in on?"

"I'm pregnant," she burst out.

"Och, Jesus buckin' Christ!" he yelled, twisting away from her and taking a few steps back. "You're jokin', aren't you?"

She wanted to swallow it, desperately sorry for what had just slipped effortlessly from her tongue, turn the clock back a few seconds and ignore that remark. It hadn't crossed her mind to go down that road until it came out of her mouth. She held her breath and began to tremble. She wanted to say, Sorry, I didn't mean it, which would have been the truth, but she stood hyperventilating on the cold pavement, shaking her head in an imitation of someone with palsy.

He took off his hat and threw it down on the ground. "Och, naw. You cannie be. We just did it once. That cannie be right. Whae else have you been see'in?" She winced as he grabbed hold of her arm and gave a slight twist. "Whae else have you been see'in?" he yelled. "Tell me it's no true, Gracie. I dinnae want to be comin' to you like this."

Grace bit her lip and struggled with the tears that were spilling down her face. "I havenae seen anybody else," she spluttered.

"No like this. Jesus fuck, Gracie. No like this." He bent down to pick up his hat and belted it against his leg, turned away and began walking up the street. "No like this," he muttered, then returned and took both her arms in a strong viselike grip.

"Dinnae," she pleaded, "you're hurtin' me!"

"Just tell me, Grace. Is this what it's come to?"

Through her tears she stammered, "I thought . . ."

"Thought what? I was a mug? Get oot o' my sight, woman! Leave me alane." He pushed her backwards and then began walking up the street quickly towards the pub.

"Wait! Dinnae leave me here like this," she yelled.

Kenny stopped again and came back, hissing through his teeth in her face. "You've bloody got me now, haven't you. I hope you're satisfied. It's what you've been angling fur aw' the time. Well I hope you're satisfied. But I'll tell you one thing—I'm no takin' that bairn o' yours. I've got nae money, so you might as well get used to it. I've telt you aw' along I wisnae ready for this."

"I'm sorry," she squeaked, holding onto his arm to stop him from leaving.

He pulled away from her grip and this time did not turn around again, leaving her to find her own way home, struggling with the consequences of her lie.

Agnes felt as if someone had placed a cast iron plate on her chest. She had missed this part of Grace's life, but somehow she knew this was the truth. Grace and Kenny had stayed together through the toughest times and it was no surprise to her that it had started this way. Grace had all but admitted to her later in life that she had trapped him because she was desperate. She didn't want to end up being an old maid. She had said that there were so many things she had been blamed for in her life, and while she had been guilty of many of them, she didn't deserve to end her years alone, living in a house where she was barely tolerated, raising a daughter she wasn't even sure if she loved. It wasn't the bairn's fault, of course, but she couldn't help herself. Every time she saw John, she wanted to separate herself even more from Harriet. The child obviously adored her uncle John, which made it almost impossible for Grace to relax at home when he was around. She wanted to protect Harriet, but she wanted to leave her behind also. Kenny was her perfect excuse even though it would take her a while to admit that this was the case.

twenty-three

"Canada!" exclaimed Effie. "Whae do you ken in Canada?"

"They're lookin' fur skilled labor in Ottawa, Ma, and I thought it might be aw' right if I went. There's nae work here worth stayin' fur. You always wanted fur me to get ahead, so I thought I would gie it a go. If I dinnae like it, I can come hame in two years."

Douglas stood next to John and took him by the shoulders. "Do you ken what you're day'in?"

"I think so. There's nae tellin' really, but I think it'll be aw' right."

"'Cause if you dinnae, we're no gonnie be here to pick up the pieces, you hear?"

"Aye, I hear you." He looked at his mother twisting her apron in her hands, giving him such a look of loss that he almost changed his mind. Then he remembered Grace, who had spat and cursed at him at every opportunity and knew it was the right decision.

"I dinnae understand you. You've no been hame five minutes and you're gawnie leave again. How do you think that makes me feel?"

"It'll be aw' right, Ma. I cannie explain it, but I have to go. It'll be easier for everybody."

"It'll no be easier for me," she said defiantly. "It'll no be easier for your faither, either."

Douglas sighed and came to stand behind Effie's shoulder. "You'll dae what you have to dae," he told his son "I've always held out hope that you'd dae better fur yourself. But why Canada?"

"I met some great lads when I was away and they telt me aw' aboot living there. It's a good life, Dad. I can make something o' myself there. I signed up for passage and I'll be gawn as soon as I get a date."

Effie sat down wearily in her chair and rested her hands on her lap. "Well, we'll have to see," although it wasn't clear what she was waiting for.

Grace told him good riddance to bad rubbish when they met on his way out the door.

❧

"I'm gettin' married!"

"Tae whae? That Kenny laddie? Well, this is a surprise. I thought he wisnae interested in marriage?"

"He's changed his mind."

Grace pulled her housecoat around her knees and sipped her tea, handing the bottle of milk across the table to Harriet for her porridge.

"When's it gonnie be?"

"Two weeks time."

"A bit of a rush, isn't it? Is everything aw' right wi' you?"

"Och, Ma, you dinnae gie me a chance, di you?"

"I'm just askin', that's aw'," said Effie defensively, scrubbing at the pot in the sink, thick with oatmeal.

"We're gonnie go doon to the registrar's office and gie our notice."

"Where are you gonnie live and what aboot that bairn?" She swung around from the sink. Harriet was blowing on her porridge.

"We'll find something. It cannie be that hard," said Grace, picking up the piece of toast and playing with it.

"So what aboot the bairn?" asked Douglas. "I hope he's gonnie take her as well. He's no much o' a man if he disnae."

"It's a lot to think aboot," said Grace, buttering some toast.

"Is she gawn wi' you?" asked Effie to make sure Grace understood the question. Grace was crumbling pieces of bread between her fingers and nails. Effie stopped drying the pot and stood still, staring at the bread crumbs. "What's go'in on?"

"Nothing!"

She placed the pot on the table in front of Grace. "You're no takin' her, are you?"

Grace looked up at Harriet, then down again at the bread crumbs she was sweeping into a pile. "I cannie," she said softly.

204

Effie's hand exploded across the side of her face and Grace fell sideways with the weight of it.

Harriet jumped down and Effie told her to go next door to Sadie's house. The child scrambled from the room but did not go to the neighbors. Instead, she sat with her ear to the door.

Effie's chest was rising and falling in great gasps. "You've got to be kiddin' me. This bairn is yours. You've done this to me before. I said that was it then, and I meant it. She's your responsibility, no mine. You think you're just gonnie walk. Well, you'll walk over ma deed body before I let you dae that. Whae do you think you are, comin' here like that? What kind o' mother just gets up and leaves the bairn behind? You're no right in the heed, you ken that. What kind of man is he? There's neither o' you any bloody good if that's your decision. You better no be thinkin' that, Gracie. I'm tellin' you, I'm no takin' it. She's gawn wi' you, make no mistake aboot that."

"But you dinnae understand . . ." Grace began to shiver. "Please, Ma, he winnie let me. I have to . . . If you knew . . ."

"Know what? You pregnant again? I wouldnae put it past you," she said dismissively, placing her hands on her hips. Douglas walked into the kitchen and put his hands on Effie's back. She turned ferociously "What dae you have to say aboot this?"

"You're no, are you, hen?" he said weakly.

Grace bit her lower lip. "If you knew. . . ." She fought every impulse in her body to lay it out on the table, to slice them apart and blind their accusing eyes with the truth. Her mother was almost bleeding from the eyes with pain at the possibility. "It wisnae like that."

"That's what you said the last time. How wis it? You come waltzing in here and tell us you're gettin' married but you're no takin' the bairn. What am I to think? What kind of dreamin' is that, lassie? I dinnae understand you."

"No, you dinnae, Ma, that's the trouble here. It's always Gracie's fault. Look at me!" She stabbed at her chest. "I'm gettin' auld and naebody wants me. Can you no understand what I'm sayin'?"

Effie stood solidly in the middle of the kitchen. "You could've had aw' the chances in the world, Gracie, and you've lumbered yourself at every turn. What can I say?"

"I tried, Ma." Grace sank to her knees on the floor and grabbed at her mother's skirt. Effie pulled away.

"It's no right, Gracie. I dinnae understand what happened to you. You could have had a hunner men by now to mirry. Tae choose one whae disnae want the bairn, that's no right."

Douglas turned to leave. Effie stuck her hand out and stopped him. "Dinnae think you're gawn anywhere," she accused. "You're in this as much as I am."

He looked at his daughter squirming on the floor and told her to get up.

Grace opened her mouth to scream, then sucked in some air, sobbing. "Didn't you have dreams once? Didn't you want something more?"

Douglas looked at Effie and then started to pick Grace up from the floor. "C'mon, get up. Dinnae be like that," he soothed. She began to rise, holding out her hands to her mother.

"I'm no pregnant, Ma. I'm really no. I want to marry him, Ma. He cannie afford her. If he could then he would, I'm sure aboot that."

Effie shook her head but stood resolutely by the table. "It's no just aboot money, Gracie. If it wis, nane o' us would have any bairns. Can you no see that?"

"But it's no fair," she screamed. "I didnae ask for this."

"No, you probably didnae," said Effie defiantly, "but you've got a responsibility here. You cannie just get up and leave."

"What aboot John? He's gettin' to go wherever he pleases and I'm left here wi . . ." Grace bit her lip and sat down on the chair. "I'm the one whae . . ." She stopped and began to sob more quietly.

"He's a laddie, for Christ's sake. This is got nothin' to dae wi' him," said Effie.

"Och, Ma . . ."

"C'mon, Gracie, pull yourself the gether. This Kenny laddie is no worth it if that's the way he's thinking," said Douglas, patting her back.

She pulled away from his touch. "Please, Ma. It's ma only chance."

"This is no a chance worth taking, Grace. Dinnae be gawn doon that road. There's nae luck in it."

"When do I get to be lucky, Ma? When is it ma turn?"

"We aw' make oor beds and have to lie in them, hen. That's aw' there is to it." Effie lifted the pot off the table and put it on the rack above the stove.

"I hate that stupid saying," Grace said feverishly. "I hate that and I hate you and all this stupid family. I wish I'd never been born."

The kitchen door opened as Harriet leaned against it, causing everyone to stop for a second. Grace stood up quickly and brushed past her at the door. "Where's Ma gawn?" she asked.

"Naewhare," said Effie, picking her up and plonking her into the chair. "I'll get you some toast."

—✺—

I blame him for it, thought Agnes, sadly. He was adamant from the beginning that he wasn't taking the bairn on and she was bloody stupid to accept it. Shaking her head to clear the tears then smacked her lips together vigorously, making a puckering sound. All this crying was getting on her nerves. In seventy-seven years of living, she did not remember feeling so bloody miserable. I dinnae ken what's wrong wi' me, she thought. I'm like a bairn wi' aw' this.

twenty-four

GRACE SPENT THE next few days avoiding everyone she knew. She wanted to swallow the lie like a spew of heartburn in the middle of the night. There were a dozen ways she could get out of this if she really wanted. She could tell him she had been pregnant and then had a miscarriage. Her period was late. She was coming down with the flu but none of them seemed right. Effie was right, even if she didn't want to acknowledge it. No matter how Harriet had arrived, she was still her daughter and her responsibility. She had wanted so badly that morning to tell her mother the truth. To tell her that Harriet was John's child and let him take the blame for a change, but she knew it would break her mother's heart, cripple her in a way that would ruin her for the rest of her life. Agnes had been the one who said above all else, their mother had to be protected from the terrible things that went on in their family. It was the unwritten law, and at that moment, every part of her wanted to know, why? Who wrote it? Nobody else seemed to be carrying the burdens.

He stood by the front door of the Eldo, smoking a cigarette holding it in his usual way, cupped in the palm of his hand. There were a few stragglers staggering out the door and on stage the band performed an impromptu jam session. They would have asked Grace to stay but she had been a shadow all night, missing the intros and singing without conviction. Al Spencer, the bandleader, asked her if she was feeling all right and received a wave of her hand. She saw Kenny standing at the bar earlier and her stomach bunched into a knot. It was now or never because she couldn't keep doing this.

"Did you get the banns?" she asked nervously.

"I got them posted. Are you still wantin' it?" he asked.

"Well . . . I wis . . . My ma . . ."

"If you're gonnie change your mind, that's aw' right wi' me," he said, almost too quickly.

"You're awfy quick to change your mind!"

"Me! It sounds like you're the one whae's day'in the changin'. Spit it oot, Gracie. I dinnae want to be standin' here for nothin'."

Grace swallowed hard. "My ma disnae want me to leave Harriet."

He took a drag on his cigarette. "That's aw' clear. I've telt you I cannie take her. If you werenae like this, I widnae be even thinkin' aboot it."

She chewed on the inside of her mouth. "Do you like me?" she said

"I widnae be wastin' ma time if I didnae," he responded gruffly.

"So you widnae ask me to mirry you even if I didnae have a bairn?"

"I dinnae think there's much to be said aboot that now."

She felt the sawing of her heart in two as she pressed her hands together to keep herself from trembling. She was the girl to have a good time with but not someone to spend the rest of your life with. Kenny wasn't any different from the rest of them.

"Your ma has to understand it's no easy," he said, stubbing out his cigarette with the heel of his shoe. "I just cannie be takin' on another man's debts."

"She's no a debt you can pay off," said Grace. "I didnae get her on credit," she spat, then regretted her outburst. He would never understand and even if she told him the truth, he would push her aside so fast she would collapse forever, truly become the one thing she despised. Every time she looked at the child, she saw her brother. She was burdened with it for the rest of her life even if she chose to leave the child behind—it would always be hers and John's. This debt had put her in a jail she could never escape from.

She couldn't go back on what she had said. It wouldn't matter to him that she was telling the truth—it would only matter that she lied. Maybe in time he would soften up and Harriet could come live with them. Effie would probably be all right taking her for a short time until they got on their feet. Since she wasn't pregnant, she would continue working and they would be all right for money. He would see how much she loved him. Everything would be fine.

❧

Kenny's mother was appalled he was getting married because she was pregnant. "Do you ken it's yours?" Her long dour face looked like a bloodhound.

His sister Cathy stepped into the conversation. "She's called Gracie and she's a singer. She's got a bairn already."

"You hud your wheesht." Kenny leaned towards her and gave her a swipe on the leg. "The bairn's no comin'."

"How did she react to that one? She's no much if she agreed to it," said his mother, shaking her head.

"Her ma's agreed to take it," he lied.

"You winnie be able to buy any mare fancy suits if you get married," piped up Betty, his middle sister. "She'll take aw' your money."

"Shut up, you," shouted Kenny. "You've got a big mooth, you ken that?"

"Aye, maybe so, but it's you whae's in trouble."

"So what are you gonnie dae, son?" asked his mother.

"I have to marry her, Ma. If she's pregnant wi' ma bairn, I've got to. I dinnae think she's been wi' anybody else since we started gawn oot, so there's no much else I can dae."

"Do you like the lassie?"

He nodded his head slowly in an arc that wasn't clear if it was a yes or a no. "We go dancin' the gether and aw' that."

"You both better learn how to dance better," said Betty.

"And what aboot the money? I'm worried for the lassies. It's no been easy since your faither died," said his mother, coming back to the old story of how she worked hard to keep everybody together when times were difficult.

A contemptible feeling of responsibility crept upon on him. "I ken that, Ma. You'll be all right, I promise."

"Just do what you have to," she said quietly. "You'll do what's right."

Effie and Douglas sat long into the night talking about what to do with Grace and Harriet. "I just cannie understand how she could walk oot and think we're gonnie take care of her. It's no right. When you and I were gawn the gether, you kent aw' the time aboot Agnes. But this laddie's askin' a lot and she's off her bloody heed acceptin' it."

"Things was different in they days. It wisnae the same way."

"It's aw' the same. You have a bairn, that's it," grumbled Effie. "She says she just wants a chance, but every chance she's got she's managed to make a hash o' it. We're no gettin' any younger and that bairn is only five and half. She says it's only for a wee while until they get on their feet, but I dinnae ken. Something tells me he's no gonnie change his mind aboot this and we'll be dealin' wi' her for the next fifteen years. I could be deed before she decides to take her."

"Aw' she wants Effie, is a man to marry her," said Douglas softly. "She's twenty-seven and it's no easy. I'd say we let her go. Keep the wee yin. We dinnae have much to say to each other unless it's got something to dae wi' the bairns. I dinnae mind. It's been that way a long time. This hoose'll be empty withoot a bairn in it."

"So you want me to gie her the benefit of the doubt?"

"Aye, I do. Gie her a chance to see if she can work it oot. The bairn'll be better off here anyway, at least until Gracie gets settled."

"Just dinnae expect me to be day'in aw' the work."

"We're aw' in this the gether," said Douglas, picking up his whittling knife.

Grace didn't know whether to laugh or cry when Effie told her she would keep Harriet. "But it's only till you find your feet, you ken. You're gettin' what you want, but I hope it's the right choice."

Kenny looked like Clark Gable and he danced like Fred Astaire, but no amount of two-stepping was going to make this marriage work though Grace clung to the notion that somehow it would all change once he really understood how much she loved him. Her yearning carried itself on each aching note she sang and each person listening longed for their lovers in the same way. But this amount of love was impossible to return. It was duty that drove him and love was a notion that belonged in celluloid dreams. If ever there had been any passion, it had died at the news of her phantom pregnancy.

On the morning of the wedding, Grace ironed her best green two-piece suit and beige rayon blouse. Douglas polished her shoes, and Harriet helped her take out the curlers that she had slept fitfully in the night before. The bags under Grace's eyes were proof enough that she had not slept well. Weary but excited, she smudged some Pan-Cake makeup on her face to cover up the dark shadows, then smiled at herself in the mirror. "Here goes nothing," she said. Grace ran around the house picking up clothes to stuff in the suitcase as Harriet watched. Since the scene in the kitchen, she had been anxious every day waiting to see where Grace was going. Still she had to ask. "Where you gawn?"

"I'm away to get married."

"Can I come?"

"No, not the day." Grace absently gathered up the hair curlers and put them into a bag, searching under the chair for the pins that held them in place.

"Are you gonnie have a poor-oot?" asked Harriet.

"Och, no now, Harriet, I've got to get gawn," said Grace impatiently.

Harriet stood directly in front of her. "Why can't I go?" she demanded defiantly. "You said you widnae take me. You told Nana you had to leave me behind, I heard you."

Grace pushed her to one side. "No now, Harriet! I'm gonnie be late." She stood on her tiptoes to look in the mirror above the fireplace, rolling her lips together to even out the lipstick. I'm a mess, she thought, almost in tears.

"Dinnae be like that wi' the bairn, Gracie. She disnae ken what you're day'in."

"I ken that, Ma, but I'm gonnie be late, and I look like who-flung-dung. He'll be aw' perfect as usual and I'm lookin' like something the cat dragged in."

"You look fine. Just calm yourself. If your gonnie start the life like this, it's no gawnie be good."

Harriet picked up John's doll and sat on the couch, pursing her lips and holding it tight. "I hate you," she said to Grace.

"You'll get over it," said Grace sharply.

Effie held her arms out with wool in them. "C'mere, hen, help me wind this. Just hold your wee arms oot and I'll put the skein on them, but hold them straight. I'll make you a nice jumper wi' this."

Harriet did as she was told but all the time watching Grace who was still gathering her things.

"Aw' right, I think I'm ready," Grace said, brushing her skirt down with her hands and putting on her peek-a-boo shoes which showed off the dark part of her nylons. "Will I dae?"

"Aye, you'll dae," sighed Effie, glancing up.

Effie told Harriet to hold her arms straight again. Harriet forgot her rage for a moment. "You look nice, Ma. Aw' sparkly."

"Aye, aw' sparkly is the right word, hen. You'll dae, Gracie. Just remember to send us a postcard. You better be gawn. Keep up your arms, wee yin, the wools aw' droopy."

Douglas shuffled in from the kitchen. "You're off?"

Grace hesitated for a moment. "Aye, I suppose," she said, then bent down to kiss Harriet on her cheek. She looked surprised and so did Effie. Turning to Douglas, she said, "You look after her."

"What's that supposed to mean?" said Effie. Douglas nodded his head solemnly.

"Nothing! I'll see you soon," said Grace picking up her suitcase. "Cheerio."

"Cheerio yourself," said Effie, rolling the ball of wool.

Outside the door, Gracie stood with her cheek to the cold plaster wall and breathed in deeply. She blinked several times to keep her eye makeup from running. Putting her head down towards the staircase, she shook her head and flicked the spilled tears off her cheek before running downstairs and out the door.

Harriet watched from the window until her mother's black and white checked coat disappeared round the corner.

That poor bairn, thought Agnes. She always got the short end of the stick. It's no wonder she ended up wi' aw' kind of problems. Whenever she was spoken about, Gracie always said he wisnae ready and then eventually it got too late. Harriet was Effie's problem, then she became mine. Agnes stared at the crack of light that was creeping under the window shade, wondering where Harriet was now. Years before she had moved to York with Effie, then she married a plumber when she was sixteen. They divorced after having two children and then she took to the drink. Agnes and William had tried to help but she wanted none of it. Agnes felt the problem was she never belonged anywhere and always carried the burden that Grace had left her behind. At one point she had actually said it was something she did, which Agnes told her was a lie. She was never able to get past it, from what she could see. It's a bloody shame, she thought, and once more wondered if there was something they could have done to help it turn out differently.

twenty-five

WHEN GRACE DECLARED her wedding vows, she promised with all heart that she would be a good wife to him in sickness and in health. Kenny said he would be her lawfully wedded husband. They got drunk with Nellie and Kenny's friend Rab before he took her back to a dingy room with putty-filled cracks facing a granite stone-walled alley strewn with years of detritus and swarming with rats.

They furnished the room with a table and two straight-backed chairs, a bed and a wardrobe, and a shelf that Kenny had built on the back wall to hold their pots and cans of food. In the dim light of the forty-watt bulb hanging from the ceiling, Grace undressed quickly and left her clothes lying on the floor as she jumped into bed, complaining of the cold. She shivered under the thin army-gray blanket that scratched her face and called on him to hurry up. Kenny took off his suit carefully and made sure the creases of his pants were perfect before hanging them in the wardrobe he had bought in exchange for some cans of corned beef that had "accidentally" fallen off a boat. He sat down on the edge of the bed taking his socks off slowly, then lay down on the narrow mattress with his back towards her. On their first night sharing a bed, Kenny fell asleep with Grace weeping beside him. It took five days of him turning his back and five nights of her pawing and begging before he agreed to make love to her. Within two weeks of her wedding day, Grace was pregnant. It was six weeks before she knew that the lie had turned into the truth. She didn't know whether to laugh or cry. It seemed all she had to do was open her legs to a cold draft and she was pregnant.

From the start Kenny wanted his tea at five o'clock when he came home, not eight o'clock when she finished her work. He expected his clothes to be clean and the house kept tidy. Grace took a job at Crawfords Biscuit factory, standing on a production line eight hours a day packing biscuits into tins for export to places she had never heard of. She complained to anyone who would listen that men had no right expecting their wives to go to work then come home to cook and clean. One old woman told her, "Get used to it, hen. It's aw' you're gonnie get."

Kenny told her to stop singing at the Eldo. He didn't want anyone thinking they his wife was for hire. Grace was flattered by his jealousy, but felt as if she were being suffocated by his control. She said she would cut it down to only one night a week. Kenny told her not now, then she cried. "It's over, Gracie. Tell them you're no comin' back," he grumbled.

Andy Galbraith told her it was a pity. "Naebody can sing like you, Gracie, but if your man says you cannie, then I suppose that's the way it'll have to be. You've got to respect that."

Grace took her wages for the week before and swallowed her resentment like an Askit powder without water, trying not to choke on the bitterness.

Grace never said she could cook, so dinner each night consisted of cans of soup, peaches that came from the docks, and bread. Eventually, he would eat at his mother's house four nights out of seven.

She took up sewing and dressed the room in brightly colored fabrics she had picked up at the rag shop and the discount material store. She made a matching cotton bedspread and pillow covers to hide the hideous gray army blankets on the bed, and found a couple of armchairs covered in brown corduroy at the secondhand store.

Kenny worked night shift when he could get it, which left Grace alone and lonely with only her sewing to keep her busy. Out of desperation one night she visited her mother. No sooner was she in the door when Effie asked, "When are you coming for the bairn?"

"Aye, nice to see you too," said Grace, putting her coat down and going into the kitchen to make some tea.

Effie was knitting. Harriet was watching her grandmother's needles moving fast back and forth. "Can I knit like that, Nana?" she asked.

"Aye, one these days," said Effie distracted. "So what's it gonnie be, Grace?" she yelled through to the kitchen.

Grace yelled back. "No the now, Ma." She poured some tea from the teapot that had sat on the back flame of the stove all night and came back into the living room. "I'm oot workin' aw' day and he's in and oot o' work wi' they damn strikes that have gawn oan." She set the cups down by the side of the fireplace. "Can't you just keep her a wee while longer?"

Effie's needles stuttered to a stop and she looked up. "Och, gie me a break, Gracie! Where have you been aw' these years?"

"It's no me, Ma," whined Grace. "I've tried but he isnae interested. C'mere," she said, reaching out her arms for Harriet.

Harriet sat on her grandmother's lap and buried her face in her neck.

"You shouldnae expect it," said Effie.

"You're gawnie have a wee brother or sister," Grace said, patting her stomach, trying to make things better.

"Again," said Effie. 'When are you gonnie stop?"

"I dinnae want one," said Harriet defiantly, getting down from Effie's lap. She stood in front of her mother. "When am I coming to your house?"

"Soon," said Grace. Harriet raised her eyes to the ceiling. "I've heard that one before," she said. "

"You see what you've done," said Effie. "Do you have an answer for her?"

None she could think of.

Kenny's family treated Grace like a leper and his youngest sister, Cathy, called her "the trollop fae Granton." Occasionally, they would go visit his family on a Sunday, but there was little conversation between Grace and her mother-in-law, a dour heavyset woman with no teeth who doted over her only son and said he didn't look as if he were eating enough. Grace knew he was eating well enough but it was from his mother's pot, not hers. Eventually, the topic turned to children.

"Do they pregnancies go on an awfy long time?" his sister Cathy asked Grace. "I widnae like to be pregnant that long. It must be hard."

"What are you talkin' aboot?" questioned Kenny.

"Nothing much," she said gravely, giving Grace a superior look with her head thrown back.

Grace stared back at her and said nothing, sipping her tea through a tightly held jaw and a curled fist ready to strike out at her sister-in-law's smug face.

"Leave the lassie alane," said Peggy, the oldest sister. "You dinnae ken what you're talkin' aboot half the time."

Grace swallowed her anger and managed a grateful smile in Peggy's direction. "It disnae matter how long you're pregnant, it always feels like too long."

"True," said Peggy, who had had her first one the year before.

"Aye, and even longer to come oot," said her husband, Bob. "She was aw' day trying to get oor Sarah oot. But now look at her—she's great, she is." He held up his daughter who giggled as he rolled her from side to side.

Kenny looked at Grace who had given up any pretense of being happy and with a toss of her head towards the door, she stood up. He put down his cup and stood to follow her.

"You're no gawn already, are you?" asked his mother. "You've just got here. You dinnae have tae leave yet."

"I've got to finish the cot the day," he said weakly before pushing Grace out the door first.

"Well, we'll see you in the week," she said. "Take some of that cake. You look like you could use it."

He declined the offer and said goodbye. Knowing glances went between his sisters but Grace ignored them. "I'll see you," she said to no one in particular.

Each weekend Kenny did a little bit more to their furniture, sanding and painting the shelves, the table, and the chairs. Now he was working on the crib they had picked up from the secondhand store on Leith Walk. It was pitted with little teeth marks, chewed on by dozens of children with sharp teeth, and it took him a whole day of sanding to get it evened out until it looked brand new. He painted it yellow because Grace said it would match everything. The table and chairs had been stained brown and the bed had a patch work bedspread made from scraps of orange, brown, and beige clothes. Kenny had to admit that for an ugly hole in the world, she had managed to make it look reasonable, but there was no disguising this hell-hole they were in. As soon as the work became steady, they would move to a bigger place.

Grace asked if she could go to the night school to learn how to do proper dressmaking. She could earn some money when she was home with the bairn, she said. "It'll only cost two pounds ten for the whole course. It'll be good to learn it. I've started day'in aw' right wi' the wee bits and pieces."

"Dinnae be daft, woman. It's aw' we can dae to keep the rent paid here. No the now."

Slamming the pot down on the table, she yelled, "That's aw' I ever hear. 'No the now. No the now.' When does it come later? It never comes later, does it? Always 'No the now.' I've been hearin' that aw' ma life. When do you think we can dae something better? I'm sick o' this. Everything I dae you tell me 'No the now.' I'm tryin', Kenny, but you're no helpin' me. What I do wi' my money is my business."

Grace was always looking for ways to spend the money, in his opinion. She had already spent last week's wages on new cups and plates, and he could have sworn she was wearing a new blouse, but she said it was an old one. He didn't know if she was lying or not, but he wasn't taking any chances. He'd seen too many clothes lately that he hadn't seen before. He had warned her about getting credit, but she told him as long as she was working and he was giving his mother a pound a week, it was her business what she did with her money.

"I cannie gie it to you and that's that," he roared. "Get out of my sight."

For a week he didn't speak to her or touch her. On the following Saturday he asked for his tea and she told him she was too busy. He should get it himself. She did not expect the slap across the mouth that came next. Grace recoiled from the blow and then picked up the black cast-iron pot that hung in the grate. "Go on," he dared her as she lifted it above her head. "You cannie, can you?" He was taunting her, begging her to do something, but instead she lowered it and put it back. It was the biggest mistake of her life.

Agnes had known about the violence from Effie. But Effie's position had been clear. Grace had made her bed and now she must lie in it. There was nothing to be done. Grace had a knack of making the wrong choices and paying the price for it. Agnes was grateful to be gone from the ravages of her sister's life, but felt burdened by the guilt, as if she could do something about it.

In they days women put up wi' a lot mare than they do the day, thought Agnes. It was they poor bairns I felt sorriest fur. They always got the short end o' the stick.

Alison had said children always pay for their parents' mistakes. It was the old sins of the fathers stuff. But Agnes said it didn't have to be. People made choices they lived with. For Alison, she had made a choice to give her daughter up for adoption and it was the right one at the time. Now she was trying to patch up the mistake by giving the girl her family history. Alison said she didn't want her making the same mistakes even though she had lived a completely different life from everyone else in the family.

twenty-six

IT WAS ANOTHER girl. Grace wondered where the justice was in that. She was named Alison because Grace liked the sound of it. On the day she was born, Kenny's sister Cathy came to the hospital to bring Kenny some sandwiches. Idling outside in the corridor, Cathy said, "She must have been awfy late."

"I heard you say that before. What do you mean?" asked Kenny, holding the sandwich in mid air about to take a bite out of it.

"Have you considered how long it's been since she told you she was pregnant? It was before you got married," said Cathy, folding her arms and crossing her legs as she stood against the wall.

"I dinnae ken what you're talkin' aboot," said Kenny. He bit down on the sandwich and started chewing on it.

"Och, sure you do," laughed Cathy. "If she'd actually been pregnant when you got married, she would be ten and half months pregnant. That would be a record."

Kenny swallowed and then began to choke as he said, "Och, that's shite. You're no makin' any sense."

"Just think aboot it. I think you've been had."

He swallowed the bread and tried to clear his throat. "Och, leave it alane, Cath. What is your problem?"

"It's no ma problem, son. It's yours," she said.

Kenny saw the doctor going into his office and put down the sandwich. "Excuse me, doctor. Grace Napier is ma wife. Can you tell me how late she was wi' the bairn?"

The doctor looked puzzled for a moment and then said, "You must be mistaken, Mr. Napier. Your wife was not late. This was a full-term baby. If anything, it was born two weeks early."

Kenny thanked him and turned to Cathy, leaning against the wall, smiling. "See, I told you so," she smirked.

Coming in close to her face, he hissed, "You're such a cunt, you ken that? You've had it in for Gracie since you first met her and couldnae stand the idea that she was takin' me away. She's ma wife, fur Christ's sake."

"Aye, well, it disnae look like she came by that one honestly, does it?"

"Whae do you think you are? You're no exactly lily white yourself, are you?"

Cathy's mouth shut tight. "Choke on that sandwich again. You might start to see things clearer," she said before walking away.

"Aye, go," he shouted. "You ken what I'm talkin' aboot."

He could not see the tears that were dripping down her face as she marched defiantly down the hallway. She had given up her baby when she was sixteen because her mother told her there would be no place for it at home. Since then, she was determined that no man would ever get within five feet of her again.

"Is it mine?" he demanded as Grace adjusted herself on the cushion they had given her to sit on.

"What are you talkin' aboot?" she grimaced, looking around at the other women in the ward.

"You ken," he said. "You werenae pregnant when you telt me you where." he hissed, trying to avoid attention from the other women in the ward.

Grace waved him away and sat up a little straighter, biting her lower lip against the discomfort of her swollen perineum and the lie that was about to be found out. "Whae have you been talkin' to," she demanded in a hushed tone. "It wisnae like that. I thought I wis, then I wisnae." She reached out towards his hand that was lying on the bed. He withdrew and sat back on the chair. "And then I wis again," she said weakly.

"But you werenae pregnant when we got married?" he asked. "You kent that before we got married, and you didnae say a thing to me. Did I no deserve to ken? What were you thinkin'? I had to hear it fae ma sister Cathy. She thinks I'm a bloody joke."

"I wanted you to be my man. I thought if I telt you you'd no be interested anymare, so I just let it be. It's oor bairn, Kenny. I shoulda telt you, but I was feard you'd send me away. I'm no tellin' you any lies now, I promise. This is oor bairn, that's nae different than before."

"How could you, Gracie?" he said softly.

"I dinnae ken," she replied sadly. "I'm daft aboot you. I've always been daft aboot you. Everybody telt me I didnae stand a chance, but I didnae care. I wanted you. You're a good man, that's why I wanted you. Can you no understand that?"

He shook his head and scraped his top teeth over his bottom lip and chin. "I just dinnae understand how you could have lied to me, Gracie. It wid have been easier if you'd telt me the truth."

"I ken that, but it disnae change anything, does it? We can still make a go of it," she pleaded. "It's no changed anything."

"I dinnae ken if I can trust you anymare."

"I did it because I love you," she cried.

The women in the next bed and across the way were all ears as one whispered to the other, "Shame."

❧

Grace sat by the fire staring at a cold grate, blocking out Alison's cries by singing to herself. She had also managed to ignore the banging on her door until the door was almost caving in and the sound of her mother's voice stampeded behind the thumping. "Gracie, you in there?"

"What the hell!" said Effie as Grace opened the door, standing in her nightgown and housecoat, her hair frizzed at the ends, bags under her eyes heavy with the color of bruises.

Grace stood with a blank look on her face, opening the door just wide enough for Effie to pass through. "Come in."

Effie had an urge to hold her nose as she stepped into the room. Alison was standing in her cot, her nappy fallen down around her ankles, streaked brown, crying for someone to pick her up. A bottle lay next to her, empty. The room stank of urine and tobacco smoke mingled with coal dust. Dishes lay in the sink with dried-on food and the bedsheets lay gray and twisted. "Good God, woman. What's go'in on here?" exclaimed Effie as she took in the scene.

Grace dragged on her cigarette and shrugged her shoulders.

Effie went straight to the crib and picked up Alison. "This bairn smells o' shite. What are you thinkin', Gracie? This is no to believe."

She laid the child down on her lap and took off the eye-burning nappy, carefully wiping the excrement from the creases of her behind with the dry part because she had a severe rash. "Och, you poor thing," she cooed. "This isnae fair, is it?"

Grace slouched across the room to the pile of clothes in the corner to retrieve a cleanish nappy.

"You're no puttin' that on the bairn, are you? It's still broon fae aw' the other shites you've left in too long." Effie took the baby to the sink and ran the tap, splashing cold water on her bottom, which made her cry even louder. "There, there, hen. It'll be aw' right." She searched for a dry towel and found a clean dish towel under a pile of dirty dishes, wiping her carefully. "You're a bloody mess," she said to the child, "your Ma disnae care." She wiped her carefully then wrapped her in a blanket. "You've got to dae better than this, Gracie," she said.

She warmed up some water in a pot and stood the bottle in it while walking the baby back and forth across the room. "Where is he?" she demanded.

"I dinnae ken," said Grace softly.

"What do you mean, you dinnae ken? When does he come hame fae his work?"

"He disnae."

"Fur how long?"

"I dinnae ken. A long time," she said wistfully.

"This is no right," spluttered Effie. "This is no right at aw'. Look at you." She reeled round on Grace. "When wis the last time you went to the bath? You're stinkin'. This is no like you, Gracie. No like you at aw'." She rocked the baby up and down in her arms, leaving her bottom naked to the room. "Do you have any cream for her bum?"

226

Grace was staring at the fire again. "Gracie! I'm talkin' to you!"

Effie searched the table for cream and found a tube unopened. "For Christ's sake, get a grip."

"He left," intoned Grace.

"Left where?" Effie put the baby down on the bed and attempted to open the window. With a shove of the bottom towards the top, it opened a crack, sending cold stale air into the room.

"I dinnae ken," said Grace, poking at her slipper with the iron poker.

Effie picked up the crying baby again and took the bottle from the hot water.

"Get a fire on, for Christ's sake, it's like winter in here."

Grace poked the grate with the poker and started to roll up newspaper balls as if in a trance.

"How can you no see this, Gracie?" she asked, looking at the cot mattress stained yellow and brown. The front of Alison's bib was gray and slimy. Clothes lay scattered on the floor and Effie could not distinguish between dirty or clean. The brown and orange bedspread had turned the color of mud. The baby ate hungrily and then fell asleep. Gracie managed to get a fire going with the small pieces of coal she had left. Effie placed the sleeping baby on the corduroy chair. "Right, then, let's get a start here," she ordered, pulling Grace to her feet.

Within an hour she had stripped the bedding and put it outside the door, washed the dishes, and swept the floor, hauling Grace around with her as she stuck rags in her hand to wipe surfaces and dry dishes. Grace followed in a trance. Effie was frightened to see her daughter like this. "When was the last time you had anything to eat?" She looked emaciated.

"I dinnae ken," Grace answered.

"Is there anything you do ken?" asked Effie. "Let's go. You're go'in' doon the bath hoose. Where is he?"

Grace was staring at the fire. "His mother's. He's no been hame for weeks," she said in a distant voice and then began to cry. "I'm pregnant again, Ma. I dinnae ken if he's comin' back."

"He'll be back, aw' right," said Effie, picking up Alison and putting her into a warm sleeping bag. "I'll make sure he does, if it's the last thing I do."

~×~

Effie waited outside the dock gates. As Kenny came through wheeling his bicycle he was surprised to see her and gave a grave nod as she approached. "We need to talk," she said curtly. He nodded again and walked on.

"I dinnae care what your differences are," she began, "but that bairn needs a faither and you're it whether you like it or not. If you've got any sense of decency, you'll take yourself hame and look after them. She's no well, do you ken that?" she added forcefully.

Kenny shook his head. "She's no been well for a very long time," he said sarcastically.

"Aye, well, she's your responsibility now. Do you want the death o' a bairn on your conscience?"

He stopped wheeling the bike and looked at her sharply. "What do you mean?"

"I mean, I found the bairn sitting in her ane shite the day in a freezing cauld room wi' a mother whae's gone daft in the heed because her man is no comin' hame."

"I didnae ken," he said weakly.

"Well, you ken now, don't you? You better get hame," she said, softening her approach. He turned the bike around and walked down Bernard Street. "Just gie her time," shouted Effie. "She'll be aw' right. You'll work it oot."

~×~

Kenny may not have shared Effie's optimism when he returned to his wife, but Grace began to believe that he really loved her after all, even if he hardly said a word except when it concerned the child, his meals, or his washing. Within a few weeks things had settled into a routine again. Grace took care of Alison, kept up with the washing and learned to do some simple cooking. As her mother would have said, she could now boil water successfully.

The room had become a prison cell and she felt trapped within its walls. The once bright fabrics had faded to a wash of muddy textures punctuated by nicotine stains and the smell of pissy nappies. The outside toilet was a midden neglected by all the tenants because none wanted the job of cleaning it first. To escape the squalor, which was worse than anything she had known on Portland Place, she took Alison for long walks in her pram and usually ended up at the shops on Junction Street or Leith Walk, dreaming of all the things she could not have.

The sign in the window said credit available. The woman in the store told her to call the Provident Insurance Company. If she took out insurance, she could take out loans against it. It was that simple. The Provi man would come every Friday night to collect the payments for the insurance and the payment for the credit. There was nothing to think about. It had helped her family out on many occasions. Grace thought it would make their living situation more tolerable, and it wouldn't cost them that much each week. She presented the idea to Kenny.

"You've got to be jokin'. That's the auldest game in the toon. Before you ken, we're up to oor necks in it. We're no gawn intae debt fur things we cannie afford." He shoved the plate of food away from him and stood up. "Dinnae get me started, Gracie."

"But it's no really. We've got an insurance policy already. We can just take oot a wee bit fur a new couch. Look at the auld yin, Kenny. It was worn oot before we even got it. The bairn could use some new claes, and I've got nothin' to wear wi' this yin I'm carryin'."

"Where di you think I'm gonnie get the money to pay for it? I dinnae need the aggravation. Forget it."

"I wid get a job if I could."

"Nae chance o' that, is there?" he growled. "We're no gawn intae debt, and that's final."

"Aw' the mare reason then, don't you think?" said Grace, pushing some minced beef and mashed potato into Alison's mouth.

"Nae mare, Gracie. Dinnae ask again."

A few days later, Kenny was dressing for a Sunday afternoon stroll in the park. Grace put on her old maternity dress with sweat stains under the armpits and put a ragged hat on Alison's head. Kenny stood at the door and viewed them both. "You're no gawn oot like that," he asked.

"I dinnae have anything else that fits," said Grace. "If we could just get a wee bit to help, it would make a big difference."

Kenny sighed. "One dress, that's aw'," he warned.

She took out a policy for five pounds and was to pay it back at one shilling and sixpence a week. It wasn't much, but it would be a help. Within a day, she had bought a new dress for herself, a new pair of shoes, a romper set and a cardigan for Alison, and some new underpants for Kenny. She began to sing around the house again and even played bouncing games with Alison. Her effervescent mood rubbed off on Kenny, who started to look around for somewhere better to live. They had to get out of the basement room or he would go mad.

He found a three-room flat on the top floor of a building that had once housed the soldiers of Mary Queen of Scots overlooking the Water of Leith, and next to a granary populated by rats and mice who made regular visits to the flats next door. The steps of the spiral stone staircase were worn smooth with centuries of wear and the plaster on the walls flaked off in chips that left ghostly shapes on the walls in the dim light. They shared a toilet with the man next door but it felt like a mansion to Grace. A real living room and a bedroom with a kitchen felt like luxury. It was next to the unemployment office and she joked it was handy for Kenny signing onto the dole. He shivered at the thought he might actually need it.

Grace returned to her sewing. She kept busy making clothes for Alison and prepared for the new baby by knitting a new shawl. The old one had been used by three babies and was now yellow and hard with too much washing. Kenny made a small bed for Alison and cleaned up the cot. The child was beginning to walk, and he took delight in her attempts to climb on the furniture. They began taking walks out in the park on Sunday afternoons to listen to the band, and once in a while, if he had done particularly well during the week at work, they went to the club on a Saturday night, where Grace would get up and sing.

He listened to the sultry sounds and regretted he had held her back. It was her radiance that had attracted him in the first place, but it was also the odor of sexuality that buried him in a possessive spirit. She sang to every man when she was up there as if they were the only ones. Everyone out there wanted Grace, but nobody could have her the way he did. She was his wife. He was Kenny Napier, the most handsome dresser in town, but when she sang, he was simply Grace's man. When she sang, it was the only time she looked fully alive.

When their son was born, Grace thought her luck had changed. She called him Michael, after the archangel, and hoped he would take care of his mother in her old age.

For Kenny, it was another mouth to feed and a body to clothe. He worried how he was going to pay for it all, especially since Grace's five pound loans kept rolling over from one to another. They had a new couch, the children were dressed in new clothes on Sundays, but the strikes in the docks over the arrival of container boats made the loading and unloading by men seem unnecessary. The trade unions called the men out, leaving them stranded at home, aggravated and bored, not to mention penniless. As often as possible, Kenny took work on cement boats, grain boats, and coal boats because they were the dirtiest jobs and paid the most. He also worked night shifts, sometimes working back to back thirty-six hours in a row.

The contrast between their living conditions and the way they dressed was the difference of five pound credit notes. It made Kenny crazy that the money was being paid out of his wages every week, but he also didn't discourage it because he didn't want his bairns looking raggie arsed like the rest of them around him. Grace made an offer.

"I'm gonnie get a job."

"Dinnae be daft. Whae's gonnie mind these bairns?"

"I'll work it oot."

"You'll spend just as much payin' fur somebody to mind the bairns as what you'd be gettin' in wages. That's just daft."

"Daft or no, I'm no livin' like this for the rest o' ma days," she said,

"It's a sight better than a lot o' people huv, so dinnae go gettin' any fancy ideas," argued Kenny. "You're off your bloody heed."

"My mother went to work, so can I," she said defiantly.

～✦～

The work was two pounds ten shillings for four hours a day at the paper mill, running huge sheets of jute through a machine that flattened it out into paper. She paid the woman up the street five shillings and sixpence a week and was out the door before she asked Kenny if it was all right.

Her credit bills did not disappear, but her argument was that it was part of her wages and it went towards paying for them. She took out a Provi check for seventy pounds, and Kenny said he was heading for a heart attack just thinking about how that was going to be paid back. Grace told him not to worry and went out to choose a new three-piece suite for their living room and a new double bed. In the grimy setting of their rooms, they looked overdressed, but Grace saw it as a sign of upward mobility. She kept the plastic on to keep it from getting dirty, and Alison slid up and down it to hear the squeaking sound it made.

At the Dockers Social Club one Saturday night, Grace spent most of the night at the microphone. Her theme song became "I'll Be Lovin' You, Always." Harry Mackintosh slid up to Kenny and told him if he wanted "to gie her up, they were aw' waitin'." Kenny didn't think much of the joke, especially when she got carried away and danced with anyone she wanted. "She's a guid dancer, Kenny," said Davie Wishart. "You're a lucky man."

"Aye, she's good, aw' right," laughed Kenny, trying to be polite. "Just watch your taes," he joked. "That's sharp heels she's got on." He tossed her an aggravated look and a shake of his head towards the front door.

Grace ignored his signals to go, then wrapped herself around one of the dockers known as Seldom. He was a tall lanky man with slick brilliantined hair. He got his name because he was seldom seen when it was time to buy the drinks. The dockers were used to nicknames like Milky Bar (he had blonde hair and looked like the Milky Bar kid), Huddybox (at the docks always asking people to hold the box, I'll be back in a minute), Special (he was fond of Carlsberg Special beer), and Errol, which happened to be Kenny's nickname because they liked to pretend he looked like Errol Flynn.

"Aw' right, Erroll," shouted Seldom as he winked and held Grace tighter. Kenny waved him away and waited for the music to stop before grabbing Grace fiercely around the arm and marching her towards the coat room.

He started the minute they were outside. She was behaving like a whore. She was showing him up. She said he was jealous. He was daft. He was stupid and, her usual comeback, "It's aw' in your heed."

He pushed her towards the bus stop and sat in silence on the way home. Once inside the house, she pushed him out of the way and he whacked her head, causing her to stumble. "Leave me alane," she yelled batting at the air with her arms as she backed up.

"With pleasure," he said before slumping into the chair.

"Stop your girning," yelled Grace as Alison clung to the side of her skirt, begging to be picked up. She was in the middle of changing Michael's nappy and pricked herself with the pin. "Shite!" She pulled back and Michael began to cry.

Kenny shaved the underside of his bottom lip with his top teeth and said, "Take these bairns away oot for some fresh air. I cannie stand hearin' them anymare."

"Why don't you get your fat arse doon to the docks and see what's gawn on. You've been sittin' aroond here like your trapped in a dungeon. How slow does a 'go slow' have to be? Any slower, then we're aw' gonnie be deed. There must be something you can dae. They cannie be gawn slow aw' this time. It's been three bloody weeks."

"Where did you get these new shoes?" he asked, looking at her feet.

"I've hud them for a while," she said dismissively.

"You never did. They're new. Where did you get the money for them?"

"It's ma money. I can dae as I want wi' it."

"It's no your money. If you're up to your auld tricks wi' the Provi checks . . ."

"Och, leave it alane. You're getting' aw' worked up aboot nothin'."

"You're oot o' work, Gracie. Do you no understand that?"

"I'll get another yin."

"Don't you understand, woman. There's nae work oot there. We had mare gawn on during the war than we have now. You're off your bloody heed if you think we're gawnie be aw'right. How are we gonnie pay the rent? We're aw'ready two weeks behind."

"It's no ma fault. You're no bringin' anything hame. What else are we supposed to dae?"

"You've been runnin' up aw' these Provi checks. Are you daft or something? We cannie keep day'in this, Gracie. I just cannie keep livin' like this."

Grace ignored Alison, who had gone from whining to crying, bringing Michael into the fray with the yelling.

"Archie Turnbull just got kicked oot o' his place because he'd been oot for three months. Nane o' us are day'in well. Dinnae make me oot to be the bad yin." Alison continued crying for attention. "Wid you pick that bairn up, for Christ's sake."

"You pick her up, she's your bairn as well. I'm sick o' aw' this and I'm sick o' you."

Kenny exploded from his chair and lurched towards the table where Grace stood next to Alison. Every impulse in him wanted to annihilate her. The rising frustration and anger threatened to engulf him in flames. He curled his fist and swung it towards Grace, who instinctively moved to deflect it, taking the blow on her shoulder, staggering under the impact with Michael in her arms. Kenny grabbed Alison with one arm and wiped the snot from her face and put her down again. She instantly grabbed hold of Grace's skirt again and howled even louder.

"Are you satisfied now?" screamed Grace. "You've got us aw' in hysterics. Is this the way you're gonnie go on, Kenny? Is this aw' we've got to look forward to?"

Everyone in the room was crying except Kenny, who had stopped his rampage, breathing deeply and defeated. "We cannie go on like this," he said desperately.

"You're a fuckin' eedjit, you ken that. You've lost it. We're no the problem, you are. And I've got news fur you. I'm pregnant again."

"Naw! Naw! Jesus buckin' Christ. Naw."

Reading it like this, Agnes didn't believe that Grace deserved half of what she got. These were awful times and everybody was in debt one way or another. Agnes had been in York with William and had heard from her mother that Grace was having a hard time. She also knew that Grace hardly ever saw Harriet and had more or less abandoned her to Effie and Douglas. It was not Agnes's business to interfere in her sister's affairs, but maybe I should have, thought Agnes.

twenty-seven

SHE HEARD THE sound of coins slapped down and his orders before he left for work. "Get yourself ow'er to the chemist and see what she has to offer. Get rid o' this thing. There'll be nae mare bairns in this hoose or I'll see myself in the gas oven." Then the squeaking of his bike as he pushed it through the front door, slamming it behind him.

Holding her aching breast in one hand, she pushed back a strand of hair that had fallen across her eyes with the other. Grace sighed and got up from the kitchen table, shuffling her slippered feet towards the living room, which doubled as a bedroom. After putting on her girdle and stockings, she squeezed herself into the orange and blue housedress that hung on the back of the door, then put on her coat and scarf to hide the hideous orange hair color that had failed to dye correctly.

Alison and Michael were still asleep, and she left them in their beds to go across the way to the chemist. Alison had been up half the night with her asthma. Grace had tried rubbing Vick's on her chest, and giving her margarine rolled in sugar to ease the bronchial tubes but it didn't help. Kenny had cursed the lot of them for the inconvenience and rolled over back to sleep.

Her feet tripped on the staircase, causing her to jump the last three steps of winding granite stone. For an instant, she thought about throwing herself down the stairs, but with my luck, she thought, I'll only end up with bruises.

She hurried down the cobbled street and headed for the bridge to the other side of the Water of Leith where the chemist shop stood next to the rag and bone merchant. The wind was a typical northeasterner blowing straight in off the Firth of Forth, which blew her sideways as she crossed the square.

The chemist shop had been there for almost forty years and Miss Thomson, the chemist, had been there the same amount of time. Grace was there more times than she would have liked because Alison had developed bronchial asthma and Kenny was always getting cuts and bruises from the docks.

The sound of the shop bell clanged unmercifully as Grace entered the shop shrouded in the mysteries of Latin names heavily embossed in white ceramic on mahogany boxes. Above them, rows of glass bottles in dark green, blue, and purple contained liquids that could kill if wrongly used. Hanging over everything was a smell that seemed to the untrained nose to be camphor or turpentine, which made Grace's nostrils prickle as she walked inside.

Miss Thompson, a tiny woman with gray hair tightly held in a bun at the back of her head, was placing packets of Askit headache powder into the glass cabinet in front of the counter and turned to see who had entered. Grace tried to smile but couldn't, then she began to cry.

Closing the glass door, Miss Thompson approached Grace, putting out her arms towards her. "There, there, hen. What's got intae you the day? C'mere, sit yourself doon," she said kindly. Grace sat down on the chair reserved for the elderly or the sick waiting for their prescriptions to be filled. "Just stay there, and I'll be right back." She disappeared behind the partition separating the back of the shop from the front, and took a glass of water, slipping something into it before presenting it to Grace. "Here, drink this, it'll calm your nerves. Tell me what's going on."

"I'm pregnant, Miss Thompson," she blurted out, "and he disnae want it."

"That's too bad for him," Miss Thompson said. "He'll have to take his responsibility just like any other man."

"But it's no like that," cried Grace anxiously. "He telt me I've got to get rid o' it."

Miss Thompson had been bending over Grace as she spoke and now stood up straight. "I see," she said slowly.

"No, you dinnae," said Grace a little too defiantly. "He says he'll put his heed in the gas oven if I dinnae get rid o' it. What I'm a supposed to dae?"

"Are you sure you dinnae want this?"

"I cannie dae anymare bairns," she wept. "I've got enough and we cannie take care o' the ones we've got. I've got to dae something."

"How many have you missed?"

"Just the one. I've had enough to ken when I am."

Miss Thompson, watched Grace's face for signs of doubt. She'd had many women in her shop trying to get something to help them get rid of it, and many of them were young girls barely out of school. But this was different. There was no signs of hesitation here. "If you're sure," she said.

"Please, Miss Thompson, I dinnae ken what else to dae."

"Wait here, I'll be a few minutes." Returning five minutes later she gave Grace a small paper cone.

"Take six of these this morning and six again tonight and see if that does it. Don't take anymare. I cannie promise you it'll work, but you can give it a try."

Grace took the cone slowly from her hands and handed over the two and sixpence Kenny had left behind on the table.

"Keep your money. You'll need it," she said.

Grace tried to smile again, but instead took her hand. "Thank you," she said.

⁂

In the kitchen, Grace unrolled the paper and stared at the yellow pills for a few minutes. He was willing to kill himself but she wasn't, and it made her sick just to think about swallowing them. She filled the black enamel kettle with water and set it to boil on the back of the stove. She would have given anything for a hot bath and a bottle of gin right now. Nausea rolled over her as she lurched for the kitchen sink to avoid throwing up on the floor. The bitter burning in her throat was the reminder that she had to stop the continual assault of unwanted pregnancies that had made her life hell. She would have to get rid of this one way or another.

Alison came into the kitchen without her pajama bottom on. "I've peed ma bed," she said sorrowfully. Grace sighed and swore under her breath. Suddenly sweating and nauseous, she sank to the kitchen floor, clutching her belly then threw up. Alison, horrified at the sight of her mother on her knees, backed up to the kitchen door, ready to run. "I'm sorry, Ma," she began. "I didnae mean it." As Grace stayed on her knees, Alison stood rooted to the floor, afraid to move in case she got in more trouble, her legs beginning to freeze from the draft under the front door.

When Grace composed herself again, she said "What are you standing there for, Alison? Go get your brother." The cramps had not subsided but she was able to stand. When Alison returned with her brother, they were both in tears. "What are you greetin' for?" asked Grace. The children didn't know how to respond. She took the wet pajamas from Alison and dressed her in dry clothes then changed Michael's nappy and took them to a neighbor round the corner.

Annie McCall was a good woman who was raising four children by herself after her husband had gone down with a whaling ship shortly after the Second World War began. It didn't matter to her if she had two more children to look after. In her mind, one or twenty, it was all the same. Grace wished she could have a small percentage of her optimism and strength.

"What am I gonnie dae?"

Annie, a staunch Catholic, told her, "God will decide, Gracie. Just watch oot fur yourself. He's lost in the drink, and it's you and the bairns that have got to be careful. It's none o' ma business, but he's belted you too many times and I'm worried aboot they bairns. I'll take care o' them as much as I can, but you've got to get him straightened oot."

"I tried to get him to gie up the drink, but he disnae understand." Grace wiped her nose with the handkerchief Annie held out to her. "He says it's the only pleasure he's got left. He's aw' I've got, Annie.

I ken there's times when I could kill him, I really could, but where else am I gonnie go? If there wis a God, I wouldnae have to keep day'in this. How much do I have to keep payin', Annie?" She began weeping again. Never in her life had she wept as much as she was doing now.

"He shouldnae have asked you to dae what you've been tryin' to dae," said Annie severely. "It's no right. I dinnae care what his excuses are."

"I'm gonnie have to have this bairn, Annie. What am I gonnie tell him? He's gonnie go off his heed."

"You tell him the truth. You both got yerselves intae this, and you're both gonnie have to get on wi' it, regardless."

"I dinnae want another one," she sobbed, clutching at Annie's hands. "I've made such a hash o' the ones I've got and I'm just gonnie make it worse again, I ken I will. I cannie dae this. I just cannie."

"I ken, hen," she said soothingly, rubbing her hands. "But you've got to. You've got nae choice."

After taking the second dose of pills she waited three more days. Nothing changed. Kenny had not spoken to her in three weeks except to ask if it was gone yet. Each time, she shook her head in the negative. Two months later, she had tried laxatives, quinine, gin, a hot bath, and sniffing turpentine. Finally, in desperation, she took a piece of wire and gingerly poked it into her vagina, causing her cervix to bleed but not enough to dislodge the child that was gradually growing to full size.

She was five months pregnant and Kenny had not put his head in the gas oven. However, he had drowned himself in alcohol as often as possible.

❧

Grace stood awkwardly at the door next to the bowl of holy water. Wondering if she was supposed to sprinkle herself with it before she entered, she nervously dipped her middle finger into the water before sprinkling it over her chest in a flurry of movement that did not relate to the sign of the cross. She didn't believe in God and thought it was probably blasphemy for her to be entering here.

240

The interior of the church was dark with only a small light over the cross at the far end of the nave. Creeping down the side aisles, she pulled her headscarf further down her forehead. If anyone were to see her, it would be difficult for her to explain her presence. Churches were for weddings, christenings, and funerals. She never considered that they were also a place for the desperate.

That morning there had been blood on her pants. A sense of hope mingled with dread washed over her as she stuck her fingers into her vagina to see if there was any more. There was only a thick, smelly mucus that clung to her fingers, and then, like the wings of a butterfly, she felt a light flutter inside her. The sensation she prayed would never come. "It's still there," she gasped. It was like a whisper inside her, a reminder that life will fight back at every opportunity. She sank down onto the wooden toilet seat engulfed by the smell of other people's piss and shit sticking to the bowl, suffocated by the dank walls, gulping back the isolation and hopelessness that clung to her like a life raft.

Thickly, through the fog of her misery, she heard Michael screaming in the house and rushed to the bedroom. Alison was trying to take Michael's finger out of the metal catch on the side of the cot, pulling it as he screamed. Pushing Alison to the side, she released the weight of the folding catch from Michael's finger. Alison was breathing hard and making a wheezing sound, crying, "It wasn't me, Ma. He got his finger stuck. I was trying to take it out."

For several dull moments, Grace heard the children screaming and crying, but it was as if she were wrapped in cotton wool. I'm the one who's stuck, she thought, until the rush of grieving children swarmed over her and she collapsed onto the floor, clutching them both. "I'm sorry," she sobbed, rocking back and forth with the children on her lap. "I'm really, really sorry," holding them as if she never wanted to let them go.

It frightened Alison to be held this close while her mother made keening sounds like a wounded animal. Scared by the intensity, but craving the warmth, longing to be held and fondled in the softness of her mother's arms, she couldn't breathe with her cheek pushed up against the buttons of her mother's cardigan and Michael's snotty face inches away on the other side. While Alison squirmed to get down, Grace held her even tighter, making it impossible for her to catch even one deep breath. After a few minutes Michael stopped crying, Grace stopped sobbing, and there was only the sound of Alison's deep whistling breath.

⹓⹓⹓

Grace hastily bowed, knelt, and put her hands together. "Why, God?" she implored, squeezing her hands together. "Why do you keep gi'en me this?" she murmured, her knees beginning to tremble. "Can you no see? Please, if there is a God up there, you have to help me. What have I done to deserve aw' this?" As she asked that question, a voice that said she deserved to be miserable resounded in her head. In response, she whispered through nose-clogging tears, "I tried, God, I really, really tried this time. I know I've sinned. I know what I've done wrong. Are you listening, God?" she said urgently, and then a little more angrily, "Are you listening? I'm sorry. I'm sorry." Her sobs saturated the front of her coat.

The silence in the church was shattered by the dropping of a metal cup. The hollow clang and bounce on the stone floor startled her, and she remembered her mother telling her that God's business is his own business and he's not interested in anyone else's. Grace rose from her knees and turned to go. Like a spirit, a priest appeared by her side. "Is there anything I can help you with?" he said kindly. "I couldn't help but notice you."

Grace looked at him blankly and shook her head, the tears streaming down her face silently. "It's too late," she moaned and started to move away.

"How do you know?" asked the priest, gently laying his hand on her arm.

There was a sharp pain in her belly and she stumbled, clutching the front of her coat. A screaming began in her head, "Not here! Not now!"

242

The priest steadied her and led her to a pew, where he sat her down. She looked up at him, searching his soft holy face for some understanding. "Is it possible to ask for forgiveness?" Her body shook with the uncontrollable grief that had been buried below all the holding on. Through everything that had happened before with her father, with John, with the death of Rita and the birth of Harriet, she had never felt such tremendous loss of herself. It crippled every part of her that knew how to hold on, to continue in life no matter what. She didn't want to do it anymore. She was tired, so tired from getting up each day and carrying on. If she could, she would lie down and let the silence of this church take her away.

The priest said, "We all want forgiveness, my dear, but what is it you want forgiveness for?"

"Everything," she said.

The pages hung limply in Agnes's hand. Grace wanted forgiveness and Agnes supposed that's all any of us want. Flexing her hands and feet she shifted her body in the narrow seat. I keep asking myself where she got all this, she thought, and I still don't know. I knew a lot o' this, but I never knew about Gracie go'in to the church. We were never allowed to go to a church. Ma would have none of it. Annie McCall was a good woman and the only one who had any time to give. If it wasn't for her, I hate to think what would have happened to the bairns. Alison was never out of her house. I suppose she must have asked her about things. Annie McCall had died with Alzheimer's thinking her daughter was her mother. But she did know Alison briefly. She remembered her as a girl and insisted they sing a song together. When Alison left she told her daughter that wee Alison had come to visit and brought her chocolates. It was one of her last lucid moments.

twenty-eight

"C'MON, ALISON, I HAVENAE got aw' day to stand here." Grace stood swaying with Michael on her hip, clutching the banister at the top of the stairs. In spite of her pregnancy, she looked emaciated, her face was sallow and pitted with spots, her hair hidden under a headscarf because it was falling out. Effie stood in the open doorway leading to her flat, watching Alison slowly clamber up the stairs, stopping on each one to gasp another breath.

"Come in for Christ's sake, Gracie. You look bloody awful. Gie me that bairn." Effie snatched Michael from her arms and gave Grace a slight push towards the living room. "C'mon, wee yin," she called to Alison, "you can make it." Alison kept her steady pace up the stairs until she was standing next to Effie. "Well done, hen. You did good."

"Can I go oot to play later, Nana?" she said, breathing heavily.

"We'll see. Let's go in and see your auntie Agnes and your cousins before we say any mare."

Effie's living room was a squall of children. Agnes had come for a visit and brought her two children Scott and Shirley. Harriet was bouncing Shirley on her lap. "Come see the bairns," she called to Alison.

"Well, what do we have here?" said Agnes. "This cannie be Alison. You've got awfy big since the last time I seen you."

"She's no as big as me," piped in Harriet.

"Naebody's as big as you," laughed Agnes. She reached over to touch Alison's hair. "You aw' right, hen?"

Alison nodded and moved away to sit next to Harriet who had gathered Shirley up in her arms and held her like a sack of potatoes. "Dinnae drop her," admonished Effie, who was that minute putting

Michael down on the floor. Scott, a shy boy, had stayed close to his mother, clutching his blanket and sucking his thumb.

"Whae's he?" asked Alison, pointing at Scott.

"That's your cousin, Scott," said Agnes. "Say hello, Scott."

"Why's he sucking his thumb?"

"Maybe he likes it," said Agnes, amused at the direct ways of the child. "Did you no suck your thumb?"

Alison shook her head. "No, But sometimes I pee the bed."

Agnes started to roar with laughter. "You're quite a character, aren't you?"

"Aye, she's a character aw' right," piped in Grace. "You look like you're in your element."

"And you look like something the cat dragged in. What the hell you been day'in wi' yourself?" She looked haunted. "Harriet, you be the big sister and take these bairns ben the hoose and play wi' them for a while. Gie your mother and me a wee break," she said gently.

Harriet held onto Shirley and took Michael by the hand. "C'mere, wee yins, let's go play." Scott clung to his mother's side and she gently pushed him away towards Alison, who took his hand and led him to the bedroom.

Grace sat down opposite her but had not taken her coat off.

"Are you no stay'in?"

She pulled off her headscarf and Agnes gasped. Grace's rich auburn hair, which had always held a good curl, was flat and in strands. "Good God, Gracie. What's go'in on?"

Agnes looked towards Effie, who shrugged. "She's no been lookin' efter herself and naebody can say a damn thing. He's got something to dae wi' it. He's gi'en her aw' kind o' bother."

Agnes's eyes begged Grace for an explanation. "Ma, can we have a cup o' tea?"

"I suppose so," said Effie, getting up to make it.

"How long you here fur?" Grace asked Agnes.

"A week. William wanted to come but he was needed at the works. He's just had a promotion to supervisor."

"I suppose he's day'in aw' right then?"

"Aye, no bad."

An awkward silence followed until Agnes stood up and came to sit next to Grace on the couch. "What's this aw' aboot, Gracie?"

"I cannie tell you."

"Cannie or winnie?"

"It disnae matter which, does it?"

"This is no right, Gracie. Look at you. You're a bloody sight. I've never seen you like this before. When is this bairn due?"

"In two months."

"In two months! Jesus Christ, you dinnae look mare than four months pregnant. Are you eatin' right?"

Grace gave a weak laugh. "Aye, for two!"

"What is he day'in aboot it?"

"It's no his to worry aboot."

"Och, dinnae talk shite. Look at the state o' you. I just cannie believe you'd let yourself go like this."

Grace gave a big sigh and searched in her bag for her cigarettes, lighting one up and blowing the smoke towards the ceiling. "I'll be aw' right," she offered.

"I bloody hope so. How's the wee yin do'in? Her asthma is no sae good."

"She has her good days and her bad days. There's no much they can dae for her."

"You should come doon to me for a holiday. It'll dae you good."

"Aye, when we win the Pools. Where's Dad?"

"Gawn doon the library. He couldnae stand the noise. I cannie say I blame him. So what's been gawn on wi' you? Not a bloody drop o' ink on paper since I last saw you. Did you think I'd gone away forever?"

Grace dragged on the cigarette some more and shook her head. "I've never been good wi' letter writing. I did send you a Christmas card last year."

Carrying a pot of tea and cups with a plate of biscuits she had baked that morning, Effie returned in time to hear the last remark. "Aye, you're lucky you get a Christmas card. She disnae come here very often either. Better get some of this down you before the bairns come back in and eat it aw'. They're makin' quite a noise in there. Harriet must be entertaining them."

Grace finished her cigarette and stubbed it out in the ashtray on the table. "I've been busy."

"We can aw' see that," said Effie, sarcastically.

"Your bairns are lookin' braw. Must be good air doon there," said Grace, changing the subject. "Do you like it there?"

"No bad. The people are aw' right, and we've got a nice wee hoose near William's mother, so we're do'in aw' right. The bairns are nae bother. Scott's like his dad. Quiet. Shirley reminds me o' you when you were a bairn. Full of energy. She's the one whae wears me oot. How aboot your two?"

For the first time in months, Grace began to relax, as they swapped stories about the children that made them laugh, grateful that Harriet had taken them out of the room and given time for some peace and quiet. Effie took biscuits into the bedroom to them and left Agnes and Grace to catch up. Agnes worried about the condition of her sister but stayed off the subject. It wouldn't make any difference what she said. Grace's life seemed to be set.

❧❦

Grace was seven months and three weeks and was standing in the queue at the butchers' when the blood began dripping down her legs. The woman behind her noticed it first and thought she had begun her period. Leaning in to tap her on the shoulder, she whispered urgently. "I'm sorry, hen, but you're bleedin' doon your legs."

Grace looked down and, seeing the pool of blood at her feet, collapsed against the woman. Without another word, three women and one of the butchers had placed her on the stool that the butchers used to cut pieces of meat on, while the other butcher ran to get his van so he could take her to the hospital. Grace remembered the smell of the meat and the faces that gathered around her, but the rest was a haze of movement as she was taken from the shop to the van and into the hospital. She remembered the nurse taking her clothes off and the doctor examining her; the shiny steel of the operating room, the clatter reverberating in her head. Hospital platitudes that were supposed to soothe her didn't work.

When she awoke the first question she asked was, "Is it dead?"

"We're doing all we can," said the nurse.

"It's aw' right," murmured Grace.

"We'll see in a while if he's going to be all right," she added kindly.

He looked like a small bird with an oversized head, thin arms and legs glowing red, showing his arteries pulsing visibly. You could have placed him in a small basket. He meowed after the doctor gave him resuscitation at birth and they placed him in an incubator. Grace did not see him for three days as she lay in a fever, conscious of the second gaping wound in her abdomen, refusing food and drink.

Kenny arrived at the hospital three hours after she had been placed into intensive care. He stood outside the window that looked on the babies in the incubators and refused to believe that this malformed child was his. When the nurse insisted it was, he began to cry.

Kenny sat by the side of the bed. "Have you seen him?" he asked. "Doctor's dinnae ken what happened.

"It was you!" Grace spat. "It was aw' they things I tried to dae because o' you!" she hissed.

Kenny moved back in his seat and then stood up to go. He put his cap on his head. "I've left the bairns wi' Annie."

"Dinnae hurry back," she said, closing her eyes and letting the tears dribble down the side of her face.

Halfway up Arthur's Seat in the middle of Holyrood Park, Annie stopped to take in the view and to allow Alison to catch up. She said the fresh air would be good for Alison's chest and a little greenery now and again was good for the mind.

Alison marched on cheerfully behind Annie, clambering upwards towards the summit, hardly stopping to take a breath. For a tenement child, it was a strange universe, as if a door to the whole world had been thrown open. On the way up they passed sheep grazing on the slopes and dogs out running with their owners. She could see fields and churches, boats and warehouses, cars, trains, and roads. The water sparkled in the distant, and the big cranes in the docks looked like birds in a dance with each other. The clouds were close enough to touch, and in the middle of the park stood a great palace that belonged to the queen. Alison felt the world was hers on this hillside.

Annie brought sandwiches and they sat down on the grass, surveying the railway station in the distance and the pillars on the Carlton Hill. "They call that the Disgrace of Edinburgh," said Annie, pointing towards it. "They ran oot o' money. Typical, don't you think?" Alison nodded her head as if she fully understood and munched on her sandwich.

"Did you ken Donald's name was because my auntie Betty says there wisnae troosers big enough to fit him?" she said seriously.

Annie threw back her head and roared with laughter. "That's a good yin. 'Donald, Where's your Troosers' I think they forgot the kilt part." She started to sing the song "let the wind gang high, let the wind gang low, through the streets in my kilt I'll go, and a' the lassie shout hello 'Donald, where's your troosers.'"

They walked past the Palace of Holyrood, pink faced and wind clean, to get the bus home.

Donald was lying outside in his pram, taking in the sunshine. "He's aye quiet, lying there like a tattie," said Annie, running her fingers over his face. "That bairn needs to be picked up mare often." She brushed his cheek with her hand and he turned his face towards the movement but she noticed his eyes held no focus. Annie wiggled her fingers in front of him. There was no response. Pulling her fingers across the space in front of his eyes, he did not follow but remained passive. "This is no right," she murmured. She clapped her hands softly, causing a slight breeze, but still he did not move. "This is definitely no right," she said, picking him up and taking him upstairs.

Grace sat in the kitchen, sewing two pieces of rags together into a small bag. Her hair hung in tufts like dried grass. Her apron was splattered with grease from fried bread.

"Do you ken this wee yin is no see'in properly?" said Annie, holding him up.

"He wis fine this morning," said Grace, putting the needle and thread down and reaching her arms out to take him. "I didnae notice anything." She was staring into Donald's face as she cradled him.

"I'm tellin' you. Look at this." Annie did the finger test again and although Donald blinked, he did not follow her fingers.

"But he's only three months auld. Maybe he's no supposed to see that well."

"Aw, c'mon, Grace. You dinnae believe that. Wake up. You're no aw' there." She looked around the kitchen. "Have you seen the state o' your hoose? It's a mess, Gracie. You've got to dae better than this." She waved her arm around the room at the dirty dishes piled in the sink and on the table, washing lying in piles on the floor and nappies unwashed. The dust and grease were settling into the grooves of the diamond pattern on the linoleum floor. The house stank of neglect. "Look at these bairns. Michael's nose has been runnin' for weeks, and Alison needs to get oot mare often. What's he sayin' aboot this?"

"Nothing."

"Well, I'll talk to him. You just take care of this yin."

Alison stood quietly by the door, watching her mother's face turn from indifference to confusion. When she had come home from the hospital, she spent all her hours in the kitchen with nothing to say, only responding when she was asked something, and then she was annoyed as if she didn't want to be interrupted. Her father was hardly home anymore, so she had to help with Michael. He was on the floor playing with a wooden car Douglas had made for him. Annie picked him up and then took Alison by the hand. "C'mon, you two, let's go. I'm takin' them to ma hoose." She was almost out the door when she turned around. "Dinnae let this go, Gracie. Get up that hospital and make an appointment. Leave a note fur that man o' yours to come and see me for the bairns."

Grace flashed her hand across Donald's face and he did not wince. She gripped him tighter and pulled him towards her, gazing into his face for signs of recognition. There was none. "What have I done?" she whispered anxiously.

❧

The doctor was a balding man with an unlined face who introduced himself as the head of pediatrics. He coughed a few times before asking them to sit down. "I have the results of the tests we did on Donald," he announced before riffling through file in front of him. "It seems there was more damage than we originally thought at the time of birth."

Grace held her breath and Kenny cracked his knuckles.

"While technically he is not blind, there is considerable damage to the optical nerves. We also noted that there was some difficulty with his motor function."

Grace began to wonder if he was talking about a car.

"It is possible as time goes by we will begin to see further deterioration in other functions as a result of the birth trauma. He is able to respond to outside stimuli only marginally. For the moment, because of his age, we cannot do a great deal, but we will continue to monitor his progress as he grows."

"I see," said Grace, trying to sound as if she did.

"So what do you want us to do, doctor?" asked Kenny.

"Nothing. We'll just have to wait and see. I'm afraid I can't tell you more than that."

❧

The news of Donald's infirmity spread rapidly to the families. Kenny told his sisters they were to tell no one, but of course, his sister Cathy could not keep a secret for five minutes and the whole of Leith was informed that Grace and Kenny had a retarded child. The response was always the same: "What a shame." No one really said whether it was a shame for the child or a shame on the parents for having it.

Effie and Douglas took the news badly. Even the death of Rita paled against this. On the day Effie came to visit Donald in the hospital, she knew there was something seriously wrong. It wasn't only that he was premature and small. That was normal. It wasn't that his head was oversized for his body or his chest had a strange shape to it. It was the quiet of the child that disturbed her the most. He didn't cry as much as he meowed from time to time, the sound barely above a whisper. Effie put her hands on him and asked, "What has she done?"

Douglas stood clasping his hands together, trying to stop himself from shaking. How could his daughter have come so far from the promise of her youth? He had tried so hard to put away the memories of those years when she was a little girl. He had loved her more than anyone in his life and somehow this was his doing. He had failed as a father. Now she was failing as a mother. She was being punished, but he could not explain why. He could not explain, but he felt the guilt in the sinews of his being.

Effie's heavy body began to heave up and down with gales of emotion that started with a slight moan and ended with sobs. For the first time in many years, Douglas placed his arms around her and pulled her into his chest, allowing the wails of injustice to be soaked through his shirt.

Donald was eight months old when the doctors gave their final verdict. He lay mostly inert until physical stimuli awakened him. The doctor said he was to all intents and purposes mentally disabled, and they should start looking for a place to put him that could give him the care he needed. Unfortunately, all the government institutions were full and they could only expect to be placed on a waiting list. Meanwhile, they should try to live as normally as possible.

Grace began to laugh hysterically. "Normally!" Kenny took her by the arm and started to lead her out of the room. "Normally! You've got nae idea, son."

The drinks trolley was just moving down the aisle when the announcement was made. "The captain has turned on the seatbelt sign so please return to your seats. We will be experiencing turbulence for the next fifteen minutes until we can rise above it. We hope it will bypass shortly." The plane started to bump, rising and falling with the air currents, but it felt like Agnes was on a stormy sea being tossed around. She gripped the arms of the chair and took deep breaths. The girl next to her said "It always gets like this when they're serving food or drinks. I swear there is a switch they turn on at that time."

Agnes tried to smile, but it wouldn't come.

"It'll be all right," said the girl. "I've been on and off planes all my life and they always get you there."

"I didnae want to come on it in the first place," said Agnes, shaking her head.

"If you don't mind me asking," said the girl, "you look like you're reading something very important because I've been hearing you sigh a lot."

"Aye, I'm sorry if I disturbed you. It's ma niece's story." She held up the pages in her hand. "It's no very easy to read. I dinnae ken why she had to put it all doon, but she did."

"Are you going to Los Angeles?"

"Aye. I've to take this to her daughter there. She was adopted, you know. She hasn't seen her mother since she was three months old. She doesn't even know her."

"Well, I hope she appreciates how far you've come," said the girl.

twenty-nine

ANNIE STOOD DONALD up against the wardrobe in her front room, coaxing him to take the few steps towards her. "C'mon, son, one step up, two steps up, just move these wee legs o' yours. Dae it for Auntie Annie. C'mon now!" Urging him forward, allowing her excitement to mobilize him, she cried out "Aye, you're a bonnie laddie, you ken that. I ken you can dae this, c'mon."

The doctors had said he would never have the freedom of independent movement but Annie McCall was determined to prove them wrong. For months she had exercised Donald's legs, pumping them up and down to get some strength into them. She would see this child walk if it was the last thing she did.

Donald gave a luscious, drippy smile, drooling onto the permanently soggy, gray bib he wore. He lifted his foot as if it weighed a hundred pounds before plonking it down in front of him and giggled. Then he lifted the other, moving forward in jerky spasmodic motions with his arms and torso flailing. "C'mon now, gie me another one. You've gone and done that much, you can dae me another one."

Donald lifted the other foot, wobbling slightly before making a perfect comeback into balance, drawing sharp breaths as he threw his weight forward. Annie cheered him on as if she were at a sporting event. Alison sat in the chair hugging her knees, willing Donald to make it, holding her breath as he jerked his way forward into Annie's arms.

Annie sank down onto the floor in tears, clutching him to her breast. "I always knew you could dae it. You're a brave, brave wee laddie," she sobbed.

Donald looked up at her with glazed dark amber eyes making a "dah, dah" sound.

255

"Aye, we're gonnie tell your dada aboot this one," she cried. "Is that right, Alison? We'll gie him the fright o' his life, won't we?"

Alison jumped off the chair and came to stand her brother up again. "Another yin," she cried. "Do it again, Donald."

Donald just grinned and sat down on the floor.

When Kenny arrived Annie couldn't talk because she was so excited. "Come and see this. You're no gonnie believe it. I can hardly believe it myself. Whae wis it that said this bairn would never walk? That bairn can walk!"

"Och, you're daft, Annie. It's no gonnie happen."

"Just you watch."

She placed Donald up against the wardrobe again. "C'mon, my darlin'. It's fur your faither this time. Let him see what you can dae. Come to Auntie Annie."

He lifted his leg unsteadily and plonked his foot down in front of him. "That's it, ma bairn, just keep on gawn."

Kenny watched with incredulity as the child he thought would be crippled, blind, and speechless for the rest of his life put one foot forward and then the other as he wobbled his way towards Annie, saying, "Dah, dah."

Donald gave a loud gurgling sound as he swung his arms out in a wide arc, almost falling over. Kenny made a motion to catch him but Annie waved him back. Giggling Donald made five steps before collapsing into Annie's arms.

"See! I telt you," she beamed.

Kenny was surprised to feel the wetness on his cheeks, wiping it with the back of his hand. "I never thought I'd see the day," he murmured. "I never thought that was possible." He would have given up the drink then and there for this one if he could.

"Well, believe it, son. This bairn is walking. All you needed to dae was gie him the chance."

Alison watched her father's reaction and felt a hardening take place inside. No matter how hard she tried, no matter what she did, she would never see that much pride in her father's eyes when he watched her do something. He would never love anyone as much as he loved Donald.

On the morning that Douglas passed away, Effie thought he was sleeping late. She left him alone until nine o'clock and then went to wake him. When he didn't respond, she checked his breath with the back of her hand and found none. Sitting down heavily on the bed, she took his hand in hers and sat there for a long time, until Harriet came back from school. "You're Gaga's gone," she said. Harriet began to cry. "He tried to be a good man," she said. She would miss the chipping sound of his carving, and the mess of wood shavings on the newspapers. With the house empty of children he had eventually become a comfort to Effie. "I'll miss him," she said.

Harriet built a shrine of his wooden animals next to his bed. His head looked frizzled up in the bed because he didn't have his false teeth in his mouth which had sunk to the back of his head. Effie had put two pennies on his eyes to keep them shut, and Harriet was afraid they would fall off and he would wake up again. She stayed out of the bedroom until they came to take him away to the morgue.

Grace arrived a few hours later and stayed only fifteen minutes. She comforted Effie with a pat on the back and said, "Tell me when's the funeral," and left.

On the day of the funeral, Effie dressed Harriet in a pink gingham dress with taffeta bows, and a navy blue cardigan with white sailing ships on it. She combed her curly hair as straight as she could and tied it up with an elastic band. The dress fell short of her knees and pinched her upper arms. Harriet felt squeezed through a tube.

"I dinnae like this dress," Harriet complained. Effie said this was not the time and the memories of Agnes doing the same thing on her wedding day flooded back. She sat down heavily on the bed and sighed. "Go see your Auntie Agnes," she said, pushing her out of the bedroom door.

Searching in the wardrobe, Effie had trouble making up her mind what to wear and changed her clothes three times before she was satisfied. Effie had long ago given up looking in the mirror, so Agnes was surprised when she went back to check her appearance twice before going out the door.

Walking down the street to the church, Effie stopped twice to catch her breath and lean against the wall. Douglas had said he wanted a church burial, which caused Effie some sleepless nights just thinking of stepping inside a church. She could still remember the cold floor under her knees in the morning as a young girl and her mother's insistence on her saying her prayers before she left for school and work. The idea of the church still gave her the chills. Religion is for fools, she had said many times.

"Aw' right, Ma?" asked Agnes, taking her arm.

Effie shook her off. "I'll be aw' right in a minute." There was a thin line of sweat on the top of her lip, and she dabbed at it with a handkerchief. "I'll be aw' right."

Grace stood smoking a cigarette against the church wall, pushing Donald's pram back and forth as he slept. Alison was running around in front of the statue of Jesus, spreading her arms out to mimic his. Michael was trying to follow her and fell down, scraping his knees on the gravel, and immediately ran howling to his mother. Grace gave a curt sweep over the graze and told him to go play.

At the church door, several people nodded to Effie when she came forward, and she stopped to talk to a few. Harriet walked slowly behind her with Agnes, casting a glance at Grace, who had not moved from the wall.

Meg, Douglas's sister, took Effie's arm as she approached and led her into the church. John had arrived from Canada and was standing apart from everyone with his wife, Helen, her hands clasped tightly around the prim leather handbag she was carrying. Her small hat sported a feather on the side, which fluttered in the breeze from the open door.

Effie stumbled as she approached the front of the church and the coffin, but she recovered and hung on tightly to Meg and Agnes, breathing heavily.

"It'll be aw' right," said Agnes.

"I'm feard o' churches," Effie whispered.

Grace waited until everyone was in the church before she wheeled the pram into the back and corralled Alison and Michael to sit beside her. John sat in the front row with his wife, Agnes, Harriet, and Meg.

"Do you want to go sit in the front?" asked an old man. "I'll watch the pram for you."

Grace shook her head. "Naw," she said, placing Michael on her lap. "I'll be aw' right here." She pulled Alison closer to her side and watched the back of John's head in the front row, leaning towards his wife. She wondered if Helen ever uncrossed her legs.

John was doing well in Toronto and had now become superintendent at an electrical power company. His wife wanted children but had suffered three miscarriages so far, with the likelihood she would be unable to have any at all. They considered adopting, but he wanted to make sure he was making enough money before they made that commitment. He hated Scotland with its miserable weather, its depressing living conditions, and the lack of hope that clung to everything he saw. His only chance was Canada. There was little reason to come back. He glanced towards the back of the church and saw Grace sitting with her three children. He wondered where Kenny was, then the thought occurred he was probably getting drunk somewhere. Grace had made some helluva choices in her life. He looked down the row at Harriet, who was now quite tall for a ten-year-old. She looked more like Grace every year. He shuddered and pulled his wife in closer to his side. Maybe they would be lucky this year and have a child of their own. Harriet was a dull annoying fact that haunted him every time he sat on these shores.

Before leaving to return to York, Agnes broached the subject of Effie coming to live with them. "Och, I cannie go there, Agnes. This is aw' I've kent, plus I dinnae have any money fur that."

"But we can help you, Ma," said Agnes, pulling her mother's hands towards her. "The bairn'll do better doon there. The air is better."

"There's nae air better than Scotland, lass," said Effie. "I cannie afford it."

The next week, she had a visit from the insurance man.

"I'm no payin' any mare insurance," she said. "I cannie afford that anymare. They'll aw' have to manage fur themselves and I'll get a poorhoose burial."

"I havenae come to take payment, Mrs. Sharp," he laughed. "I've come to tell you your man left you a wee bit o' money when he died."

"I hope it's enough to pay for his funeral expenses," grumbled Effie.

"Aye, and there should be enough left over for you. You see, he had over a thousand pounds in premiums. He's been payin' it a long time."

Effie opened her mouth and made a blowing sound out of it, then started laughing. "A thousand pounds!" she kept repeating. "Did you say a thousand pounds? I had nae idea. A thousand pounds! We could aw' go on a holiday wi' that money. Are you sure that it's right?"

The insurance man was smiling broadly and took off his hat. "He signed it all to you, Mrs. Sharp. It's yours."

"Well, I'll be . . ." She slapped her hands against her thighs.

Agnes reiterated her offer to her mother and Effie realized there was nothing keeping her now. John was in Canada and Grace was a virtual stranger to her daughter and her mother. She knew it hurt Harriet every time she saw her mother. Whenever Grace did see Harriet, she was always bad tempered, trying to cope with her three children, and inevitably gave Harriet little notice or none at all. Grace was making an attempt but God knows, she thought, it was hard enough even for somebody who really wanted to do a good job. In Effie's opinion, Harriet would be better off away from her mother. There was nothing to be gained staying in Scotland.

thirty

GRACE STOOD BY the gabled window washing dishes, watching the men in the granary window next door smoking cigarettes. Sally Gordon called up from below "Jesus, will you die for us?"

"Naw, he's just going to swing for us," caterwauled her sister Myra.

Clutching the great hook that swung the sacks of grain into and out of the warehouse, Davie Moffat, teenage heartthrob of Leith, dangled from it, causing the girls to gasp. He was called Jesus because his long blonde hair reached to his shoulders. In an age when most men were still doing Elvis and duck billing their hair, Davie was great entertainment.

"Don't get your knickers wet, girls," shouted his mate Paddy. "He's no dying for you yet."

Davie started laughing, rubbing his belly with his free hand, then lifted his shirt so they could see his stomach muscles. "No nails yet," he called down, swinging back and forth across the expanse of the door.

"Och, you're off your heed," yelled Sally.

The kitchen window was partly open. Grace yelled "You lassies need to find something better to do."

"Aye, missus, we can see you too," Davie yelled back, sticking out his tongue and rubbing it round his mouth.

"Shite!" said Grace, scrubbing at the pots. She didn't hear Alison coming in the kitchen door.

"Ma, I've got a new song. Do you want to hear it?"

She turned quickly with the wet rag in her hand. "God, Alison, you made me jump."

"Can I sing for you?"

She had been listening to the radio and on hearing her mother sing around the house, she decided she wanted to be a famous singer. In a rare moment of intimacy, Grace said she had wanted to be a singer, but with bairns that was the end of that. Alison thought she could take up where her mother left off.

"Go on then, hurry it up. I want you to take Donald down the stairs for me and give him some fresh air."

Donald was sitting in his special high chair, strapped in so he wouldn't fall out. His eyes were not focused on anything special, just staring at the wall. Alison gave him a pat as she walked past him, just like a friendly dog, then launched into the Eartha Kitt version of "Big Spender."

Her mother started laughing when she did the hand motions and body gestures, slapping her behind with her hand when she sang, "So let me get right to the point, I don't pop my cork for every man I see."

"You've got no idea what you're singing, do you?" Grace laughed. Donald gurgled.

"Do you like it, Ma?" Alison asked breathlessly.

"It wasn't bad," she offered.

She sang the chorus again and her voice got louder.

Grace raised a soapy hand and turned around again. "Enough, I have work to get on with. Take Donald down the stairs and see if Michael is still down there. I don't want him wandering off again down they docks."

Paddy shouted "Got yourself an Eartha Kitt there, missus."

Grace told him "Shut your gob, you. Get on wi' the work they're paying you for."

Alison swallowed the song under her breath and continued humming as she took Donald out of his chair and placed him in his pram, tucking his long legs behind the bar so they wouldn't catch while bumping down the stairs. With each step the pram gave a jolt and Donald laughed at the motion. Alison felt a little wheezy but clung on to the pram handle, feeling the jarring ripple of each step reverberate up her arms. By the time she was four steps from the bottom, she had to stop for a minute to let Bobby Freeman trundle a barrow out of the hardware store back room. "All right, hen?" he asked as he passed her.

"Fine, Mr. Freeman," she wheezed.

"Just give me a minute," he called. "I'll help you down the last few stairs."

"It's all right, Mr. Freeman," she said slowly, "I'll manage."

He gave a nod of his head as he slammed the barrow into the back of the van that was parked with its back door wide open before dumping a few boxes inside.

As she bumped the pram down to the outside, Jesus rushed forward to help her down the last few steps. "You'll be gettin' arms like mine if you're no careful," he said. "Here, go round the corner and get yourself some gob suckers," then handed her tuppence and winked before taking a big sack of wheat off the lorry that was parked alongside, resting it on his broad shoulders before he walked it towards the big green door of the granary. "How's the wee one the day?" he called back.

"All right."

"How's your Ma?" shouted Paddy.

Alison looked up towards the window. "All right, I suppose."

"Her Ma's all right, eedjit. Alison, get that bairn across the square for some sun."

"Aye, Mrs. Napier," yelled back Davie, slinging the sack down onto the warehouse platform. "How's it going?" he yelled up, flicking his long hair over his shoulder and tossing her a puckered kiss. "Still watching *Crackerjack*?"

Grace gave a shrug and closed the window. "Bloody riff-raff," she muttered. *Crackerjack* was a favorite children's show and at five o'clock on a Friday night, they would all be gathered round the television set. Since they were the first ones in the neighborhood to own one, it usually meant other kids from the neighborhood crowded into the living room to watch also. Kenny had to put a cardboard box over the dials to stop Donald from playing with them because he had developed a thing for all kinds of dials and buttons and took every opportunity to push or pull on them. Alison's favorite program was *This Wonderful*

World, a series of documentaries on the world around us. That year she asked for a world map for Christmas.

"What do you want with a map? You plannin' on leavin' us?" asked her father sarcastically. She wanted to say in a minute, but said nothing. Instead she escaped to the books she either borrowed or stole from the libraries.

Occasionally, Annie's oldest daughter, Ellen, would take a book from the bookbinders where she worked and give it to Alison. Her most treasured book was *Tanglewood Tales* by Nathaniel Hawthorne. She loved mythology and history, imagining herself the heroine battling Minotaurs and slaying dragons. Then she discovered dance, twirling and sliding, prancing and swooping up and down the small hallway of their flat, adding pirouettes, pliés, points, and arabesques to her repertoire. Grace told her to pack it in. The neighbor downstairs banged her broom on the ceiling to tell her to cut it out. She spent nights dreaming she was the star of the dance academy and did her barre practice on the railing that ran along the harbor wall. She wanted to dance and she wanted dance lessons. Grace told her there was no money for nonsense, but was the first person to buy herself a Persian lamb coat before anyone knew there was such a thing as a Persian lamb, or even where Persia was. Alison could have told them since she had already tracked her way across half the globe to India. Grace's neighbor Kate wanted to know what was wrong with sheepskin. "We've got plenty of sheep in Scotland, why bother going to Persia for it?" It caused a great gale of laughter over drinks on Saturday night at the club.

"Och, you're daft," said Mel Maxwell, who had just returned from Australia. "It's a type of sheep shearing."

"Sheep shite!" said Kate, though she couldn't help but admire the glossy brown wool elegantly layered on Grace's back.

There never seemed to be enough money, but Grace continued to accumulate things other people only dreamed about. She grew tired of the five o'clock in the morning visit to the wash house, so she ordered herself the latest model washer. It could heat the water and spin the clothes almost dry. It also doubled as a water heater for the aluminum bathtub on Sunday nights. After years of going to the local bath house each week, taking a bath in the kitchen was total luxury, especially for Alison who listened to the latest music on Radio Luxembourg each Sunday night while soaking in the tub. The children got new shoes every three months whether they needed them or not, and a new coat each winter. After Grace had taken dressmaking classes, she spent weeks sewing elaborate dresses for Alison to wear at the Docker's Christmas party each year. She would not have her daughter under-dressed.

Work had picked up at the docks, but Kenny still had to queue each day to be chosen from among the crowd. His reputation as a hard worker was well known, so it was rare that he returned home empty handed. There were plenty of grain, cement, and coal boats to work. There were also plenty of whisky and beer boats. The favorite among the Dockers was the Carlsberg Special boat. Pallets of beer would come from Copenhagen every few weeks, and with great dexterity the Dockers opened the beer bottles, drank the beer, and folded back the gold foil without showing any signs of tampering. Between the beer and the whisky that flowed out of the distilleries of Leith, it was hardly surprising there were so many alcoholics in the docks, and it was amazing that more men didn't get killed doing their job. But getting killed was the least of Kenny's worries.

The rain was falling in a hard slant that soaked through everything, leaving the dampness collecting in the bones. Kenny had just finished hauling sacks of cement onto a boat bound for Leningrad and was ready for a beer at the pub. He could taste the chalky flavor of cement settling under his false teeth and gave a spit to clear his mouth out. A beer would be just the thing, he thought.

Cycling to the dock office, he parked his bike against the wall and joined the queue of men waiting for their wages. The men were in a good mood, looking forward to the weekend and a chance to relax at the Docker's Social Club on Saturday.

As he approached the window Kenny nodded to Kenny Scott, who was giving out the packets of money. They had wound up in the same hospital in France during the war, sometimes getting their mail mixed up because they were both named Kenny. He turned away from Kenny and spoke quickly to the man who shared the office with him before picking up a small piece of paper from the desk. "I'm sorry," Kenny Scott said almost in a whisper. "I can't give you your wages this week. The bill collectors have taken it." He showed him the piece of paper that stated he had forfeited the right to wages because he was three hundred and forty-five pounds in debt.

Kenny felt a heat rise in his neck and face, as if he had been standing in the sun all day then blinked a few times letting it sink in. He felt as if the scummy water that engulfed the grimy ships sitting in the harbor was drowning him.

"You're joking, aren't you?"

Kenny Scott shook his head. "I wish I was, son. I'm sorry."

George Watson was right behind him and had heard it all. He leaned in towards him.

"If there's anything I can do for you . . . ," he whispered.

Kenny cut him off with a nod and walked past, the vein in the side of his head throbbing so hard he could hardly see where he was going. He fumbled in his trouser pocket and found two shillings, two sixpences, and three three-penny bits. Just about enough for two pints of beer. They can all bloody starve, he thought.

The family was sitting around the fire, banked high with coal briquettes, trying to ignore the draft from the living room door that gnawed through everything like a steel cutter. The hot glow was giving them tartan legs but nobody cared. All eyes were on the television watching *Perry Mason*.

They heard the front door slam as he came in. Grace looked at the clock. It was nine o'clock. She knew he had been out drinking since he wouldn't be home at this time if he was working the night shift.

"Where's my buckin' dinner?" he yelled as he took off his coat, ignoring his work boots, which were all muddied from staggering through the gutters on his way home.

Like a gale force wind gusting through the room, everyone moved back from the fire and Grace stood to get his dinner from the oven. Alison moved out of his chair and sat huddled with Michael and

Donald on the couch, eyes glued to the television. She had been climbing on the social security roof and had ripped her skirt and scratched her leg and was waiting for her mother to let him know all about it. There was no telling how her father was going to be. He was like a tinder box just waiting for the fuse. She had already felt the rough edge of his belt many times over the years and prayed Grace wouldn't tell him.

Kenny sat down heavily in his chair and immediately closed his eyes. His greasy hair, regularly oiled with paraffin oil, engraved itself further into the permanent circle of oil that adorned the back of the Naugahyde chair. His fingernails, shining white from cement, were entwined across his chest. The coals in the grate slipped quietly as they settled, and Alison's shoulders came back to rest in their usual place, two inches from her ears. Donald had fallen asleep and was slouched against her. Michael sat on the floor with his eyes still glued to the television.

The plate was hot as Grace set it down on the small folding table in front of him. With his eyes still closed, he spread his legs out and knocked it over, splattering the plate of mince and potatoes on the carpet and onto his boots.

Instantly, he was awake and sitting up. "Jesus buckin' Christ! Can't I get my dinner without there being' a buckin' mess to clean up? What am I supposed to eat now?" he roared.

Grace spooned the mess from the carpet back onto the plate. "I've got mare in the kitchen, Kenny. Don't get so bloody worked up," she said cautiously, moving his feet to scrape around the edges of his shoes. Suddenly, he bounced forward with outstretched arm, and crack!—his fist connected with her cheekbone.

"I got no wages the day, thanks to you," he raged.

As she crumbled to the floor, he smacked her again, and she hit the side of the fireplace. Alison's shoulders hugged her ears and she drew her legs up under her, pulling Donald towards her for protection. Michael scurried under the table. Grace screamed for Kenny to stop, then grabbed the poker and swung wildly in his direction, missing his ear by inches. Taking advantage of the chaos, Alison skidded off the couch and took refuge under the living room table behind the lace tablecloth that draped to the floor, leaving Donald alone on the couch, knowing nothing would happen to him. He was the untouchable.

Grace swung the poker again and then released it to strike the carefully painted door Kenny had finished the weekend before. She was screeching and backing up towards the living room door. "Get out of here! Get out of here! I'll kill you, you stupid bastard! Don't you touch me again! I'll swing for you! You're a stupid drunken bastard. Get out!"

Donald began to cry on the couch. Michael grabbed hold of Alison and clung like a life-raft to her. The living room door slammed as Grace ran into the kitchen.

Over the sound of hard breathing, the sonorous voice of Perry Mason deliberated some argument to the jury. For a brief moment, Alison thought he was acting in their defense.

Kenny's teeth ground over his bottom lip while his mustache bounced up and down. He rubbed his ear and snorted like a bull ready to charge. His entire jaw was locked from the ears down to his shoulder as he stood up and came towards the living room table.

Alison whispered to Michael to keep quiet, but he whimpered and began to fuss. Kenny reached under and found Alison first.

"Get out of there," he yelled. "What do you think you're doing?"

She held on to the big claw-legged table, but her strength was no match for his. The tablecloth and the vase that sat on it tumbled to the floor.

"Don't, Dad. I didnae do anything!" she cried, struggling to escape from his grip. "Let me go!"

"Let you go! You're a nosy little bastard, aren't you? Always tryin' to find out what's going on, aren't you? You're just like her, aren't you? All trouble! You're all buckin' trouble."

With each angry cry, the thick massive hands that a few hours earlier had slung heavy sacks of cement and huge containers of whisky onto boats pummeled their way into her soft flesh. With each new blow, she curled further and further into herself to escape them. "It wasn't my fault, Daddy," she cried, trying to make herself smaller and smaller and take the brunt of his blows on her back. "Don't hit me," she sobbed.

She felt her mother pull on his arm, yelling that she was the one he wanted to kill. He pushed her aside and continued beating on Alison until Grace picked up the vase and brought it down on his back.

He turned with a roar and caught the vase in midair as she was bringing it down a second time, and he threw it across the room, where it shattered against the wall. Donald and Michael were crying hysterically in harmony, and Alison had curled into a fetal position huddled on the floor. "Get out," shouted Grace. "Don't come back here again."

Kenny cursed the lot of them and strode out the door, slamming the door behind him. Grace collapsed beside Alison, holding tightly until she stopped shaking, then scrambled towards the couch pulling the three children into her arms. When the sobbing died down, they were staring at the faces of Perry Mason and Della Street, unable to make sense of anything.

Agnes buried her face in her handkerchief and made no attempt to hide the fact that she was crying.

"Are you all right," asked the girl in the next seat. "Can I get you something?" Agnes shook her head, wiping her tears. "I didn't know half of it. I was only there a few times. She never told me. I knew Grace had had a hard time with Kenny. He never had much patience. There was a lot of women in they days who put up with that shite. But I didn't know about the bairns. If I had, I would have done something about it. I feel so ashamed."

"I think you need to stop reading this book," said the girl. "It's not good for you."

"It might not be good for me, hen, but I have to finish it now."

thirty-one

FOR TWO YEARS Donald was left in Alison's care while her mother went out to work at the biscuit factory. She learned how to change him, feed him, and play with him, but she never learned how to bring school friends home without frightening them. With his long gangly legs, a lump of nappy around his bum, a hump on his chest, and a mouth that constantly drooled in a loopy smile, he looked totally insane. Although he could walk a few steps, he never comfortably went beyond the length of the living room. On the street, he walked with most of his weight on the arm of the person guiding him. Annie had been right—he would walk—but he would never be independent. His eyesight was still limited and his speech patterns only a mimic of what he heard. He called her Dason and Michael became Dikel. Everything began with the "D" sound, including his favorite word, Dugger. He would always say it with a laugh, as if he knew it was a bad word.

When he took to having epileptic fits, Grace found that the safest thing to do was shove a wooden spoon in his mouth. Very soon, they had all learned how to do it. It scared Alison at first, but she got used to waiting out the seizures that left him twisting in a backward swim of contortions on the floor. After he took a short sleep, he would get up and be happy once more, as if nothing had happened.

In adding this to his list of disabilities, nobody asked how Grace was coping. In early photos she was a young, vivacious redhead with an easy smile, but she had become a frizzy-haired, skinny woman with breasts that looked like flattened doughnuts. Tired and irritated most days, she complained about everything. She worked five nights a week and the only time she looked a little better was on Saturdays

271

when she went to the club. But even then she had the look of a woman worn down to the bare boards. She never looked happy except when she'd had a few drinks; then she would become obnoxious, flirting mercilessly with the men at the club or with the neighbors in front of Kenny. He showed his displeasure by keeping his distance and going to bed early. If he was in a particularly bad mood or if he himself had been drinking, he would take out his revenge on Alison and Michael. They learned to stay out of his way as often as possible, but it wasn't always possible. While Alison took care of her brothers Kenny drowned himself in the bottles of whisky he stole from the boats. They all developed a keen sense of impending danger which resulted in an overcautious approach to life later on. She was fiercely protective of Donald, and because of this was dismissive of Michael as useless, since he couldn't change a nappy or make dinner. Donald followed her like a puppy, and when she lay in bed at night, she sang songs to help him go to sleep.

When the news arrived from the Department of Social Services, Grace and Kenny had been waiting nine years for a place at a home for the mentally and physically disabled. Grace read the letter several times, her hands shaking, muttering to herself, "What am I going to do?" until she could stand it no longer.

"What do you think I should do?" she implored Annie. "I don't know if I can let him go after all this time. I just can't imagine what it would be like."

Annie's soothing voice stroked her anxiety. "It's no easy, Gracie. No after all this time. I would have the same problem myself. You know how I feel. He's a brilliant bairn and he's come a long way, but he's no going to get any better. I can see how much strain it is on all you. That wee lassie of yours doesn't have much of a life. If he was mine, I'd hold onto him, but you've got to do what you think is right."

They had a week to give their decision, or the place would go to another child. Kenny sat in silence for a long time, staring at the fire.

Finally, he said if Donald went away he'd get better care. His epilepsy was getting worse. The day care complained it was hard work. Nobody thought to mention anything to Alison until she saw Grace packing a suitcase with his things.

"But where is he going to go?" she asked

"Away to the hospital. You'll see him again," Grace said.

She packed Donald's clothes in a small brown suitcase, making sure he had his transistor radio. It was actually Alison's radio, given for her eleventh birthday, but when Donald discovered that he could change the channels by pushing the buttons, it became his radio, and he clapped it to his ears all day, punching the buttons until the station changed to something he liked.

"But where's he going?" she insisted. "Where about is it?"

Grace continued folding his sweaters and pants, matted in the front from continual wetting. "He's going away," she said, catching a sob in her throat.

"But what's wrong with him?"

"Just get out of my sight, Alison. Leave it alone."

∝℣∽

When the bus arrived from the hospital to take him away, Grace and Kenny walked him downstairs, his legs taking one step at a time until he felt balanced, supported on his father's arm. A young man took Donald's hand and his suitcase and told Grace he would take good care of him. Donald strained to look backwards towards them, pulling away from the hand that held him in a strong grip. He cried out, "Dah, dah," then changed it to "Dason," before the young man pulled him in tighter towards him.

"Away you go, now," said Grace, choking on the tears she was holding back. "I'll see you soon."

In the front seat of the bus, Donald's head lolled towards the window as he looked at them standing outside.

Alison had climbed up onto the kitchen sink to watch from the window but saw only the top of the bus. The men from the granary, including Jesus, stood respectfully at the second-floor loft door.

Annie stood on the corner, wiping her eyes with her apron. It seemed as if the whole neighborhood had come to see Donald go. The square was crowded with bairns who had stopped their play.

Grace pulled away from Kenny's arm, and stepped onto the bus and hugged Donald fiercely around his shoulders, smothering him with kisses. "I'll see you soon," she said in choking bursts.

The children outside had begun to get restless and started jumping up and down, waving to Donald. "All right Donald. See you the morn. See you next year. See you when the sun shines." Grace began to cry and the young man lifted her gently down the stairs to Kenny whose face was set like steel before leading her away as the bus slowly drove across the broad pavement.

Alison held on to the kitchen tap, feeling a sickness descend like a stone into her stomach, holding back the despair, the loss, the guilt. She wanted to cry so badly, but knew it served no purpose. She was eleven years old and knew little of a life outside the care of her brother. She had dreamed of a life free of his care, where she could go out without organizing her life around him, where she could invite people round and not have them stay five minutes before they decided it was too scary being there. She loved him but she hated him too. He was an annoyance, an embarrassment, and a yoke around her neck. It was hard for her to see, but her mother had felt many of these same emotions all her life.

Grace used the excuse that it was too far to go to visit Donald every week, but Alison and Michael had not gone to visit him once in eight long months. She was surprised when Grace said they were all going out to Fife to see him.

After changing buses at the Edinburgh bus terminal, they arrived at the hospital two hours later. From the outside it was a beautiful stately home set among trees with a large lawn out front and rows of neat little red flowers along the borders near the front entrance.

Inside, institution white paint and long lines of beds lined the walls of each ward and the smell of disinfectant coated the air. Drab white curtains hung in folds around each bed, a few missing the correct hooks to hang them properly. Children lay in cots railed in like prison cells, a few were sitting in chairs grinning at nothing in particular, their eyes flat. Nurse aids were in various acts of feeding or changing them. A laughing child came loping down the hall with a nurse running after him.

Alison gripped Michael's hand and stayed next to her mother as a nurse walked slowly towards them holding a child's hand as he clumsily slid and bounced from side to side. His trousers were falling down and seemed to be wet.

Grace recognized him first and cried out, "Donald!" then ran towards him. Hearing the familiar voice, his face lit up and he struggled to get away from the nurse, gurgling and laughing as his legs kept sliding in opposite directions. The nurse was practically carrying him in order to keep him balanced. Annie would have cried if she could have seen him in this state. Grace took his struggling body into her arms and collapsed onto the floor, mingling her tears with his drool.

In that moment, Alison fully understood that her mother and father had only ever truly loved one person in their life. That nothing she could say or do would ever bring her closer to the love they were now giving their son. It had been a mistake to send him away.

Kenny bent down to pick up Grace and Donald from the floor and thanked the nurse for her help before leading them towards the garden in the back of the building.

"Would you like a cup of tea?" asked the nurse. "Maybe the bairns would like a biscuit."

No one said anything as they walked away.

Sitting on the bench, suspended above the grass they were forbidden to walk on, it was clear how much ground he had lost. They tried singing songs with him, but he had forgotten most of them. They played hand games, but he had lost the coordination he had struggled so hard to find. Michael played peek-a-boo, but he sat looking at the grass. They wanted to make him laugh, to see some of the spirit that had held them all together, but the laughter had disappeared from his lips. He looked at them as if they were the mad ones. His eyes had lost some of their sparkle, his dark hair was greasy, and his pants looked unwashed. Alison was sorry she had been so mean to him. All the times she had taunted him with bananas, which he hated, all the times she had called him names. He should have been home with me, she thought.

Kenny tried to get him to walk to him, but he could only stumble a few steps with Alison hanging on to his shirt. Grace held him on her lap, a tall, skinny boy with extraordinarily long fingers, and stroked his hair in between puffs from her cigarette.

Alison suggested they bring him home, steal him away, and Grace hesitated for a long second before saying, "He's better off where he is."

Three months later, when the knock came at the door, Grace was in the kitchen getting their tea. When she answered the door, a keening of wounds held for too long crashed through her barriers, cascading into a waterfall she was helpless to stop. Frightened by the intensity, Alison and Michael joined the fray, unable to comfort their mother because they didn't know how.

It was all so long ago and so much water under the bridge, but Agnes couldn't help but be back there again, reliving it all. She had felt sorry for her sister so many times—she had been a stupid bugger, but in the end she had not asked for everything that came her way.

Shortly after Donald died, Grace was deep into depression and had come to visit in York. After two days she had said practically nothing to Effie and had completely ignored Harriet, who had been looking forward to her mother's visit. Grace said she had a bad headache and Effie said she should see a doctor. Agnes knew that this was a heartache that had scarred her sister beyond anything that had happened before. The losses she had endured, the cavalier attitude she adopted to cover it all up, were all gone now. All of the guilt and remorse that she had never been able to explain to anyone came struggling to the surface, engulfing her in the darkest parts of her existence.

Alison had heard snippets of stories, rumors, and passing remarks that she had built into full-blown fantasy during her early life, but after Grace died, she wanted Agnes to put all the jigsaw pieces together for her. She said she was laying the ghosts to rest. Reading this book, Agnes had no idea how she had resurrected these ghosts. When the family gathered together on special occasions and after a few drinks, the "Do you remember?" stories began, most of the time it was trivial things, meant to amuse. No one ever spoke about the day-to-day horrors of getting by, of losing children, of having their hopes crushed. These things were better left unremembered. They were the bricks and mortar of what held them up through the years, and to start chipping away at them would bring the whole house down and expose the life for what it was. Like the weather in Scotland, it was gray with a chance of sunshine. Nobody held their breath waiting for the break in the clouds.

Agnes had found herself a good man who provided well for his family. She had three children she loved deeply and counted her blessings every day. When Grace collapsed on her sofa that day and sobbed her heart out to her, Agnes made a vow that she would do everything she could do to help her and her children, but with the distance between their two *houses and the passing of time, promises slipped away only to show up on Christmas cards each year.*

When Grace died, Alison wanted to know where she came from because she had to make sense of it for her own child. Well, it looked like she had found more than she bargained for, thought Agnes.

With less than two hours to go before landing in Los Angeles, Agnes knew she would not finish the story. She knew what would matter the most to this young woman was why her mother gave her up for adoption. That was the part that lingered in every abandoned child's mind. Why did she leave me when for three months she had tried to make it work? Alison said it was her journey to make sense of it. Agnes wondered if you could ever make sense of things like that.

candle in the wind

one

THE GUSTS OF wind blowing down the alley could have frozen fish. I stamped my feet on the pavement to keep warm and scanned the length of the street. Maybe I should have gone into the pub, but if I missed him, it would be Saturday night suicide. Waiting was the only option. I was waiting to pick up speed outside the Deacon Brodie pub, just down the hill from Edinburgh Castle.

I rubbed my hands together, noticed the ink stains on my fingers, and applied some spit to rub them off. It only made my hands colder. My mother had insisted I take a typing course when I left school at fifteen. She said it would keep me out of the bonds and the factories but I typed so badly I'd lost two jobs already. I was always getting my hands dirty from the carbon copies and then spreading it onto the pages I was supposed to be typing up neat and tidy. At the end of the day, I was probably as dirty as if I had worked in the bonds where my mother worked putting labels on whisky bottles.

I searched the High Street to see if I could see his lumbering walk and twitching arms coming up the street. A car pulled up outside the police station down the road. It was a drug squad car, a black Austin-Healey, and when we saw them we usually moved along *tout de suite*. A poor sod was hauled out of it and led inside. It made me think of my brother Michael who had just been sent up to reform school for breaking and entering again. This was the third time he'd been busted. The first time, he broke into our electric meter and took out two months' worth of shillings. My mother didn't want to believe it was him and only found out because nobody had actually broken into the house to do it. She knew it wasn't me because I was at work all day. She let him go with a smack round the head that time, but then the stupid bugger did her gas meter and she got really pissed, so she sent for the police. He got off with a warning, but if he was reported again, he would be up for it. I never did think Michael was one of the brightest light bulbs in the shop, and he proved it by breaking into a metal yard with a mate and got cornered by a policeman as they jumped over the wall. That earned him probation for a year. Then he broke into a pawn shop and tried to sell the watches back to the same man. Now he was in Linlithgow Boys' Reformatory doing six months to a year. I told him last time that if he was going to do something, then at least make it worth his while and stay out of jail.

I stood against the wall out of the wind and the pub door swung open. A guy staggered out and fell against me as I backed away.

"Are you looking for a bit of company?" he slurred.

I didn't answer him as I moved further down the street. He followed me.

"Why is a pretty thing like you hangin' around in the cold? You in the business?"

"Fuck off!"

"Oh, feisty language, eh? That's no way to treat a potential customer, is it?"

"Get away from me, you ignorant bastard."

He looked at me as if I were a piece of meat on a hook and then staggered towards me. "Listen, titless, I'll do what I want to do, won't I?" He grabbed for me and I swung my bag at him and backed up some more.

"C'mere, you bitch," he grunted and lurched forward again.

An arm grabbed him as he lifted his hand to me. Joe, six feet three inches and built like a brick shit house, stepped in front of the guy, at least seven inches taller than him. "Piss off. Go on, get out of here or I'll wipe the flair with you." The man yelled "bitch" then staggered down the street towards the police station. "I'm sorry I'm late, hen," he said in a nervous voice, looking up and down the High Street.

"God, Joe. I'm glad to see you. I thought I was in for some real trouble then. He thought I was on the game. Stupid fuckhead. What do I look like?" Joe gave a grin and then shook his head. "Don't answer that," I laughed. "So what you got the night?"

"The usual. Take your pick. Blues or bombers," he said, his eyes darting all around him.

"I've been waiting on Sheila but she seems to be takin' her time in gettin' here. I'm a bit a skint this week—I just got fired yesterday. . . ."

"I don't need to hear your life story," Joe interrupted. "C'mon I've got to get doon the Bridges."

"I've only got a pound for the night."

"I tell you what," he said, rummaging in his pocket, feeling for the envelopes neatly folded into the lining. "I'll give you fourteen blues for ten bob, how about that? You can owe me the next time I see you."

I handed him the ten shillings and he held my hand as he passed over a handful of blue pills which I put in my coat pocket. "You're great, you ken that," I said. He huffed his shoulders and was about to walk away when Sheila came running round the corner, her coat wide open, her frizzy brown hair blowing behind her. "Oh, God, I'm sorry," she said breathlessly.

"Where you been?" I shouted. "I've been freezin' my arse off here waiting for you."

"I'm sorry. My Ma was in a bad mood and wasn't going to let me out. She lent me her nylons last night and I put a hole in them. I had to find another pair before she would let me go. Hi, Joe. Gie me a pound's worth. It doesn't matter what. I'm easy."

Joe gave her the pills and she put them in her handbag. "Take care of yourself, Alison," he said, slouching off down the road. I started to walk away from the pub.

"Where are we goin'?" asked Sheila.

"Down the café." I said.

"Aw, can't we go to the pub, Alison? I'm in need of a drink. My Ma was a real bitch about these nylons."

"Listen, I lost my job yesterday because I was takin' my time when I should have been hurrying up. My Ma took three pounds and I had to beg Joe for the blues the night."

Sheila pulled her coat around her. "Aw' right, stop your moaning, let's go. I'm bloody freezin'."

Inside the café it was warm and quiet. We ordered two cups of tea and I heaped three spoons of sugar into my cup. "You're disgusting," said Sheila. "That's sickening."

"You want to hear sickening stories," I said, then told a story about a girl I knew at school that ate petroleum jelly out of the can. We laughed hysterically about the all the possible repercussions of doing that until the tears rolled down our cheeks. We didn't hear the man in the café ask us to quiet down. On the third time, he came and stood by the table. "Quiet down, or leave," he said.

I told Sheila to behave herself, but that only seemed to throw her into fits of laughter again. I couldn't help myself. I knew we were being offensive, but the very idea of behaving ourselves was ridiculous.

The doorbell tinkled and we looked up. Standing in the doorway were two boys in blue. I poked Sheila and we stopped the hilarity immediately by putting our hands over our mouths.

The café man turned red in the face. "I'm glad you're here. I've asked they lassies to quiet down and leave, but they don't seem to understand."

They planted themselves in front of us. "I understand you ladies have been asked to leave," one said.

"I didn't hear that," I said. "He asked us to be quiet. I'm sorry we're no very quiet, officer." I had a desperate urge to start giggling again, and almost peed myself holding it in.

"They were not bloody listening, that's why," yelled the man, who had returned behind the counter.

"I'm sorry, shir," I said stupidly. "We're leaving now, if that's all right?"

"What are you girls doing here anyway? How old are you?"

"I'm fifteen. My Ma knows I'm up the town," said Sheila.

"Fifteen, eh? That's awfully young to be traipsing about up the town. Maybe you two need to come over the street with us. We'll give your parents a call and see what they think."

Sheila moaned and I gave her a nudge. My heart had set up a rhythm like a bongo drum, and I was doing my best to keep my breath steady without holding it. "Oh, they don't have a telephone, sir, and they're probably out themselves." I had a tremendous urge to pee. "Can I go to the toilet before we leave?"

"She's no using my toilet," the man shouted.

I shrank into my coat and stuffed my hand into my pocket, feeling the pills floating like loose buttons in the corner of the pocket. I was going to flush them but that took care of that, so I began to poke my finger through the lining of the pocket, crumbling the pills with my fingernails as I worked it. I knew I should have taken them in the café, but I didn't want to take them too early. There was a long night ahead. I couldn't go home until at least eight in the morning when I'd tell my mother I'd been sleeping over at Sheila's house.

The police station was a warren of small rooms originally built as a Customs and Excise house in the eighteenth century. We were led into a room with a vaulted ceiling and no windows. The walls were painted institutional blue with a black border, which was chipping at the edges of the ceiling. Wooden benches lined the wall and a long dark mahogany table stood in the middle of the room. The walls had posters of smiling policewomen and stern policeman exhorting you to join the most valuable profession in the world. I couldn't think of anything more worthless than them right now.

A policeman sat at the table, reading a newspaper. From time to time someone would come in and talk to him, then they would look at the two of us sitting quietly in our terror, and leave. My imagination was on overdrive. I had given them my name and address and they told us to sit tight. Sheila kept giving me nervous glances, occasionally looking down at her bag as she did, but I said nothing for fear of giving something away.

Slumped in my coat with my hands deep in my pockets, I continued crushing the pills into tiny pieces, trying to reduce as many of them to dust as possible before forcing the dust down through the torn lining towards the hem. I had taken up the hem of my coat recently, and it had a thick turn at the corner. That was my final destination as I casually pulled that part of the coat towards me.

"Excuse me, sir, but I need to go to the toilet very badly. Do you think I can go?"

He smiled at me for a moment and then said, "You just sit tight until someone comes back from visiting your Ma and Dad." He went back to reading his newspaper.

An hour later, two policewomen arrived. Both had neatly curled brown hair under their flat-topped hats, wearing heavy black shoes that would have done somebody some real damage on a Saturday night. One was wearing bright coral lipstick, like the kind my mother would wear. Immediately, they were all business and the man left the room.

"Right then. Let's have your coats and your bags up here."

I broke into a sweat immediately and stood up. I did a quick check to see how much more I had to crumble, which wasn't much, then dropped it through the hole and took my coat off. I prayed she wouldn't find it.

"Your shoes also."

I unzipped my boots and took them off, noticing at once that there was a hole in my stockings where my big toe stuck through. I felt undressed.

The woman with the coral lipstick patted me all over, paying particular attention to the crotch area, before telling me to sit down.

Sheila had been sniveling the whole time. The policewoman at the table went through her things first as the other one patted her down.

"What's this?" She held up Sheila's makeup bag and emptied the contents onto the table. Out fell the mascara and the lipstick with the half-empty bottle of Almay foundation, and in a little clitter clatter like tiny little sweeties, the blue pills fell onto the tabletop.

"They're my Ma's," she bubbled through her tears.

"Your Ma's?" she said slowly.

"Aye."

"Does your Ma have medicine like this as well?" she asked me.

"No, Miss. I don't have anything like that."

Sheila gave me a look that could have killed.

"Go sit down," the policewoman told her, and she returned in her bare feet because she wasn't wearing any stockings at all.

I watched the woman go through my handbag and then she started on my coat. She turned the pockets inside out and saw the hole and like a bloodhound, she started patting and feeling the edges of it. I thought she was about to give up when I saw her catch the turned-up corner and feel the lumpy material. I knew at that moment I should have paid more attention to my mother's sewing instructions, but I thought there was no way she was going to get in there. Suddenly, she ripped the hem of the coat and opened out the material. Out of the corner fell the pill dust.

---※---

Agnes shifted uncomfortably in her seat and rubbed her aching eyes. I've never read so much in my life, she thought, and especially, not this kind of stuff. She's put out all her dirty washing here. I don't know if this lassie in Los Angeles will want to know all this. I don't know I'd like to hear that my mother wanted to make an abortion of me. We all do desperate things but we don't all need to put it out there for others to see. I don't think I can stand much more.

two

I sat with my mother outside the courtroom door, waiting for the summons. Amid the low mumble of conversations and the occasional slap of leather soles on the marble floors, I wheezed. I had woken that morning with a bad asthma attack. The ephedrine didn't help. Instead, it gave me the feeling I was sitting on top of an engine in a car that wasn't going anywhere. I tried coughing to release the pressure but it wasn't working.

When the clerk of the court called my name, my mother gave me a push. "I'm so sick of showing up to these places. I didn't think it would be with you." She blew her nose and smoothed her coat downwards before walking me in.

I was about to sit down again when the clerk told me to remain standing. I noticed the coat of arms above the Judge's seat with a scale on it, and wondered how much dope you could weigh on it. The barrister behind the desk looked bored and kept scratching his head under the ash-colored wig he was wearing. The clerk read off the complaint and asked me how did I plead? I looked at him vacantly, until my mother gave me a nudge.

"How do you plead?" he asked again. The judge looked tired.

Suddenly, I wanted to plead poverty. I wanted to plead ignorance and I wanted to plead innocence, but instead, I shrugged my shoulders and pleaded guilty.

The judge gave me a lecture on the use of drugs and sentenced me to two years' probation because of my age. As an afterthought, he suggested I make an appointment with a court-appointed psychiatrist for evaluation. It was a shame that I was wasting my time in his court on such stupid matters.

❦

Dr. Simpson was probably in his early forties with warm eyes that melted into crinkles around them when he smiled. His beard was thick and showing signs of gray, but without it he probably would have looked baby faced. He smiled at me as he said, "Welcome," then pointed to the chair I was to sit in. When we were settled in, he asked "Tell me why you are here."

"You've got the papers," I said, trying to be smart.

"Yeah," he said slowly, "but I want you to tell me why you're here."

"Because I got busted."

"For what?"

"A few blues, nothing important."

"I see." He sat for a moment studying me before looking down at his file. "Okay." He said this slowly making some notes. "How long were you using for?"

"You make it sound like I've been doin' heroin or something. It was only a few lousy pills."

He made some notes on his pad again and waited. I waited for the next question.

"Okay. Why don't you tell me a bit about yourself?"

He seemed to be fond of the word okay. Like John Wayne in the movies, it kind of swaggered from his lips.

"There's no much to tell." I sat for a few minutes swinging my crossed legs, admiring my shoes, before I looked up again. He was still waiting.

"I'm fifteen and I hate livin' in Scotland. I'm thinking of runnin' away as soon as possible to London."

He nodded and made a note on his pad. "Tell me more."

"My mum and dad dinnae understand me, and I can't stand my little brother. My job sends me to sleep every day."

"Well, that's a good start," he said, smiling.

I wished I hadn't been so damn smart-alecky.

"Tell me why you want to run away, Alison?" he said softly.

The softness in his voice made me want to cry. I tried coughing it back, but it didn't work.

"I hate my dad." I said, suddenly pissed with the doctor and pissed with myself. I wanted to shock him with my honesty. "I'm the one who gets all the punchings. He beats me up almost every day. My Ma's no help. She just tells me to stay out of his way." Then the tears began. "I dinnae ask for it all the time," I said, feeling like a six year old.

He leaned forward in his chair and asked softly, "How long has he been beating you?"

Swallowing the sobs, I mumbled, "I don't know."

He sat back and shook his head.

"Does he beat your brother too?"

"Aye."

Sighing, he made some notes and then pushed a box of tissues towards me. I blew my nose and sat up straighter.

"Ma said he was just trying to keep me from making a mistake. That's her excuse whenever he beats me up." What the mistake was I had to figure out for myself. I had made many in the years I had lived with them, but in my opinion being born was the worst one. If childhood was supposed to be a happy experience, then someone had forgotten to deliver the barrel of laughs.

When I was late, he was waiting for me. When I forgot to wash the dishes or take the rubbish out, he was waiting for me. If he'd had too many, which was often, he would get mad about something and decide to punch me or my brother for it. We were never allowed to talk about the bruises on our backs, or the arms. We ran into something was always the response.

There were genuine accidents. A broken arm and black eye I sustained after tripping on the carpet in the hallway of our house after heading for the doorpost. That earned me sympathy and a new swimsuit that embarrassed me when it fell down over one nipple as I was having my picture taken. Then there was the broken leg and a broken nose. I fell off the wall of the men's toilet while trying to see what was on the other side. Then someone yelled "You're faither's comin'," and I pushed my brother, he pushed me, and he won. I spent two weeks in the hospital on that one.

I seemed to spend a long time in hospitals as a child and actually enjoyed it. It was more often about the asthma than anything else, and after the first two or three days when they got it under control, life was a haven of sanitary joy. The nurses were great and I took baths in the deep porcelain tubs that I could almost swim in. People brought me juice and sweeties, and on the occasion of my broken bones, my mother gave me a Dutch doll in national costume. Sometimes it was hard to leave. I thought at one point, I should be a nurse. I was getting plenty of experience in taking care of people, so it seemed a natural place to go.

But that altruistic thought disappeared when my brother Donald died. I'm not sure what happened, to be honest, but something disappeared with him. Perhaps it was the way my mother and father took to the bottle, or because I was always out of the house as late as possible so I wouldn't have to come in and find him in a bad mood again. But one thing led to another and I was always in trouble. Usually it was something simple like coming home later than I was supposed to. That's when I would find him waiting for me with his bludgeoning fists. Taking the fetal position is good way to save your face, but it cripples the back. After a few thuds and curses, Ma would step in and start to haul him off. She was a poor referee because it took her a long time to stop the fights. Of course, beating me and my brother did not seem to cause my father any anxiety because after it was over, he simply went to sleep or had another drink. It took a little longer for me to recover.

It seemed I could never do anything right for that man. Nothing was ever good enough, even as he used to tell me, "If you're going to do a job, do it right or don't do it at all." That phrase haunted me all my life. It has made it impossible for me to do anything halfway. I guess that's why I'm such a perfectionist, I joked only half-seriously.

But it was on the issue of being like my mother that made him the angriest. "Don't you turn out like your mother," he would tell me when she was sobbing into her cups after a night out, or when she was flirting with someone after a night of drinking. He would tell me this almost conspiratorially, as I sat there trying to watch television while they did their arguing or their partying. I wasn't sure what he meant. To me, she just looked unhappy and most of it was his fault because he was such a mean bastard.

When Donald died my mother cried for six months and played Jim Reeves records ad nauseam. Her favorite was "Nobody's Child," and she sang it whenever she'd had a few too many. And then, as if deciding there was nothing more to lose, she went out to work at the whisky bonds putting labels on the bottles and spent her wages on whatever she wanted. She went to the hairdresser's, bought clothes, spruced up the furniture and the curtains, and rarely cooked because she could afford Birds Eye frozen food. By this time I was thirteen and my brother almost twelve. She figured we were old enough to take care of ourselves. Most nights she wasn't home until six or seven, and by then we had defrosted our own dinner and done whatever homework we were supposed to do. She rarely checked to see what we'd done, and those few times when she did, she dismissed us with, "It looks all right to me."

We took to marauding the street until ten o'clock at night, hoping that he was either asleep in the chair or in his bed before we got back. He was always arguing with her about something or lost in depression, staring at the fire. It was creepy and we hated coming home. If we were unlucky, he was waiting for us with his rage firmly contained within his curled fists, and all we could do was duck and crouch to take the worst of it.

By age fifteen, I had left school, lost my virginity to someone whose name I forgot almost instantly, and taken my first amphetamine.

"Does taking the speed make it better?" Dr. Simpson asked gently.

"Maybe. I can forget about it. I hate the aftereffects though."

"Why do it?"

"Because it gives me a break."

"I see," he said, looking at his watch and then folding his papers together.

"I'm sorry, we have to end now. That's it for this week, but I'll see you next week."

He must have been reading my mind because he followed that up with, "Don't forget the court needs you to be here each week." When he stuck out his hand to shake mine, I stood up and took it. "Be careful out there," he said. I nodded and went on my way.

On the bus home, I kicked the seat in front of me, causing the bus conductor to give me a warning. "How could I have been so stupid?" I muttered. "How did he do that?" In forty minutes he made me identify the very thing that made me angry all the time and the one thing I didn't want anyone to know about. I kicked the chair again and got kicked off the bus.

On the sixth visit he shook my hand in his usual "Hail fellow, well met" kind of way, and I sat down without saying anything.

"How are you?"

I shrugged my shoulders and studied the backs of my hands.

"What happened this week?"

Staring at my hands made it easier to stop the tears from falling. I did not want to cry again. I was getting sick of crying during these sessions. Somehow this room was like some vast toilet bowl that I kept emptying all my shit into. I was exhausted.

"This is no good for me comin' here. It just stirs things up and it's no going to help anything, is it?"

He reached forward and touched my hand. "It can if you want it to."

"That's just it, isn't it? I went berserk this week, you know. I started crying and mauling all my Beatles posters down off the wall. My Beatles posters! Do you know how important they are to me? My dad was ready to start in on me but I slammed the door on him. I'm having these awful dreams about being killed and trampled to death and I can't breathe."

When he calmed down, Dad asked me what I was doing. I told him I was rearranging my room."

"Have you done any drugs lately?"

"Naw!" I said angrily, and then looked back at my hands again. It wasn't entirely true. I had found some great Lebanese hash that took the edge off things.

Taking a deep breath, he sat back in his chair. "So what do you want to do?"

"I'm sick of this. It's no going to get any better as long as I stay here. I need to go somewhere else."

"Where would you like to go?"

"London. I can get a decent job down there for starters. I know somebody who could take care of me."

"But you're only fifteen."

"A know that."

"Do you think that's the answer to your problems?"

"Probably not. I'm just *angry* all the time." I said through gritted teeth, feeling the hot swell of tears coursing down my cheeks. "Everybody thinks I'm off my head. They just don't get it. My dad says I'm worthless and I'll never amount to anything. He says I'll end up just like my Ma. She used to have dreams. She was going to be a singer, but then she had bairns and that was that. I've got a half-sister I hardly know, and a brother I can't stand. If I stay here, do you know what's going to happen to me? I'll end up with a drunken bastard who spends his nights at the pub just like my Dad, he'll give me three bairns and I'll have to work in the bonds or something. I'm no going to do that. I don't know what I'll do, but it's no going to be that."

He stared at me, waiting for something else, and I stared at the picture of a flower on the wall that sucked me into the ochre red and yellow of its petals. My mind was yammering incoherently and most of what I was feeling told me I had gone too far. This doctor wanted to stop me from doing something stupid but it was too late for that.

"Alison?" he asked gently.

Biting my lip to avoid crying, I whispered, "I don't want to end up like them, all bitter and drunk. I want more out of my life. I'm no stupid, but everybody seems to be thinking I am. I'm scared. I drink too much when I'm no supposed to. I take the pills to forget about everything, and I've had too many laddies whose names I can't remember. My dad tells me I'm going to end up like my mother. He says I'm going to get pregnant and if I do I'm no to come home. I've actually thought about doing myself in, but that's stupid. Nobody would care anyway." I was blubbering now and frantically searched in my pocket for a used tissue. He pushed the box towards me and put his glasses down on the table.

"Let me tell you something that I don't think anyone else has ever told you before," he said leaning forward. "You are magnificent."

I looked up sharply then looked down at the torn tissue in my hand. It was too difficult to look at him when he said things like that.

"You are brave, courageous, and unique, and don't let anyone tell you otherwise. You could have refused to turn up here for these appointments. You were not force marched here every week. It took guts to keep coming here. It's not easy doing this, and you've had a lot to deal with. I don't think you're stupid or mad. In fact, I would say you are anything but. You might be one of the sanest people I've ever met. You should have stayed at school. What do you think London will give you?

"I just want to get away, that's all."

"Just think about whether that's a wise choice. That's all I ask. I wish we could continue to work together longer, but I was only given six weeks. I can recommend further counseling, but I don't know if they will approve it or not."

I had a hard, bubbly feeling as if something were screaming to get out. The word "sane" bumped up against the panic and fear repeating like a record stuck in the groove. I nodded my head but couldn't say anymore. He took my hand and held it firmly for a few seconds staring into my eyes. I held on until he dropped it.

—m—

Agnes was shaking her head. We can never tell what we're doing to our children until it's too late. We all try to do what's right, but who knows. There're no easy answers. There are always two sides of a story, but she was sure Alison didn't deserve half of what she got. She was always too smart for her own good. The questions she asked were always direct but she rarely got the answers she asked for. Too busy, too tired, too ignorant for the most part. But there was always another side to the story. It was a pity Grace wasn't around to tell it herself.

three

THIRTEEN MONTHS LATER, the train ride from London to Edinburgh seemed to take forever. I swallowed my trepidation like heartburn and watched the landscape change from industrial England to the rolling green hills of Scotland. When I left, my father had made his thoughts clear. "If you find any trouble doon there, dinnae come hame here with it."

My mother said it was stupid of me to be leaving, and asked only two questions. "Who are you going with?" and "Where are you going to stay when you get there?" I told her I was going with a girlfriend who had a cousin with a flat in Acton, and I could get a job easily. She said, "Do what you like. You always do." I thought she was glad to get rid of me.

The train moved slowly through the green rolling hills until the sea emerged in a long stretch of white peaks under the endless gray canvas of turbulent Scottish skies. I was clinging to a small part of me that wanted to believe there was someone at home to save me but knew the truth of the matter was that there was nothing there for me. But when you've got nowhere to go, home still looks like the place to be.

When the train rolled to a stop at Edinburgh's Waverley Station, I sat a long time in the carriage before making my way through the station towards the bus stop on Princes Street. My father's rage loomed in my head. My bag felt heavy. It was pouring rain, the bus stop was drafty, and my shoes were leaking. Huddling into my navy blue pea coat, I felt a headache coming on from the wet smell of wool that stuffed my nostrils with dampness.

❧

I wasn't sure I was pregnant at first. After a year of living in London finding new jobs every few weeks, changing bed-sitters to avoid paying the rent, and spending all my spare cash on beer and hashish, I found myself sharing a grubby bed-sitter with twenty-foot ceilings, two beds, and an orange box bookshelf, lit by a Chinese paper lantern hung over a solitary sixty-watt light bulb. The windows were stuck shut with paint, but that didn't stop the drafts from slicing through the room. We had a gas stove at one end of the room and a gas oven at the other. Both were kept on twenty-four hours a day until the room was stifling. We paid for the gas by breaking open the gas meter and recycling the same shilling each time the meter started to run out.

I started throwing up and blamed it on the cinnamon toast I'd been eating for a month.

"You need to see a doctor," said Sue, the anorexic want-to-be model who seriously wanted to emulate Twiggy.

"Och, I'll be fine once I start eatin' properly again."

"That's not your problem," she announced in her thick Geordie accent. "I don't eat, and I don't get sick like that."

"You've got other problems," I said.

A week later I was still feeling queasy every day and throwing up in the mornings.

"It was that idiot you slept with in Holland Park," she announced. "I bet you what you like. He's given you something. Go see the doctor before you end up in the hospital."

❧

The waiting room was in the basement of a townhouse off Portobello Road, heavy with dust and soiled magazines that lay scattered over the table and chairs. I sat in a black leather horsehair chair sagging low to the ground, cracking under the weight of too many large bums.

The doctor's office was on the well-lit first floor, and I was called to it by way of an intercom that hung on the wall. There was a strong smell of camphor and tobacco smoke hanging over the files stacked on his desk. I noticed his white coat was buttoned up the wrong way, giving a skewed look to his collar. His greasy black hair was combed straight back from his forehead, reminding me of my father. His name was Dr. Singh and he gave a polite smile and that little nod of the head that Indians do before he waved for me to sit down.

He took my pulse and then my blood pressure, saying, "And what do you think the problem is today?" in his singsong voice.

I wanted to say, if I knew that I wouldn't be here, but instead said, "I've just been sick all the time."

"Have you been eating?"

I lied.

"I see," he said, pushing the stethoscope across the table to make room to write on his paper. "Do you think you might be pregnant?"

He could have said do you think you might be dying and he would have received the same response. I gasped and felt the room darken momentarily. It was a forbidden thought shoved away from me several times during the last two weeks.

I must have turned white "Are you all right?" He offered me a glass of water. I refused.

My breathing was shallow and I searched in my pocket for my inhaler. I took two puffs and apologized.

"You are here to get help with your asthma?"

"No. I'm fine," I said rather loudly. "Isn't there some kind of test I can do? I mean, you have to prove it, right?"

"Oh, yes. We can take care of that right away. Just give me a little sample in this." He handed me a plastic cup that looked as if it had been used a few times, "and come back in two hours."

My hand trembled as I took it from him. "The bathroom is just along the corridor on the right."

The toilet seat was cracked and the light wasn't working, so I was forced to leave the door ajar as I placed the cup under me to take a pee. None would come out. I kept thinking rain, running water, until I flushed and then I got a trickle. I hoped it was enough to tell.

The breath caught in my throat, and I wasn't sure if I would ever breathe again. Fear swelled in my stomach like a giant balloon, and I gasped before sitting down. It had to be the gigolo from Holland Park. He was so smooth with his candles and Vivaldi.

The doctor poured me a glass of water in a water-stained glass, and I took a sip but was unable to swallow. My mind was under siege, you're pregnant, you're pregnant, see what you've done. He must have made a mistake.

Seeing my distress, he asked kindly, "Is there anyone here who can be of help to you? Is there a person to whom you can talk? Where are your mother and your father?"

I looked up at him as if he were speaking a foreign language. He told me I should go home.

"There are options available," he said as he opened his door. "We will be talking about them later when you are ready," he said gently, steering me to the front door.

I spent most of the first two days after leaving the doctor's office sitting in Henekeys pub on Portobello Road, talking with anyone who would listen. Everyone had his or her own ideas. Tim thought I should just get rid of it. "Nobody needs to have a baby who doesn't want one," he said. "There are enough bastards in the world."

Big Gus said he thought I should keep it. I would get used to having a kid around. He said he had a boy up in Newcastle and his mother seemed to be doing all right.

Gladys told him if she was all right in Newcastle it was probably because he was down here with nothing better to do. He was probably doing her a favor. "You probably don't know what to do with yourself, do you?" she said to me. "Have you told your mum and dad yet?"

I nodded my head in the affirmative and said nothing.

As soon as I could put words in my mouth, I called my mother.

The phone booth at Notting Hill Station felt like a refrigerator empty of nourishment. The evening rush hour was in full stream but I didn't hear the rumble of trains rushing through the tunnels and the ticket barrier calump, calump, calumping. I heard my mother's disapproval and I heard my father's condemnation. I heard "Get lost" and I heard despair wailing across the telephone dial tone.

I hoped I would find sympathy with this woman who had had bastard children herself. I thought she would understand.

The phone rang and rang and I was about to hang up when she answered. "Hello." There was no answer from my end. "Hello," she said again. "Is that you, Alison?"

It broke the freeze and my voice trembled. All my rehearsed lines disappeared and I was holding on like an over wound spring. My throat lost its lubrication. "Hi, Ma. It's me." Then the dam gave way and I surged forward. "I'm sorry, Ma. I didn't mean to. I need help, Ma." The sound of my mother's gasp was barely audible, and the momentary silence that followed was deafening.

"Oh, Alison! Don't tell me that. I don't want to hear that. You can't be. Good God. Don't come home here. Your father'll kill you. What in God's name are you going to do with yourself? You can't be right," she said.

I held my breath to stop myself from crying, while voices in my head were telling me to run; run away as fast as I could. But my feet were stuck to the concrete floor of the phone booth as I gathered up my sob and put the phone down.

Gladys's face was disheveled, pockmarked, and wrinkled. It looked like someone had made room for their baggage. With her bright purple hair and multilayer colored fabrics, she could easily have stepped out of a circus. She held my hand and watched as the tears trickled down my face before leading me to the toilet.

"Listen, Alison. I can get someone to get rid of this thing for you. I know an old woman who lives up in Chiswick who helps girls out for about fifty pounds."

I shook my head violently. "Fifty pounds! No, I can't do that. First of all, I've got no money. Secondly, I . . . No like that."

"But you're not going to keep it, are you?"

"I don't know," I said. A part of me wanted to keep it. To hold it, to give it cuddles and dress it up in nice clothes. Nobody could tell me what to do with it. I would take it strolling through Kensington Gardens, the perfect loving, caring mother cherishing her child. In reality, most of the people pushing prams in Kensington Gardens were the nannies of which I could have been numbered. The rose-colored paint was chipped at the edges but that didn't matter. I wanted to feel there was something that belonged to me. That loved me. That I could love back.

"It's a lonely life with a baby. A single room and social security are not very romantic. You won't be able to sit around the pub every night with a baby in the pram next to you."

"But I don't know what to do. What do you think?"

"If it were me, I'd get rid of it, but I can't tell you that," she said. "This is your decision and if you decide to go ahead with it, then give that baby everything. Don't shortchange it the way we were shortchanged. But think about this hard. Your life is not your own anymore."

The next day, I found blood on my pants and thought my troubles were over. I couldn't tell if I was disappointed or not.

When I showed up at Dr. Singh's again, he asked me outright if I wanted the baby. I said, "I don't know," and he phoned for an ambulance.

The hospital bed was hard and I felt encased in white curtains and stiff sheets. The sound of carts rolling back and forth across the linoleum floor and the clatter of stainless steel bedpans as they hit the stainless steel shelves on the trolley rustled the isolation. I should have been used to the sounds and smells of hospitals, but I always felt overwhelmed in the early days of being there.

A nurse poked her head around the curtain and asked if I needed a bedpan. I wanted to go to the toilet but she said no then jammed it underneath me. I sat perched over the flat stainless steel pan and tried to go but nothing would come. When she left and closed the curtain again, I jumped off the bed and did a few jumping jacks before the guilt crept over me and made me stop. Cradling my belly, I wondered if I could actually be a mother. Then I heard a group of feet approaching and scurried back under the sheets.

The medical staff arrived en masse like witnesses at an execution. A tall, imperious man wearing a navy blue spotted bow tie with a terrible pink and white striped shirt under his white coat stepped forward with a clipboard in hand. As he read the notes, I noticed his fingernails were immaculately manicured. He looked up at me with a well-placed smile on his lips and said, "Good morning. I'm Dr. Skinner."

Turning back to his students, he said in his imperial manner, "This young woman is eighteen years old, seven weeks pregnant and presently indicating the possibility of a spontaneous abortion."

I felt as if I were in a nineteenth-century operating room being readied for dissection, intimidated by the students and his regal presence. He turned up the corners of his lips and asked how I was doing today. The rush of anger was overwhelming.

"When can I have an abortion?" I snapped.

He blinked twice, and the students shuffled their feet and looked at each other and then at him, waiting for his response. "Well! We'll have to talk about that, won't we?" he said, bending down towards me.

I was suddenly ablaze with decision. "I don't want this. You can't make me." I felt like I was four years old again, behaving in a way that I was never allowed to do when I was four.

He smiled again, but this time the corners of his mouth didn't turn up, only opened wider. "Well, dear." His voice patronized the air around him. "I know that's what you want, but I'm not sure you understand the position you are in. Abortions cannot be handed out just because you want one. They are not so easy to dispense like medicine. It's a grave decision to take away a life. I think you and I need to have a little chat." He waved his hand and the students stepped outside the curtain. I could hear them whispering amongst themselves.

I felt overwhelmed by his sweet-smelling aftershave and his supercilious smile. He pulled up a chair and sat right next to me, almost taking my hand but stopping at the bed's edge.

"You know there are many people out there who are unable to have children, who would desperately like to have one. Now . . . ," and he leaned in a little closer, "The world needs strong babies from strong girls. What do you think? You could make somebody very happy. Don't you think you should revise your idea of having an abortion? Adoption is not such a bad idea, is it?"

Stupefied by his patronizing airs, my resolve was swamped in turgid muddy thinking. I was going to make someone else happy! My mouth wouldn't open, too stunned to give a response. I was allowing this man to make my decision for me. I was giving in to the old fear of authority, the one that said I should "respect my betters" even when I knew that my "betters" were no better than me.

He patted my hand and stood up. "We'll keep an eye on you for a few days," he said as he pushed open the curtains to the waiting supplicants.

I didn't stand a chance in the prestigious world of the obstetrician to the royal family who was doing his slumming on Wednesday mornings at the local National Health Service hospital.

The voice of Alison telling her story felt as if she were talking to the world. Agnes had never known this part of the story because Alison rarely spoke to anyone in those days. It was as if she had no family and wanted to erase all of it from her life. Grace had told Agnes she was worried about her, and Agnes had advised Grace to go to London and take her home immediately. Grace said there was no point—Alison had always done as she bloody well pleased. Most of the time Grace had no idea what she was up to, but when she was caught by the police for drugs, Grace phoned weeping, asking why everything she ever touched turned to shite. Agnes tried to make her feel better by suggesting that Alison would find her own way. She hesitated to say there wasn't much to come home for.

The plane started an up and down motion and the seat belt sign went on. The pilot apologized for the turbulence, as if he could control it, and suggested everyone stay in their seats. It felt like a roller-coaster ride as it dipped on the current, sending gusts of nausea through Agnes. She was trying to read and ignore it but it was hard to concentrate. The young girl leaned over and said "Just take some deep breaths and it will be fine. They don't usually last too long. Don't worry, the plane will be fine. It just feels like it's dropping out of the sky, but it isn't really."

four

Standing at the front door of our flat, I was drenched, tired and really scared about what was waiting on the other side. I had lost my front door key so I rang the doorbell. Mother looked me up and down as I walked in. "You look like something the cat dragged in. Make yourself scarce, he's no in a very good mood."

"Hello, Ma. Nice to see you too," I said, putting my bag down in the hallway. I brushed past her and went into the living room.

He was sitting in his usual chair by the fire, wearing a vest and baggy pants, huddled over a newspaper. His glasses were perched on the end of his nose, and a glass of whisky sat next to him on top of the electric fire. He turned his head. "I suppose you must be wantin' something."

My mother's presence behind me felt like a whisper being strangled. "I'm going to the hairdresser's," she said. "I'll be back in a couple of hours. If you need anything, you know where it is."

I had heard that line for years. I still wasn't clear where I could find what I needed. I followed her out to the front door, and as I lifted my bag she said, "Don't get him all worked up, Alison. It will be miserable the night if he's in a bad mood."

"What about me?"

"We'll talk when I get back. Just stay out of his way." She pulled on her rubber boots and took the umbrella from the coat rack.

"It's pourin' of rain. Your hair'll get soaked."

"I'll take a taxi back," she said, then was gone with a slam of the door as I stood, wondering whether I should heed her advice or not.

I felt damp and chilled and the hallway was freezing. The corporation said they would put in central heating, but that was two years ago and there was still no sign of it. I dumped the bag inside my bedroom that was now full of old sheets and towels that smelled like they'd been lying around since the Reformation. My mother's ironing board and iron stood by the side of the bed. I had forgotten how small the room was. I had had many a Sunday afternoon twist and shout with my boyfriends in this room before I left home. My Ma would stand outside the door and yell for me to come out, always before we got to the penetration stage. It was as if she had a sixth sense about it. I always wondered why she never barged right in if she knew what I was up to. It was probably amazing I didn't get pregnant before I left home.

It was cold and I was shivering so I went into the living room to get some warmth.

He lay there with his arms folded across his chest, fingers intertwined together, eyes closed. This was the image of my father I would remember the most. We had quite a few photos of him in this position, always with his head slumped to the side and his mouth slightly open. He snored a lot until my mother kicked him and told him to wake up. In the later years he would complain but he didn't curse anymore.

I sat down across from him on the other side of the fireplace watching the steam rise up from my socks. The Naugahyde chair squeaked as I moved. My mother tried to soften the effect by using cotton chair backs, which kept sliding down until they lay in a wrinkled mess in the crack. The couch still had the original plastic wrap on it. Plastic on plastic. Your legs usually stuck to it if you sat there long enough, leaving wrinkles on the backs of your thighs.

The lizard eye opened. He had this way of raising it only high enough to get the contour of who was there, and then he would shut it again if he was uninterested. He closed it and gave a couple of smacking sounds with his lips.

I picked up the newspaper that lay at his feet. It was the usual tabloid nonsense. He probably only looked at the pictures since it was well known my father was illiterate. Not once in my life did I ever see him pick up a book, and when my Ma died, he didn't even know how to fill in the checkbook. It was sad I suppose, but I didn't think so at the time. I just thought he was an ignorant bastard.

After five minutes I put the paper down and stood to look out the window. The rain was coming down in buckets and I wondered about Ma's hair. The squeak of the plastic caused him to open both eyes this time. Without moving his body, he said, "What are you home for? I thought you were off in London livin' it up. Couldnae do withoot us? Run out o' money, did you? Well, dinnae expect any here. I havenae got any."

In all my years, most of what I had gotten from him was stolen when I raided his pant pockets or found some money lying on the fireplace. But there wasn't much. He counted every penny.

I sat down again to face him. "I don't need any money." I hesitated. He gave me his "scunnered" look that said you're annoying me.

Suddenly I couldn't help myself. "I've come to tell you something."

"What's eatin' you? You've been fidgeting since you came in the door. I hope it's no what I think it is. If it is, you might as well leave right now."

I looked into my father's red eyes and blurted out, "I'm sorry. I didn't mean to," and started to cry.

"Jesus buckin' Christ! I don't want to hear that. Who's the father? Do you know?"

Through my tears I saw his upper lip curl over his lower one, a fine layer of sweat shining through his mustache. His fist was curled up tight causing his biceps to bulge. When he stood up I thought for sure he was going to wallop me, but he walked past to the drinks cabinet under the window and poured a glass of whisky, which he drank before turning around.

I was holding on so tight my muscles were shaking. I had come home to lay this burden at his feet, to tell him that all his words of warning had achieved the exact things he didn't want. I had succeeded in being like my mother, as he had predicted. There wasn't a chance in hell I could be anything else.

He stood waiting for an answer. I would have preferred to say it was someone I was madly in love with, but the reality was I didn't know who the father was. It could have been the guy in Holland Park but I wasn't going to go knocking on his door. I had only slept with him once. There were too many I could lay the blame on.

He turned back towards the cabinet and poured himself another. The half-pint bottle was almost finished. It was one of the specials my mother handpicked from the whisky bonds. I held my breath and waited for him to make the next move.

He sat down again with the glass in his hand, grazing his top teeth over his bottom lip.

"What do you think you're going to do now? Between you and your brother, there's been no peace. He's away in Dunfermline. They gave him a year this time. I don't understand what gets into you two."

That was a familiar phrase. Like something had possessed us and made us do it. It seemed to take care of the blame issue quite nicely.

"I don't know," I said feebly.

"You can't stay here. I'm no having all the neighbors talking about you." He stared at me, expecting an answer. I stared at the floor.

"Well, if you don't know, I don't know what to tell you." He turned his attention to the fireplace, and I took this as a cue to leave. I had nothing more to say, and if I did it could end up in a serious argument, not to mention the weight of those fists, which he hadn't used on me in three years. I went into the kitchen to make a cup of tea and heard him settle back onto his chair again as it squeaked under his weight.

It wasn't as if I was getting any surprises here because I knew what the reaction would be, but I held on to the illusion that you could always go home. Like Dorothy in The Wizard of Oz, my little piece of Kansas would always be waiting. But like Oz, there were so many illusions it was hard to find my way back home, if indeed there was ever a place I could call home. I spent my life in search of that until I finally figured out that it isn't somewhere you can touch. No matter what anyone says, you can never go back home once you've left.

My mother returned an hour later, her hair an impeccable auburn, coiffed to perfection and lacquered within an inch of its life to keep it looking good for the next five days.

"You told him," she said, standing in the bedroom door.

I nodded.

"What did he say?"

"He said I'd get no help in this house."

"He's no goin' to put up with it. He's never been good at understandin' these things." She had tears in her eyes. "I'm sorry you had to go through this, hen." Her voice was wavering. "If it's money you need, I can help you a wee bit."

"But why, Ma? You had a bairn, didn't you? You didn't have to do this yourself, did you? You had Nannie to help you. It's no fair. I wanted to have an abortion, but they wouldn't let me. The doctor told me I could go make somebody very happy if I gave it up for adoption. I don't want to make anybody happy. How about me being happy for a change? What am I going to do?"

"Aye, I had a bairn, but you probably noticed she didnae live with us. He disnae understand these things. It's no his fault."

"How can you say that? It's always been his fault. He's a drunken bastard!"

"Sssshh. You wake him up and he's like a bear wi' a sare heed. I see the bottle's empty." She had a look of panic on her face, and for the first time I really understood how vulnerable my mother was with him. She was now making more money than him but that didn't matter. There was this odd thing going on between them that gave him the authority. I swore no man would ever hold me down like that.

"So that's it. I just have to get on with it."

She looked tired and completely drained of energy. "I can't do anything else."

"Well, I might as well go then," I said angrily. "There's no point."

The rain had turned to drizzle and it was growing dark. I had no idea what time the train was leaving, but I couldn't sit in that house any longer. I had to get away and figure out what I needed to do. I could see in my mother's face that she didn't think much of my chances for survival. I put on my shoes, which were still damp, and picked up my bag. As I struggled to control the tears, I was suddenly full of resolve. I would have this baby and I would show them I could do it myself. I didn't need them or their approval.

"You can stay the night," she said weakly.

"I'm going." I pushed past her into the hallway.

"At least take this," she offered, giving me a five pound note. "It's all I've got right now."

Both of us stood at the door, separated by our grief, telling ourselves it would be all right. But it was all lies—that had always been our way. Never tell the whole story. Only enough to make the lie believable. Even when we thought we were telling the truth, it was a variation of the lie. To tell the truth would be to expose the pain, and we could never do that.

"Take care of yourself," she said as she watched me going down the stairs.

"Aye, right!" I said, pulling my coat tighter around me.

When the train stopped in York, I thought about Auntie Agnes. It had been at least five years since I had last seen her. As the train conductor blew his whistle, I impulsively grabbed my bag and jumped off the train as it was pulling away.

"Sleeping, were you?" he said. I nodded and looked down the platform towards the buffet. I would take a cup of tea and figure out what I was doing next. It was ten o'clock at night, and I only vaguely remembered her address. It was totally ludicrous of me to jump off the train because I had no money for another ticket to London. The buffet was empty except for a man and a woman sitting in the far corner kissing. I sat down at the counter.

"Where you headed to, lass?" asked the old man behind the bar.

"London."

"Oh, you'll have missed the last one," he said kindly.

I nodded.

He leaned over towards me and said quietly, "There's a waiting room at the end of platform 6 that has a nice fire in it. You can bide there until the five forty-five comes through. Nobody will bother you." He winked.

I sipped the strong tea and eyed the dried-at-the-corners ham sandwiches. I was hungry but I didn't want to spend any more money. If I had to I would hitchhike back to London. It wouldn't be the first time. He saw me looking at the sandwiches.

"Has thee eaten t'day? Tha looks fair peekit."

I confessed that I was a little hungry, and he pushed a plate of sandwiches over the counter. "There's nobody going to eat them tonight. Shame to waste them."

I was grateful for the food, as I had eaten nothing since the morning when I left Kings Cross Station, and ate it too quickly, causing a great burp to arise. The couple in the corner started to snigger and the woman pointed at me.

"That good, eh?" the barman asked "Where you from? It's not from around they parts, is it?"

I told him and his face lit up. He said he'd had his honeymoon in Selkirk because he was posted up there during the war. "Technically, I was too old for service, but they was desperate," he said conspiratorially. "Bloody shame for the war, but good for me. My wife's a Scots lass. Still got the tongue. I suppose it never leaves your," he said.

Suddenly I remembered where Auntie Agnes lived.

"Do you know where Willis Street is?" I asked

He lifted his cap and scratched his head, and then he gave a rub of his stubbly gray beard with his left hand before picking up the glass to polish it. "I'm not rightly sure," he said slowly. "There's a Willis Street about fifteen minutes from here, just past the old gate. Would tha be the one?"

I sat up straighter, suddenly full of energy. "Aye, that's the one." I suddenly remembered the old Roman walls that ran round the city. "It's near the Roman walls," I said.

"Everything's near the Roman wall around here, pet." He laughed heartily at his own joke. "It's not that difficult to find. Here, I'll draw you a map." I was ready to go when I realized I didn't know which number.

"Do they have a phone?" he asked.

"Yeah. My Ma talks to her all the time."

"Well, why didn't you say that in the first place, girl? We can find them in the phone book." He pulled out a thick book from under the counter, and we began to look through the list of Rankins in the city. William Rankin was last on the list. The address said 25 Willis Street.

"Thanks so much," I beamed. "I really appreciate the help."

I was about to go when he said, "Don't you think you should call them before you go?"

"No, I'll surprise them," I said, with more energy than I'd had in days.

I thought I could read the map but as I slogged through the winding streets in a slow drizzle of rain I began to wonder. The wall ran all the way around the city, and as I followed it, it was now twenty-five minutes instead of fifteen, and it didn't feel as if I were any closer. It was nearly eleven, and I thought by now they would be asleep so maybe this wasn't a good time. I was soaked through and was feeling thoroughly miserable again. You're so stupid, I told myself. You couldn't find your way out of a paper bag. I passed a pub that was just letting out and asked someone if they could tell me where Willis Street was. "You're in it," he said, waving his arm at the barely readable street sign tucked behind an advertisement for Bovril. I felt like a complete idiot and thanked him before looking at the numbers. I was at 76 going up, so I retraced my steps, realizing I must have passed it.

"Oh, my God!" exclaimed Agnes when she opened the door. "What are you doing here?"

I stood dripping on the doorstep, apologizing for disturbing her so late at night. "Why didn't you tell me you were coming?" she asked, pulling me inside. "Look at you, you're dripping wet. Get these things off you and come in to the fire. You gave me quite a fright when that doorbell rang."

I followed her into her cozy living room filled with souvenirs of holidays and photographs of her children, leaving my shoes, coat, and bag in the front hallway.

"Come in to the fire. You'll get your death. William's been in his bed for an hour, but I always have trouble sleeping so I don't bother until about one o'clock. Let me make you a cup of tea. Just you warm up there and I'll be back in a minute. What a surprise this is." She shuffled off to the back of the house to make tea and left me sitting comfortably by the electric fire. It was so warm in her living room that I fell asleep in the chair before she got back but awoke when she placed a plate of sandwiches and chocolate biscuits next to the beautiful bone china teacup and saucer.

"You look like you're no feelin' well," she said gently. "Here, gie me that jumper. It's all damp. I'll give you one of our Shirley's. That'll fit you." She left again to fetch it and seemed to be taking delight in this midnight adventure. "Wait till William knows you're here. He'll be tickled."

I drank the tea and ate a sandwich. So far I'd said practically nothing—she was so excited at my being there and hadn't given me a chance. But now that I had everything I needed, she sat down opposite me and leaned forward, surveying me. "So what's brought you here in the middle of the night? I don't think it's because you missed me."

I was in the middle of sipping my tea when I began to cry, causing the hot liquid to run down my chin. I put the cup down carefully and continued to let the tears fall. She fell onto her knees and came to rest beside me, putting her arms around me and pulling me into her large bosom. "There, there, hen, it must be pretty big if it brought you here."

My nose was beginning to run and I felt ashamed to be letting it drip all over her, so I pulled away. "Do you have a tissue, please?" I blubbered.

She pulled out a hankie from her sleeve. "It's clean. I haven't used it the day."

I blew my nose and sat up straighter. She waited patiently for me to say something, watching my face with a look of such sadness that I almost started crying again.

"I'm pregnant, Auntie Agnes."

She didn't say a thing. Just nodded her head and went to sit in her chair. She closed her eyes for a second and gave a big sigh. "Have you told your Ma?"

313

"She doesn't want to know about it—neither does he."

"She can talk," she said. "What does she think she's playin' at? I've got to speak to her. This is no right."

"I don't know what to do, Auntie Agnes." I started crying again. "She didn't want me there. I went hame and she told me I would have to work this one out. It's no fair. She should be able to understand?"

"Aye, she should. That one more than anybody else should, but I don't know. Things are very queer and I don't get the sense of them ever. Let's talk about this the morn when you're feeling a wee bit better. I'll give you Shirley's bed. She's at Nottingham University now," she said proudly. "Billy and Scott are sleepin' already. C'mon, give me your wet things after you get ready for your bed and I'll dry them out for you."

I settled into Shirley's bedroom, a pastel pink confection of sweet teenage heaven. I never would have wanted a room like this, but it was somehow comforting anyway. There were posters of David Cassidy in various degrees of toothbrush smiles and the neatly emaciated Karen Carpenter staring dolefully at her brother in a pose that didn't look like a sister and brother. The bedroom was warm because the house had central heating, and I tossed the covers back to get some air. Agnes had taken my clothes and my underwear and was planning to wash them. I fell into a deep sleep, oblivious to the world until she awoke me with a cup of tea in the morning. It took me a minute to remember where I was, and then I smelled the bacon and eggs.

"When you're ready, I've got a breakfast ready for you. William's gone to his office and the boys have gone to school. I didn't want to wake you because you were so tired last night. You'll see them the night. I've left you a dressing gown at the bottom of the bed."

I didn't want to get out of this bed ever. "I'll be there in a minute," I said, feeling like I wanted to drift back to sleep again, but the smell of the eggs and bacon meant she was going to a lot of trouble and I didn't want to disappoint her.

Examining the framed family pictures in the living room Agnes asked. "Do you remember everybody?"

"They've all changed a lot," I said. I had spent most of my life trying to ignore where I came from, I knew Agnes and William and their kids because we were occasionally sent there during summer holidays. It was great to be away, but I always wanted to go back home. In our house, the only pictures out were school ones until the age of nine or ten, and an old one of my dad when he was in the Army. All the rest were stuffed away in boxes in the wardrobe. Years later, after my mother died, I found them. It was not surprising to see that most of them had my mother or father with a drink in hand.

"You look like you need feeding. C'mon, sit yourself down. Agnes's ample body leaned across the table as she placed an enormous plate of eggs, tomatoes, bacon, and fried bread in front of me.

Waiting until I had finished everything she then brought me a piece of cake. "I made it this morning. You should have a wee bit before it gets cold." I was ready to burst, but I nibbled on her lemon cake and found it delicious, so I ate some more. Stuffed would have been an understatement. I was now fed for a week.

Agnes was working the armholes of a jumper she was knitting, making small talk about the children and their schooling, how proud she was of Shirley for getting a place at Nottingham to study archaeology, "although I don't know what she's going to do with that," she said. William was doing well at Rowntrees and had just been promoted to district manager. He was in good health and so was she, and that was all that mattered. Everything else was secondary. "So what are you going to do?"

"I don't know. My father told me I wouldn't get anything at home."

"Aye, well, he would, wouldn't he. He hasn't changed. What would you like to do?"

"I don't know what to do. I've no got anywhere I can go right now."

"Well, you're welcome to stay here as long as you like, hen. Shirley's no comin' back for a few weeks."

"I'll no stay long," I said quickly, "I can get the train the morn."

"There's no need to go runnin' off so fast," said Agnes. "I think you better talk to me about what's happening."

I told her the whole story about the hospital and what happened at home without crying once. She listened carefully without interrupting

315

until I admitted that. I wanted to get rid of it, but I couldn't. "What chance can I give it?" I asked.

She sat quietly for a moment, casting off and picking up the stitches on her knitting. "You know you're no the first one wi' this problem, don't you?" She looked up and over her glasses.

"I know about Harriet, if that's what you mean,"

"I ken, but I wasn't talking about her. Your Ma had another bairn. Her name was Rita. She died when she was three. It was an awful thing."

My mouth fell open and then closed as I wiped away the tears from my face with the back of my hand. Agnes reached forward and gave me another hankie. "She had two bairns before me? She's no helpin' me and she was the same way!"

"Aye, I suppose, but dinnae blame her. She's been blamed enough. I think it's him. He's the one she's up against. It's always been that way. You know that, don't you?" she said breathlessly.

"Why didn't she tell me?"

"Your Ma's no been very good at tellin' things straight," she said slowly. "It's always been a problem."

I thought of all the occasions I had asked her about what it was like when she was a girl. How did she meet my father? How come Harriet never lived with us? I never once got a straight answer. "What am I supposed to do, Auntie Agnes?"

"Given what I've seen over the years, I would suggest you go for the adoption. It's the fairest way to the bairn. Take what happened to our Harriet. She didn't get much of a chance. She tells me she's happy, but I don't believe it. I think she's been drinkin' too much. I can't say I've ever seen that lassie really happy. She's always looked for ways to get into trouble. William's tried talking to her, but she doesn't want to hear anything we've got to say. She just does as she wants and doesn't care. The same as your mother used to be. She's the same bloody way. Don't make the same mistakes, hen. I think you're better off giving it away. Dinnae do the same things as your mother. It will only make you miserable."

All the times when I thought I was doing what was best, I was only putting my nose where it wasn't wanted. With all of them, all I tried to do was protect them. They all wanted for something I could never give them. I tried all my life to keep away the resentments and losses I never wanted to deal with. I wanted to feel I had been right all my life but that wasn't what was happening. I've done my best to take care of my family. There's not been a time when I've not been some kind of mother to some-body. Always willing to step up and take over. Always willing to protect.

Everybody wanted something. Mistakes were all over the place. Not one person knew how to forgive until Alison. It was no accident she sent me on this journey. She talked about the need to forgive, but it was me who needed to forgive. I judged Grace for all the mistakes she made. I judged Douglas for not being the father I always wanted. And I judged my mother when I tried to protect her and failed. Alison knew that, which is why she wouldn't let me say no. This wasn't just about Lauren. She knew I would read this, she thought, with a certain amount of bit-terness creeping in. She knew what she was doing.

Shuddering, she wiped her eyes with the handkerchief she carried up her sleeve. "How am I going to give this to that lassie?" she murmured. "What am I going to tell her when I get there?"

five

SHE WALKED INTO the waiting room with a file in one hand and a cup of coffee in the other. Her hair was a careless sweep of black tendrils folded into a clasp to hold it together, and she wore a skirt of ethnic print that looked as if it had been bought at the Oxfam shop. She dropped the file but before picking it up said, "Hi! I'm Lisa Sawyer. Sorry I'm late," and stuck her hand out, shaking mine in a strong grasp. I stood back a little from the force of a personality that was cheerful and precise.

"Come, we'll go to my office," she pronounced, giving me a wide smile. I wasn't much in the mood for smiling, but I followed her as she rushed down the corridor towards a small cubbyhole of an office, very sanitary, with a small desk and two chairs and a poster of a mother holding a baby and "Every Child a Wanted Child" written under it. She saw me studying it and said, "Would you like a cup of tea or coffee? We don't have any biscuits because we just ran out."

I shook my head from side to side.

"It's okay. You can relax. I'm not going to eat you," she said gently, sitting down opposite me.

The doctor had said I should go speak to the adoption agency just to see if that's what I wanted to do. I was four months pregnant and had not yet been able to give a straight answer about whether I was keeping the child or giving it away. To be honest, I didn't want to make the decision. I wanted it made for me. And in the indecision, I found it difficult to get out of bed in the morning and go to work. The doctor at the prenatal clinic suggested I talk to a social worker.

"You want to tell me a little bit about yourself?"

I sat dumbly in the chair, feeling as if someone were turning a screw in my back, waiting for me to start talking.

She waited patiently for a few minutes. "You don't have to make any decisions today," she said kindly.

"I'm sorry," I blurted out. "I'm just not sure what to do."

"You don't have to do anything right now, dear. You've only just arrived." She smiled. "This is not the time."

I shrugged and twisted the ends of my shirt. My belly was beginning to swell but not enough to make me look like I was pregnant. I put my hands over it.

"Whatever your decision, it's not only for the good of your baby but for you, and nobody's going to push you one way or the other. You can trust me on that." She reached over and took my clasped hands into hers; staring into my face I immediately wanted to withdraw. "I'm here to help you."

Nodding, I let her warm grasp melt some of the tensions. "I know," I whispered.

"Look, let's leave the question of the baby aside for the moment. Let me ask you something else. What did you have for breakfast this morning?"

I smiled for the first time. "Toast and tea."

"Me too! That and a little yogurt. That's what I have every day. Do you like your tea with sugar or no sugar?"

"None."

"Great. I'll make you a cup of tea. I think it's what you need."

She turned to the kettle on the table and began making me tea. While busying herself with cups and tea bags, she told me how many cats she had and how much her husband loved walking in the Scottish Highlands. She said she had spent a year in Edinburgh doing her graduate studies and found the rain a little hard to take. She asked if I knew the Barleymead pub in the Grassmarket, but I didn't. She asked what I liked to do but I couldn't come up with anything beyond reading. When I'd drunk my tea and the chitchat had ended, she said it was a good start and she'd see me next week.

I felt disappointed. Nothing had been settled.

The following week, she asked, "What do you see yourself doing in the future?"

The future was something I couldn't see at that moment. I shrugged my shoulders. "When I was in school, I had this daft idea that I could help kids who were growing up in the same situation that I did. I had a retarded brother who died, and maybe I could do something like that, you know, help with them. But I haven't got the qualifications. As my Ma says, 'You can't live on dreams.'"

"Dreams are what take us to the next place, Alison." I hesitated for a moment.

"My Ma says they get you in trouble."

"They can, but it's a shame to stop yourself at the gate. Many great things have been done because people dreamed."

"It's all rubbish. My Ma says I've got too much of the gift of the gab."

She wrote something down on a piece of paper.

"Here, I want you to call this number and make an appointment. It's for an IQ test. Maybe that will convince you."

"I'd be wasting my time."

"Up to you. What are you really afraid of?"

I started laughing. "I might find out I'm really stupid."

"What if you're wrong?"

⎯⎯⎯⎯⎯⎯

On the day of the test, I almost didn't go because I felt nauseous most of the morning. As it turned out, the test was a breeze except for the math questions. I had never been any good with numbers, and no one had given me any support with it at school. I was the one who got four out of a hundred on math tests and lived through the agony of it being broadcast to the classroom when they gave out the results. But I could write rings around everyone in English class, though in the long run it didn't matter. They sent me off to David Kilpatrick Secondary School, affectionately known as Daft Kids, because I didn't have the math to get into Leith Academy, where my friends were going.

"Must have made a mistake," I said when she read the paper. "I guessed half the answers."

She laughed. "These are not idiot results," she said. "I think you better start thinking about what you want to do once this baby is born. Maybe you should consider going to college, take a diploma in teaching. You'd probably make a good teacher. You can do it if you want to."

"In my family, we're bloody lucky we made it to secondary school. Most of us left when we were fifteen or younger. I can't afford to go to school."

"Think about it. I'm a believer in dreams."

six

I WAS LIVING on low wages and borrowed clothes. I ate lamb stew for weeks on end because it was cheap, and picked up free vegetables at the Portobello Road market. It was stupid to think I could keep a baby. I could hardly feed myself.

As my belly grew larger, I had moments of great tenderness as you squirmed inside of me. Like every mother-to-be in the world, I watched fascinated as a hand or a foot rose out of my smooth, swollen abdomen like a mole, catching my ribs as you carelessly struggled to make room for yourself within the small space. At times like these I honestly believed I could do it. I could be a good mother to you regardless of what Agnes had said about family history. Somehow I would learn how to be a mother like the ones I saw on television. I would love and be loved in return. It would be easy.

I wanted to keep you with all my heart, but my head kept getting in the way. I spent many sleepless nights imagining how it could be with us, then remembering how it was for my mother, and finally wondering what I was thinking. I couldn't escape the idea of adoption. It seemed to override every fantasy I had about taking care of you myself. I could have said it was the family history, my mother's negativity, my father's brutality, my Auntie Agnes telling me to give myself a chance, but somewhere in amongst the confusion I knew I didn't want to raise another me, full of frustration, fear, and insecurity. I didn't want to create another Harriet, abandoned by her mother and left to figure out who and what her parents were. I felt sure there were other stories hiding in the closet that I didn't know about. Every family has their secret children. Every family has a story. For your sake I had to make the decision to give you away. There was no other choice that made sense.

In my seventh month I had an overwhelming need to see my mother and invited her down to London for a visit. She had never been to London, and I had not seen her since my visit to Scotland, although we had talked on the phone from time to time. To my surprise, she accepted the invitation and came for three days.

Walking towards me at Kings Cross Station, she gasped as she caught sight of me and almost dropped her suitcase. I had an urge to run into her arms and bury myself there, but then just as quickly pulled myself together. I took the suitcase from her. "Did you have a good journey?" I asked formally.

"No bad. I see you've no been feeding yourself right." She pointed towards my belly, which was quite small. The nurse at the clinic told me I needed to eat more because I could use more weight. "Are you all right?"

"I'm fine," I said. I was in fact pissed off that she had come. The push/pull of wanting/not wanting my mother, rejecting my mother, left me hating my mother. Any elation I may have felt that she was coming disappeared in my disapproving manner. I wasn't exactly clear at that moment why I had invited her at all.

We shuffled along the platform and down to the Underground. The whole time, she kept twisting her head to take it all in. "It's awfully busy here. Are you no feard getting around?"

"You get used to it," I said, putting a ticket into the barrier for her.

When we got home she inspected my room with a head butler's eye. "You certainly learned how to keep your room neat and clean. You didn't do that when you were home."

Defensively, I told her, "I've learned how to take care of myself quite well."

"You have, have you. Well, dinnae mind me. I can do for myself. I know you've got work to go to, so I'll just amuse myself." She was staring at the small fold-up Zedbed that I had borrowed. It was narrow and short, and I had already decided I would sleep on it for the time she was there. She was still standing with her coat on and I wondered if she was actually going to stay.

"Don't worry about the bed, I'll sleep on that one."

"Don't put yourself out for me," she said, taking her coat off.

We both slept fitfully that night. My mother moved a lot, releasing great sighs as she turned over, and the springs of the bed ground under her weight. When the sounds changed to sniffs, I lay still, trying not to intrude on her moment. For three hours I watched the bedside clock flip through time, my mind clamoring with questions about Harriet and Rita. The isolation was drowning both of us. My last thought before drifting off to sleep was to ask her how she had gotten pregnant with Harriet.

I was washing the breakfast cups and plates when I let one slip from my soapy hands onto the floor. "Fuck!" I shouted. "Fuck! Fuck! Fuck!" I repeated as I picked up the broken pieces.

She looked up from the magazine she was reading. "Are you all right?"

I stood up slowly, soap suds clinging to the broken pieces. "No, Ma, I'm not all right. I'm not sure I've ever been all right." I placed the cup in the dustbin and dried my hands.

"Och, don't start, Alison. I've had enough with your father. I thought we could do this with a wee bit of peace and quiet. I guess I'm no so lucky."

"No, you're not!" I said defiantly. "How come you've never explained to me where Harriet came from and why she never lived with us? I know you told me because Dad had a problem with her, but that's no all there is, is it?" My carefully learned speech patterns were radically deteriorating as we spoke.

"Well, aren't you all worked up this morning? I heard you rolling around in your bed last night. Couldn't sleep?"

"Aye, and I heard you crying so isn't it about time we stopped this stupid game? Isn't it about time you told me the story?"

"It's nobody's business but mine. Who do you think you are barging in like that? And you're wrong, I wasn't crying last night. I must have got some dust up ma nose because it was itchy."

"This bothers you, doesn't it, Ma?" I rubbed my belly angrily. "You're having a very hard time seeing me like this, aren't you? I knew you would. All these months I never came home. You know why?"

"Too feard?" she said, slamming the magazine down on the table.

"I knew you'd be having a hard time with this and I knew I'd get bugger all if I came up."

"Get a better control of that mouth. Who do you think you are, talking to me like that?"

"I've had it with you, Ma. Just tell me the whole story, no just the part you want to. I know what's gone on. I went to see Agnes."

"I bet she didn't tell you much. She's a closed mouth."

"You're wrong. She told me mare than I wanted to hear," I said.

My mother looked fierce as she said, "What did she tell you?"

"Everything!"

"Shite! She didn't tell you half of it," she said smugly. "I know Agnes. She's no one to come clean."

"So what is there to tell, Ma? What about Rita? How did you feel, Ma? How did you feel?" My rage hurled the words at her like bullets.

Ma hung her head and shook it from side to side. "There's no point."

"But there is a point. I want to know. I need to know. Don't you see?"

My mother's green eyes flashed angrily, and her mouth made a chewing motion. "All I can see is you stirring up all the shite. What do you want to do that for, Alison? I've never understood you. All your life you've wanted to know stuff that's none of your business. This is none of your business, so you might as well shut up right now."

"I can't, Ma. I can't go about like this for the rest of my life. I'm talking about giving my bairn away. Do you understand what that means? Do you know how much that hurts?" I gasped out the last word, feeling the gaping hole in the middle of my chest. "It doesn't go away, Ma. It never goes away."

She twiddled with the buttons on her cardigan before looking up with a misty film over her eyes. "I know," she said slowly, "but I can't be going into it now. Just leave it alone, Alison. Don't go getting all worked up about it. See what you're doing to yourself."

"I can't help it, Ma. It hurts too much." I dropped to my knees in front of her.

"Don't," she muttered. "It's too hard."

"Things were different in they days," she said, in a faraway voice.

"I know, Ma, you've always told me that. You told me that about Donald, about you and Dad, about Nana and Harriet. That's no an excuse." My palms were sweating and the muscles in my back felt like metal ropes twisted together, rigid as steel. I never wanted to be like my mother, doing the same things over and over again, following down some blind alley lined with bleeding hearts, stripping myself of any chance to break out of it. I wanted to know who this woman was who called herself my mother. I wanted to know my place in her history. I did not want to be handing this down to my daughter if I had one. I would not have secrets that would cripple her. I felt like a dog gripping a towel, refusing to let go.

"So what's it to be? Are you going to tell me or do you have to leave?"

She stood up and began folding her nightgown into a smaller and smaller bundle, straddled over the suitcase, full of uncertainty. "You've always been such a persistent bastard, Alison!"

I stood up and faced her defiantly, now feeling enraged that she was walking out on me. "I'm no the bastard, Ma. Remember, there were others before me, although I must have come pretty close. You were married in March and I was born in December."

She looked up from her folding in surprise.

"I checked your marriage certificate, which I found in the box in the wardrobe with all the other papers. There wasn't much time wasted."

"You've developed quite a mouth on you, you little sod."

I slumped into a chair and let out a big sigh. "You're no leavin' me much alternative, are you?"

Ma twisted her mouth hard and looked around my single room, neatly made up, no dust, clean dishes, alphabetically arranged books and records, and not one single piece of art on the walls. "It's too neat in here," she announced, then sat on the bed, giving it a tug on the corner to straighten out the bedcover.

"You don't give anybody a chance, do you?" she sighed.

I waited.

"Harriet was a big mistake," she began, dismissively. "I didn't ask to get pregnant with her."

"What does that mean?"

"You know bloody well what that means."

"No, I don't." I was not going to make this easy for her by guessing what it was she was saying. I wanted her to say it.

"Don't be like that, Alison," she whined. "It's no easy. This wasn't my fault. It was . . . ," she faltered.

My defiance was rooted to the chair."What!"

"It was my brother," she whispered. It was him who . . ."

The plaster could have been falling from the ceiling, raining chips of paint and dust, and I wouldn't have noticed. I thought she was going to tell me she was raped, but this left me speechless. I had an urge to wash my hands, but if I had moved she would have stopped her story. My slimy uncle John from Canada. I had always suspected that he was capable of something. He was always playing games, putting his fingers up your sleeves and touching your legs. I didn't like the feel of that man ever. He always had a sweaty face, and he had a big belly, which made his shirt buttons look like they were about to pop.

Her voice floated in from the edges of the room, and I heard her say, " . . . I couldn't live with myself after that. You have to understand what I felt like every time I looked at her. It wasn't the bairn's fault I couldn't look after her."

"Does Dad know this?" I demanded. "Is that why he refused to live with her."

"It wisnae like that. Nobody knew the story except your auntie Agnes. She was the one who found me. She didn't tell you that part, did she?"

I shook my head.

"I knew she wouldn't," said my mother, almost smiling.

From my basement window I watched the passing feet on the

street above. Outside, the dustbins were piled high with the rubbish from the flats above, partially camouflaged by the curtains on my window. My mother's freckled face was bright red and wet with perspiration. She took off her cardigan.

"Does Harriet know this?"

"No!" she exploded. "And don't you think you're going to tell her. She shouldn't have to know about this. I'm only tellin' you because you pushed me so far." The anger was creeping back into her voice. I pushed back with an involuntary urge to see her suffer some more. "I heard there was another bairn before Harriet. Was that a mistake also?"

She was twisting her wedding ring, a bent oval of gold, shaped by years of slapping labels on whisky bottles.

"I don't know why you're doing this. This is none of your business. This is no helping you."

"You had two bairns before you married, Ma. I don't want that."

"This is no easy."

"Truth never is, Ma," I said coldly.

She paced the room a couple of times and I waited patiently. Finally, she sighed and sat down again. "Her name was Rita. She died when she was three. I was a bairn myself. I didn't have the sense to know the difference and wanted to give her away, but your nana said no way. She had a heart problem and died just before Harriet was born. I'm no making excuses. I'm just tellin' you what it was like. It was all a bloody mess. There now, are you satisfied?"

"How come you didn't let me know any of this? Maybe it would have made a difference."

"When was I going to sit down and tell you this? You have to be stupid to think that. I'm no proud of what I did. Look at you—you're out to here and all I can think of is, it's my fault. I thought I was protecting you, but I didn't, did I? Do you think I sent you away that night and didn't think about it again? Well, you're wrong. It's just him and me now. If you came hame your father would hold it against you for the rest of your days. He's always had trouble with that, that's why he wouldn't have Harriet. He said it was because we couldn't afford it, but I know better than that. If you're thinkin' of given up this bairn for adoption, it's the best idea, if you ask me. Give it up and start all over again. Give yourself a chance. Don't be like me."

She was crying and I began to cry. "I don't know how to," I sobbed.

"Aye, I know," she said, coming over to put her hand on my head. "I really do."

—⚉—

"Ladies and Gentleman, the captain has turned on the no smoking sign. Please fasten your seat belts, store your tray tables in front of you, and place your seat backs in the upright position. We have begun our descent into Los Angeles International Airport."

"Are we there?" asked Agnes anxiously.

"Almost," said the girl, adjusting her seat. "I can't say I'm ready."

"Me neither," said Agnes, nervously looking out the window at the foothills of the San Fernando Valley, dotted with blue swimming pools. "What am I going to say to her?" she whispered."I want to go home."

"It'll be all right," said the girl. "Is your seatbelt fastened?"

"I'm too fat for this seat," said Agnes. "I think I ken how a sardine feels."

"Did you get to finish your book?" asked the girl. "It looked like a difficult read."

"Aye, it is, and no, I havenae finished yet. I dinnae ken if I want tae."

"What's it about?"

"History. A long time ago," said Agnes folding up her tray table.

"Where's your husband? Is he not coming with you?"

The girl touched her belly affectionately. "I don't have a husband," she said. "It's a long story."

"They all are," said Agnes, piling the pages together. "Do you live in Los Angeles?"

"No, my mother does. She's going to have a fit when she sees me." The girl tried to smile at Agnes, but it faded on her top lip. "No doubt she'll have a few things to say."

Agnes rubbed her eyes wearily. "Just give her a chance. Expect her to be shocked. She has to make her adjustment."

The girl patted her belly and spoke to the rising mound. "You're not going to let that bother you, are you, little one?"

"I think I've kept my behind in one place for too long," joked Agnes. "I suppose you could say I've been getting my knickers in a twist." She started laughing, an uncontrollable gale of emotion sweeping over her, feeling stupid but unable to stop. She was almost at the point of tears *when she looked down at the pages in front of her, the words a blur as she fought to control the immense weight of emotions sweeping over her.*

She hoped to God that Alison's daughter Lauren would be waiting for her. She had told Agnes, "I don't want to see her." When Agnes told her that she wasn't coming with her mother but with a book written by Alison about her family history, Lauren's tone of voice changed slightly. "Why don't you just send it?" she asked. "Because I'd like to see what you look like," said Agnes in between holding her breath. "I can send you a picture," said Lauren. To which Agnes responded, "I need a holiday."

—∿—

The officer at Immigration Control asked in a very precise manner how long she was there for. He looked surprised when she told him three days and then asked if it was for business or pleasure. "I've come to deliver something," she said innocently.

He stood up out of his chair and peered over the counter at her bag. "Must be pretty important," he said unsmiling. He scanned her passport and studied his computer. Agnes closed her eyes, visibly trembling as she stood waiting. "Are you all right, Ma'm?" the officer asked when he noticed her pale face.

"I don't know where to go," she said anxiously, looking beyond immigration to the baggage claim.

"Just check the flights on the carousels, Ma'm," he said helpfully. "You pick up your bag then follow the signs to the exit." The officer handed her the passport. "You have a nice day, Ma'm."

She thought they were awfully polite in America as she lifted her canvas bag with the manuscript in it, Agnes did not remember it feeling so heavy when she began the journey. Scanning Customs Hall she saw the pregnant girl waiting by the carousel. "I'm sorry to bother you, hen, but can you help me get my bag?"

"No problem," she said, "what does it look like."

"A wee brown one," Agnese said, "you can't miss it."

She was perspiring heavily, clutching her bag waiting for the baggage carousel to move. The Customs Hall was enormous, with hundreds of people searching for bags, queuing up to go through inspections. Panic struck her squarely in the chest. *What if she's no here? What am I going to do? What a stupid old woman I am, I'm way out of my depth here.* Her headscarf was askew and her raincoat, which she had not taken off the whole way, was crumpled beyond hope.

Seeing her bag emerge from the other side of the belt, she grasped the girl's arm. "That's it. That's my bag." The girl lifted it and gave it to Agnes. "You have a safe trip in Los Angeles."

Agnes thanked her and walked over towards the line forming to get through customs. On the customs form she had marked down that she was

332

not carrying any fruits, vegetables, animal products, or large amounts of money. It asked the value of gifts but she didn't know how to answer that. He put a pen mark across it and handed it back to her. She wondered how many checkpoints you had to go through in the United States before you were allowed to enter. Finally, she handed the form to a burly customs man and emerged into the arrivals hall.

She had to stop and take her breath for a minute. There were hundreds of faces peering in her direction. Many were holding signs up with people's names on them. She scanned the lineup but saw nothing with her name on it. I'm lost, thought Agnes.

Surrounded by a sea of people she stood like an island in the middle, reeling with the impossible expectation that everything would be all right. I've got a phone number and I can find a hotel, she told herself. I can get a taxi. She looked at the signs to see where the taxis were, then waited a few minutes longer, watching the faces as they came into view, hoping one of them was for her. All around her people talked and laughed as they greeted old friends and family members they had not seen in some time. She was envious of their joy and the ease in which they seemed to travel. She would not go so far away from home again, she thought.

Then out of the rush of people meeting and greeting, she saw a small sign with "Agnes Rankin" written on it, held up by a tall good-looking boy with dark curly hair. She was so excited she forgot where she was. "Yoo-hoo," she called. "Yoo-hoo." Almost everyone in the vicinity turned to look at her.

He hesitated before coming over. "Are you Agnes?" he asked.

Agnes was out of breath. "I'm so glad to see you, son. I didn't think anybody was going to be here. Are you from Lauren?" She gathered up her bags, struggling under the weight of them.

"She's over there," he said, pointing across the hall.

Agnes followed his gaze and almost began to cry. She looked just like her mother when she was younger, except she was taller. Her long blonde hair was tied back into a pony tail, and she was wearing a simple white T-shirt with black pants and sandals. She looked so fresh and clean and shy.

"I'm Ben," he said, sticking out his hand, forcing Agnes to drop her bag again. "Aye, and I'm Agnes," she responded, taking his firm grasp in her limp hand. "As if you needed to be told," she joked.

"Let me take your bags."

"Just the one, son. I'll carry this one." She hoisted the bag with the manuscript onto her arm, and they began moving towards Lauren, who had not moved from her spot.

Lauren watched her boyfriend Ben help Agnes and thought, what a sight! She looks like a peasant in search of a field. My mother could give this woman a makeover, but she'd probably need two weeks. I hope she isn't staying long.

As Ben approached, he raised his eyebrows at her and gave a slight shake of his head. It was his way of telling her to behave. She was sometimes too quick to say the wrong thing.

"Agnes, this is Lauren," he said. "I know you two will have a lot to talk about," he added mischievously.

"Hello, Mrs. Rankin," she said sweetly.

Agnes ignored the formality and rushed on in. "I'm so happy to meet you, hen. I've been wanting this for a long time." She stuck out her hand and Lauren accepted it limply, trying to avoid the soft, sticky texture of Agnes's skin.

Just then, Agnes's legs started to fold and she dropped the bag, causing the binder to fall out. Ben lurched forward to grab the bag, but it was Lauren who caught Agnes, struggling with the weight of her.

"Are you all right?" she asked anxiously. "You don't look so good."

Ben began restoring the contents of the bag while Lauren held her arm. "It's no wonder you let this go, it weighs quite a bit," he said. He hefted the bag and held it out to Lauren. "You should feel the weight of this thing."

Lauren shook her head and declined it. "Can you take this?" she said, reaching down for the small bag.

Before he took another step, Agnes lifted her canvas bag from his hand. "No, it's all right. I've carried it this far, I can carry it the rest of the way. I'm all right, son, just a wee bit puggled, that's all. I'm no used to going such a long way." Agnes leaned on his arm and recovered her balance.

Ben held her tightly. "I think we should get you into the car. Can you walk?"

"Aye, it takes mare than six thousand miles to knock me down."

Lauren was staring at the large canvas bag. Agnes followed her gaze then broke the spell with, "You know, you look just like your mother."

Lauren snapped her head up quickly and then tried to smile, but it wouldn't come. "Actually, most people think I look like my dad," she said tartly. "What hotel are you at?"

"She doesn't need to go to a hotel," said Ben, a little too enthusiastically. "We've got room, haven't we, Laur?"

Lauren tossed him a look that said, I don't believe you just did that, and then responded as brightly as possible, "Sure!"

"I've no booked anything yet. I thought I'd find something no very expensive, so don't go to any bother for me. I'll be fine with any bed at this point. I could sleep on the flair here."

Lauren did her best to disguise her disgust at the idea, but it didn't escape Agnes's notice. "Oh, don't worry, hen. I'm only kiddin'." Lauren gave a waxen smile as they headed for the exit.

seven

MY TWENTIETH BIRTHDAY came and went without fanfare. Christmas was more of the same. On New Year's Eve I sat at home with a bottle of sparkling apple juice and a bag of crisps watching Bing Crosby and Grace Kelly in *High Society*, envious of their highballs and flirtatious camaraderie.

It was five in the morning when I sensed the first sensation that something was wrong. The bed was wet and I thought I was back in my childhood again afraid to wake up to the truth. Then a wave of tightening muscle extended over my belly slamming me back into the present.

When I arrived at the hospital, the nurse asked if I had anyone with me. I forced a laugh and told her I didn't know who it was yet. She didn't get the joke but continued filling in my information form. "How long in between each contraction?" she asked.

I had no idea. They were coming regularly and I was doing the breathing bit in between. I'd managed to take a Tube to the hospital when the contractions were still ten minutes or so apart. I figured I had time. According to the books, I needed to be three minutes or less before it started getting serious. I was coming out of Paddington Station when I doubled over with pain and had to grab hold of a banister to stop myself from falling. "Maybe three or four minutes," I gasped.

"Right! Let's get you upstairs," she said decisively, pulling in a wheelchair. "Get in."

The journey to the delivery room was a blur. I was breathing and huffing and trying not to hold my breath, but I couldn't keep it under control. I started to moan out loud, and in the moaning I heard all the rage, the stupidity, and the desperation pushing their way out of my body and splattering all over the walls of the hospital. I wanted my mother, Auntie Agnes, Lisa—anyone who could come and hold my hand and tell me it was all going to be all right.

The stirrups were cold when they placed my feet in them. A nurse held my hand. "We need you to push, Alison," said a voice from the bottom of the bed.

I didn't need to be told. My body was bursting apart at the seams with an unbelievable urge like wanting to take a shit and you can't find a toilet close enough. It had a will of its own and my face felt like it was exploding with the effort. "Hold it!" the nurse yelled. "You're almost there."

"Noooooo!" I screamed, letting all the years of holding it in dissolve in that one moment of complete surrender to the forces of nature.

"You'll tear," warned the nurse. Everyone was yelling and I was screaming and it felt as if there were too many hands on my body and I wanted them all to go away. "You'll tear if you don't hold it."

And in a burst of air and a wailing that could be heard far across the desert, I felt a searing burn trace its way from my anus to the front of my vagina. In the release of a burden far greater than I could manage to support, your shoulders were pushing me aside like a rugby player in a rush, until you lay slippery and wet between my legs. I tried to sit up to see what you looked like, but the nurse placed a hand on me gently and told me to lie back.

"It's a girl," the doctor pronounced. "Congratulations."

It was my first slide into a huge wormhole of never-ending longing.

When I awoke a few hours later, a nurse was checking my temperature while holding my wrist and keeping an eye on the watch pinned to her uniform. I could feel the fullness in my breasts and I ached all over. Sliding my hand across my stomach, the empty sagging skin reminded me of what I was missing. "Where is she?" I asked softly.

"She's in the nursery, dear. Just get some rest."

"I need to see her," I said. "I want my baby girl."

"There, there, love, just relax. You need your energy." She picked up a white paper cup with two pills. They looked big enough for horses. "Here, swallow these. They'll help dry up your milk."

I took them and weighed them in my hand as she poured me a glass of water.

"Are you hungry? You've missed lunch but I could find you something."

"I want to see her."

"Maybe later," she said, patting my hand. "Just take these and you'll feel better."

I looked at them again as she stood waiting for me to finish. To be so full of promise and then emptied overnight seemed a cruel joke. The milk I was being asked to dry up was to feed my baby.

I started to cry and she closed the curtains around the bed. "It's only going to make it harder on yourself," she said. I was still holding the paper cup. "Come on. Let's get this down you. You'll feel much better soon."

But I didn't want to feel better. I wanted my baby. I wanted you. I wanted to see you, to touch you, to smell you, to see that you were all in one piece. I wanted you close to me, to feel your skin on mine, to know that you were mine. I swallowed the pills and almost choked on them, causing them to spew back out onto the bed, narrowly missing the nurse's uniform as she jumped back.

Lisa arrived with a mixed bunch of supermarket flowers. She was not smiling when she sat down. "How are you?"

"Where have you been?"

"What's happening, Alison?"

"I want her back," I said defiantly. "I don't want to give her away." I sounded petulant but I didn't care.

"I'm not sure that right now is the right time to make that decision."

"I've had lots of time. I want my daughter," I said a little too loudly. Other visitors looked in our direction and she sighed when she returned her gaze to me.

"Where do you think you'll go with her? You wanted to give her a chance, didn't you?"

"I want a chance. She's my baby and I don't want anyone else taking her." I bit my lower lip, trying to stop myself from crying again. I was doing too much of that. "You have to let me keep her, Lisa."

She placed her hand on top of mine and I withdrew. "It's not my decision, Alison," she said, pulling back on the chair she was sitting on. "It's yours, but I strongly advise giving this some serious thought before you barge ahead."

"I have," I moaned. "It's all I think about."

"Please. You have to tell them. I can't give her away. She's mine, can't you see that? She's all I have. She needs her mother. I can be a good mother. I don't care if we have to struggle. It doesn't matter. I can't give her up. It's too hard," I wailed, feeling all that raw emotion burning its way through my skin and exploding into emptiness. "I want her. Now!" I screamed.

Lisa stood up and reached over to hug me. I shrank back into the bed and pushed her away. "Let me have her," I pleaded.

She stood back. "If that's really what you want. If it's your decision I'll do what I can to make it easy on you." As she walked away, I felt as if I'd just lost a friend.

Half an hour later you were brought to me.

I forgot everything I had ever thought about giving you away when you were placed in my arms. I wept all over your sleeping face. You were so tiny, so fragile and helpless. I drank every detail of you until I felt dizzy and giddy with the pleasure. I memorized every puckered expression on your face. I was your mother and it didn't matter what was in front of us. We would be together. We would make it work. I could feed you, change you, worked night and day to keep you. You were mine. I called you Caitlin.

The following day I was shocked to see Agnes standing by my bed with a big smile on her face and her arms open wide. "I came to see you and the bairn," she said, folding me into her arms. She hugged me tight until I pulled away.

"Who told you I was here?"

"Your mother phoned me."

"My mother?"

"Aye, she's worried about you."

"Aye, right!" I said. I had called her the day the baby was born. All she had to say was, "I hope you're going to leave her at the hospital." There were no "Congratulations! Are you all right?" involved in the conversation.

"She's a braw bairn, I'll give you that." Agnes leaned into the cot and placed a half-crown under the small pillow. It was good luck to give a child some silver when it was born. She also handed me a packet wrapped in brown paper. "So what about you?"

I shrugged and sat down on the edge of the bed, pulling open the paper. "I'm all right. Just sore on the bottom end." I undid the tissue paper and then gasped. "This is gorgeous, Auntie Agnes. Did you knit it?" I held in my hand a finely knit wool shawl in a delicate shade of ecru, soft to the touch and delicately laced. It was an exquisite shawl that must have taken months to make. "Did you knit this for her?"

"Aye, I thought she needed something to keep her warm. What are you going to do with her?"

"I'm keeping her," I said a little too defiantly.

"Do you think that it's a good idea?"

I shrugged again. "We'll manage." I folded up the blanket and placed it on the crib.

"That's the part I'm nervous about," she said. She took off her coat and hat and sat down on the chair next to the baby's cot, giving it a slight push to start it rocking. "She's a bonnie bairn. You used to have blonde hair."

"Now it's mousy brown," I said, "and greasy." I ran my fingers through my stringy hair and pulled it tight. "Why didn't she come?"

"She said you and she were not gettin' on."

"Haa! That's the least of it."

"It doesn't matter. You're making a big mistake if you take this bairn away, you know that. You don't know what you're gettin' yourself into. It's no fair to the bairn or you."

"That's what my social worker said. Why is it that everybody seems to think I'm incapable? I'm not like my mother plus I don't need anybody. I can get a job and do it myself. We're going to be all right."

"Listen, hen," she said softly. "I'm no here to tell you what to do. I'm here to see if you're going to do the right thing. I just don't want to see you hurt. This bairn needs a chance. You've no got two halfpennies to rub together. Give her a chance," Agnes said, touching your cheek, your eyes wide open staring at her.

"I've tried, Auntie Agnes. I just couldn't let her go." Reaching into the crib, I picked you up and took you into my arms. "She's all I've got."

"You can come and live with us in York. I'll see to it that you get to go back to school. Your uncle William says we can do for you what we would do for our own bairns. There are good jobs by us. You don't need to feel so far away from everybody."

I looked at you and you gave a windy smile that passed across your face like a shadow. "I can't," I said.

After a cup of tea in Lauren's apartment, Agnes oohed and aahed over the dishwasher and the disposal unit in the kitchen sink in her discomfort at being there, making silly noises because she didn't know what to say. She was out of place, and had no idea how she was going to get through the next day or two. Lauren tried to connect with her but made no attempt at conversation other than the politeness of how was your journey. You must be tired. Ben took her bag into the spare bedroom and insisted she take a nap. "She's out of a Thomas Hardy novel," Lauren said to him in the hallway. "I can't understand a word she's saying."

The bedroom was ablaze in floral curtains, a floral bedspread, and floral pillows in shades of blue, violet, and pink. A chintz nightmare, thought Agnes. Taking off her clothes she laid them carefully across the armchair, then collapsed onto the soft pillows and in a few minutes was asleep. An hour later, she awoke in a panic, clutching her nightgown, confused as to where she was. "What am I doing here," she moaned, then reached down to the bag on the floor. "I have to get this finished," she said, picking up the manuscript.

eight

LISA FOUND ACCOMMODATION for us with her friend Carol in exchange for babysitting her two children. It was a small room furnished with a single bed, a table, two chairs, and a crib, all compliments of the Department of Social Services. When I took all my books and dishes from my old bed-sitter, it felt like home. The view from this room was even worse than the one I had just left. It backed out onto a brick wall, and I joked that I could count the bricks when I wasn't sleeping.

At first it was wonderful. You ate, you slept, I changed you and watched your every move. I stroked the fine down hair on your cheeks and watched you turn your head towards my finger in search of a bottle. My breasts were dry and no amount of suction would bring it back.

Then it began. Every night around five o'clock, about the time when my energy was giving out, you began to scream, pulling your knees up into your chest and your face to turn bright pink. Carol told me it was probably colic resulting from gas bubbles. She told me not to worry; it would stop before you started school. I tried gripe water, rubbing your stomach, walking and bouncing you, but nothing worked. You screamed each evening for an hour, sometimes two.

I started taking long walks with you in the pram, regardless of the weather. Anything to get you to sleep and to find some release from the wall of sound that surrounded us. I began to feel tired no matter what time of the day it was, my patience diminished with each passing day.

꧁꧂

I heard you crying as if from the bottom of a very deep well, and as I struggled to shake off my sleepy head, I glanced at the clock. It said two a.m. "Right on time," I murmured.

Staggering across the cold floor to the kitchen, I warmed up the bottle from the refrigerator. When I returned you were in full soprano belt. It was cold in the room, so I wrapped you in Agnes's shawl and pulled the bedcovers up over my legs. After you had taken half a bottle, you pushed it away and began to cry again. I thought it must be your nappy, so I changed you and still you cried. "Not again," I said pleadingly. "I'm tired. Just go back to sleep." But you had no intention of going back to sleep. I put you down because I was told to let you cry for a few minutes, not to get in the habit of picking you up, because then you'd always expect it and I would never get any peace.

The room shrank to the size of a postage stamp as you continued crying. I picked you up and began pacing. The bricks on the wall outside looked awfully close. "Shush!" I admonished. "Shush. Please stop. You'll wake up the entire house." I held you tighter against me, bouncing you up and down violently. "What do you want?" I pleaded, but this only caused you to become even more anxious. I picked up the half-empty bottle but you spat it out. I put you on my shoulder and patted your back to get the wind out of you. I held you tighter and forced the bottle back into your mouth and then you vomited. You howled even more intensely. I gritted my teeth, drowning in the maelstrom of my violent temper and your insistent cries. I had to do something, so I slammed you onto the bed, leaving you shrieking and red faced. Turning away towards the window, I clawed at my face as if I were trying to rub myself out of the picture. Leaning down towards you, I hissed in your small, helpless face, "What do you want from me? What do I have to do?" Sobbing, I turned to the window and the wall and asked, What am I doing? How could I have been so stupid as to believe I could do this? Self-pity swarmed like an itch over my whole body, covering me in a depression I could not break out of.

I wasn't prepared for the violence that finally took over.

The nappy pin was stuck in the cotton cloth and wouldn't go through to the other side. Your legs were working up and down like peddling a bike as I pushed and pushed, trying to get the pin through. Your cries sucked in every bit of air there was in the room, and my mouth was getting tighter and tighter as I insisted that I would get this to work. "Shut up!" I screamed with a hoarse, whispered voice, pushing the pin through to the other side and stabbing my finger. "Fuck! Fuck, fuck, fuck!" I hissed, sucking the blood from my finger.

Suddenly, without warning, I was ready to murder you. Not just the thought but the actual act of it. I picked you up and slammed you down on the bed, causing your head to bounce off the mattress. I pushed my face inches from yours, and like the girl in the film *The Exorcist,* I screamed in a contained deep, guttural voice, "Why? Why are you crying? Don't do it! Don't do it! You hear me. Don't fucking do it," and I slammed my fists inches away from your head. "I'm fucking fed up with this." I picked you up and began shaking you so that your head wobbled back and forth. "I don't want to feed you. I don't want to change you. I've done it and I'm not doing it anymore. You hear me? Do you hear me, you!" I was spitting on your hysterical face "I can't do this. I can't be your mother. I don't know how." Sobbing and clutching at your clothes I threw you back down on the bed again. "I hate you. I hate this mess we're in. I hate it all." You were screaming in fear and my hysteria promised to annihilate both of us. Kneeling on the floor by the side of the bed, I punched my fists into the mattress and put my face into the covers. "Get it! Get it! Get it!"

Just as suddenly as it started, the madness subsided and I scooped you up, the nappy hanging from your leg as I held you tightly to my chest. "I'm sorry," I sobbed. "I'm really sorry. I just can't do this anymore. I just can't. I'm sorry," as my tears mingled with yours and the warm rush of urine soaked the front of my nightgown. Sobbing, I held you close, putting your mouth to my empty breasts until you fell asleep in my arms.

The next day, Lisa came on one of her weekly visits. "How are you coping?" she asked. She could see from the dark circles under my eyes that it wasn't well. But I lied anyway.

"Great. I could use a bit more sleep but that's all. Isn't she doing great? She was making purring sounds this morning like a little engine. I think she's trying to sing." I never mentioned my depression, my inability to cope, or the thoughts that kept creeping in every night that this was a big mistake and I should be giving you up right now. Even as every fiber in my body cried out to give you away, I kept insisting I could do it.

❦

I called Agnes. We had not spoken since that day at the hospital when I had more or less dismissed her.

"Hi, hen. How's the bairn?"

"She's great. She's getting big."

"And how are you doing?"

"No so good. I'm . . ." I couldn't finish the sentence. "Oh, Auntie Agnes. I don't know what to do. It's hard."

"I know that, hen." Her voice was soothing and warm. "Do you want to come up here for a wee while? We've got the extra bed. It's no bother."

There was silence for a few seconds while I pondered what to do. "Can I?"

"Get yourself on the next train. Just give us a bell when you know what time, and your uncle William will meet you at the station."

I held the phone for a few minutes after I hung up and wondered if I should go. Outside the phone box you lay asleep in your pram. Your blonde hair clung in wisps to your scalp, and your forehead had a little frown on it as you slept, as if you were worrying over something in your dreams. Suddenly, it became clear what to do. I would take you to Lisa's office and leave you there. There was no point in postponing it any longer. I was a danger to you. After last night, I had no idea what I could do next. It scared the hell out of me to think I was that close to wanting to annihilate you.

I called Agnes back. "I'm sorry, I can't come. It's no the right time."

"You're going to be all right?"

"Aye, I was just feeling a bit panicked, that's all. I'll be fine."

346

"I'm worried about you."

"I'm all right, honest."

"Why don't I believe you?"

"It's just hard, Auntie Agnes."

"Give her up, Alison. Let her go. She'll be better off with people who can take care of her properly. I've said it before and I'll say it again, do the right thing for her and for you. You deserve a chance and so does she. If you really love her, give her up."

"I know that, I really do, but it's so hard, Auntie Agnes. I never thought it would be this way."

"Unfortunately, we all learn the hard way, hen. Give her up. Don't do the same stupid things that your mother did. Maybe for once somebody in this family will do it right."

⟨≈⟩

As soon as I walked into Lisa's office, I thrust you into her arms. "I can't keep trying to make this work. I should have listened to you." She took me gently and sat me down. Just this gesture was enough to make me cry. "She was crying and crying and I couldn't stop it and I wanted to hit her so hard. I didn't want to and I didn't want to be mean to her," I sobbed, "but I can't do this. I'm so sorry. Keep her safe before I do any damage?"

Lisa sat cradling you and then placed an arm on me and said, "Stop!"

I couldn't. "I'm not a mean person. I'm really not. I just don't know what I'm supposed to do here. Look at her. I don't deserve her. She hasn't done anybody any harm. Please!" I was out of air and gasping for breath because my asthma was kicking in and I was so tired of crying.

"Don't, Alison! Don't!" She held me tight, squeezing us both, mother and child together. "You tried. You really did. You gave it your best. You needed to do it this way to understand. You have to know that."

My sobs had turned to hiccups, and I searched in my pocket for my inhaler. The aching pain in my chest felt like a black hole that sucked all the life out of me. I had brought you into this world and now I was abandoning you. I wondered what it would do to you. How you would feel about me. I didn't want to do it this way, but I knew how destructive I could be. I had seen the destruction that came from frustration and disappointment up close. I did not want it for you. I wanted you to have a better life. I couldn't do it so someone else should. And through all this, I hesitated when Lisa asked, "Are you sure this is what you want?"

Suddenly ashamed I said, "I don't know."

She carefully put you back into my arms. I wanted more than anything to put you back inside my body so that I could be with you in a way that made it easier for me.

"I'm not sure I can do this." Then you smiled at me. "I need her for two more days," I said.

"It won't be any easier in two days," Lisa advised.

I nodded my head, all the while staring at your perfect face. "I know. Just two more days."

nine

FOR THE FIRST time in weeks we both slept through the night but I awoke with a jerk, afraid something had happened to you; that maybe I had smothered you in my sleep because I had taken you to bed with me. You were sucking on your bottom lip, and as I watched you I knew for sure that I had no choice. It was the only way you could be happy. I had too many demons circling around me, and you would end up inheriting them as long as I was still fighting them. Patience and love were something I would have to learn. Agnes was right—we both deserved a chance. I had dreams of getting out and away, and I had tied myself to the post by having you. It wasn't your fault, it wasn't my fault. It just was, and that was all you could say about it. I had to move ahead and leave all the craziness behind. I hated my mother and father, and I didn't want you to end up hating me.

There were five children on the doorstep, and the entrance hall was crammed with Wellington boots, school blazers, raincoats, umbrellas, and bikes. Mr. and Mrs. Price, the foster parents, stood quietly by their children, smiling at me as I approached. She was a small, thin woman with a long chin that made her mouth look too small for her face. Mr. Price towered above her, his balding head glinting in the glare of the winter morning sun. The youngest child, Tamsin, clamored to hold you immediately, but her mother held her back gently and told her to be patient, there would be plenty of time later.

I was feeling sick to my stomach, and there was a thickness in my throat like I was choking.

"Come in, come in. It's cold out there," urged Mrs. Price. "I've made some tea, would you like some?"

Lisa led me to the living room, where I sat down on a sofa that was falling apart from too many jumping children. The coffee table in front of me had crayons, books, and magazines strewn on it, and I began to wonder how I could leave you in such a mess as this?

She placed a cup of tea in front of me and passed a plate of biscuits over. At once, the kids made a dive for the plate, and she whisked it away from their grasp. "Our guests first. Where's your manners?"

"Sorry," came the chorus of voices. "We forgot."

Mrs. Price smiled at them and passed the plate towards me again. I took a small biscuit out of politeness and put it on my saucer.

"Would you like to see where Caitlin will be staying?" asked Mr. Price, standing up and almost hitting his head on the lampshade that hung from the ceiling.

I looked at Lisa, who said, "Go ahead. You can leave her with me if you like." She held out her arms.

Shaking my head, I said, "No," and then proceeded to follow him upstairs, clutching you to my chest. As I passed the children's rooms, I noticed they were cluttered with toys, books, and clothes thrown all over the floor. Maybe having five children, and now a sixth, didn't leave much time for housekeeping. I understood it a little since I never seemed to have enough hours in the day to sit down with one baby.

"Here we are," he opened the door to a small room. "This is where she'll be sleeping. You can be sure the children are going to take good care of her. They love it when we get babies to look after. Don't you, Tamsin?"

I was not encouraged. The children took care of the children. She smiled sweetly and pushed her father into the room. From the door I saw a crib with wooden slats that needed a new paint job. Above it hung a clown mobile and next to it was a changing table. On top of the crib was a quilt made from odds and ends. A large tree outside the window caused shadows of light and dark to play across the room. "Is there anything I can do to make this easier?" asked Mrs. Price from behind me.

My heart was pounding in my ears. I hesitated allowing my heart to catch up with my words. "I think she'll need feeding soon. Can I feed her before I go?"

"Of course you can, love," she said sweetly. "You don't have to rush. We're not in a hurry, so take your time. You know, you're welcome to come anytime you like."

Walking downstairs in front of me, she said, stopping on the stair and touching your shawl, "She'll be safe here, I promise you that. We look like we're all of a mix-up here, but we're okay. I've never had a child in my care that didn't thrive."

I tried to smile, but it wouldn't come. I had a stuffed-up feeling and an urge to leave but held you tightly while I tried to swallow a sip of tea. The threat of tears made it difficult to swallow. Lisa gave my arm a pat then an uncomfortable silence settled on the room. Lisa coughed to clear her throat.

Suddenly, I stood up. "Would you take her, please? I'm sorry, I have to go now. I can't stay any longer. I'm sorry." I gave you one last kiss then handed you to Lisa.

"I'll call you," I said to no one in particular, slamming the front door.

"Alison, wait! Let me talk to you for a minute." Lisa was following me down the street but stopped when I started running. The houses on either side of the street were a blur as I jumped out of the way to avoid a passing car, the driver tooted his horn and raised his fist at me as I ran, hoping the station was in that direction. There was a searing pain in my chest and my body felt like it was drowning as I sobbed and gasped for air, unaware of the cold chill blowing through my thin blouse. I wanted you and I wanted my freedom, but I knew I couldn't have both. I couldn't go back to see you because then I'd have to say good-bye all over again. I wanted to run and keep running until I couldn't run anymore. I began wheezing and tried to ignore it, gasping for intakes of breath, my lungs collapsing inwards towards to a heart that was now in pieces.

Dulwich railway station was in sight just as Lisa caught up with me in her car. "Get in," she shouted as she drove slowly alongside me. "It won't do you any good to keep running. It's a long way to central London."

I stopped and stood gasping for air. "Get in," she shouted again. I reluctantly opened the door and sat down, searching for my inhaler.

"Are you all right?"

"NO! I'm not all right," I screamed, causing her to brake the car and pull over to the side. "What the hell am I doing here, Lisa? What did I just do?"

"You did what was good for you and for the baby," she said softly.

"I don't believe that," I yelled. "I think I'm doing what everybody else wants me to do. You included. I don't think anybody gives a fuck about me."

"I understand you feel that way, but you're saying that because it hurts. You know it's not true."

"I don't know what's true anymore. I don't know what I'm supposed to do with any of it anymore." Lisa watched me, my face soaked with snot and tears."It's sooo hard. She's all I've got. What am I going to do now? Where am I going to go? I can't go back to Carol's. I can't be in that room again. Oh, God. It hurts. It really, really hurts." I felt as if my chest were being crushed under the weight of the car.

Lisa said nothing. There was no way she could say she knew how I felt. She had never given away her child.

ten

"I THINK I'VE found some great people for her," she said, "Can we talk about it?"

"I guess," I said miserably. Every night I second-guessed myself about whether I was doing the right thing, and every night I had to talk myself into the "yes, you are" business. I read Kalil Gibran's *The Prophet* and took marginal comfort in his wisdom that your children are not your children but part of life's longing for itself. They come through us but are not ours. My mother took that one to heart. I wanted to find you the perfect parents, the loving mother, caring father, who would give you everything you needed. I clung to the Madonna image for you. You would be spared all the pain I had gone through.

"She's had a couple of miscarriages and a child who died at birth. They've been trying for four years. From what I can see, they look very promising, I'm only going ahead with it if you approve."

"If you're sure they're the right ones," I said," then go ahead."

"Nothing is guaranteed, Alison, but I'll bet my record on them. I think Caitlin will be happy with them. You'll be giving them a wonderful gift."

I almost threw up on that one. She sounded like the doctor at the hospital telling me I would make someone very happy.

"I don't want to be giving gifts," I said

"Can we just talk about this?" Lisa asked

It was two days before she came to visit me with a thick file in her hand. She took out a picture of the couple. I wanted to hate them, but they looked so normal. She was wearing a brown and beige striped shirtwaist open at the neck to reveal a small gold chain, her light brown curly hair was cut short, and she had a warm smile. He was sitting next to her holding her hand, wearing an Oxford shirt and khaki trousers with slip-on shoes that showed he was wearing no socks. They looked like they were on holiday in a garden full of rose bushes. There wasn't a drink in sight. In my family pictures there was always a drink in front of my parents.

"Where was that taken?" I asked.

"Their house. It's quite a big house and she would have her own room. They decorated it for the child who died a year and half ago."

"That's too bad," I said. "It looks like the kind of house I used to dream about." I was surprised at how warmly I was feeling towards them. "They look nice. Will they really take care of her?"

"If I didn't think so, we wouldn't be having this conversation."

"How soon do they take her?"

"I don't think we'll be ready for the exchange for at least another two months."

"She'll be at least six months by then."

"Yeah, but they will be visiting with her at the Price's before then. They have to get to know each other."

"I suppose," I said wistfully. "It seems like such a long time."

"It will go fast."

I didn't think so.

❦

I called my mother and said I was coming home for a weekend. I'd been working as a temporary secretary and there was no work lined up.

"Are you all right?" she asked. "We've been worried about you because we haven't heard anything for weeks. Your Auntie Agnes phoned me."

"Was Auntie Agnes worried, or were you?"

"Don't start, Alison. Are you comin' home or no?"

"Aye, I suppose."

"We're having a wee party. Your auntie Cathy is coming."

"You two are awfully chummy," I said, remembering how hostile she had been towards us during most of our growing up. She hardly ever came to the house unless it was something very special like a Hogmanay party.

"I'll see you the morn," she said.

❦

The welcome home was as if nothing had happened to upset my life. My mother asked if I was all right and my father ignored me. Mother spent the day in her usual way, at the hairdressers, then came home to put the frozen food specials out on the table and made sure there was enough beer, vodka and whisky. I noticed the new television and beta tape recorder.

"Another provi check?" I asked

"No, it's no, you cheeky sod," she said. "I paid for that with my own money. It's good. The picture is much better than the last one we had."

"Maybe you can put it in the bedroom when you're having your party, I said. "I could watch a film."

"Why did you come up here?" she asked "All you ever do is complain."

❦

I was sitting on the couch between the two of them with my eyes shut pretending to sleep, feeling as if I was a book in the middle of nattering bookends that'd drunk too much. "Are you keeping her here with you?" Cathy asked my mother leaning over me. "If she was mine, I'd make sure she went into the bonds where I could keep an eye on her. You were no right in the head lettin' her go to England like that."

"Aye, I know, but there's no talking to them these days. They all do what they like."

"Where's the bairn now?"

355

"She's given it up."

"It's the best. It's no something you want to put up with, is it?"

My mother shook her head. "No, I suppose no," she said.

I almost choked and began to cough violently. I stood up quickly and went to get some beer to stop the spasm. Their short memories were amazing. Cathy had given up her son at age 16, and Mrs. Virgin Mary, Full of Grace, well . . . enough said.

My dad was talking to Cathy's husband, Mike. After many years of insisting on her spinster life, she had married a widower. Dad had hardly said a word to me since my arrival earlier in the day except to ask, "Are you home to stay?" I told him not likely. He said, "Good." I began to wonder once more why I bothered with the charade of family.

I went to their bedroom because my bedroom was filled up with coats. I pushed the door closed behind me and lay down on the bed. After a couple of minutes, I heard the roller ball pop off the door catch and the hall light streaked across the room, then the door closed again.

I turned around and sat up quickly.

"What are you crying for?" My dad was slouching against the side of the wardrobe. "I heard them talking out there. They're drunk."

"I know that, Dad," I sobbed. "I don't deserve this. They all talk like they're saints or something. I know I did wrong. I'm paying for it. No you, not them. Me!" I stabbed my fingers into my chest. "Who gives them the right to talk about me that way?"

"C'mon now, let it go. They'll no even remember the conversation the morn." He was smoking a cigarette, and the glow from the end sizzled when he took a drag.

"Aye, but I will." I pulled myself up into a sitting position. "Do you know how much it hurt me when you said I couldn't come home?"

"Who said you couldn't come home? I never said that."

"Yeah you did. I heard it from Ma. She told me you would have a fit."

He hesitated for a moment. "I never said that, It wisnae me. Just ignore them all."

You lyin' bastard, I thought. How could you. He had sat on the end of the bed facing me, keeping his distance, and then his voice changed to a softer tone.

"Why don't you go and do something with your life? Don't be wastin' it." He dragged on his cigarette again and when he exhaled he said "No like us."

"You're right, Dad. I have been wastin' it. But I'm not anymore." I slapped my hand over my face and dried my eyes. "I've made up my mind. I'm going back to school in September and then I'm going to university. I've had it up to here with this shite."

The bedroom door opened and my mother walked in, putting on the bedroom light. "What's going on here?"

"Nothing," he said, rising quickly from the bed and walking past her.

She stood for a minute looking at me, chewing on the inside of her mouth. "You going to your bed? I'll get the coats off next door." She then turned and went across the narrow hallway, leaving me to figure out what had just happened.

❧

When I returned to London, Lisa had sent me a letter saying papers were ready to be signed. Holding the letter in my hand, I began to tremble and then I threw up in the kitchen sink. I waited three days until she called me to see if I had received it. I lied and said I had only received it that morning. "The adopting parents are anxious to sign. Can you come to my office tomorrow during your lunch hour?"

"How is she doing?" I couldn't even say your name for fear of what it would do to me.

"She's fine. Thriving, I would say. I saw her last week, and she's put on quite a bit of weight. I think the Price children are feeding her too often. They get excited when it's time for the bottle."

"Must be a different formula from the one I was feeding her." I took a sip from the tea I was drinking.

"How was your visit to Scotland?"

"Miserable."

"Need to talk about it?"

"No."

"Okay," she responded guardedly.

"Okay," I said. "When do you want me in?"

"Tomorrow at one?"

"Okay."

I put the phone down and threw my cup across the room, where it exploded against the wall, splattering the plaster with tea stains. "Great, now I'll have to pay for the repair," I shouted, searching for the bottle of QC sherry.

❧

"It says here that I willingly consent to the adoption of said minor Caitlin Napier. Do I?"

"Only you can answer that, Alison. I can't do it for you."

I looked at the legal papers, all neatly bound together with pink legal ribbon. "So where do I sign?"

She put her hand on the file. "I have one question I need answered once and for all. Are you absolutely sure you do not know who the birth father is?"

"I told you when we first met that I had no idea," I said gruffly. "If I did, then I would have said."

"It's important. The judge needs to be reassured that you are making this decision without anyone else coming in later to claim her. I'm trying to protect her interests, Alison."

"I have no idea. Look, can we just get this over and done with? I can't stand all this waiting around."

"I know it's hard, but you have to know that we're doing everything we can to make sure that these are the best people for your baby. I want the best for her and for you. Trust me on that."

I read the papers again. Petition for Consent to Adoption. I didn't want to read the fine print. "Where do I sign?"

She pointed to the last page. My name was typed on the bottom next to theirs. I took the pen from the desk and signed it then dated it. "There. Is that good?"

Lisa slid the papers back across her desk and closed the file. She stood up to come around the desk. I pushed the chair back and walked to the door. "Give me a call when you need me."

When the final documents were ready, I asked only a couple things. I would be allowed a letter and a picture of you each year as you were growing up, and I wanted you to know who I was. If that was agreeable, then we had a deal. The adopting parents agreed on the understanding that I would not attempt to make physical contact with you. I would have taken a postcard if it could keep me connected to you in some way.

On July 27, 1970, the court made it official. My child became their child. You belonged to them now.

I cried for several hours, and then went to the pub to drown myself.

eleven

"WE DIDN'T EXPECT this," said Agnes, shaking her head. "No your mother. She always thought it would be him first, especially wi' that." She looked at my father snoring in the corner. His neck was wrapped in a thick scarf to cover the gash in the side of his neck. Cancer had eaten its way through his lymphatic glands and his tongue. His mouth was open and I pushed his mouth upwards to close off the offensive black gaping hole where once his tongue sat. It was a terrible thing to think, but I thought he had it coming to him. But my mother's death was the greatest surprise. She was the tough one. I almost collapsed when I got off the plane from London and had to be taken in a wheelchair to the first aid room. Now we were sitting in a pub with everyone getting drunk and singing. Agnes and I huddled in the corner trying to ignore everybody.

"What was it about her, Auntie Agnes?"

"I don't know myself, hen. It always seemed to me queer that she put up wi' as much as she did. But Gracie had her own ideas about things. She didn't think much about anybody interfering. I don't think I can tell you anymore than that."

"But you know!" I said earnestly. "You've been there all the way through. Was she ashamed or something? I would really like to know who my mother is, Agnes." My father grunted in his sleep and then gave a swift suck in as he dribbled, but did not wake up.

Agnes sighed and leaned a little closer to me. "Do any of us?" she asked simply. "Do we really see our mothers or, for that matter, our fathers," she gave a nod in his direction, "as people? I'm your auntie. Do you see me? Or do you see your auntie, your mother's sister? I can't tell you who your mother is anymore than you can. She's my

360

sister. I can tell you what she went through, but we didn't go in for all that psychology stuff. That's you. That's what you're interested in. You figure it out. Your Ma had a hard life, harder than any of the rest of us. That's all I can tell you. You have to work out the details for yourself. What brings you to this place now?"

"I don't know. Lots of things, I guess. I made a big mistake when I gave the bairn away. I should have kept her."

"No you shouldn't have," said Agnes vehemently, "and I'll tell you why." She leaned towards me. "You would have done her no bloody good." She returned to her original position. "Look at what you've been going through. Look at the state of you!"

I opened my mouth and closed it again. "How could you say that? You saw me in the hospital. You saw what I was going through. I didn't want that to happen. I couldn't let her go."

"But you did, didn't you, hen? You must know you did the right thing."

"Yeah, I did, because you and Lisa Sawyer convinced me it was the best thing I could do for both of us," I said nastily.

Her voice softened. "But you saw for yourself how hard it was, hen. Three months is a long time to be keeping a bairn and then giving it away. We were just trying to save you from that."

I sat silently for a few minutes and Agnes waited. "Why do you have to know, hen?" she asked. "What good can it do you?"

"Maybe if I can understand it will make things easier for me, that's all. I'm seeing a therapist right now and I feel like there's so much I don't understand and I want to. Maybe if I understood a little bit about where my mother came from, who my grandmother was, what she was afraid to tell me. Look at Harriet over there." Harriet was sitting with a drink in her hand, playing with her necklace, not talking to anybody. "We're all so unhappy. I feel like I've been living with a lot of secrets that nobody is talking about. Do you know what I mean? I'm not making much sense." I stared at my father; his jaw had dropped again and the gaping black hole in his mouth lay open. I shuddered and felt sorry for the man.

"I just get a feeling that there's something. I can't really tell you what it is, but you're the one person who really knows what happened. You can tell me."

Agnes shook her head. "Aye, I can tell you something but I can't tell you everything. You have to decide what it is you're looking for. Sometimes it's hard to tell where a story really begins, and I certainly don't know where it ends." She sat silently for a moment and then took a breath as if it came from the soles of her feet. "Your nana had me before she was married, so I guess that makes me the first bastard in the family."

I could feel the wind blow through my hair. "You mean Nannie . . . . ?"

Agnes folded her arms across her chest and leaned back. "Now where would you like to go from here?"

*Agnes felt the full weight of the history bury her in a rockslide of emo-
tions she could no longer ignore. She bit into the back of her hand to stop
herself from sobbing out loud, and her body shook and jiggled under the
impact of holding back the sobs so they would not be heard on the other
side of the door where Lauren and Ben sat waiting for her to wake up.*

*This reading had come to epitomize her whole existence, as if she were
caught in a time warp outside of her real world. Almost as if it were the
last flash before she died, just like people who had near-death scares. Her
world of children and grandchildren and a happy home seemed as far
away as another galaxy.*

*Agnes had tried to protect the people she had loved all her life, but the
overpowering sense of failure she felt reading this story, was the failures
she had tried so hard to ignore.*

*I never complained, she thought, and I never realized until now how
much I hated it.*

*She had abandoned Grace when she had needed her the most, aban-
doned her mother because she was tired of being the one everyone turned
to because she was capable and never complained. Not once did anyone
ask how Agnes was feeling. They all took and never once asked if she
wanted anything back.*

*She was tired of the secrets; tired of the tragedies that kept piling up
one on top of the other, ruining every life that came into it; tired of being
the capable one. Alison had asked her to deliver the truth, to sweep aside
all the negatives and try to set things straight for the future. Why me? she
thought. Why did I deserve this?*

*Alison had dug deep into an abyss no one wanted to visit again, least
of all Agnes. She had not been sent here to answer for her mistakes, but
they had been tossed in her face. How much responsibility for that lay
with previous generations, she couldn't be sure. It was clear that whenever anybody tried to make a difference, they somehow couldn't. There
were too many odds against them. Agnes was just one of the pawns in
the game. She had escaped the poverty, the ignorance, and the oppression,
but she had not escaped the weight of guilt, of having escaped. They had*

all wanted something better, and she was the only one who had seemed to make a difference in her life.

She thought Lauren was the lucky one because she had escaped the agonies of survival, but perhaps she was wrong. Perhaps Lauren was just as much a part of the secrets and lies by omission. She had been sent away, but it didn't change anything. The history was still there. The unanswered questions still remained. The place of belonging that comes when you know who your mother and father are—that's what Alison had tried to bring her.

This was why Agnes was the one to make the journey. She was the last link to this. Alison wanted to wipe the slate clean, make amends for lives gone terribly wrong, and for the children who suffered because of it. She was trying to appease her guilt. She wanted to know if she had done the right thing. Everyone had lived their lives in so much dread of life. They had refused to see the light that shone in the darkest places, and Alison had refused to carry it over to her grave.

The poison was the lies and secrets that kept everyone distantly longing for something else, too afraid to step away from the history that weighed them down, not even recognizing what it had done to them, until Alison had put it all down in a book.

Agnes sobbed into the pillow to keep her sorrow quiet. How she had fooled herself that she had escaped the worst horrors. She was drowning without realizing it and would have gone to her grave with it if Alison had not insisted she take this to Lauren.

"We all made mistakes," she said out loud. It sounded so easy to say, but it had taken her a lifetime to understand.

twelve

BEYOND THE SHADOW of the bed came the sound of coughing and deep breathing. A nurse sat at a table with a small lamp lit above her head. She had said it was too late for visiting, but Agnes had insisted, saying she had not come six thousand miles to be turned away because she was five minutes late.

Approaching the bed, she recoiled at the sight of my withered body lying flat with only a small pillow under my head. Agnes had been gone for less than a week, but it felt like it had been months. An IV was attached to the back of my right hand. Agnes gasped when she saw me and dropped her bag.

I moved my eyes but my body remained inert. "Is she all right?" I whispered, my lips sticking together.

Agnes leaned over me and bent her head towards my face, kissing me softly on the forehead. "What are you sayin' hen?" she asked. "How is she? She's grand. She looks just like her mother. You'd be proud of her."

I tried to smile and raised my hand towards Agnes's face. "What about you?"

"You knew, didn't you?"

She brought my hand down carefully, holding it like a bird with a broken wing. "I didn't know it would be so hard," she said, fighting back the tears. "I was only tryin' to do my best."

"I know," I said breathlessly.

Agnes bent down to kiss me and a trickled tear ran down the side of my face feeling like a caterpillar walking on my skin, then pulled from her large canvas bag the large red mohair scarf she had been knitting. "I finished it on the plane," she said, tears now streaming down her face. "It will keep your shouders warm."

She placed it over the top of my body, small as a sparrow, and straightened out the edges. "Like Max Factor," I said hoarsely.

Agnes sat down on the chair next to the bed and held my hand.

On the far side of the ward, the door to the hall opened throwing a streak of yellow light across the floor. A thin shadow passed in front of the nurse's desk and a voice called softly "Mom!"

glossary

Aboot	About
Aw'	All
Awfy	Awful
Bairn	Child
Braw	Wonderful
Cauld	Cold
Cannie	Can't
Couldnae	Couldn't
Dae	Do
Day'in	Doing
Dinnae	Don't
Disnae	Doesn't
Doon	Down
Fae	From
Faither	Father
Fur	For
Galoot	Idiot
Gie	Give
Gi'en	Giving
Go'in	Going
Gonnie	Going
Hame	Home
Havenae	Haven't
Hud yer Wheest	Quiet or Shut up
Ingin'	Onion
Lassie	Girl
Nae	No
Oor	Our

Oor...................	Hour
Oot...................	Out
Ow'er	Over
Sae	So
Sare..................	Sore
Shouldnae.............	Shouldn't
Telt	Told
Whae	Who
Whair.................	Where
Winnie	Won't